The Will
to Win

Also by Suzanne Higgins

The Power of a Woman
The Woman he Loves

The Will to Win

SUZANNE HIGGINS

POOLBEG

Published 2005
by Poolbeg Press Ltd
123 Grange Hill, Baldoyle
Dublin 13, Ireland
E-mail: poolbeg@poolbeg.com

13 5 7 9 10 8 6 4 2

A catalogue record for this book is available from the British Library.

ISBN 1 84223 187 1

Typeset by Patricia Hope in Bembo 12/15
Printed by CPD, Wales

www.poolbeg.com

About the Author

Suzanne Higgins was a radio and television presenter on RTÉ, where she presented the highly acclaimed Great Giveaway Show for several years. She also presented several successful television programmes before "retiring" after the birth of her second child. She subsequently started to write.

Her debut novel, *The Power of a Woman,* was a national bestseller and its sequel, *The Woman he Loves,* was a number one bestseller.

Suzanne is married and lives in south County Dublin with her husband and four children. She is currently working on her fourth novel.

Acknowledgements

First and foremost, I have to thank my two dear friends and seriously good readers – Judi Pleass and Helen O'Rian. They were resilient enough to wade through a very rough first manuscript and brave enough to suggest where improvements could be made. Thank you, ladies. (Ber, you're included there too!)

I want to thank everybody at Poolbeg Publishing who made me Number 1. The day I got to the top of the bestsellers list is one I will never forget! Particular thanks to Paula Campbell, Emma Walsh, Conor, Lynda, Aoife and of course Gaye Shortland. Thanks also to Phil, Kieran and Anne O Sullivan and Brona and Sarah (gone but not too far!). There is a very dynamic, hardworking team behind the scenes at Poolbeg. Thanks to each and every one of you.

Thanks also to my agent Jonathan Lloyd. I'm also deeply indebted to the Irish booksellers who are so generous and kind to me.

Thanks too to Pat, Adina, Helen and Belin who help me so much at home. Folks, without you I simply couldn't write! I'm very grateful.

Thanks as always to the Duffys, the Higgins and all the in-laws for the unconditional support, love, patience and toner cartridges! I could go on but I won't. Michael? 'Thank you' seems like too small a tribute. Would you settle for floccinaucinihilipilification? (hint: you're the opposite!)

I want to thank my great friends Jenny, Josephine, Paula, Sarah, Suzanne, Ashling, Debbie, Gail and Ann.

A particularly big thank you goes to a very generous group of women who have been so welcoming and encouraging to me. They are the writing super divas: Marita Conlon-McKenna, Sarah Webb, Clare Dowling, Martina Devlin, Marissa Mackle and Joan O'Neill. You're an inspiration, ladies. I want to especially thank Cathy Kelly, novelist extraordinaire and one of the most generous people I know. Cathy, if you hadn't been so giving of your time and encouragement I genuinely think I might not still be writing. I owe you! Thank you.

And last but not least – my four little angels. I love you. Thank you for giving me enough space to write but not enough to forget my priorities. You're still number one!

And finally, thank YOU, the reader, for buying my book. I really hope you enjoy *The Will To Win*. If you have any comments please log on to my web site: suzannehiggins.com

Love Suzanne

For my daughters,
You are Magnificent!

"If you want to seek revenge,
You should dig two graves."

CHAPTER 1

Fiddler's Point had never seen so much action! Up high, seagulls squawked in excitement as they feasted their eyes on the fuchsias and scarlets below. Feather boas flocked together as the kitten mules click-clacked into the picture-postcard church. And higher again, helicopters hovered impatiently, their importance diminished by the fact that they had to queue to disgorge their precious cargo of Ireland's richest and most influential.

The residents of Fiddler's Point looked on with great amusement. They were used to the super rich in their midst. The Judge family had lived there for over a hundred years and, in fairness to them, while they were a little eccentric, they had brought much-needed income and jobs to the village. Fishing was the primary reason for Fiddler's Point to exist at all but when James Judge the First started making bootleg whiskey back in 1899, the village rapidly gained a second source of income and an unrivalled reputation for wild nights.

Frank Delaney had his fishing trawler out six days a week and it felt strange not to be out on the Irish Sea at lunchtime on a Saturday but his wife, Tess, wouldn't hear of it. As soon as she got the nod from her old employer Rose Judge, wild horses wouldn't have stopped her. Tess had been informed that she was "most welcome to sit in the back row of the church" during the marriage ceremony. Rose had made the offer the previous week as both women walked out of Mass together. In all probability it was just an impulse of the moment on Rose's part, but Tess accepted instantly. It certainly wasn't the warmest invitation she had ever received but what the heck! It had been many years before that Tess had worked up at Dunross, the Judge family mansion. Tess ironed and polished alongside Mrs Bumble when they were both young. Mrs B was now head housekeeper at Dunross. Tess gave up work when she became pregnant. She and Mrs B had remained firm friends ever since but Rose Judge was a good deal more distant. It was quite clear that she believed staff should know their place.

Frank, Tess's husband, had no interest in going to church – ever, let alone to see the young Judge lad get married but Tess had begged her husband and she didn't usually ask him for much so he gave in. She had put up with him for close on forty years. Surely he could afford her this one little favour and, anyway, his three boys could fish well enough without him.

Frank and Tess were one of the first couples to arrive – such was her excitement – so they got to see the church fill. The bride's friends arrived in droves. A flock of giddy young things, they were laughing and looking beautiful – carefree and happy. Tess watched them fondly and remembered back to when she thought the marriage of her friends was a novelty. The old maxim was true: youth was wasted on the young. Frank recognised several ministers and of course the Taoiseach who was looking particularly well - heeled. Tess was much more interested in the executive wives, the women that were around her age – mid to late fifties – and there were plenty of them. Their jewels dazzled her and the clothes – well, Tess's eyes were out on sticks. That said, she wasn't jealous because she was contented with her life. She loved Frank and every day she counted her blessings for the three strapping sons she had, but she did like to see how these people lived. It was a little like stepping into a society magazine. She didn't know the make of clothing they wore but she knew quality when she saw it. The older women were dressed in cream or pastel-coloured suits, many of them embroidered in gold. Others were decorated with the more traditional pearls. They wore softer tones which were kinder to lined faces, Tess noted with resignation. The pretty young things wore feather-light fabrics made of strong, bold and vivid colours; their beautiful limbs were wrapped in soft angora and shimmering silk shawls. All of the Judges' guests looked so healthy with their Mediterranean or Florida suntans. Then she looked at her Frank. Ironically his tan was just as good, courtesy of the windburn aboard *The Ashling*, his boat. For a second, Tess's mind went back to her own dear Ashling, the only daughter God had sent her. It was after her three sons had been born and Tess wanted to call her Ashling – the Irish for 'dream-vision' because it was like a dream coming true to have a little girl at last. Her dream was very short-lived, however, and after just one precious hour in Tess's arms, Ashling went back to God. It was the only tragedy in her life but it was one Tess knew she would never quite get over. Some years later when Frank was able to afford his own modest fishing trawler, he asked his wife if maybe he could call it *The Ashling*. She thought it would be a nice way to keep the memory of her little girl – her little dream, alive. She pushed that thought away now. Her sons were out on *The Ashling* today. Hopefully they would have a good catch.

Bringing her mind back to the present, Tess rubbed her dress down with her hands as if to smooth out imaginary creases. She patted her hair which had been freshly set that morning. Her husband glanced at her and gave her a wink. Frank had insisted that she buy herself a new dress for the wedding. It had been ages since she had bought anything new and she felt very smart. She had what Frank referred to as a full figure and a substantial bust. Normally she was quite happy with her figure but today it was a little difficult not to feel self-conscious. Tess also stood nearly as tall as her husband but the advantage of this was that she was able to see right up to the top of the church.

The place was beginning to fill. Expensive and heavy perfumes hung in the air, each vying for supremacy. There was a ferocious racket outside as the powerful engines of the helicopters thudded a monotonous beat while they hovered and eventually landed. Then Tess caught her breath as the President glided past, nodding and smiling at notable people she recognised in the little church.

"Jesus, this is better than anything you'd get on the telly," Frank muttered, laughing lightly.

Tess shushed him as Rose and her husband, James Judge the Second, marched up the aisle. She was the mother of the groom and today was her day. She walked up the aisle as if she were royalty but Rose Judge actually looked a lot more like Joan Collins than she did any queen. Despite receiving the invitation from her, Tess didn't really like Rose. Nobody in Fiddler's Point did. She was a snooty, stuck-up cow and she was certainly milking today for all it was worth. That said, she was frightfully glamorous. The lilac-coloured suit she was wearing particularly suited her colouring and naturally it was expertly made. Everything Rose wore was tailored to flatter her petite hourglass figure. Her eyes sparkled like diamonds as she glided up the aisle.

Then Tess's heart softened as Cameron escorted his grandmother, Victoria Judge, up to the front of the church behind his parents. It's really *his* day, she thought fondly. Cameron had grown up in the village. He and Tess's boys had played together every day of their childhood. Then, of course, their life paths had diverged as Cameron was sent off to be educated in England. That was the Judge family tradition.

Naturally, Tess Delaney's boys, Matt, Mark and Luke, went to the local boys' school. It was ten miles up the road in Wicklow town. Although the Delaney boys and Cameron Judge never fell out, the relationship that they had had when they were nine and ten years old was gone, probably forever.

Tess watched Cameron as he gently guided his grandmother into the designated seat – not that she really needed help. Even well into her nineties that woman's mind was still as lucid and clear as a crystal champagne-flute. Tess, however, was sad to see that Victoria's body was definitely growing weary. This was the first time she saw the old lady succumb to using two walking sticks instead of one. It would be a dark day in Fiddler's Point when Victoria Judge died. Granny Vic, as everybody knew her, lived at Dunross and had done so ever since she married into the Judge family herself some time back in the 1920s. Victoria was a wise old owl and didn't suffer fools, or Rose, gladly.

Safely deposited, Cameron left his grandmother and moved back down the aisle to greet his guests as they arrived at the church door. He was such a composed-looking gentleman, Tess thought. Most grooms were nervous and a little pale as they waited for their brides to arrive but not Cameron. He oozed success and wealth. He had his father's height at six foot two and he looked terrifically confident. One would think he spent a lot of time in the church, he looked so comfortable there – but that certainly wasn't the case. One of Cameron's talents was just that: looking confident and at home no matter where he was.

He had a perpetual tan from spending his summers in the Judge's Caribbean villa, in Barbados. Cameron's winters glided by with him skiing in Switzerland and Colorado. He was devastatingly good-looking with a fit athletic build. His face he had obviously inherited from his mother. Cameron's eyes, like hers, were set wide apart and were azure blue. His danced with life and mischief, however, while hers were considerably cooler and more distant. Cameron's nose was perhaps a little too prominent (as was Rose's) but his mouth was wide and lit up his entire face when he smiled, which he did almost perpetually. They both had Greek God bone structure and quick minds but it was the charm which Cameron employed to such deadly effect that drew people to him like bees to honey. Rose was equally proficient at turning on the charm when she wanted to, and as such you never knew whether she was really being nice or just saying what you wanted to hear. Rose Judge really was a very unsettling creature, Tess reflected.

Everyone knew that today was Cameron's birthday because the much-anticipated wedding had been covered in so many magazines.

Today, September thirtieth, Cameron was thirty-five years old. Ireland's most eligible and handsome bachelor was about to marry a beautiful young lady called Samantha White. Surely she was the luckiest girl in the world.

Samantha looked absolutely stunning. She usually looked good or even better-than-good but today she was really spectacular.

Her two best friends were fed up that she had shut them out.

"We're meant to be helping you, Miss White," Gillian shouted through the closed bedroom door.

"I don't need any help, Gill! Thank you very much," Samantha answered.

Gillian threw her hands in the air and went back to her own bedroom to get her cigarettes.

"What about your make-up? Shouldn't I do it for you?" Wendy suggested. "You know I'm a trained beautician!"

"When did you last do somebody's make-up, Wendy Doyle? You may have trained as a beautician a million years ago but it's been a long time since you actually donned the white coat and got your hands dirty!"

Wendy harrumphed. "I do my own make-up every day, you know. Don't think that I've lost the touch!" Then, having run out of arguments, she banged on Samantha's bedroom door. "OK, sod your make-up, just let us see you! We're your bloody bridesmaids and that gives us certain privileges. Come on, Sam, open this bloomin' door!"

Samantha had secretly wanted to get to the church without anybody other than her hairdresser seeing her. It was a silly old romantic notion really and it was pretty obvious that her two oldest friends weren't going to settle for it. When she first got engaged and began to think about the wedding, she played with the notion of not having any bridesmaids at all. She thought the concept was totally outmoded. Sam didn't need anybody's help to get dressed or to do her make-up. She did it by herself every day of her life. What suddenly made her so incompetent on the day of her wedding? Her mother-in-law wouldn't hear of it, however.

"No bridesmaids? What a sweet notion!" Rose's smile held the warmth of crushed ice as she looked at Samantha. "But totally unrealistic, of course. Marrying a Judge, you will need an entire fleet of bridesmaids and flower girls, perhaps even a few page boys if we can find any." She was off.

From the outset, Sam knew she wasn't going to win that particular argument. Her one consolation was that it could have been a lot worse. Her sisters-in-law had point blank refused to play any part in the wedding. Rose had asked them to be bridesmaids or at least maids of honour but they balked at the idea of wearing ribbons and frills.

Samantha had received a similar response when she asked Cameron's niece, Zoë. The seven-year-old she-devil simply refused to be involved. As the first-born grandchild of the Judge dynasty, Zoë was appallingly spoilt and generally a very brazen child and Samantha was delighted that she refused to be involved no matter how hard her grandmother tried to convince her.

Samantha wasn't scared of her future mother-in-law but she did hate the way she managed to manipulate everyone around her. She had been very difficult to deal with over the wedding arrangements. Sam was quite happy to stand up to her but it was the look on Cameron's face, her dear sweet Cameron, that stopped her. He looked pained to see the two women in his life disagree on anything and so Samantha inevitably backed down for his sake. It wasn't really worth the hassle.

There was another loud knock on the door. Clearly her friends weren't going to take no for an answer and anyway they *were* her bridesmaids.

She took one last look at herself in the full-length mirror and nodded. Even she was happy with the outcome.

Gillian was back and full of renewed vigour, having lit up. "Come on, Samantha, you've got to let us see you sooner or later. It may as well be sooner so you can save yourself all this verbal abuse through a bloody door!" She took another sharp drag.

7

"OK!" The bride was at last worn down. "I'm coming. Now you have to give me your honest opinion."

Wendy, Gillian and Samantha were already in residence in the exquisite Rathnew Manor, in County Wicklow. The wedding reception was to take place there later in the day. The girls had checked in the previous evening, as had Rose and James Judge. Wendy and Gillian were sharing a luxurious and very large double suite. Samantha's was a slightly more modest one down the corridor. That was because she was moving into the massive bridal suite later in the day. Samantha still hadn't seen it because Cameron had wanted it to be a surprise. He made her promise not to sneak a peek but rumour was that it was quite out of this world. She crossed her room and unlocked the bedroom door. Her two best friends stood in the doorframe and stared at her, their mouths wide open.

"Oh my God!" Wendy gasped. "Samantha, you are *sooo* beautiful!"

Then Gillian spoke, "Christ, Sam, you really look like someone out of Hollywood or something. You look absolutely amazing!"

"I'm so glad I chose ivory rather than white," Samantha studied her own dress. "The off-white suits my colouring better and look how well it works with your goldie-coloured dresses."

Gillian coughed on purpose. "Excuse me, this shade is actually champagne − not goldie!" She smiled at Samantha.

"Sorry but we do complement each other perfectly," Sam beamed.

"You look divine," Gillian added.

Delighted with the praise, Samantha sashayed back into her bedroom and did a regal three-hundred-and-sixty-degree turn for them. "So, you approve," she beamed.

"God, have you lost even more weight?" Gillian asked, stubbing out her cigarette and lighting another in the same motion. "That's it! I'm never eating again."

"No, Gilly," Samantha said sternly, "I haven't lost any more weight and you know bloody well how I feel about cigarettes. They don't help you to look better." She saw Gillian raise her eyes to heaven. Now was not the time for a fag-nag and so she changed the subject.

"But the heels are a good bit higher than I'm used to, so I do look taller than usual."

"Will you be taller than Cameron?" Gillian asked

"Hardly – in these," she flashed her three-inch stilettos and continued, "I'm about five foot eleven but Cam's six foot two."

"And all man!" Wendy added with a dirty laugh. "Samantha, you're a lucky girl to get him but, Christ, he's a lucky man to get you. I've never seen you look so good and that's saying something."

The bride had chosen to go for a figure-hugging, particularly flattering design of dress. The tightly-fitted ivory satin bodice was hand-embroidered with the faintest image of tiny, barely visible, roses. These complemented the ones in her hair. The bridesmaids walked around her slowly to see the exquisite garment from all sides. The detail on the back of the corset was equally breathtaking. What looked like a hundred satin-covered miniscule buttons ran down Samantha's long and slender back. The skirt was simple, fluid and slightly clingy, and contrasted starkly with the boned structure of the bustier.

"Sexy," Gillian smirked.

"It's not at all bridesy, is it?" Wendy agreed.

"Well, I didn't want to look like one of those meringues, if that's what you mean," Sam laughed. "One must always try to look good, even on one's wedding day."

The slim A-line silk skirt draped elegantly down the bride's long legs, much more seductively than most wedding gowns would. Then a long train stretched out at the back. Samantha took a few paces forward to show how the train spread out behind her.

"Wow, that's long!" Gillian said.

"It's called a semi cathedral train, if you don't mind. A bit impractical for dancing later."

"But so romantic," Wendy sighed. "You're a princess."

"The Princess Bride," Gillian agreed. "And you still bloody well manage to look seductive."

"My God, no veil!" Wendy gasped. "What will Rose Judge think?"

"It'll be too late by the time she sees me." Samantha grinned wickedly.

"How could I wear a veil with this kind of dress, anyway?" she scoffed. "And I love flowers so I had teeny tiny roses put in my hair."

The girls studied Samantha's head. Her long blonde curly hair was gently clipped up into soft rings. In the centre of each curl was a miniature champagne-coloured rose.

Gillian studied her old friend. "Samantha, you've done what you always said you'd do."

"What are you talking about?" Wendy asked, but Samantha was smiling at her bridesmaid for remembering.

Gillian explained. "When Samantha and I were little girls, Wendy, she always said that when she got married, she'd have flowers in her hair."

"What a memory, Gilly!" Samantha was chuffed with her oldest friend. "That's why you're my nearest and dearest friend."

"Well, I'm afraid I haven't been around for that long," Wendy sniffed, a little jealous that the other two had more history than she did with them.

"Hey, we three have been flatmates for ten years now and barely a cross word in all that time. You can't get much closer than that," Samantha reminded her.

"I know, it's just that you guys go back even further –"

Sam interrupted Wendy in a motherly tone. "Now, girls, you know I love you both just the same." Then she raised her arms in the air. "Group hug!" she shouted and the three girls hugged in a tight little circle, but the bridesmaids took care not to crush Sam's dress or incredible hair creation.

"I think I'm going to cry," Wendy, the softest and most emotional of the three announced, so the other two pulled back.

"Now now, it's far too early for that," Samantha reproached her, trying to lighten the mood somewhat.

"You really do look amazing. Did your hair take ages?" Gilly asked, having the sense to change the subject before Wendy started to blubber.

"What do you think took me most of the morning? Mind you, both of you look fantastic, too. Obviously the resident hairdresser is pretty good."

"Yeah, she was lovely, not that we were particularly complex hair-jobs." Wendy laughed as she flicked her light brown bob.

"Gilly, your hair is even more shiny than usual," Samantha said admiringly.

Gillian shook her head, making her dark auburn hair sway gracefully. "Thanks, it does have a heck of a sheen when I get it blow-dried professionally."

"She looks like a henna ad," Wendy agreed.

"Except mine is all natural." Gilly winked at her friends.

Wendy returned to openly ogling her friend. "But you, Sam, you look like some goddess of old or ancient queen out of Celtic mythology."

"Hey, less of the 'ancient', if you don't mind," Samantha quipped.

"Ah, Sam, you know what I mean," Wendy defended herself. "At thirty-five, you're a child bride by today's standards."

"Sure, look at the two of us. Still young, free and single, having seen thirty-five come and go." Gillian laughed.

But for the first time, Samantha thought she detected a slightly bitter tone to her old friend's comment. "So, you really think the dress is OK?" she asked, moving back onto safer territory.

"Do you think you'll be cold?" Wendy asked, indicating Sam's bare shoulders and arms.

"Oh, I have a lovely stole." Sam crossed the room and picked up her long silk wrap. Like the bodice, it was decorated with a trim of finely embroidered silk roses.

"The detail is incredible," Gillian said.

"Thank you," Sam beamed. "I must admit everything has been entirely hand-stitched. I could have bought a small house in Dublin for the cost of this dress."

Despite her best attempts, Gillian felt a bitter stab of jealousy.

"And as for the colour!" Wendy continued to gush. "When we saw the swatch you gave us, we had no idea that it was going to suit your colouring so well – you really do look like – like –" Wendy couldn't find the right words to describe her friend.

"I've got it," Gillian piped up. "You look like the Lady of the Lake in the Ballygowan ad on TV."

Samantha and Wendy looked at Gillian for a moment and then burst out laughing.

"Typical Gilly! You always have to think of the advertising angle. You're just a media babe through and through," Samantha smiled.

Gillian shrugged, accepting the compliment of sorts. "Well, if I am the media babe, where's my drink?" She clicked her heels together just like Dorothy in *The Wizard of Oz*. "Everyone knows we marketing Madonnas do our best work under the influence. Surely it's time for some champagne."

"Great idea!" Wendy rushed over to the phone and called room service.

Then it was Samantha's turn to admire her bridesmaids' beautiful raw-silk dresses. They had opted for a more traditional style of dress, with bodice tops and fitted skirts cut to the knee. At Gilly's insistence, there was a very flirty slit at the back. The champagne colour was very flattering to their fair Irish complexions and particularly enhanced Gilly's pale cream skin and deep auburn hair. They looked terrific but both bemoaned the fact that God hadn't graced them with Samantha's figure. As they were both a sexy size fourteen, with any other bride their hourglass curves would have looked stunning but they agreed that next to supermodel Sam it was difficult to compete.

"Any man's fancy," Samantha told them as the champagne arrived.

"Well, our boobs are our best assets so we may as well display them to their full advantage," Wendy said as she practiced her best smoulder in Samantha's full-length mirror.

"Absolutely," Sam agreed. "Just don't display too much of them until the elder lemons have gone to bed tonight."

"As if," Wendy exclaimed in mock horror. The fact that she had, on occasion, flashed her boobs when she was drunk didn't particularly bother her.

"OK, what will we drink to?" Samantha asked as she poured the Bollinger into three fluted champagne glasses.

Wendy and Gillian each took a glass from her and the three of them held their champagne high.

"How about – to old friends and new beginnings?" Gillian asked.

Wendy and Samantha looked at each other and smiled. They spoke at exactly the same time: "Media babe!" they teased their friend.

"What?" Gillian pretended to look hurt.

"You're so bloody fast with the buzz phrases," Wendy explained, "but this time, in fairness, it really fits. What was it you said again?"

"To old friends and new beginnings!"

The three girls clinked their glasses, repeated Gilly's toast and then took a large gulp.

When the phone rang in Samantha's room, Wendy answered it. "Both the bride's and the bridesmaids' cars have arrived, along with that extremely cute little brother of yours," she announced.

"OK, girls, this is it. Are you ready?"

"Ready, willing and able. How about you? Are you OK, Sam?" Gillian touched her arm as she asked.

Samantha knew that Gillian wasn't talking about Cameron Judge. She wasn't talking about the fact that Samantha was going to marry the only son of Ireland's richest dynasty. She wasn't referring to the mother and sisters-in-law from hell. Gilly wasn't even talking about the photo shoot with *Hello!* magazine later that day.

What her old friend was alluding to was the fact that Samantha was about to get married without any of her own family there other than her adorable little brother, Ricky. Where would she be without Ricky? Samantha heaved a great big sigh to release some repressed tension. Then she nodded gratefully at Gillian.

"Yes, I'm fine. Really. Thanks. Today is going to be a great day, so let's get the show on the road, as you would say, Gilly."

Gillian studied Samantha's face for a moment and then nodded in approval and gave her a kiss.

Next Wendy kissed Samantha. "See you in church," she said as the two bridesmaids teetered out the door.

"Yes." Samantha waved goodbye, feeling a lot more insecure than she looked. "See you at the church."

Chapter 2

Suddenly the room became deafeningly quiet. Samantha crossed her suite to look out the large bay window. The view was magnificent. She was looking out from the back of Rathnew Manor with its exquisite panoramic views of the Wicklow Mountains in the distance to the north. It also had beautifully manicured lawns, sweeping down to the lake. She noticed that the Judges' helicopter was no longer parked on the helipad. Obviously James and Rose Judge had already gone to Fiddler's Point.

She sighed as she realised that they hadn't phoned her to say hi and bye or to wish her luck. But then again, why should they, she thought sadly. They weren't that kind of people. The Judge family were cold and aloof, not like her. The one exception to that rule was Cameron. He had passion and he was full of life. Cameron lived every moment like it was his last and he ran Judges' Whiskey with that same massive energy. It was his great-great-grandfather who had founded Judges' Whiskey and Cameron was honour-bound to continue the family business. A trickle of nervousness tingled over her as she considered the fact that he was the only son and she would be expected to produce at least one boy to continue the family business.

A clear, long, slow wolf whistle brought Samantha back to reality with a pleasant thud.

"Babe-alicious," Ricky crooned at his sister.

Samantha swung around at the familiar voice.

"Wow, big sis, you really do scrub up well," he grinned at her. "If you weren't my sister, I'd file you under 'e' for 'edible' in my chick-tionary."

"Yeah, and if you weren't my brother, I'd file you under 'n' for 'never' in my dick-tionary."

Ricky tried to look hurt but he couldn't sustain it. He crossed the room to his sister and took her hand.

"Can I at least kiss the bride?"

"Of course, you old rogue, you know that I love you," she smiled.

He kissed her so gently on the hand and then on the cheek, she barely felt it.

"And I love you too, Samantha. You're all the family I have and I'll always be there for you. You know that, don't you?"

She laughed. "What is this? The little pre-nup pep-talk?"

"Yeah, I guess it is. I know you love Cameron, but if he ever does anything to hurt you, just call. Promise?"

"Promise," Samantha beamed at her little brother. She really did love him to distraction. "You're very good to me, Ricky, and you do know that it works both ways. If you're ever in trouble, just call. It doesn't matter where you are or what you've done, just call and I'll come running."

Ricky had put his arm around her waist and was walking her towards the door but he broke into a rendition of 'You've Got A Friend' when he heard her say 'just call'.

Sam serenaded him right back in pretty awful harmony. The two were just at the door when Ricky spotted the nearly finished bottle of Bolly.

"Oh, look!" he said in his naughty-boy voice.

"Help yourself. My tummy is churning a little, I can't really drink, but I don't particularly want to appear at the church on time so I guess we have a few minutes to spare."

Ricky recycled Samantha's glass and filled it to the brim with the remainder of the bottle.

"Steady on, old boy, I want you to be able to walk up the aisle with me, not stagger."

He took the entire glass in one swallow. "Ha! It would take more than that to make me stagger."

Samantha tensed up and a shadow crossed her face. As usual Ricky saw her change in mood. He had always been very empathetic to his sister.

"Relax, big sis. I'm not turning into a lush. I'm thirty years old, for God's sake. I'm meant to drink like a fish."

"Yes — but Mummy —"

"That woman was born an alcoholic. She didn't become one by drinking the dregs of a bottle of champagne." Then his tone softened. "Have you spoken to her since you went to see her?"

"No, that was a month ago today. She just yelled and shouted at me and I ran out of the house. I'm not trying any more, Ricky. I mean it this time. She's out of my life forever. If I never see her again, it will be too soon."

"Wise decision. Look at me, I never go to see the old soak and I'm the better for it."

Samantha felt a stab of disloyalty wrench her already jittery stomach but she suppressed it. "Yeah, I guess you're right."

"I know I'm right. Now let's go and party. Hey, by tonight you'll be Mrs Samantha Judge and one of the richest women in the country — pretty cool, heh?"

"I'm not marrying him for his money. Surely you know that, Ricky?" Samantha's mind flashed back to something she had read somewhere: "*Marry a man for money and you'll spend the rest of your life paying for it.*"

Her brother saw the panic rising in her beautiful face. "Hush, Sam, you're getting all worked up. I know you love Cameron and that he's crazy about you. You're a perfect match, like peas in a pod. Believe me, everybody knows that you two are good together." He looked at her reassuringly. "Everything will work out just fine, trust me."

She nodded and smiled, visibly relaxing at his words of encouragement.

"God, that feels better," he said as he put the glass down on her bedside table. "Hair of the dog and all that."

"Did you have a late night last night?"

"Did we ever?" Ricky laughed. "Cameron and I sat up until the small wee hours up at Dunross. Cam's best man Vinny and his brother-in-law David were with us and so was Caroline's boyfriend, Marcus. God, Sam, that's some pad!"

She ignored his praise for her future home. "What time did my fiancé get to bed at?" she asked but her tone was light.

"Damned if I know. I passed out around five this morning. But we had to see him off properly. It was his last night as a single man. You understand, surely, sis?"

She laughed. "Well, I am happy that you get on so well with my husband-to-be."

"That I do," Ricky smiled as he spotted Wendy's barely-touched glass of champagne on another table. "To be honest, he's the brother I never had. We're like soul mates. I'd say we'll be buddies for ever."

"Oh, Ricky, that's such a relief. I was just standing here before you came up thinking about what cold people the rest of his family are. His sisters, I mean, and as for his bloody mother!"

"Yeah, they're all a bit dull, but strictly between you and me, Rose wasn't all that prim last night."

"Christ, Ricky, you didn't seduce my future mother-in-law, did you?" she teased.

"Nah, relax – mind you, she's still one sassy broad. She's quite sexy even though she's old enough to be my mother. Ugh! But I tell you she was bloody well flirting with me last night. When I told her I had Spanish blood, she couldn't get enough of me. I told her my real name was Enrique Garcia and she practically jumped me."

Samantha burst out laughing, "And where was Cameron when his mother was trying to have her wicked way with you?"

"Ah, she's smarter than that. She waited till he was out of the room. I'm telling you, she's a real goer that one."

"Stop, Ricky. I don't believe you."

"Would I lie to you?" But he laughed jovially as he spoke so Sam knew to take him with a pinch of salt. "She even told me I could have the maintenance contract for the Dunross estate as soon as she fired the crowd who do it at the moment.

"You told her about your new business enterprise?"

"Yep, and she was most impressed. I'm telling you, this landscaping business is a licence to print money, Samantha."

"I believe you, little brother." She saw him staring at Wendy's glass. "Go on," she smiled. "It's not like you're driving."

Ricky had crossed the room in a flash to rescue the lonesome glass. "Yeah, James came into the room in the nick of time and pulled her off me. I swear it was a close thing."

She could tell by his tone that he was exaggerating quite a bit and she laughed at him as he happily opened his mouth and throat and downed Wendy's champagne.

"OK," he said as he wiped his lips with the back of his hand. "We've delayed this long enough. Now come on," he took her by the arm, "our Merc awaits."

By two o'clock, the area around the little church in Fiddler's Point was jam-packed with cars. Three stretch Mercs took up the entire space in front of the little chapel, which had been built some two hundred years earlier before such parking problems had been anticipated. Stashed along the narrow streets were the visitors' cars.

The first time Samantha saw the village of Fiddler's Point, she fell in love with it. Just ten miles south of Wicklow town, the roads were absolutely dire but it was well worth the effort to get there. If the Irish tourist board was looking for a quaint old Irish fishing village to market Ireland to the outside world, this was it.

Fiddler's Point was home to Judges' Whiskey. By the time James Judge the First was thirty, he had become so wealthy he was able to build the mansion, Dunross Hall. After him, it was his son Edward who continued the family business. It was also Edward who had been married to the ever popular Granny Vic, as she was affectionately known. Victoria and Edward Judge were married in

1927. A year later, their first son, Charles, was born. For eleven blissful years they lived a privileged luxurious life, although sadly for Victoria she didn't get pregnant again.

In 1939 Edward went off to do his bit for the war. When he got back in '44 he was a very different man. He had lost his *joie de vivre* and he had become very withdrawn. But the one great surprise for everyone was that Victoria then became pregnant again at the grand old age of thirty-four. Their first son, Charles Judge, was sixteen years old by then and he was desperate to get involved in the war. Against Victoria's wishes, Edward granted the boy permission. In early April 1945, Charles Judge was killed in what was his first combat action. Heartbroken and blind with despair, Victoria gave birth to James Judge the Second on the thirtieth of April 1945. It was the day that Hitler committed suicide. The war was over.

For Victoria, however, the misery continued. Her first-born had died only weeks before her second son had even come into the world. The war and Charles's death destroyed Edward too. He couldn't forgive himself for permitting his son to go to war. Edward never came near his new son, James. Instead he buried himself in the distillery.

That baby, James, was Cameron's father. Now it was Cameron's turn to run the distillery. He was the fourth generation of Judges to dominate the Irish whiskey industry.

Samantha knew the story inside out because of the fact that she had worked for them for the last five years. In fact, it was she who introduced the notion of doing visitor tours around the old distillery. The tours had been fantastically successful giving Fiddler's Point yet another financial boost. It quickly became apparent that after a forty-minute walk around the distillery, the busloads of tourists were keen to stop and take photographs of the pretty little town. Fiddler's Point soon had its own coffee shop and a separate gift shop. Ordinarily there wouldn't be enough business in the small town to keep them busy but the tours were a daily occurrence now. Droves of people descended upon the village, spent their money and headed off again. Yes, Samantha thought with satisfaction, Fiddler's Point owed a lot to the Judges.

Coming from the direction of Wicklow, as they were today, the first indication that the village was just ahead was the new petrol station on the right-hand side of the road. Then, a little further along on the left just before the road fell into a steep hill, stood the statue of the Dancing Fiddler.

He stood about ten foot high but, as he was usually seen from a distance, he didn't seem very big – quite the opposite. The Fiddler was cast in bronze, making his features piercingly clear. The veins on his hands stood out in relief. His eyelashes were clearly visible and although larger than life, up close he seemed quite alive.

The Fiddler's demeanour made him look like a friendly sort of chap. His face was permanently etched in a broad smile but his laughing eyes focused intently on his hands and fingers as if to make the fiddle really sing. With a flat cap balanced precariously on the side of his head, he danced to the tune he was playing. It was a constant source of wonder to Samantha how he could be made of something as heavy as bronze while his feet looked light as air. His little companion, a dog, also made of bronze, appeared to run about his feet. The animal was looking up at the fiddler, jaws open and tongue sticking out to the side. He looked like he was panting. His ears were pricked up and his head was tilted. It was as if only the two of them could hear the wonderful music. Samantha loved the Dancing Fiddler because he looked so happy, without a care in the world. Surely Fiddler's Point was a happy place. She was not surprised when she was subsequently told that the Dancing Fiddler was a gift from the Judge family to the people of the village.

Just after the Fiddler, the road took a steep dive and there at the bottom of the hill lay the peaceful little village. It had become quite a respectable size. In fact, lately, the locals had stopped calling it a village. Now it was a small town – not that Samantha knew exactly what differentiated a large village from a small town. Whatever it was, Fiddler's Point was at that stage of development. It had two ladies' clothes shops, a small supermarket, the obligatory chip shop and now there were the new outlets because of the ever-increasing tourist trade. The Fiddler's Rest was just one of the many pubs and of course there was the church with Father Carroll's house just next-door. The row of shops and the church looked out to sea and behind them were a couple of small streets. That's where the residents of Fiddler's Point lived. Over the last few years the roads around the village had been resurfaced and upgraded. Now there was a carpark just opposite the beach and a pretty, if small, promenade making the most of the tiny sandy beach. Just beyond the carpark was the hotel, The Anchor. Two miles further out that road was the magnificent estate of Dunross.

Looking down on the village now from the top to the hill, Samantha was utterly shocked at the chaos that lay below. It was positively packed. She saw three choppers parked on the small carpark down by the beach. There were throngs of people hovering around the church, none of whom she recognised, except of course for Wendy and Gillian. They were already being photographed by a guy who looked disturbingly like a professional. Then she spotted a TV3 van.

"What the hell is going on here, Paul?" she asked her driver.

"You're marrying a Judge, Sam. You're Irish royalty now," he answered simply.

Paul Smith was the Judges' personal driver. His credentials were impeccable. Ex-SAS, he had experience body-guarding many of the world's most famous and he was happy to 'drive' for the Judges. He had worked for them full-time for the last four years. Samantha knew that he had got into some sort of trouble in a shooting incident in England prior to working for the Judges and that was why he was happy to keep a relatively low profile in County Wicklow. That was all she knew about his background. Cameron had told her the rest was all a bit hush hush. Whatever it was, Samantha didn't really mind. He had always been a perfect gentleman to her and she certainly felt very safe when he was around. Sam was sure that he could quite happily handle any unwelcome attention she received on her wedding day.

"What happened to the small and intimate wedding I requested?" Samantha wailed.

That was, of course, before Rose Judge got her hands on the guest list. After the old bat had done her stuff it was now something loud and showy. The worst part about it was that she held the trump card, or should that be 'Trump' as in Donald Trump card, Samantha thought furiously. Rose was paying for the whole show and as such there wasn't a damn thing that the young bride could do. She had hoped that Cameron would stand up to his mother but he never had in the past so why start now? No, she was going to have to get married the Judge Way. That was the sad reality of her situation. She made herself push those thoughts out of her head as the large Mercedes gently inched its way past the expensive cars parked on both sides of the road. It missed thousand-euro wing-mirrors by millimetres and Ricky winced.

"How many people are coming to this bash anyway?"

Samantha sighed, "God knows at this stage. I got panicky when the number went over two hundred but Cameron explained to me that it was business and not to worry about it. Looking at the amount of cars here, I would think you could double or even treble that number."

"*What*? You are exaggerating, aren't you?"

"Ricky, can't you see what I see? Although, I do know that a good deal of the invitees are political."

"You mean politicians?"

"Oh, yes, they're all here, I gather, but what I meant was that there were a lot of political invitations. You know: we couldn't have the MD of the Radisson group of hotels if we didn't invite the MD of the Doyle group too. These people are important to us. They sell oceans of booze for us and so the list just got longer and longer."

"Which does better business, these days?" Ricky asked his sister. "Judges' Whiskey or Gracias?"

"Well, it's hard to compare, Ricky – they're completely different products. You know that. And there's such a wide range of Judges' Whiskey, covering their entire whiskey portfolio from the standard whiskey to their posh and expensive vintage blends." Then she beamed at him. "And then there's Gracias – my baby, my wonderful long-neck alco-pop!"

"It looks like a beer to me," he argued just to tease her.

"Perhaps, but it doesn't taste like beer!"

"No. It's sweeter. But it looks like a beer in a long-neck bottle with frosted glass and it's a gold colour."

"That's no coincidence, little brother. We're going after the beer-drinking market. The fact that it's sweeter is also attracting a larger female market share too."

Ricky slapped his forehead. "And here we are thinking that we can freely choose what we want to drink in a pub of a Saturday night! You business types really have all of us corralled into different market shares and personality profiles, don't you?"

Samantha giggled. "Yep!"

"And you practically own Gracias! This makes you quite a good catch, Sam!"

"Ah, my dear old fiancé and his family hold quite a shareholding too, you know."

"I know, but you're still a major player, girl. How did you get so smart?"

Samantha reached over and kissed her brother on the cheek as Ricky continued, "And of course, now you'll be a Judge too which means probably even more shares for you."

"Hump off, Ricky. You hardly think that's why I'm marrying Cameron. You know how much I love him. The money and shares are just a fringe benefit." She scowled, "And it works both ways. I guess what I've already achieved will now belong to me and Cam as opposed to just me. So really it's a win–win situation. I just think of it as a financial perk!"

"Yeah, like this wedding." He looked out his car window again. "So this is a sort of a corporate do?"

"In a manner of speaking, yes. Don't forget, Cameron is now the Managing Director of the Judge group. Since his father retired last year it's Cam who meets all of these people on a regular basis. So obviously they expected an invite to his wedding."

"Christ, I think you should have eloped."

As she watched the seemingly endless stream of Mercs, Jags and Porches along the road she nodded. "I'm beginning to think you're right."

At last, the bridal car made its way to the doors of church. All the stragglers had been shooed inside. Now only the bridesmaids were standing outside with their driver and a few others. They were smiling broadly and preening as they waited for Samantha. Ricky was out of his side of the car in a flash. But bodyguard Paul was faster, and it was he who opened Samantha's door.

Then Ricky offered his arm to his sister. "Your hand, madam," he smiled at her.

Sam took his hand and gracefully alighted from her car. Suddenly there were two strange men beside her.

"Smile, lovey," one said and a bright flash went off in her face.

"What the –?" Ricky was momentarily stunned. "Who the hell are you?" But in one fluid movement, Paul had armlocked one of the men and snatched his camera. He smashed it to the ground with such force that even Sam got a fright. The camera broke into several expensive-looking bits.

"Oops," Paul smiled through gritted teeth at the man he was holding firmly.

Just then another two bouncers who had been hovering at the door of the church came bounding down and quickly man-handled Paul's prisoner and the other photographer, who had been stunned into inaction, off into the distance.

"What the hell was that about and who in tarnation were the bodyguards?" Samantha asked angrily. "Will somebody please tell me what the heck is going on?"

Wendy and Gillian came rushing over.

Gillian spoke first. "I know one of those photographers. He's a freelance and does a bit of work for *The Sun* and *The News of the World*. They must be down to get a few shots of the wedding of the year.

"They can't just bloody well barge in here without an invitation."

"That's exactly what paparazzi do, Samantha," Gillian explained patiently.

"Well, who saw them off?"

This time it was Ricky who replied. "I assume your dear old hubby arranged security for such a posh wedding."

"He's not my hubby yet," she snapped and then continued, "He bloody well better not have!"

"Why not?"

"I expressly said that I didn't want security. Well, except for Paul, of course." She smiled at her driver who was hovering within earshot and scanning the carpark for any more unwelcome guests. He smiled back, understanding her wish for a more intimate gathering.

Then Samantha frowned again. "I had the same argument with *Hello!* magazine. I'm not famous and it's my wedding. It's personal to me, not a bloody news article. I mean, heck, this is a wedding, not a rock concert!"

Ricky could see that it wouldn't take much for Samantha to throw one of her rare but powerful temper tantrums. She was usually a very serene person but if she lost it, she really lost it. Bloody pre-wedding jitters, he thought.

"Sam, sis, think about it. You said yourself that there are a lot of political heavies and VIPs inside. Those bouncers could belong to any one of them. Surely the President comes with her own security?"

"Not today. I discussed it with her on the phone when she accepted the invitation to the wedding. She said that she was off duty. This was a personal invite so she and her husband would be coming alone. She's incredibly normal like that. She didn't want to take away from my day."

Ricky persevered. "Anyway, isn't it just as well that there was added security? Not that Paul didn't have the entire situation under control." Ricky stared at the driver, secretly amused and impressed to have actually seen him in action.

"I suppose," she agreed, not sounding very convinced.

"And anyway, one problem has just eliminated the other because those photographers will keep the bouncers busy for at least the next ten minutes so any late arrivals won't be frisked. OK?"

Samantha loved her little brother and he had a point. She looked at her bridesmaids and pasted on a smile. "Ready, Gill? Ready, Wendy?"

"Ready!" they chorused.

"OK then, let's go get married."

When the organist started up, the packed church rose to its feet. Gillian and Wendy glided up the aisle, smiling beatifically – perfect angels. Then Samantha, arm in arm with her brother, followed. She didn't know that she was smiling but she was. She could hear the gasps of approval but they didn't really register. All she could see was the sandy head of hair that belonged to Cameron at the top of the church. His square shoulders were held proudly and he was looking straight at the altar. Samantha had made him promise that he wouldn't turn around to see her as she walked up the aisle.

"Why the bloody hell not?" he had laughed.

"Because it's bad luck," she explained. "I want to come up to meet you at the altar." In truth, she wasn't sure that it was bad luck at all. She just wanted to be up close to him when he saw her so she could see the expression on his face. Samantha had really pulled out all the stops to make herself look good for her wedding day and she desperately hoped he would approve.

As she neared the top of the church, she caught sight of James and Rose. He was smiling and nodding in approval. She, on the other hand had an expression of horror followed by begrudging approval on her face. There was nothing she could do about it now, Sam thought with pleasure. Rose had made it quite clear to Samantha that she expected her to dress in a traditional manner but, guessing by her expression, it looked like even Rose was conceding to the fact that Samantha looked absolutely amazing. When she looked back again to the strong square shoulders of her fiancé, Sam was disappointed to see that he was in fact looking back at her.

"I couldn't help it," he mouthed as he smiled and studied her from head to toe.

What the heck, she thought as she and Ricky reached her groom.

"Take good care of my sister, Cameron," Ricky whispered as he shook the hand of his soon-to-be-brother-in-law. Then the two men, so fond of each other, bear-hugged.

"You know I will," Cameron promised as he squeezed Ricky.

"Oh, and Happy Birthday," Ricky added.

"Thanks," Cameron laughed. Then he looked into Samantha's eyes. "And what a birthday present! My God, you're gorgeous," he whispered.

"You weren't meant to look back," she scowled, but her eyes were smiling.

"I couldn't stand the suspense. Relax, it's too late for any bad luck now. We're both here and in one piece. Right?"

She nodded in agreement as they mounted the single step up to the priest together.

Not overly religious, Samantha and Cameron had kept their service short and sweet. Father Carroll was an old family friend of the Judges and he made the whole affair pleasant and amusing. She was five minutes into the service before she spotted the TV3 film crew on the side of the altar. Samantha was justifiably stunned. What were they doing there? Surely Cameron hadn't sanctioned that? Then again, there was no way they would have been there if he hadn't. Perhaps it was a friend of his who worked in TV3, doing a special wedding video for them. Maybe Cameron wanted to surprise her. Then her attention was drawn back to the service.

"Now," he said in his friendly tone, "just before I make it all official, is there any reason why anybody here can see any good cause, legal or otherwise, why these two lovely people can't be joined together in the sacred unity of marriage?"

As the usual deafening silence fell upon the crowd at this point, the two inner doors at the back of church groaned open.

"Me!" was screeched from the back of crowd.

It was so loud everybody in the congregation, including Samantha and Cameron, turned around.

The female figure was a small and skinny one. She wore a navy headscarf and a light sandy-coloured trench coat, belted tightly around her miniscule waist. Under the hem of the coat were two spindly legs that looked more suited to a bird than a human being. The Jackie Onassis sunglasses covered practically all of her face, but Samantha instantly knew who it was.

"Mother," she whispered.

Cameron, who had never met Sam's mum, had heard his bride. More importantly so had Father Carroll. Cameron's eyes scanned the back of the church. Where the hell was his extra security?

"Me!" she shouted again from where she stood. This time with even more conviction.

Father Carroll coughed to clear his throat. "Is there something you wish to say, madam?" he asked politely but even at that distance, he had noticed the brown-paper bag that she clutched desperately in her right hand. It obviously concealed a bottle of something. Her stagger was the other give-away that she was under the influence of alcohol as she tried to lurch a few feet further up the aisle.

"Me!" she repeated even louder if that were possible. "I know why they can't get married and so do his family, by God, but they won't say. Too bloody proud!"

Father Carroll could feel the crowd getting hostile. To stop a wedding was one thing, but to insult the hosts of what was promising to be the biggest social Who's Who event of the year – now that was just going too darn far.

"Madam, if you know of a reason why these two fine young people can't get married, please share it with us," the priest commanded. Then he added, "Please tell the congregation who you are."

Kathleen White Garcia hovered for a long moment. From behind the safety of her large dark glasses, she let her eyes rest upon her only daughter. She shook her head miserably and Samantha saw her mouth the words "I'm sorry," to her. Then she raised her voice again. "My name is Kathleen Garcia," she said proudly, and she raised the brown-paper bag up over her head as if summoning all her remaining courage and energy into one single action.

"The bride and the groom can't get married," she announced

loudly to a stunned congregation, "because the bride and groom are in fact brother and sister!"

Then Kathleen collapsed onto the floor unconscious, the glass bottle smashing as it hit the cold church tiles.

Then there was silence.

CHAPTER 3

Tess Delaney responded without even thinking about it. This strange little woman who was obviously completely out of her mind with the drink had just collapsed in the middle of the aisle and nobody was moving a muscle. The whole drama had happened just beside her pew at the back of the church and so, instinctively, she simply stepped out and tried to help. She wanted to get the lady onto her feet but failed. Despite Tess's larger frame and this intoxicated woman's small size, the woman was a dead weight in her unconscious state. Tess looked up with panic on her face. She feared that the woman might have died.

"Is there a doctor in the house?" she pleaded. Still nobody moved. Then, after a split second, which felt like an eternity, it was Samantha who tore down the aisle.

She had dropped her flowers at Father Carroll's feet and run at full speed. She was so fast, she had reached her mother before either Wendy or Gillian had yet moved. Cameron was rooted to the spot with sheer horror. Then Ricky, the ever-faithful little brother, ran after her.

Frank Delaney was a little shyer than his wife but, when he saw how she needed him, he quickly stepped out of his pew.

As Ricky reached his mother's limp body, he realised that he hadn't actually seen her for some five years. In that time he had grown bigger and stronger. Sadly, she had grown smaller and weaker. Everybody watched him as he carefully tried to overstep the shards and retrieve his mother from the pool of shattered glass. He was able to lift her as easily as he might a small sleeping child. The glass crunched loudly under his feet. Other than the grinding of the broken glass, the silence was absolute. Now that he had her in his arms, however, he didn't quite know what to do with her.

Tess's heart went out to the bride – the poor girl's face was flushed and wide-eyed with panic. "Samantha," she addressed her by name, even though she had never actually met her before, "don't worry – Frank and I will take this poor unfortunate creature home with us. You go back up there and go on with your marriage service."

"It's not quite that simple," Ricky explained. He dropped his voice to a whisper. "This woman *is* our mother."

Samantha was staring at her mother in Ricky's big strong arms. She reached out and held Kathleen's hand as it hung limply down by her side. Frank just stood there, acutely uncomfortable, waiting to be told what to do.

Tess couldn't believe her ears. Did that mean that there was possibly some grain of truth in the crazy woman's ranting? Surely, it had to be some sort of mistake. She thought quickly. She addressed Ricky. "Look, give her to Frank and we'll take her home. We live nearby. Don't worry, we'll look after her." Then she spoke to Samantha. "You go and talk to Father Carroll," she suggested. "He'll know what to do."

Frank Delaney took Kathleen Garcia's limp body from Ricky. Then Tess gestured to her husband to get the heck out of the church. Sam stood by the doors, which, just a brief while earlier her mother had walked through. Ricky, as always, stood by her side.

They watched Tess and Frank walk out through the doors of the church, Frank's strong broad back practically obscuring the fragile load he was carrying.

31

"Samantha?" Ricky tried to break into her trance.

"Mum," Sam whispered, "how could it be?"

"Sister," Ricky tried again. He gently touched her arm so that he might be able to guide her back up the aisle. Samantha blinked as if she was coming out of a daydream or in this case a living nightmare.

"Come on," he urged as she began to respond to his gentle encouragement.

Samantha's mind was in a whirl. Christ, had that really happened? She looked at her brother who was smiling reassuringly.

For the second time in twenty minutes, Ricky and Samantha walked up the aisle together. This time there were no smiles from the congregation, no sharp gasps of admiration at the bride's great beauty. This time the congregation either examined the floor or closed their eyes in pretence of prayer.

"Don't worry about that. She's a nutter. You and I know that. Come on," he whispered.

Samantha nodded mutely. Some of her little curls had come free when she ran down the church and now she looked very vulnerable and more in need of his protection than ever. Ricky thought his heart would break. Jesus, he was going to have his mother locked up after this. "That woman – she's a vindictive, malevolent, stupid –" he stopped himself before he got too carried away. Samantha was watching him with huge worried eyes. "Sorry, sis."

They had reached the altar again and Ricky guided Samantha back to a very sombre-looking Cameron who thrust her bouquet back into her arms.

"You dropped these," he said coolly.

"Is everything all right?" Father Carroll asked the totally dazed bride.

"Of course it is," Cameron snapped. "Let's get this thing over with."

Samantha looked at the friendly face of the priest and then at Cameron's furious scowl. Then she turned and looked down the centre of the church. There was no sign of her mother or those lovely people. The only evidence that anything had happened at all was the puddle of liquid that had spilled from Kathleen's broken bottle and the twinkling bits of glass that refracted the sunlight mockingly back to her. Who were those kind people? Where had they taken her mother? They had said they lived nearby – but hadn't said where exactly. That meant that she didn't know where her mother actually was. Then Samantha looked over at Ricky. In the pew behind him stood a positively furious Rose Judge. Did she know anything of what her mother was ranting about? James Judge looked utterly shell-shocked.

"Samantha?" Father Carroll was trying to bring her back into the service but she was somewhere else.

How could her mother think that Cameron and she were brother and sister? Was it possible? Sam knew that Kathleen was her mother. Could it be that Pablo wasn't her true father? Had her mother once known James Judge? She looked at Cameron's father again. He squirmed where he stood under the weight of Sam's glare and began to study the intricate design of the church tiles about his feet.

"Samantha!" Cameron snapped.

She jumped, as did half the dumbstruck congregation. She looked at her fiancé with her huge sad eyes brimming with tears. Very gently she shook her head at him. "I'm sorry," she whispered. "I have to find out what just happened."

Cameron grabbed her wrist and clenched it tightly, although he did try to do it as discreetly as possible. "Don't be stupid. You know your mother is a madwoman. She's just doing what she does best. She's wrecking your life."

Samantha glanced at the priest and then over at her brother.

Ricky stepped up to the threesome, sensing her need for support. "Sis?"

"Ricky, you said it – she is vindictive, she is malevolent but she's not stupid. This wedding would have been in her interest if only for financial reasons." Samantha's eyes were beginning to clear and her tone was definitely firmer. She glanced at the priest and smiled in embarrassment. "Sorry, Father Carroll." Then she turned to Cameron. "Darling, you heard what she said – we have to find out what –"

"Bollocks," he whispered urgently through clenched teeth. He turned and smiled confidently at the waiting congregation, then he turned back to Sam and continued through gritted teeth, "We're hardly going to back out now just on the strength of the rantings of some old lush."

"That's my mother you're talking about, Cameron."

"Yes, Samantha, but you know as well as me she's a bitter old woman who lost touch with reality a long time ago."

"Are you sure about that?" the bride's eyes flashed.

"You leave this church now and you'll never meet me at the altar again – Samantha, I've never been more serious in all my life."

"Cameron," Father Carroll's soft friendly tone had evaporated and in its place was some considerable authority, "perhaps we should resolve this little issue before we proceed." He was firm and placed his hand on Cameron's wrist, the one that gripped Samantha's. The groom had the sense to let go. "Go in peace, my child," he blessed Samantha.

With that, she turned again to her fiancé, "I'm so sorry, Cameron. I do still love you more than anybody on the planet."

Then she turned on her stiletto heel and in one fluid movement left him standing at the altar. She stopped for a brief second to stuff her beautiful bouquet of ivory-tinted lilies and champagne-coloured roses into Wendy's hands and then she shot off back down the aisle and out into the September sun.

Paul had been sitting up against the boot of his large black Merc, keeping a secure eye on the peace in Fiddler's Point. The photographers were nowhere to be seen and the two extra bodyguards were walking around the perimeter of the church. He jumped when he saw Samantha come running out. She had her delicate ivory dress scrunched up in her hands, bringing it right up above her knees. Glamorous she was not. She squinted in the glare of the September sunlight. The little church had been so dark.

"Which way did they go, Paul?" she asked urgently.

"Who? The photographers?"

"No, the man carrying my mother – and his wife?"

"Your mother?" he gasped.

"Which bloody way?"

"Sorry, I thought it was some guest who had fainted," he explained. "They went around the back of the church and I don't think they came back. Maybe one of the other bodyguards saw more than that." He stood up as if prepared for action but Samantha was already gone in the direction that he had pointed.

The two bouncers were having a discreet cigarette around the back.

"Did either of you see a man carrying a woman coming this way, with another woman?" she pleaded.

They were startled at the surprising intrusion and one nodded as he jettisoned his still-lit cigarette. "We helped them home. The drunk began to wake up and she became a little difficult."

"Where did they go?"

This was the first time Samantha had ever been around the back of Fiddler's Point church. She and Cameron had been to Mass there a few times in the run-up to the wedding just for the sake of appearances but she had never actually bothered to walk around the building. There was a smaller carpark filled to the gills with guests' cars there. It led out onto another little street which was mostly made up of housing as opposed to shops. One of the men ran to the church gate.

"They went down there. Number 9, I think it was. It had a red door," he added as Samantha ran past him in the direction he was pointing. She moved remarkably well for a woman running in three-inch stilettos and holding up a three-foot bridal train.

It was only five doors up as the doors climbed in uneven numbers. "One, three, five," she passed two little girls who giggled at her strange appearance. Suddenly Samantha remembered something that the lady had said in the church: "Frank and I –" She turned to the gigglers. "Does a man called Frank live in that house?" she asked them, pointing to Number 9.

35

"Frank Delaney, yeah, he lives in there, missus," said one of the girls. "But you're too late," she added with a little smirk.

Samantha stopped in her tracks; maybe the girls had seen them leave for the hospital or something. "Why? Is he gone?" she asked in alarm.

"No – worse," she laughed. "He's married!" The two guffawed and tore off towards the town centre.

Samantha ran up and banged on the door. It was Frank who answered.

"Thank God, you're here, pet," he said. "I don't know how much longer we could have contained her. She was ranting something awful a few minutes ago. She might be under the influence but she's a fairly determined woman and she's surely determined to stop your wedding."

"Thank you, Frank? Isn't it?" Sam looked at the man with the kind eyes.

"My name is Frank Delaney and my wife is Tess. She's the good Samaritan," he smirked. "She's in with –" He couldn't bring himself to say 'your mother'. He coughed and continued. "Come in, anyway."

Samantha stepped inside obediently. He led her into a small dark room just to the right of the front door. She figured it was their lounge. There was only one sofa and it was very worn. The Delaneys were not rich people.

Tess looked up. She had only just managed to get Kathleen to lie down and close her eyes. Samantha looked so incongruous in the room. Her beautifully designed wedding dress was already looking the worse for wear following her sprint from the church. Her fine features and painstakingly arranged hair only served to accentuate the incongruity. It made her look like a princess in a slum. She rushed to her mother's side and fell to her knees on the floor next to her head.

Tess winced. The dress wouldn't stand much more of that kind of treatment.

"Mummy, what have you done?"

Kathleen's eyes snapped open instantly when she heard her daughter's voice. She scrambled for Samantha's left hand. Sam realised that she was looking to see if there was a wedding ring on it. Kathleen took a deep breath and flopped back down on the couch, relieved to find the bride's hand was still ringless.

"Oh, Sami, Sami, my little Sam!" She used the chant that she had always sung to her daughter when she was a baby.

Hearing it again had a devastating effect on Samantha. It was her private little piece of her mother that nobody else knew about. To hear her mother rhyme it off again peeled back the years in a flash. Samantha burst out crying. "Why did you have to come today? What are you playing at, Mummy?" The tears flowed as she dropped her head onto her mother's arm.

Kathleen was too weak or too sloshed to sit up. "I'm so sorry, my little angel. I should have told you long before but I didn't know."

"What the hell didn't you know?"

"I didn't know you were in love with *him*."

"Cameron?"

"He's a Judge. They're poison."

Samantha ignored the slur on the Judges. "I tried to tell you last time I saw you but you wouldn't let me. You went crazy as soon as I mentioned the Judges. Why? You knew I was working for them. I told you when I got the job years ago. You knew that, didn't you?" she pleaded, willing her mother to admit that she had made some terrible mistake.

"Yes, I knew. Do you not remember me going crazy and telling you to get away from them and work somewhere else?" Samantha heaved a huge sigh. "No, Mother. I remember you getting utterly drunk and telling me that they were evil and I remember me explaining to you that it was the booze not the actual family that was bloody evil."

Kathleen found the energy to nod in agreement. "Yes, darling, I agree with you there. The drink is no friend of mine but neither are the Judges."

"You know the Judges? How?" Samantha asked, her voice shaking. She asked even though she didn't want to know the answer.

"Take my hand, little Sam," was all Kathleen managed to say. Her voice was very weak.

"Talk to me," Samantha pleaded, secretly wishing her mother to stop. She took Kathleen's hand and squeezed it hard. "Talk to me! What did you mean at the church today?"

But Kathleen did not respond.

Samantha continued through great big sobs. "Pablo Garcia is my father. He lives in Rioja in Spain. I haven't seen him for thirty years but he is my father. You told me. I even remember him. Pablo is my papi." She employed the Spanish word for father that she had used so often as a little girl. "Or – or – did you mean that Cameron is yours? Or that I'm *not* yours? Help me, Mum, I can't bear this!"

Kathleen lay on the little sofa, eyes shut, mouth closed. Samantha shook her mother gently. "Do you hear me? Don't pass out on me now, Mum! Tell me! Was it a lie?" she pleaded. "Why do you hate the Judges? Did they hurt you? Mother, talk to me! Wake up and tell me you're lying."

But Kathleen lay there as if she were dead.

Tess and Frank Delaney had long since left the room. They sat at their little kitchen table at the back of the house. Frank pretended to study the newspaper and Tess rocked gently to and fro, her eyes closed as she chased off a quick decade of the rosary. Neither she nor Frank could help overhearing Samantha's cries, though.

Tess opened her eyes and stopped rocking. "Should I go in, do you think?" she asked her husband.

"I don't know," he answered unhelpfully.

She stood up and then sat down again.

The decision was taken from them, however. Samantha barged in the door.

"Come and help, please!"

Tess was up in a flash. "What's wrong, pet?"

"She won't talk to me. I think she's passed out."

Somebody was knocking on the front door. Frank answered it.

"Hi, I'm Sam's brother, Ricky."

"You'd better come with me so," Frank said simply.

They followed Tess and Samantha into the little front lounge. With four adults standing and another lying on the sofa, the small room was now very crowded. Tess rushed to Kathleen. She quickly felt for a pulse. She looked at her husband solemnly. "Frank, call an ambulance."

Samantha covered her mouth with her hands. "Christ, don't say she's dead. Have I killed my mother?"

CHAPTER 4

Back at the church, Rose Judge did what any self-respecting mother of the groom would do under the circumstances. She fainted.

Father Carroll had just started into a little impromptu speech about life not always going according to plan and how only God had all the answers when she collapsed into an undignified heap beside James Judge. No one was happier than Cameron. He had been absolutely mortified as he stood at the altar bolstered up by his best man, Vinny. What really kept him vertical however was his pure and unadulterated rage. Samantha was in deep trouble. Never ever had he been so humiliated. The marriage was definitely off, that was the first thing, and she was probably fired too. Jesus, she was finished – nobody treated a Judge like that. Then Rose fell over. Cameron ran to her side.

"Is there a doctor in the house? It's my mother," he said clearly, confidently and loudly across the congregation.

He was instantly attended to by three GPs, a thoracic surgeon, a paediatrician and two oncologists. This was the chance that Cameron needed. He scooped his mother up in his arms and ignoring his flotilla of surgeons, he carried her out of the church, much as Frank Delaney had done with Kathleen White just ten minutes earlier. Vinny tried to help by getting everybody to stand back to give them space.

Cameron wasn't even sure at this point whether his mother was faking it or not. He wouldn't put it past her, but her health was not really his primary concern just at the moment. Getting out of that godforsaken church was.

"Paul!" Cameron called to his driver. "Get the two boys to confiscate all of the TV3 film footage. OK?"

"Got it, boss."

Cameron felt some of his old power returning. "Better still, see to it yourself. I'll get one of the ministerial Mercs to take me and Mum to the hospital. That way we can go a heck of a lot faster than if we take one of the bridal cars."

"I'm coming too," James Judge announced. He had followed his son straight out of the church.

"Is she all right?" Paul looked genuinely concerned as the pack of medics and a few of the more ghoulish guests oozed out of the church just behind Cameron.

For the first time Cameron actually looked down at his mother. Her eyes were rolling badly. Christ, he thought nervously, she definitely wasn't faking it.

"OK," Cameron spoke severely, "let's get Mum to Wicklow General. That's the nearest."

"What do you want me to do about all these people?" Vinny asked his highly agitated friend.

"Tell them all to sod off back to wherever they came from. To be honest, Vinny, I only recognised half of them anyway."

The best man nodded mutely. The-wedding-is-off speech was not a very pleasant task and one that most best men managed to avoid.

Minister Bill Boggan's Merc was the closest to Cameron. His chauffeur was sitting in the front seat having a little snooze. Cameron didn't even ask permission. He just got a hovering doctor to open the back door and they deposited Rose onto the back seat with as much dignity as they could.

"Son, I have to go with you."

Cameron had never seen his father look so shaken. He must love the old lady still, he thought.

"Mummy!" Stephanie came running out next, followed by her seven-year-old brat Zoë and the nanny who was carrying baby Amy – the youngest Judge. Bringing up the rear was Stephanie's poor long-suffering husband David Neilson.

Cameron grabbed his sister. "Steph, not now. Let us get her to the hospital and we'll let you know what's what as soon as we know."

Stephanie looked at her older brother. "This is all your bloody fault, I hope you realise."

"Please, Stephanie," Cameron controlled his temper as he scanned the carpark for cameras, as always thinking of his public image, "we'll talk later." He looked around for her husband. "Dave, could you help a little here? I've got to get Mum to the hospital. Why don't you lot head back to Rathnew Manor? I'll see you there later."

Wendy and Gillian, the two deserted bridesmaids, were hovering just outside the church door. The weather had clouded over and it looked like rain was imminent.

"We really need to support the family," Gillian said to her friend.

"You're absolutely right," Wendy agreed. "How?"

"OK, what if I keep an eye on Cameron and you go find Samantha? Are you happy with that?"

"Damn sure. I think you're getting the short straw there, Gilly. Have you seen the scowl on him? It would curdle cream."

Gillian shrugged and grinned. "It's a nasty job, but someone's got to do it." She ran off towards Bill Boggan's Merc just as Cameron was getting in beside his still unconscious mother. James Judge was getting in the front seat beside the driver.

Wendy watched Gillian say something to Cameron and then climb in beside him as David Neilson dragged a now-bawling Stephanie Judge-Neilson away from the long shiny black ministerial Mercedes. Then Wendy went off in search of Samantha.

Cameron was in a thunderous mood in the back of the car. His mother had stirred and mumbled something but then seemed to lapse into unconsciousness again. Despite his concern for his wife, and to Cameron's great annoyance, James was smoking, something he only did on occasions of great joy or tension. No prizes for guessing which one this was, Cameron thought darkly.

"Would it be wise to phone ahead, Mr Judge?" the chauffeur asked nervously.

"What?" Cameron's mind was elsewhere.

"Your mother, sir. Would it be prudent to phone Wicklow General and tell them we're coming so they're ready, like?"

"Oh, yes. Thanks – er, what's your name?"

"John, sir."

"Yeah, John, phone ahead. I assume you have a phone in this thing."

"No, sir, but I have my own mobile. We can use that."

"Yeah, thanks, John. I don't have my phone on me today. I didn't really think I'd need it." He laughed coldly. "Just shows you – you should take your mobile with you everywhere these days, shouldn't you, Gilly?"

She felt very uncomfortable. Perhaps this wasn't such a good idea. You could have cut the atmosphere in the car with a wedding-cake knife. The one small consolation was that in the minister's car, they could overtake everything and travel at speeds significantly above the legal speed limit. The only thing to overtake them was an ambulance.

"There's another poor old sod. Jesus, what a day," Cameron sighed.

Then he leaned forward and squeezed his father's shoulder. "Hey, Dad, are you OK?"

"It's your mother," James explained. "She looks pretty bad." He tried to turn so he could get a better look at her in the seat directly behind him. "You don't think she's had a stroke or anything?"

"Relax, Dad. Mum is always fainting. You know that. I think it was just the shock. Hey, speaking of shocks – what do you think of bloody Kathleen White? What was she doing calling herself Garcia? She's obviously a psycho."

Gillian watched him. He obviously didn't know about Sam's Garcia past and so he continued.

"She was something else, wasn't she? Total nutter. She should be locked up. How does Samantha live with that in her life?"

He wasn't remotely upset or frantic about what Samantha's mother had said. It was quite obvious that he knew there was no truth in it. This made her slightly more comfortable. "Well, to be honest, I don't think she sees much of her mum any more," she explained. "Samantha and Ricky had a party for his twenty-fifth and her thirtieth, five years ago, back at home in Salthill. They paid for the whole thing themselves and, against their better judgement, they invited her. It was a sort of last-ditch effort to get the family back together again – well, the three of them at any rate. Anyway, she ruined the entire night. Kathleen embarrassed them and made a holy show of herself courtesy of the drink, as usual. Heck, she's an alcoholic. Isn't that what they do? Anyway, I remember that it was back then that they both vowed to cut her out of their lives." Gillian looked at Cameron and James Judge. They were both listening to her intently and so she continued. "Well, it was only because Sam was getting married that she went back home to Galway, to visit her mother again last month. But she never got to tell her about the wedding or anything. No sooner had she mentioned Judges' Whiskey but Kathleen went wild, calling poor Sam every name under the sun. Exactly as she had done years ago when Sam first told her she was working for Judges." Gilly looked out the window as the Wicklow landscape sped past. "Well, that was that for Samantha. She promised herself that she would never see or even attempt to see her mother again."

"What about her father?" James Judge asked.

"He lives in Spain. He's Spanish. I think Kathleen kicked him out or he might have walked out on her – I'm not sure which, after Enrique was born."

"You mean Ricky?" Cameron asked, genuinely amazed to realise how little he knew about his girlfriend's family.

"Yes. Sorry – Ricky. I must have called him Enrique because of the Garcia thing coming back."

"What Garcia thing?" Cameron asked nervously.

Gillian explained. "Samantha and Ricky's father is a man called Pablo Garcia. They changed their name back to White when they moved to Galway. It's Kathleen's maiden name. I suppose they thought it would be easier to settle in with a more anglicised name. Remember that was thirty years ago. Ireland was very insular back then."

James Judge lit another cigarette and stared straight ahead as he spoke clearly. "So Kathleen White was in fact – once upon a time – Kathleen Garcia? Is that what you're saying, Gillian?" But still he looked dead ahead.

"Yep, but that's all ancient history," Gillian said.

Cameron looked shocked and slightly less confident than he had a brief while earlier.

Rose began to groan.

"Mum," he turned his attention to his mother, "Mum, are you all right?"

"Oh, my, everything is spinning. Where am I?" Rose asked, sounding genuinely lost.

"We're on our way to the hospital. You fainted. We want to check out that you're OK."

John, the driver made his phone call to Wicklow General and was happy to report that a private room would be set aside for Mrs Judge.

When Samantha and Ricky got to Wicklow General Hospital's Accident and Emergency department they were treated like royalty. The ambulance man explained Sam's dress by saying 'The Judge Wedding,' and there the confusion started. The room that had been set aside and considerably spruced up for Rose Judge was quickly occupied by Kathleen White. She had regained consciousness again and she was ranting profanities. "He's a bastard, a bollocks. He never loved her, he loved me."

Samantha was mortified. "Mother, please shut up. We'll all be arrested for disturbing the peace."

"Ah, he's only a bugger, James Judge. I was too good for him all these years – that's the truth and all."

The nurses sniggered as they half heartedly tried to calm her. This was not a side of Rose Judge you ever got to see. *The Mirror* had been tipped off by their photographer down in Fiddler's Point and they had a reporter posing as a patient with a sprained ankle. He was really sorry he didn't have a camera with him as he watched the woman he thought was Rose Judge throw her tantrum. This was just too good to be true.

Back at Fiddler's Point, Wendy couldn't find Samantha anywhere. The church crowd had dispersed incredibly quickly. Most of them were terrified of being photographed by *Hello!* magazine at the fiasco of the year. Any of the younger ones who still wanted to party decided to grace The Fiddler's Rest with their presence and they were getting well stuck in. At last, Wendy found Tess Delaney's house following a discreet tip-off from one of the security guys. Tess didn't want to say too much, only that they were worried about Kathleen's health and Ricky and Samantha had taken her to the hospital by ambulance.

Then Wendy ran out of steam. She wasn't really ready for the Fiddler's Rest but she also realised that she had no means of transport back to Rathnew Manor. Would she even bloody well stay there that night? All her clothes were there so she had to get back to collect them if nothing else. Feeling just a little useless, she headed back to the church in the hope of bumming a lift back to the Manor.

Good old reliable Paul was still standing sentry. He had whisked Victoria Judge back to Dunross Hall and returned to the church in case any more Judges needed him. Everybody else was gone. He was sitting against the bonnet of his car, much as he had been earlier. Like Wendy, Paul wasn't sure where to go next. If nothing happened soon, he would head back up to Dunross. Not much point in hanging around the church.

"Thank God, a familiar face," Wendy smiled as she came around the corner.

"Oh, hi, Wendy. Any news?"

"Well, it looks like Samantha's mother has been rushed to Wicklow General Hospital and so has Cameron's mum. So I guess that's where all the action is now."

"Do you want to go up there?" he offered.

She looked at him and smirked conspiratorially. "Right now? Not really, to be honest."

"Good, neither do I," he grinned. "I have my phone on. If they want me they'll call."

"Has everybody else gone?" she asked.

"Yep, the only one that was really lost was Minister Bill Boggan. He had no transport because Cameron hi-jacked his car to take his mother to hospital. Anyway, a gang of lovely young things took him off to The Fiddler's Rest and he didn't seem too perturbed in the end."

"Yeah?" Wendy smiled shyly.

"What the hell happened today?" Paul asked eventually, feeling that this was the first time it was acceptable to actually ask such a question.

Wendy studied Paul's face for a moment and then she shrugged. "I may as well tell you, considering it will probably be in all the papers tomorrow. Paul, the wedding is off, for the time being at least," she said.

He looked baffled. "Because Samantha's mother passed out and then Mrs J fainted too?"

"It's not *because* they passed out, it's *why* they passed out," Wendy explained. "It would appear that, according to Kathleen, Samantha's dear old ma – well, she said that Cameron and Samantha were brother and sister."

Paul burst out laughing. "But that's bullshit!"

"Is it? How would you know? You weren't with the Judge family thirty-five years ago, were you?"

"No, I was only ten years old, thirty-five years ago, thank you very much, but I still know that that's bullshit, Wendy."

So you're forty-five, she thought, and no ring.

"Think about it, would you," he continued, oblivious to her private little fantasy. "That poor woman was raving drunk – she probably didn't know what she was saying. And if she wanted to stop the wedding for some crazy reason, she'd probably have said anything that popped into her head!"

Wendy thought about this for a moment. "I guess you're right. Kathleen is obviously having delusions again. Thanks, Paul. You're the voice of reason." She was wondering if he was single. At six foot four he towered over Cameron Judge and Ricky White and that was saying something – they were big boys. Paul was also very broad and Wendy was fairly sure that he knew how to use his muscles. *Yummy*, she thought, but then she forced her mind back to the matter in hand.

"Paul," she smiled sweetly, "about that lift?"

CHAPTER 5

The air was blue when Cameron Judge reached the admittance desk in the Accident and Emergency ward at Wicklow General Hospital.

"What the hell do you mean you had a room for her, but it's suddenly become occupied?" he yelled at the young nurse on desk duty. He slammed his hand down on the white counter top making the pen-holder and in-tray jump in terror. "Who is your supervisor? I want to speak to someone in authority here." Cameron scanned the ward.

"I'm so sorry, Mr Judge, sir, but we understood that the lady who arrived about half an hour ago was Mrs Judge – your mother, sir."

How could they mistake his mother for anyone else, he wondered furiously – morons! He leaned over the counter so he could whisper to the nurse. But his body language was overbearing and aggressive. "Do I need to tell you who I am? Have you any idea how much money we've donated to this – this bloody hospital over the last I don't know how many years! Damn it, there's even a Judge ward somewhere in this –" He stopped himself just short of saying 'kip'.

Wicklow General Hospital was, in fact, a fine facility. It had undergone a massive expansion over the previous five years due to the huge swell in the Wicklow county population. Hence all the fundraisers. Thanks to the Judges' creative accountants, however, every handout that they made to the hospital went under the heading of charity donation and as such it was tax deductible. It hadn't actually cost too much. He changed tack slightly.

"You are aware that it was the Minister's driver – Minister Bill Boggan, that is – it was his driver who phoned ahead to get this room organised?"

The girl on reception was on the verge of tears. "I'm sorry, Mr Judge. Just as soon as we get a free bed, we'll get your mother sorted out."

He stormed away from the desk. It was utterly futile talking to that little twerp, he realised. He would have to find a doctor or matron himself.

James Judge and Gillian were sitting in the waiting room with all the other patients, waiting to be seen. Rose was fully awake now but she was very weak and shivering badly. She sat between them looking particularly frail and petite. Gill had found a blanket and wrapped it around the older woman. Then she wrapped her arm around Rose protectively. Gilly reckoned that Cameron's mother had gone straight into shock. She was staring at the floor mutely. Her eyes were glazed over and she was still shivering despite the blanket and Gillian's hugs.

She was still completely unresponsive.

"What seems to be the problem? Why the delay?" James asked uncomfortably.

"They've bloody well given Mum's bed away. God knows how it happened but now we're stuck in this mess until they can get her another one. Christ, what a day!" He forked his hand back through his hair, something he always did when he was under pressure.

Gillian tried to assist. "Does Rose have a private doctor who might be able to help us?"

James shrugged. "Her personal doctor is Paddy Ryan. He would have been at the wedding today only he's away."

"Where is he? Could we talk to him?" Cameron asked hopefully.

"I have no idea, son. You know these doctors – it's some damn medical junket. He's probably in the Caribbean or the Far East."

Then from the corner of his eye, Cameron saw a woman come out of an office. She particularly caught his attention because she was in a blue uniform as opposed to the more prevalent white. She had to be the matron, he reasoned, as he jumped to his feet. If she was in charge, she was bloody well going to sort this situation out. Judges didn't wait to be seen – people waited for the Judges. He strode confidently across the ward but stopped dead in his tracks when he saw who was following in the matron's footsteps.

"Samantha!" he gasped.

She looked up, as did the matron.

"Cam, oh thank God you came!" She rushed across the ward to hug him, attracting the attention of everybody in Accident and Emergency. Cameron was still in his formal morning suit. He wore black trousers with a very fine grey pinstripe running through it and his tails were the same shade of grey. His cummerbund was black – always conservative and classically chic, that was Cameron. The only colour concession he had made for his wedding day was the rose in his buttonhole. It was a pale cream colour, like Samantha's ivory wedding dress.

Cameron side-stepped her hug and simply took her wrist in his left hand. He held her to the side as if she were a child who would be dealt with presently. Sam stopped short at this treatment. Then he addressed the older woman.

"Are you the matron?" he asked, mustering as much charm as he could.

"Yes, I am. And you are?"

"Judge," he thrust out his right hand to shake hers. "Cameron Judge. We phoned you en route to the hospital to let you know that we had an emergency. My mother –" he gestured over his shoulder to where James, Rose and Gilly sat, "my mother has taken some sort of a turn. She needs medical attention straight away."

"Yes, I thought there was some sort of confusion," the matron agreed. "We thought this young lady's mother was your mother and I'm afraid she has Mrs Judge's room." Matron began to stride over to Rose. "Not to worry – we'll sort this out."

Cameron, however, stood rooted to the spot. He whispered urgently at Samantha. "*Your* mother has taken *my* mother's bed? What the hell are you playing at?"

"Me? I didn't even know Rose was ill, Cam." She tried to pull her arm away. "We had to call an ambulance for Mum. She went into a coma and when we got here they said that they were expecting us. I assumed that the ambulance guys had phoned ahead."

Cameron continued to speak quietly but he still managed to spit the words at her. "I'm quite sure that your 'ambulance guys'," he mimicked her voice in a most unflattering manner, "did phone ahead but do you not think that the service you were getting was just a little privileged for a bloody lush?"

Samantha yanked her arm hard and this time she did manage to free herself from his grip. It was quite obvious he was going to make this as difficult as possible.

"Stop calling her that. My mother is sick. It's not her fault. And as for the service we got – it was perfectly fine. When we got here one of the nurses asked me was I from the Judge wedding and I simply said yes. Bloody hell, I do look the part!" She stared at him defiantly, matching his glare.

Cameron dropped his gaze first and stormed back to his mother, father and Gillian.

Sam stood in the middle of the ward, aware of all the eyes on her for the first time. She was a miserable sight. Most of her hair had fallen down at this stage. Her dress looked worn out and she suddenly felt like that herself. If she was Cinderella at the ball earlier in the day, it was well after her personal midnight now, she realised miserably. Everybody had seen her fiancé storm away from her in the middle of a crowded ward. It wouldn't take much more to make her cry. She ran back to the sanctuary of her mother's little room.

Matron gave Rose Judge a quick assessment and assured them she was in no immediate danger. However, she agreed that Rose needed a thorough going over by a doctor. The problem was that there were no beds for her and she might have to wait for a few hours.

Cameron was positively mutinous. "You let that bloody *nobody* take your last available bed and now you're telling me that there's no room for my mother? Matron, tell me that you can fix this."

Even the usually unshakable matron knew that this was a big mistake. If the Board of Governors got wind of it, she could find herself back on night shifts faster than you could say cash donation.

"I could make a few calls," she offered. "It might be that they have a much nicer room available in Vincent's Private, in Dublin. To be honest, Mr Judge," she was addressing Cameron, "the room that your mother-in-er – the other woman is in – well, it's just a small boxroom off the ward here. We don't have any private facilities in Accident and Emergency and I'm afraid the hospital is full – overflowing in fact. I could arrange for an ambulance to take Mrs Judge straight up to Vincent's now and she could get settled into the private clinic for a few days. She might need the rest, after all she's been through –" Matron didn't dare refer directly to the fact that there had obviously been a hastily cancelled marriage but it was pretty obvious from what everybody was wearing, their thunderous mood and hostile behaviour to each other.

Cameron scowled at the matron but he wasn't talking, he was listening. She took this for assent. "Let me just go and make that call. I won't be two minutes," she added.

Mercifully, as far as the matron was concerned, Vincent's Private declared that they had a room for Mrs Judge and would be honoured to have her there.

"Will you take the ambulance?" she offered. James was just about to accept when Cameron realised that it was the one Kathleen bloody White or Garcia or whatever the hell she wanted to call herself had just got out of.

"We have our own transport, thank you very much," he said stiffly. "Just ensure that Vincent's Private know we're on our way and try not to botch it up." His tone was so withering even Gillian squirmed.

The matron seemed to have been beaten into submission. "Again, I am so sorry for the confusion. Had I known, I would never have given your fiancée's mother —" She stopped herself as she felt the weight of Cameron's venom increasing.

He ignored her efforts to placate him. "Come on, Mum. Come on, Dad." He helped Gillian get his mother to her feet again. Then an orderly appeared with a wheelchair, which he did accept. Slowly they made their way back out to Bill Boggan's ministerial Merc which waited patiently for them in the strictly no parking zone.

As soon as his parents were settled back into the car, Cameron announced that he needed a quick private word with Samantha. He headed back into the hospital and over to Kathleen's room. Cameron managed to catch Samantha's eye as she spoke to a nurse who was connecting Kathleen to drips and various medical-looking machines. She nodded to him and excused herself from the medic. Together they walked back out to the main foyer.

Cameron donned his most sincere, concerned-looking expression. Gently and lovingly, he took both her hands in his.

"Samantha, we have to talk." He smiled warmly and lovingly at her. Cameron knew his girlfriend. He knew that sincerity and affection were the best tools he had to manipulate her with. "Do you have any idea what happened to us today?"

She smiled at him, relieved that he had cooled down a little. She desperately wanted this whole mess do go away so they could get married. "Well, I'm damned if I know. They're telling me that Mum is simply out cold from the amount of booze in her system. Because she fell, they have to keep her in for the night, just to make sure that she hasn't concussed herself. In other words," she sighed heavily, "she'll be fine — as usual."

"Jesus, what a mother!" Cameron groaned.

"Hey, I didn't pick her. There's nothing I can do about it."

He forced himself to stay calm. "I know, I know. Look, we have to go to Dublin. To be honest, I think Mum is OK. She's just traumatised but we're just going to get her checked over."

"Cam, I'm really sorry about the bed mix-up. I swear I had no idea. I didn't even realise that your mother had a problem. What happened to her?"

"She fainted. I think it was the shock."

"Oh, God."

Then he smiled. "We're in Bill Boggan's Merc, so we should get plenty of attention."

"What – the Minister Bill Boggan?"

"The very same."

"And he's from Dublin South so you'll be in his constituency."

"Yes, so I think they should take good care of us," he said confidently.

"Perhaps, but you'll also get tracked down by the press pretty damn fast too."

This annoyed him. "Look, Sam, when are you going to be able to get your mother talking and get her to retract what she said?"

"What?"

He knew his fiancée needed a little encouragement. "In all fairness, I've never heard such bull. Get her to make a full and public apology and we can let this matter drop."

"What do you mean 'let the matter drop', Cameron? What exactly do you mean?" She sensed trouble.

"Well, what she said – it's positively slanderous, Sam. It could ruin our good name. You understand I'm talking about you and me and the rest of the Judge family. Don't forget I have two sisters. Stephanie and Caroline will be affected by this – not to mention Mum and Dad, if we let it become a scandal."

Samantha could feel her blood beginning to boil but Cameron was on a roll.

"Our name is our business. I mean Judge *is* the Irish for 'whiskey'. If the Judge family name gets tarnished, so too does the whiskey."

"I don't need an economics lesson, Cameron!"

"OK, OK, but surely you see where I'm coming from, darling. It's all about public confidence." He was going into one of his little speeches, Samantha could tell. She took a step back from him.

"I'll call you when I have some news," she cut him off.

Cameron knew he was losing – she wasn't warming to his charm. Maybe he could seduce her into submission. "Well, I'll see you back at Rathnew Manor later, I assume."

"Hardly, Cameron. I'm not going to leave my mother here alone."

"Where's Ricky?"

"He's around somewhere. He's probably gone to the canteen for some coffees but I'm still not leaving Mummy like this."

"Jesus, Sam, you'll have to sleep at some stage."

"Well, I'm not bloody well sleeping with you if that's what you're getting at, not after what Mum said. Christ, what if it's true, Cameron?"

"Bull. She's a drunk, Samantha."

"Perhaps, but that doesn't make her a liar." Then it was her turn to storm away from him. She went back into her mother's room and closed the door so he couldn't or at least shouldn't follow her.

Cameron watched her stomp off. Bitch, he thought, as he headed back out to his car.

The trip to Dublin was terrible. Cameron's bad mood had deteriorated into a truly filthy one. It was positively palpable. He snapped at his father about smoking when his mother was so ill and he nearly bit off poor Gillian's head when she commented that the weather was worsening. Then he yelled at John the driver when he nearly missed his turn into Vincent's Private. When they eventually got to the hospital, Cameron commanded the chauffeur to help James take his mother into the hospital.

"I need to think about damage limitation here, John," he explained. "Oh, and can I borrow your phone?"

The driver was delighted to get away from the young Judge for a while even if it meant lending the pup his phone. He really did seem like a nasty piece of work.

Paul was just arriving into Wicklow General Hospital with Wendy when his phone began to ring. He let Wendy go off in search of Samantha and answered his call.

"Yellow," he answered jovially.

"Paul, where the bloody hell are you?" Cameron Judge's voice thundered down the phone line.

"Cameron, hi. I've just taken Wendy to meet Samantha and her mum. We've just arrived at Wicklow General."

"That stupid bag is just drunk."

Paul decided to stay silent as he listened to Cameron's tantrum.

"Surely your loyalty is to the Judge family and not to that lush?" he thundered on.

"Sorry, Cameron. I kinda thought Samantha was part of the Judge family now," Paul replied coolly. He was too old to take this shit from that young twerp. "Anyway, I actually thought you were here too. Where are you? Do you need a lift?"

"It's OK. I've got Bill Boggan's Merc. I've just taken Mum to Vincent's Private. Just keep your phone on. I'll call you if and when I need you. Got it?"

Why do I work for this guy? Paul wondered yet again. He's nothing like his father. That's when the first ripple of doubt about Cameron's bloodline entered Paul's mind. Could the old woman be telling the truth? Surely not.

As he hung up his phone the heavens opened and it started to bucket down. Wendy was just coming back out of the hospital with her arm around a sobbing Samantha White. The bride didn't seem to care about the downpour, although she was shivering. She had her arms crossed over her thin figure in an attempt to stay warm. Paul's heart went out to her. No, he decided, there's no way that that angel is related to the thug on the phone.

Cameron snapped his phone shut.

"Useless asshole," he snarled aloud.

"Who?" Gillian asked. James had suggested that she keep Cameron company while he got Rose settled.

"Paul, our driver. He's in Wicklow General chauffeuring Wendy to Sam, if you don't mind. I mean, I ask you? Who's paying this guy's wages?"

"How did you get on with Samantha?" Gillian ventured.

"Uptight bitch," he grumbled.

"Is she being difficult again?" Gillian Johnston closed the distance that was between them in the back seat of the car.

"Can you believe it? She's taking her mother seriously over this whole mess. She's staying at the hospital tonight."

"I call that unreasonable," Gillian whispered quietly into his ear. There was nobody around to hear her, but she wanted the excuse to be close to him. With the tip of her tongue, she licked the outer rim of his ear playfully and then she continued. "Well, if that's what she really wants, you and I can stay in the bridal suite," she purred. "It'll be even better than last night, I promise."

Cameron glanced sideways at her. The look was almost contemptuous.

"You know, you're not nearly as good a friend to Samantha as she thinks you are."

"What are you talking about? I wore this *thing* for her, didn't I?" She touched her skirt. "It's vile," she scoffed.

"I thought you looked amazing coming down the aisle."

Her eyes brightened, "Did you really?"

"Yeah, poor Samantha thought I had turned around to see her. I was actually looking at you. Christ, Gillian, you're gorgeous. I much prefer your curves to Sam's anorexic look. There's no flesh on her at all."

Gillian dropped her hand onto Cameron's lap on hearing all this lavish praise. She began to stroke the inside of his thigh.

"Don't get me all excited now. Not unless you're going to finish what you start," he grinned lasciviously at her.

"Why the hell are you marrying the silly cow if you love me and not her, then?" Gillian asked for the hundredth time.

"Now now, darling, we've been through this time and again. You know I had no choice. It's just business. Thanks to dear old dad's mind-boggling lack of foresight combined with Samantha's bloody good negotiating skills, she owns a significant shareholding of our most exciting new product – Gracias. It was her idea to recycle the old distillery pots from Judges' Whiskey. Dad was just going to sell them off and she managed to talk him into letting her use them to produce a new drink. Gracias is simply a flavoured and coloured alcohol but its genius is the way she has sold it into the market. Samantha came up with the concept, the logo – everything – albeit with my help, but she was the one to run with the whole Fiesta campaign. Nobody could have seen it being so successful. Damn it, the woman is selling bottled happiness. The girl got lucky. She produced the right drink at the right time."

"But surely the whiskeys are more profitable," Gillian was unconvinced.

Cameron shook his head. "You would be amazed how popular those alco-pops have become. We can't make the stuff fast enough and there's no maturation time necessary. It's a bloody licence to print money." He pulled his zip down and put Gillian's hand on his now hard dick. "You know as well as I do – oh yeah, that's good – that the entire business was spawned off the back of Judges' Whiskey. Damn it – it's Judges' baby. The bloody problem is she has a too big a shareholding in it. Marrying Sam is the easiest way to amalgamate the two businesses again."

"What if she doesn't want to be amalgamated?" Gillian stressed the 'mated' part of the word as she ran her index finger around the head of his penis.

Cameron looked surprised. "Why ever not? You know wedlock. The general idea is we share everything." What Cameron didn't say was, as Gracias grew in popularity, Judges' Whiskey sales were, in fact, slipping for the first time ever. The company was in no real danger *yet* but the 30 per cent shareholding of Gracias that he and his family owned was now taking in almost as much revenue as some of their smaller whiskey labels. Non-vintage was under particular pressure. The vintage whiskey and the Royal Judge 20, which was their twenty-year-old whiskey, were doing fine. Gracias was really rocking the boat, however, because the revenue it was throwing up was quite startling.

Cameron's main concern, and that of the accountants of Judges' Whiskey – and indeed of his mother Rose – was that while they did hold a thirty per cent stake, Samantha owned thirty-one per cent of Gracias. Samantha had been shrewd enough to negotiate her shareholding with James Judge way back when the shares had no real value. The older man's point of view was 0% of nothing was nothing and so he had been far too generous. Now Cameron had to sort the situation out. Samantha had financed the deal with a venture capitalist who took the remaining thirty-nine per cent of the business. The harsh reality was that, hypothetically, Sam could team up with the venture capitalist to have a controlling interest in Gracias and that was just too risky for him. She had to be brought into the fold.

"Still," Gillian wasn't sure, "Sam is funny like that. She's smart. You know how hard she has worked to build up that drink. I can't see her handing it over to you easily. She has a good head for business."

"Yes and you *give* great head – now put me out of my misery here," he commanded, gently grasping the dark auburn hair. As Gillian set to work, Cameron laid his head back on the ministerial headrest. There was no way Samantha White was going to keep Gracias. The long-neck bottle was being sold into the market as a Latin American fun drink. The fact that it was made in the old Judges' Distillery in Fiddler's Point didn't even seem to occur to the hundreds of thousands of party people who drank it so thirstily every night.

It was his by birthright, Cameron thought furiously, but Gillian soon soothed his temper. She was bloody good at blowing him. Thankfully the Merc had tinted windows because this gave Cameron just enough time to come and get his zip back up before John the chauffeur got back to the car.

"Mr Judge, sir, your mother has been given a private room and she's resting comfortably. Your father asked me to fetch you. Mrs Judge is asking for you."

"Very well. Don't wait," Cam answered the driver as he got out of the car. Gillian was fixing her hair as best she could.

"Where do you want to be left, honey?" Cameron asked her politely as if she were just another friend. It was the one thing that really unnerved Gillian: he was very happy to have her undivided attention when it suited him but outside of that he treated her like just another friend of Samantha's. Well, all that was going to change now. If Samantha wasn't going to marry him, she, Gillian Johnston, bloody well was and she knew just how to go about it.

"Rathnew Manor, please," she smiled warmly. "Will I see you later?" she asked lightly.

"We'll see," he winked at her as he closed the car door. She slipped down the electronic window to speak to him once more.

"Cam, I still have to give you your birthday present,"

His eyes lit up. "Wasn't that it?"

Gillian gave him one of her most alluring smiles. "No, darling, that was just a taste of things to come."

John coughed and interrupted what looked like quite a flirtatious conversation. "Will you require me to come and collect you and your parents later?" he asked.

"No thanks, I'll call the chopper." Cameron smiled warmly at the driver. "It'll be able to land on the hospital helipad." Then he shook John's hand and slipped him two one hundred euro notes. "Thanks again for all your help today. Lovely car, very comfortable back seat."

The driver grinned brightly. Two hundred euro forgave a lot of verbal abuse. He expanded his chest as if he personally owned the car.

"Thank you, sir. It was a pleasure meeting you."

"No, no," Cameron afforded him one of his broadest grins. "I assure you, the pleasure was all mine."

CHAPTER 6

Wendy had been a very welcome addition when she arrived at Wicklow General Hospital. Even though Ricky was always by his sister's side and as faithful as any brother could be, he didn't really know what to say to cheer Samantha up but Wendy did instinctively.

"Christ, Sam, it's just never a dull moment around you!" She smiled brightly at her dear friend as soon as she saw her in the Accident and Emergency unit.

"Wendy," Samantha rushed across the room and gave her a big hug. "How did you get here?"

"Paul drove me up and you can say a big thank you to him too because he had the bright idea of stopping off at Rathnew Manor on the way here so I have a nice change of clothes for you in the car." Wendy had also taken the opportunity to quickly change herself. There was no way they were going to have a wedding at this stage.

"Oh, Wendy, you're the best friend a girl could have."

Because it had started to rain heavily, Paul moved fast. As soon as the girls appeared outside to get the clothes, he guided both of them back into the hospital's doorway out of the rain, while he got the bags.

Paul looked at Samantha, his eyes brimming with sympathy.

"How are you bearing up, Sunshine?" he asked as he gently dropped her large Louis Vuiton bag beside her feet.

An emergency with her mother she could deal with. Hostility and confrontation with her fiancé she could handle. But sympathy? No way. Samantha covered her face with her hands and collapsed onto Paul's massive chest. Rather awkwardly he wrapped his arms around her as she sobbed and shook like a child. It wasn't exactly what Paul had meant to happen. He wasn't particularly good at dealing with girlie emotions. But Wendy helped. As Samantha howled into Paul's expansive shirt she stood very close to her friend, wrapping her own arms around Paul's, enveloping Samantha in a double-cuddle.

"There, there, Sam, let it out," Wendy spoke softly. "No bride should ever have to go through what you went through today. Don't worry, we'll get to the bottom of it. To be honest, it probably looks a lot worse than it really is." Samantha continued to cry but Wendy knew that the poor girl was listening and so she racked her brains for other pearls of wisdom and comfort. "I think your mother really does love you. She's just sick. You know that, Samantha. She's been, well – *unwell* for decades now. It was just the idea of losing you in marriage that pushed her over the edge. Not that it's your fault," she added reassuringly. "We'll get her better and then things will be OK. I'm sure by this time next year, you'll be happily married and we'll look back on all of this and laugh."

Paul stood as still as a statue, huge biceps wrapped around the skinny fragile bride. He felt like marble but she seemed to be happy within the security of his arms.

Wendy continued, "Cameron loves you, Sam. That's all that matters – damn the rest of them."

Samantha glanced sideways. Her face was incredibly pale and her eyes were developing bright red rims from the crying. Tears streaked down both cheeks. She looked a real mess. Wendy decided to take a risk. "Jesus, Sam, forget *that* crisis. We have an even bigger one on our hands."

Samantha tilted her head inquisitively.

"You want to see how *bad* you look." She winced but her eyes sparkled with fun. "We have *got* to get you to a mirror and do some repair work." It had the desired effect.

Samantha laughed out loud and wiped away her tears. "Yeah, I reckon I do look a bit of a mess."

"And if you don't mind me saying," Paul looked down at her affectionately, "you're shaking like a leaf. You must be freezing in that dress."

"I don't know where my stole is, I lost it somewhere along the way," Sam sighed, then she reached up and kissed Paul on the cheek. "Thanks for minding me, Paul. You give great hugs and you're a real pal."

In all the years he had worked for the Judges he had never been the recipient of any sort of affection from them. No Judge had ever spoken to him like that. He was quite positive that there was no way she was related to that shower.

The girls went in search of a loo and Paul went up to the canteen.

"You dote, Wendy, this is just perfect," Samantha gushed as she pulled out a pair of Ralph Lauren blue jeans, a T-shirt and her chunky cotton, cream-coloured Lynn Marr jumper. She sounded almost normal.

"Well," Wendy smiled, "I figured it might be a long night and it was better to be dressed for comfort than for glamour. Not that you don't look amazing in those size four jeans – wagon!"

"Hey – that's American sizing," Samantha defended herself as Wendy undid the hundreds of buttons on the back of her friend's wedding dress.

Sadly, Samantha pulled her tired and slightly torn, much crumpled bodice off. Then slowly and deliberately, she pulled the soft flowing silk skirt up and over her head. It moved like liquid. "And anyway," she added, "if I'm not stating the obvious, I'd much rather be you than me right now, if I could."

Wendy couldn't argue with that.

For a brief moment, Sam held the feather-light skirt of her wedding dress and stared at it in quiet contemplation. Then she picked up the exquisitely detailed bustier. She traced the outline of the delicately embroidered roses on the bodice with her finger. Her lower lip began to quiver again as she thought about what might have been. "It wasn't meant to end like this," she whispered. "I should be dancing with Cameron right now. Surely it's time for the first waltz?" Her voice was small and weak and beginning to crack.

Wendy wouldn't let her friend dwell on the events of the day. "Should I have brought runners or boots?" she asked loudly.

Samantha looked up. "Oh, I don't really mind."

"Well, I went for the boots. Better to kick ass with." Wendy chuckled.

"Jesus, whose ass am I going to kick?"

"That remains to be seen, Samantha, but you know, we have to get to the bottom of this. Either your mother is delusional or she just saved you from making the biggest mistake of your life –"

Samantha looked panic-stricken. "God, you don't think that it's possible, do you?"

"No, Sam, I don't. Paul and I were even talking about it on the way up here. There's never been the slightest evidence of any link between you and the Judges. Your paths only crossed accidentally when you went for that job interview. I don't think there is any way in hell that you guys could be related. So chances are that it's your mom you're going to have Holy War with. Are you ready for that, Sam? It's going to be difficult."

"I don't know what I'm ready for, Wendy." She pulled her jeans up and got into her T-shirt and jumper on autopilot.

Wendy took her by the hand and plonked her onto a loo seat in the cubicle next to the sinks. "Well, look on the bright side. Being a hospital, everything is spotless here, so sit still and let me do your make-up. You really are in a bad way, you know. No more crying. OK?"

"I don't know if I can promise that."

"Well, let's just try and be positive."

"Even that's a tall order, Wendy. What is there to be positive about, tell me? What was meant to be the best day of my life has just come crashing down around my ears. I think my fiancé probably hates me. I did embarrass him by running out on our wedding in the very public eye of a bloody TV3 news team and God knows how many photographers lurking around."

Wendy winced. "I forgot about the television crew. OK, that's not so good but think of Rose. It would almost be worth it just to see her taken down a peg or two."

Samantha looked at her friend in surprise. She hadn't thought of that.

"You're brilliant, Wendy," Sam smiled. "I'd love to know how the old wagon is taking it all – although you do know she is in hospital?"

"Ha," Wendy laughed. "That was just to get her out of the limelight I bet, clever old bat."

Samantha chuckled, "And as for the sisters. Well, Caroline is not so bad – a little wild and certainly most unorthodox but she's not as bitchy as her mother or sister. Stephanie could do with taking down a peg or two as well."

"Jesus, what a family," Wendy sighed as she applied a fairly hefty layer of foundation. She saw Sam eyes dart towards hers, however. "The family, Samantha. Not dear old Cameron. We all know he's perfect." She winked.

"But what if it's true, Wendy? I can't even get my head around that. What did Mum mean? She could have meant that Cameron is her son or that I'm – I'm –"

"Don't try. It's just too outlandish to be true. Don't worry."

"But if it *is* true, you know what that means, don't you?"

"Samantha, stop."

But it was too late: Sam had already got there, in her mind. "I've been sleeping with my brother – oh, Christ!"

Wendy snatched the eyeliner pencil. "Look," she waved it menacingly at Sam's face. "He's not your brother. Now stop thinking like that or I'll give you black eyes."

"Wendy," she pleaded "What *if*, just *if* –"

"Samantha – stop it right now or I'll get cross."

Sam slouched down on the toilet lid – defeated.

Then Wendy's tone softened. "Do you know what you need? Is your mum definitely sleeping for a few hours?"

"Probably for the night. They sedated her because she was so hyper. Why?"

"You need a stiff drink. Why don't we head across the road to the Wicklow Arms and have a couple of bottles of Gracias?" Wendy grinned from ear to ear mischievously. "Ricky and Paul can escort us. It's just the medicine for you and to be honest it's just what I need too."

"Let me check on Mum first," Sam said as she pulled her boots on.

"Well, before you go anywhere you better try and get a brush through your hair. It's half up, half down at the moment."

"Thanks," Sam took the brush from her friend and began to remove all the tiny hairclips that had been inserted so delicately and meticulously that morning.

"Did you know that Gillian was minding Cameron and Rose all afternoon?" Sam asked. "She was here earlier although I didn't get to speak to her."

"Now there is a real friend." Wendy smiled. "I'm delighted to be here with you but she is an angel looking after the Judges."

"She is a good friend, isn't she? But so are you, Wendy."

"Sure, this is nothing." Wendy smiled as she took out the last clip from her friend's hair. "Now keep brushing. Your make-up is perfect again, even if I do say so myself. I'll go and find the men and meet you at the front door of the Accident and Emergency ward after you've checked on your mom. OK?"

Samantha stopped brushing her long blond hair for a second and looked at her friend. "Is there something going on between you and Paul that I should know about, Wendy Doyle?"

"Phwaw, what a man," she giggled. "But in answer to your question, no, Sam. There is nothing to know . . . yet. Not yet."

In Dublin, the private room in St Vincent's hospital was a quiet and peaceful place.

"Cameron," Rose's voice was weak. "Come to Mother, precious."

"I'm here, Mother. Rest," he urged.

Secretly he hated the appalling way she spoke to him – as if he were still a child – but there was no way he could change the habit of a lifetime at this stage. He crossed the room and sat down on the side of her bed.

He took her hand in his. "Rest, Mother. You've had a ghastly day. Just try to sleep for a while." Thankfully, she closed her eyes.

Cameron looked around the room for the first time. This hospital was considerably more salubrious than Wicklow General Hospital, he noted with jealous pleasure. It was bright and pleasant enough, for a hospital. The room was sufficiently large to accommodate her bed, two visitor's chairs and a small table. Behind him there was a door that presumably led to her ensuite bathroom. There was also a built-in wardrobe, remote control television with a video player. Next he spotted the fridge – how convenient he thought. The colour scheme was pink and grey, a little dated perhaps but at least the curtains and bed linen matched. One wall was dominated by a large window and a door that led out onto the balcony.

James Judge had excused himself for a few moments. He told his son that he was going to the canteen to get a cup of coffee or indeed something stronger if it was possible. It had been a hell of a day for him too. Cameron heaved a great sigh. Surely *he* had had the toughest day of all of them. What the hell had happened? Today was meant to be the best day of his life. Some bloody birthday, he thought miserably as he glanced at his watch. It was after seven already. Where had the afternoon gone? Rose began to snore lightly – well, there didn't appear to be too much wrong with her by all accounts. Just then a nurse quietly opened the door and glanced in.

"Everything OK?" she whispered.

He nodded and granted her a killer smile. She gestured to him to come out of the room. "Hello," she smiled, "you must be Cameron." She extended her hand.

"Guilty as charged," he smiled into her pretty dark brown eyes as he shook her hand. "And you would be?"

"Emily," she grinned. "I settled your mother into her room when she arrived."

"Thanks a million."

"Can I offer my condolences on your day or whatever it is you're meant to say about situations like this." She looked a little less comfortable.

Suddenly Cameron realised that this was going to be the world's worst-kept secret. Damn it, he was still in his morning suit. He hated when people knew his business.

He had no choice but to play the hand he had been dealt. "Well," he sighed, "I still don't quite know what happened today but to be honest right now I'm more worried about my mother. Can you tell me what happened?" Smoothly and effortlessly he moved the conversation away from himself.

Emily's back straightened. This was her area of expertise. "Well, we do want to carry out some tests on her just to be on the safe side. They'll be done tomorrow morning. But it would be quite reasonable to assume that she fainted from shock today. She's a little frail —"

Cameron had never thought of his mother as frail — petite, yes, but frail? Never.

"And she is sixty-one after all —"

"She's not sixty-one," Cameron interrupted, a little taken aback. "Mum is in her mid-fifties, maybe fifty-five."

"Well now, Cameron if that's what she told you, I'm sure that's what she wants you to believe," Emily winked conspiratorially. "But I assure you, we're old pros at getting the real age out of mature ladies. If you ask them their date of birth as opposed to their age they find it more difficult to tell little fibs." She tipped the side of her nose. It annoyed Cameron enormously. Then she continued, "Look, there's no point in worrying about your mother until we've done those tests. OK?"

"Do you think there's any cause for concern?" he asked, suddenly realising that there could be more to her fainting than shock.

"We don't know," Emily explained again patiently. "What about you? When was the last time you ate?

He shrugged and forked his hand through his hair.

"Cameron," Rose called from her room. There was a panic in her voice − desperation. They both rushed in. "Now, now, Mrs Judge, you're not to go getting all uptight again." Emily's voice had changed into a more authoritative one. It wasn't nearly as friendly. She was definitely in charge.

"It's my son," Rose explained. "I need him near me."

"I'm here, Mum. It's OK. I'm not going anywhere." He glanced at Emily.

"Would you like something to help you sleep, perhaps?" the nurse offered.

"That's a good idea," Cameron answered for his mother. He didn't particularly fancy the idea of holding her hand for the next five hours while she moaned about the destruction of the fabulous Judge family reputation.

"Will it make my mind muddled?" Rose asked nervously.

Strange question, Cam thought. The notion of a muddled mind suddenly felt quite appealing. Anything to escape the fiasco of the day, he reasoned.

"No, not at all. It will just make you sleep," Emily explained as she headed out of the room to fetch the promised elixir.

"You know, your view is really quite spectacular," Cameron said brightly, hoping to keep his mother's spirits up. "You can see the entire park area of the hospital. Tomorrow when you're feeling a bit better, you might like to have a little walk around the gardens. What do you think?"

"Darling, come and sit next to me. There's something I have to tell you."

God, maybe she really is sick, he thought with a sudden grip of cold fear about his throat. He returned to sitting on her bedside and holding her hand.

"Mother, what is it?"

She looked at his beautiful face, his vivid blue eyes now full of worry, and his strong jaw line clenched in tension. Cameron was her favourite child. He always had been. He was quite simply magnificent. He had her intelligence and his father's charm. "I do so love you, darling."

"Mum, you are getting all maudlin on me – now come on, snap out of it. Aren't you well? What's wrong?"

Rose studied his face for a few moments longer and then almost imperceptibly, he saw her nod. It was as if she was reaching a decision within her very soul. He watched her gathering up her strength and resolve.

"Firstly, I have to tell you nothing is seriously wrong – well, perhaps with the small exception of today's theatrics. Lord knows what the papers will make of that mess. No, that's not what I'm talking about and no, Cameron, I'm not sick so you can put that right out of your mind." She smiled reassuringly at him.

That was all he needed to know. His mother was the strongest influence on his life. He really did adore her. He also noted that her tone had changed too. She was back to being the usual Rose – strong – authoritarian – the boss.

"No, what I have to tell you, you need to know because we may have a small fight on our hands. Not a war, just a small altercation but you need to be equipped with the facts."

He listened intently.

"It appears that Kathleen White *did* cross paths with us some years ago. I never realised it before because back then her name was Kathleen Garcia."

"What?" His voice came out as a squeal. It sounded almost feminine to him. He coughed to clear his throat but he still felt a nervous tingle down his spine, unsettled that there might be even an ounce of truth in what the old lush had said.

Rose was firm, however, even from her hospital bed. "Now, now, don't fuss, Cameron," she spoke impatiently as if he were a giddy child that had to be tolerated. "That's just the sort of reaction I would expect from Stephanie or perhaps even Caroline but not you." Her words had the desired effect. He froze and listened obediently as she continued. "The truth is, Kathleen, or Katie as we called her – she has always been a little – well, odd. She was married to our gardener, Pablo."

"Ha, that's funny because Ricky is into landscaping too. I wonder if he knows that his dear old father was our gardener?"

"Cameron, don't be flippant," she snapped at him. "Well, there's more. I'm afraid even back then she was fond of the drink and –" Rose looked uncomfortable and unwilling to go on.

"Yes, Mother," he smiled broadly.

She realised then that he was actually enjoying this. Cameron was obviously so furious with Samantha that he was happy with the idea of his fiancée's humble origins.

She looked saddened. "Well, eventually we had to let them go because her behaviour was just so irregular. She had all sorts of fantastic notions. She once accused one of your father's friends of having his way with her."

"An affair?" he grinned.

"Against her will," Rose explained quietly but she kept her gaze on the pink bedcover.

"Rape?" Cameron looked genuinely shocked.

"Who knows with her?" Rose waved a delicate hand in the air. "She was quite quite mad most of the time and I do assure you nobody ever laid a hand on her – nobody would have wanted to. She was always too thin and quite quite wild."

"I thought you said that you could never be too rich or too thin," he teased his mother but she glared at him. Wrong time for that particular comment he realised as she continued.

"Anyway, I think I heard that they had moved to the west. I suppose Pablo wanted to get her away from decent people."

"Jesus, I wonder if Sam knows any of this?"

"I very much doubt it. If her father has left the family, her mother is hardly likely to tell her. I'm not sure what Katie would even remember from those days."

"Well, she bloody well remembered the Judges this morning." He grumbled.

"I rather think it was their connection to Samantha that she was dwelling on as opposed to us, darling."

"What a mess!"

"Yes, it is really. I just thought you should know before it all came out in a mixed-up manner from that poor confused woman's mouth."

He looked at his mother and smiled softly.

Emily knocked lightly and entered without waiting for a response. "Here we are now, Mrs Judge. This should help you to sleep like a baby."

Rose took the tablet obediently and swallowed it with a little sip of water. Then, after Emily left, she looked back to her son. "Cameron, I assume it goes without saying, that what I have just told you is privileged information. Naturally it stays between you and me."

Cameron gave his mother a discreet nod and just the hint of a smile, "Naturally, Mother. Naturally."

She smiled at him indulgently. "Good. Now I must say I am exhausted. I really have had enough of this day," she yawned.

Within minutes, she was asleep.

CHAPTER 7

The Wicklow Arms was refreshingly busy. It was, after all, a Saturday evening.

Wendy didn't even try to hide her dismay when she heard that Paul would not accompany them.

"It's not a reflection on you," Samantha tried to console her friend. "Cameron and James needed the car. He *is* their driver. That's his job, remember?"

"I know, but it's a Saturday night, damn it," Wendy scowled. She had found Paul in the canteen just as James Judge phoned him from Dublin. Apparently Mrs Judge had been doped and the men were told to go home for the night, Wendy explained to Ricky and Sam. "So poor Paul has to drive all the way up to Dublin just to bring those guys back to Rathnew Manor."

The weather was getting worse and the chopper had been grounded. "What bloody good is a chopper if it can't stand a little rain?" Wendy whined now, as she sipped her bottle of Gracias.

Sam smiled sympathetically at her friend. "Choppers don't like storms and trust me having flown through a few force fives with Cam, it's not something I would recommend you try."

"Speaking of flying, Sam," Ricky examined the frosted glass on his bottle of Gracias, "weren't you due to fly out on your honeymoon on Monday? What will you do about that now?"

Samantha shrugged. "Well, I don't think Cameron and I can exactly leave together in the current circumstances." She slapped her forehead in anguish. "And it was going to be my first time in first class – shit, shit, shit!"

"Hey, maybe this whole situation will be sorted out by then and you two can get away together, after all," Wendy tried.

"I very much doubt it," Sam sighed. "I'm not sure if Cameron is even talking to me at the moment."

"Of course he is," Ricky added. "He loves you. Sure – he may be a little mad about the scene today, but love conquers all. He'll get over it."

"By Monday?" Sam raised an eyebrow.

The three of them looked at each other and laughed uncertainly.

"Jesus, what a situation!" Wendy sighed.

"Ricky," Samantha looked at her little brother, "do you know anything I don't know?"

"What do you mean?"

"Well, did Mum ever say anything to you about Dad or about the Judges or anything really?"

"Sister, you above all people know that Mum and I were not the closest and as for Dad? I don't even remember him. Mum said he walked out on us and that was enough for me. I've spent my life trying *not* to think about him. My life is good. I have you, as far as family is concerned. My landscaping business is starting to really take off and there's absolutely nothing wrong with my social life," he scanned a predatory eye over the new arrivals into The Wicklow Arms. "I don't want or need them."

"OK, OK, sorry – I just wondered if there was something I was missing, something Mum might have said to me years ago and I have been deliberately suppressing, but for the life of me I can't think of anything. As far as I know Mum and Pablo were married in England. They came back and lived in Galway. You and I were born. The marriage fizzled out after a few years and Pablo went back to Spain. End of story."

"Yep, that's pretty much it in a nutshell," Ricky agreed. "And good riddance to both of them, I say."

"Did your father make any efforts to stay in touch with you?" Wendy asked gently.

"Yeah, I think so. In the beginning. I seem to remember getting Christmas presents and birthday cards from him but they sort of petered out after a few years," Samantha said.

"That's unfortunate."

"Hey," Ricky's joviality sounded a bit forced, "life's a bitch."

The girls looked at one another. "Charming," Samantha said.

"Charming," Wendy agreed.

They ordered another round of Gracias and did their best to avoid talking about the hellish day they had had. Crisis or no crisis, for Ricky it was still a Saturday night. After a brief hour with his sister and her friend, he found himself up at the bar, being chatted up by two pretty young things.

"He just can't help himself," Samantha explained.

"He's not much fun to go out with, is he?" Wendy commented. "It doesn't take him long to desert you."

"No, he's like a moth to the flame when there are a few single women around. Actually change that, when there are simply women about – they don't have to be single."

Wendy nodded. "Yeah, you've been out of the single circuit for a long time, honey. Believe me, it's dog eat dog out there," she gestured at the gangs of young people who were descending into the pub in their packs. "Take my advice, hang on to Cameron. He loves you. You love him and trust me: you do *not* want to have to wade back into *that*."

Samantha looked at the eager new arrivals, drinking and flirting – Saturday night party people. From her jaded perspective, it didn't look too appealing. Her life had been heading towards nights in with a blazing fire, perhaps a few dogs lounging on the floor – possibly toasted marshmallows – not this. The pub was so warm, she had already peeled off her jumper. She was grateful for the T-shirt.

"Do you think you should perhaps phone Cameron?" Wendy asked tentatively.

"I don't know what to say if I do."

"Just say hi."

"I can't," Samantha looked panicked. "Something is stopping me and I don't know what."

"You're just a little embarrassed about today. Don't be, I think you did the right thing, Sam. But you do still love him, don't you? I mean that hasn't changed, surely?"

"No, no, yes, I do still love him. I can't imagine living with anybody else and I even want to have his babies." Then she covered her mouth with her hand. "Oh, God, I'm not sure about that last bit." Samantha looked at her friend with genuine terror in her eyes. "What if the stuff mum said is the truth? Jesus, have I been sleeping with my brother? Christ, that's so disgusting! Imagine if we had a baby – I can't bear to even think about it!"

"Stop!" Wendy almost shouted. "Sam, please stop! You're going to make yourself crazy. OK, that's that. I've got it sussed now. The first thing you have to do is to talk this out with your mother. She has to explain her actions today. You won't be OK until she does that with you."

This seemed to calm Samantha down somewhat. "Yes, you're absolutely right. I have to talk to Mum and maybe Pablo too."

"Yeah, he could shed some light on this. That's a great idea. Well, your mum is nearest so why don't we start there?"

Samantha put her hand on her friend's shoulder. "Wendy, you're really the best friend in the world but this is something I have to do alone."

"Are you mad? There's no way I'm going to let you face her alone."

"I have to. She might clam up in front of you."

"Hello? Are we talking about the same woman here? The lady who stopped the biggest society wedding of the year just a few hours ago. I don't think she's going to get crowd shy in front of you and me."

"Sorry, Wendy, I'm going in alone." Sam rose to her feet and so her friend jumped up too.

"Please, at least let me wait outside her room for you."

Sam looked over to Ricky and instantly caught his eye. He excused himself from his two female companions and worked his way through the rapidly-filling pub, back to his sister. "Are you guys going?" he asked, looking surprised. "It's early days yet, girls."

Sam laughed at his infinite enthusiasm for the opposite sex. "I'm going to hang around back at the hospital and Wendy is going back to the Manor now. Would I be correct in saying that you would rather stay here for a little while longer?" she asked playfully, poking her brother.

"Would you like me to come with you, sis?"

"No, thanks. To be honest I'd like to be alone for a while, if it's all the same to you."

Ricky nodded and glanced back at the two girls at the bar. They waved at him and giggled. "I think I'd like to stay here for a little while longer but I'm on the mobile if you want me, Sam."

She reached up and hugged him. "I know, little brother, thanks. I'll call you if I need you, I promise." Then Ricky headed back to his new playmates.

Wendy tried to stay with her friend one more time but Samantha wouldn't hear of it. "Mum's asleep. I probably won't even get to talk to her until the morning. Go home, Wendy. I'll call you as soon as I have some news."

Her friend looked crestfallen. "I don't even know where to go, now. What are you doing after the hospital? Will you go back to the Manor or back up to Dublin?"

"Where would I go in Dublin?" Samantha asked.

"Well, *our* flat of course."

"Will you have me back in the apartment?"

Wendy looked shocked. "Will I?" She threw her arms around

Samantha. "I was dreading you leaving. You know that we never advertised for a new flatmate."

Samantha hugged her friend by way of thanks.

"Right," Wendy put down her bottle of Gracias. "I'm going to stay in the Manor at this stage because it's getting late and we have the room anyway. I'm sure Gillian is back there now. If we don't see you tonight, we'll just take all your stuff with us when we check out tomorrow morning. OK?"

"Perfect. Thanks, Wendy."

"Hey, for nothing. Anyway by then you'll probably have phoned from the honeymoon suite in the Manor – where you'll be busy putting things right with Cameron. I'm telling you, Sam, I'm sure your mother was just in her own little dream world."

"God, I hope you're right."

"I know I am," Wendy assured Samantha. Then she took her leave in a taxi back to the Manor.

Sam stood outside the Wicklow Arms alone. She didn't feel the rain that was beginning to penetrate her jumper and flatten her hair.

"Hello, darling. Need some company?" A voice beside her interrupted her thoughts.

"What?" She swung around and was facing a man in his forties. He looked like he had just stepped off a building site. His jeans were covered in white cement powder and the cuffs of his old faded jumper were frayed. His smile was bright and friendly, however, and most definitely non-threatening. His friends poked fun at him. "She's out of our league, mate. Leave the lady alone!"

Samantha smiled shyly at her suitor. "Err, no thanks, I'm just going now."

"Ah, that's a shame," he smiled at her and then winked. "Maybe next time, darling."

She didn't answer – just nodded and grinned weakly. If they had any idea of the day she had just had. For one mad moment she seriously considered heading back into the pub with her new building buddies but common sense prevailed. Samantha took a deep breath and made the short but daunting trek across the road, back to Wicklow General Hospital.

David Neilson leaned his back against the bar as he looked around the largest drawing-room in Rathnew Manor. He watched his wife, Stephanie Judge, hold court. Turning slightly, he rested one elbow on the counter as he swirled two large blocks of ice around his glass of whiskey. Naturally he was drinking Judges' Whiskey; to do anything else would be tantamount to treason and easily grounds for divorce. Although that idea had its merits, he mused, as he studied the ice gradually slow down and eventually clink to a satisfying stop. He swirled the glass again.

"Jesus, David, anyone could be forgiven for thinking you were the one jilted at the altar, you look so down." It was Marcus Haywood, Caroline's boyfriend.

I should have been so lucky, he thought savagely. Then he forced himself to smile. "Hi, Marcus, no, no I was just lost in thought. Poor Cameron, all the same. What an experience!"

"Hell, yeah, I don't envy him. How has your wife been bearing up? It's not a great day to be a Judge. Poor Stephanie, she must be embarrassed by all of this." Then he lowered his voice, "You don't think there's any truth in the rumour, do you?"

David looked at Marcus and asked incredulously, "What rumour? Have you heard any more since the wedding service?"

"Well, nothing concrete. I did hear a few whispers about the Judge men over the generations. Evidently they have a bit of a rep. You know – the potent Judge libido, but I guess you'd know all about that already!" He tried to cajole David into a more jovial mood.

"Maybe it's just the Judge *men* that carry that gene," David sneered as he turned away from the room and towards the bar. He also downed his whiskey in one shot, Marcus noticed.

"Oh, Dave, the Judge sex drive is infamous. I don't want to start slurring Caro's good name but let's just say she's a beautiful, loving and certainly a very affectionate woman," Marcus smiled contentedly.

David raised his glass to the barman to indicate another of the same and then he looked at Marcus. "Is that so? Well, I'm happy for you but let me just warn you that if you're really serious about Caroline Judge, have a very and I mean *very* hard look at her mother. When I married Stephanie, she was young and fun and definitely the most *affectionate* woman I had ever met. In fact she was wild and I loved her for it. Now look at her!" He glanced at his wife. She was sitting by the fire in a most luxuriant deep burgundy-coloured armchair. The fire was ablaze and particularly welcoming especially as it had started to rain outside. But in this most ideal setting, Stephanie wasn't sitting back, enjoying the sheer carnal pleasure of the moment. No, she was sitting on the edge of the seat, holding some other guest's hand and wiping her eyes with a well-used tissue. She was the picture of misery. Marcus felt sorry for her.

"She's genuinely upset, David," Marcus reasoned. "The family are going to be really embarrassed by today's events, especially if it turns out to be true."

"How the hell could it be true? No, Steph's upset because she loves being Queen Bee and she doesn't know what it is to have to be humble."

"From Queen Bee to Bumble Pie!" Marcus laughed but David looked at him severely and so he stopped.

"No, it's much more than that. Stephanie Judge is a very spoilt lady who expects everything to go her way all the time. If it doesn't, there's a crisis – histrionics – total meltdown." He took a new glass of whiskey from the barman and continued, "And believe me, there's nothing I or anybody can do that's good enough for her then."

"Hey, steady on there, David. Has it occurred to you that today has taken its toll on you too? Cut her and indeed yourself a little slack. OK, Steph might be a little emotional but she's a good woman and she loves you and the girls."

David laughed. "She loves Zoë, I'll grant you that. In fact she loves Zoë too much. Poor kid is spoilt to bits, don't tell me you haven't noticed. Even I see it and I'm her father. I love Zoë more than anybody on earth along with my other daughter, Amy, but Steph is turning her into a monster by giving her everything that she wants. It's not good for a kid. And poor Amy? The baby is just a fashion accessory. Amy's sin is that she wasn't a boy. Stephanie always planned on having two children, a boy and a girl and poor darling little Amy mucked that up."

"Jesus, David, that baby is a little doll. Both kids are the image of you but I'm telling you Amy is going to be a knock-out. You'll have to lock her up when she's older."

Depressed though he was it cheered him that Marcus had mentioned how the girls both looked so like their father. It was David Neilson's good looks that attracted Stephanie to him in the first place. He glanced at his own reflection in the antique mirror hanging on the wall behind the bar counter. His hair was still blond, although not quite as smooth as it had been when he was a student. Now it was a little rougher in texture and there was a generous scattering of grey starting to appear. His jaw-line had been excellent and in fairness, he was still a good-looking man but he had lost the lean toned skin that once stretched over his fine bones. In its place he had a softer jaw-line thanks to too much Judges' Whiskey. His eyes were dark brown. Both Zoë and Amy had the same dark eyes. He was still attractive enough if perhaps a little rougher round the edges than he had been.

Marcus continued, "And as for having two girls – well, that just means that you'll have to go again and we both know how much fun that is!" He slapped David on the back.

Dave Neilson's mood darkened even further. He couldn't remember the last time he had had sex with his wife. It was probably when they were trying to conceive Amy.

Marcus's girlfriend, Caroline Judge, was up in her room in Rathnew Manor. She said that she needed a lie-down after the excitement at the church and Zoë had volunteered to keep her company. They lay side by side on the huge, super king-size bed.

"Are you feeling better?" Zoë asked. She was obviously getting a little impatient now that the Big Big Movie was over.

"I feel fine," Caroline smiled broadly. The quick snort of coke she had taken in the bathroom a few minutes earlier had soothed her rattled nerves. Caroline had not been looking forward to the wedding. She hated pomp and ceremony. She loathed most of her fuddy-duddy relatives, except for Granny Vic, of course. Anyway none of that mattered now; the day had been gloriously cancelled and she didn't have to sit through any mind-numbing wedding speeches.

"I'm bored," the younger girl whined.

"So am I," Caroline responded.

"What should we do?" Zoë asked her aunt.

But Caro was up already and started to tickle her niece. "I just wanted to get away from all those losers downstairs," she explained.

"No, no, please don't tickle me!" Zoe screamed.

Caroline jumped on top of the seven-year-old. "What's the matter, baby, can't take the heat?" She continued to tickle her.

"Please stop, I'm going to pee!"

It worked: Caroline instantly hopped off her niece.

"If you want to pee, please use the loo. I don't want any golden showers just yet, thank you very much."

"What's a golden shower?" the seven-year-old asked.

"Ask your mother," Caroline chuckled visualising her sister's face when confronted with that one.

Zoë slipped off the bed and wandered into the bathroom. "Wow, this is nice," she enthused.

"Yes, it's certainly big enough," Caroline agreed. She had checked it out for herself before Zoë's arrival. For a period manor house, the bathrooms were surprisingly modern in design, at least hers was. The floor and walls were fitted out in dark marble. To the left were two huge sinks shaped out of a single piece of enamel. This was embedded into the same dark marble, leaving oodles of room for the myriad complimentary shampoos, body balms, moisturisers and emery boards. There was everything a woman could want – well, almost.

"Shit, the coke," Caroline whispered to herself as she heard Zoë flush the toilet. She rushed in to her niece and checked that there were no drugs lying around but the coast was clear and, anyway, the little girl was much more interested in a hand cream that she had just found.

"Can I have this?" she asked.

"Yes," Caroline answered, relieved to notice her wash-bag untouched. She casually picked it up and brought it back into the bedroom. It might have aroused suspicion had anybody seen her putting her wash-bag in her bedroom safe but there were no witnesses. Zoë was still enthralled with the bathroom.

"I love all the lights," the little girl said, smiling back at her own brightly lit reflection.

The mirror behind the sinks covered the entire wall and it had recessed lighting along the top and down both sides.

"Here's a good one," Caroline said as she stroked the large mirror. "They have heating behind the mirrors."

"Why would they do that?" Zoë asked.

"So the glass doesn't steam up when you're having a bath. Pretty cool, heh?"

"Brill."

The bath was bigger than even the ones at Dunross – definitely made for two. Caroline tingled with pleasure as she thought of Marcus, her fairly-new-and-rapidly-becoming-serious boyfriend.

"Is it a Jacuzzi bath?" Zoë asked as she examined the little holes along the sides.

"Yep."

The shower was also a double but it looked more like a sex toy than a shower. There was the standard shower head. Then Caroline found the multiple water jets, vertically built into the three marble walls of the shower. They went right down the sides – about twenty-five sprayers in total.

"Is it a Jacuzzi shower too?" Zoë asked when she spotted the same holes in the shower.

"No," Caroline explained. "It's a super sprayer. In the bath it's bubbles of air that come out of those holes. In the shower it's jets of water. You get sprayed from the sides as well as from the top."

As if all of that wasn't enough there was another hose too, only it didn't have a shower head. It had an exhilaratingly narrow nozzle. Caroline giggled when she saw it. Her sister had once had colonic irrigation and couldn't sit properly for a week. Steph had said it was the most unpleasant experience of her life. Perhaps it was time for Caroline to find out for herself.

"What's that one for?" Zoë duly asked when she spotted the thin hose.

"I have no idea," Caroline Judge lied.

One thing was certain, if she got Marcus into the bathroom later that night, they were going to have the cleanest sex of their lives.

CHAPTER 8

"Wendy!" Gillian wasn't able to hide her surprise when her flatmate walked back into their bedroom at the Manor. "What are you doing back here – I mean, I thought you were minding Samantha. I reckoned you guys would be back in Dublin by now. Sam is hardly coming back here after today's shenanigans?"

"God knows what she'll do next. I have been with her all day but half an hour ago she sent me away. She wants to talk to her mum alone so she's gone back to Wicklow General Hospital. What are you up to? You look like you're getting ready to party."

Gilly stood in the middle of the beautiful suite that they had been sharing. She was wearing a large fluffy white towel wrapped snugly around her body and a similar, only slightly smaller one in turban-style around her head. Her skin had gone rosy pink from soaking in a hot bath but it shone thanks to a heavy layering of body moisturiser.

"I've just had a bath, that's all." Her tone was defensive but Wendy picked up on the underlying hint of guilt.

"Why? What are you up to, Gillian? Have you got a man in there?" Wendy laughed and rushed into the bathroom, ignoring Gilly's protests of innocence. She scanned the room. There was nobody there. Then she swept back the curtain that was still drawn across the bath.

"Gillian, how could you?" She came out of the bathroom and stood at the door. "That's my bloody Lancôme conditioner. You know what this means, don't you?" She brandished the badly squeezed tube. "This means I get to use your body firming gel."

Gillian shrugged nonchalantly. "Fine, in fact you can have it, Wendy."

"What?"

"I've decided I don't need to firm up any more. I like me just the way I am."

"What the hell's got into you?"

Cameron Judge, that's what got into me and I like it, Gilly thought with delight but she just smiled at her old friend. "Nothing. Can't a girl just be happy with her body?"

Wendy thought about this. "No girl I know." Then she changed the subject. "I assume you're staying here tonight, then?"

"Well, the room is paid for – thank you very much, Rose Judge. So we may as well enjoy it. Obviously the dinner and the band for later have been cancelled but I did hear a rumour that there's still a free bar."

Wendy looked at Gillian. "Hey, why did you wash your hair? The hairdresser did such a good job this morning."

Gilly swallowed. She couldn't exactly tell her old friend that she had to do it after her back-seat blow-job with Cameron. "Oh, I just wanted to freshen up. Now, tell me are you coming down for something to eat with me? I'm starving."

"Food? What a wonderful idea. I haven't eaten all day. Just let me grab a quick shower, although I'm not washing my hair for a week – it's so straight and shiny. Then I'll tell you all about Samantha." Wendy went into the bathroom and started to run the water.

"Fine," Gilly replied absently.

"And you can tell me all about Cameron. How is he bearing up?" She yelled over the noise of the shower.

Gillian lay down on her bed and thought about Cameron – wonderful, adorable Cameron. She had just been talking to him on the phone. He was on his way back from Dublin and he wanted to meet up later that night, when things had quietened down. Wendy had walked into the room literally just as she had hung up. Gillian knew that she was going to have to be a lot more careful for the time being.

"Cameron is going to be fine. Naturally he's still shocked by the whole episode but I guess it will all be OK as soon as the dust settles." Gilly closed her eyes and imagined what it would be like to be Cameron's wife.

"I agree." From the sound effects Wendy was obviously under the shower at this stage. "It's all a storm in a teacup. I think even Sam is coming to terms with that. I'd say they'll be back together in a matter of weeks."

Gillian's eyes snapped wide open again and she stared at the ceiling. Over my dead body, she fumed silently.

Back in the village of Fiddler's Point, Frank Delaney was beginning to lose his patience.

"Look, woman, if you're that uptight about the whole thing why don't you make a few phone calls and try to find out what happened to her?" he suggested.

"Sure I wouldn't even know where to start. What was her name again?"

"Kathleen someone or other," he said as he changed the television channel.

Luke Delaney walked into the small lounge. "What's wrong with you, Mum? Is it that woman from this afternoon?"

"It is, son. She was in a very bad way when she left here in the ambulance and I just wanted to be sure that she was all right."

"Why don't you phone Wicklow hospital?"

"I couldn't do that. I'm not even related to her and I don't remember her name."

Luke sat down on the small sofa beside his mother. It was the same sofa that Kathleen had ranted and raved on earlier that day. Tess was sitting bolt upright and rubbing her knees with her hands, something she did all the time without even knowing it. Luke and his brothers had already heard all about the action in the village earlier that day. As soon as they came in from the boat and off-loaded their catch, they went for their regular drink in The Fiddler's Rest. Usually it was a quiet place, even on a Saturday. That evening, however, it was sheer pandemonium. There were literally reams of gorgeous young girls with their partners, all dressed up to the nines. There was a photographer getting them to do all sorts of antics and there in the middle of it all was a minister no less. He was going to regret his rendition of *Islands in the Stream* by Sunday morning, Luke was fairly certain.

As soon as they saw the action in their normally quiet pub, his brothers had forgone their habitual pints. Instead they rushed home, showered and wolfed down their evening meal.

"I think there's a bit more fishing to do yet today, Mum," Mathew had said with a wink and a smile.

"Wait up!" Mark yelled to his brother as he kissed Tess goodnight. "We might be late, Ma," he added with a grin as he rushed out after Matty. Luke wasn't nearly as interested. He reckoned that the girls had all been drinking for over six hours by that stage and anything you could catch at that time of the evening wasn't really worth having.

He had eaten his food at a more relaxed pace and then he went upstairs for a shower and shave. They didn't shave in the mornings because they were always anxious to get out on the sea early. Mark had even taken it a step further and grown a beard. Luke didn't like the idea of that at all, however. As the only redhead in the household, he didn't fancy a red beard.

Luke had very fair skin with a liberal scattering of freckles across his forehead. His eyes were captivating, the palest blue possible. His mother used to tease him that girls would drown in those eyes but he paid no heed. Since he was a teenager Luke had worn his hair to shoulder length and was attractive in a rugged and poetic sort of way. But he was chronically shy.

He was definitely the closest of the three boys to his mother. The other two were quite wild and rarely in the house. Luke was a reader and stayed in with her regularly while the other two were gone off in search of devilment in Wicklow Town. Luke was as tall and broad as his father and, just like Frank, he was a gentle giant. It distressed him to see his mother so addled.

He took Tess's hand. "Would you like me to drive you up to Rathnew Manor? Maybe the bridesmaid is up there, the one you said came to the house after the ambulance left."

"Wendy – she was lovely. I don't even know if that's where she's staying."

"Well, at least it would be a start."

Tess Delaney looked uncertain. She regarded her son nervously. "What would I say?"

"Why don't you let me think about that?" He gave her a reassuring smile and squeezed her hand gently.

She didn't reply. She just looked at him with anxious eyes. He took this for a yes.

"Come on, so." He rose to his feet and, because he was still holding her hand, he pulled her up gently too.

"Dad, I'm taking the car. You're not going out, are you?"

"Me? And where would I be going with all the pubs full of that wedding crowd?"

"We won't be long, Frank. You'll be OK, won't you?"

"Of course I will," he smiled at his wife. After all these years, she still thought he wouldn't survive five minutes without her. The lovely truth of it being that she was probably right.

Luke took his mother out of their little house and they headed off for Rathnew Manor. They were barely out the door when Frank switched over to the TV3 news. It was one of the last stories on.

"*And finally,*" the woman newscaster smiled into Frank's living-room, "*one of Ireland's biggest society weddings didn't go quite according to plan today when a mystery guest interrupted proceedings. Cameron Judge,*"

Managing Director and major shareholder of Judges' Whiskey was to marry society girl Samantha White who also works for the company. The wedding was to take place in the village of Fiddler's Point in Wicklow earlier this afternoon. The ceremony was cancelled, however, when it transpired he was allegedly marrying a lady he was in fact closely related to: his sister. The family were unavailable for comment this evening." Another broad smile for the viewers as she continued. *"I'd say he needed a few strong whiskeys himself after that experience. And now for the weather . . ."*

Frank turned the television down. Those bloody Judge men had a great deal to answer for. Why couldn't they keep their trousers on? Fiddler's Point would be better off without the Judge family, he decided, and that poor girl was no more a society girl than he was!

Fifteen minutes later, Luke and Tess Delaney pulled up outside Rathnew Manor. The family had dined there one time only. It was to celebrate Frank and Tess's thirty-fifth wedding anniversary a few years previously. She was quite shy this evening especially on account of the fact that the Judge family were in residence and the day had been such an unmitigated disaster. Luke, however, had no such concerns. He may have been timid around girls but when it came to helping out his mother, he wasn't easily embarrassed. He took her by the elbow protectively and walked into the Manor with her.

Luke smiled at the receptionist and explained his mother's involvement in the day's events. Then he simply asked if the bridesmaids were staying in the Manor that evening. They wanted to speak to the one called Wendy.

Five minutes later Luke, Tess, Wendy and Gilly came face to face. Luke's reaction was instant and absolute. He was struck by what felt like a thunderbolt. He had never experienced anything like it before. Whether it was the way she walked or the way she talked, or the manner in which she held herself, he couldn't say – but he knew he was wildly attracted to her. The hairs on the back of his neck stood on end, his mouth went dry and he was trembling slightly. Luke stared at the woman who had just walked into his life. He could actually feel his heart beat through his massive ribcage. It was clanging so loudly in his ears he wondered if other people could hear it too.

"Luke, Luke," his mother was gently shaking his arm.

He snapped out of his suspended animation and looked blankly at his mother.

"This is Wendy, the lovely girl I told you about."

Luke looked at Wendy. He hadn't even noticed her. "Oh, hi."

Then he looked back at Gillian.

It was quite apparent to Wendy that Tess's son wanted to be introduced to Gilly. "And this is my friend, Gillian. She was the other bridesmaid."

While Tess smiled hello to Gilly, Wendy reflected that she might just as well have said that Gillian was the Queen of Mars as far as Luke was concerned. She had seen Gilly have that effect on men before. Samantha might have been way and above the most beautiful of the three flatmates but Gillian was the sexiest. She smouldered in a passive sort of way. Wendy and Sam used to tease her that she must give off some sort of scent which only men could pick up on but, whatever it was that Gillian had, it attracted men 'something powerful'.

Luke had obviously fallen for her. Wendy smiled to herself. Another one bites the dust, she thought mildly. Then she turned her attention back to Tess Delaney.

"Thank you so much for all your help this afternoon."

"Well, that's just it, you see. I was so worried about that poor woman – Kathleen, was it? Is she going to be OK?"

"Oh God, nobody called you back! I should have done that, Mrs Delaney. Things have just been so hectic today, we haven't even had dinner yet."

"Oh, I'm sorry, luv. I shouldn't have come."

"No, yes, I mean you should have. Only I never thought to ring you. I'm the one who needs to apologise."

As Wendy filled Tess in on the events of the afternoon, and assured her that Kathleen White was going to be absolutely fine, Gillian walked over to the window of the Manor to see if there was any sign of Cameron with his father.

"The weather is getting really bad now. Not a night for going out." Luke had come up beside her.

She turned sharply and looked at him. She was slightly startled because she hadn't heard him walk up behind her. "No, definitely not," she agreed. "Although you came out."

"Ah, well, it was better than staying in and listening to 'er nibs fret."

"Very kind of her and indeed you – Luke, isn't it?"

He put out his hand to shake hers but he felt awkward and clumsy. His hands seemed to have grown. "At your service," he smiled, trying to hide his emotions.

Gilly shook his hand. "I saw your father in the church today. You're more like him than you're like your mother."

"You remember my father out of a church full of people?" he grinned disbelievingly.

"He was the one to help Sam's Mum, wasn't he?"

"Oh, yeah."

"You do look quite like him, except for the hair of course."

"Yeah, the red hair is a bit of a mystery. Do either of your parents have auburn hair?" he asked, anxious to maintain a conversation, no matter how lame. Under normal circumstances he would not have dreamt of asking such a naff question but this was no normal circumstance. He was fantastically drawn to this woman and her wet auburn hair was extremely sexy, slicked back from her face.

"No, now that you mention it, they don't." Reaching up to stroke her hair, she suddenly regretted the fact that she had washed it. His own mane was considerably lighter in colour than hers, but equally striking. In fact he was quite an attractive man in a Fionn MacCumhail sort of way. She granted him a smile.

"What do you do, F – er, Luke?"

"I fish," he said simply. He was proud of his profession. He was the third generation of Delaneys to be a fisherman and they had never lost any of the family to the sea.

"What do you fish for?" she began to flirt. "Buried treasure?"

He smiled and shrugged. "Not much of that in the Irish Sea. No, mostly whiting, hake, plaice, a little haddock."

"You really do fish fish." Gillian realised that she had never actually met a bona fide fisherman before. Some of the guys she knew on the marketing circuit in Dublin went to the Caribbean or the west of Ireland to fish for shark — but haddock? That was a new one. Gillian was slightly stumped for conversation.

"Is it a rewarding profession?"

"It suits me."

"Is it lucrative? I mean is it a sustainable job?" She was unsure of herself.

Luke laughed. "You obviously haven't been following the news lately. No, the fishing industry is in crisis in this country — unless, of course you own one of those huge offshore fishing tankers."

"Do you?" she asked hopefully.

Luke looked at Gillian. She might be gorgeous but she had no idea about fishing.

"Are you serious?" he laughed at her. "Sure there's only a couple of them in the country. No, I fish off my dad's boat, *The Ashling*, with him and my two brothers. There's not much cash in fishing as a job now, but I like doing it. That's why I'm still at it."

Gillian looked genuinely confused. "But what do you do about money? How do you live?"

He thought about this for a moment and then he smiled at her. "Simply," he explained.

"You mean you live simply?"

"Yes. It's a good way to live."

"But what about clothes? Food? Holidays?"

Luke laughed at her. He examined what he was wearing — a faded pair of jeans, an old pair of runners and a jumper his mother had given him three Christmases earlier.

"I don't know. I suppose I'm not really bothered by clothes. As for food, we have all the fish we would ever want and I'm not really one for the holidays."

Oh my God, Gillian thought in wild panic, I've met my polar opposite! This was the first time in her life she had come across somebody with whom she had genuinely nothing in common. She would live and die for clothes, couldn't give a hoot about food and needed at least four holidays a year.

"Cameron," Luke looked over her shoulder and saw his old friend walk in the front door of the Manor with his father a few paces behind.

"Luke, God, it's good to see you. How the hell are you?" The two men bear-hugged. It was as if the years that they hadn't seen each other just melted away.

"How am I?" Luke laughed and put his arm around Cameron's shoulder. "Sod that. How the hell are you bearing up? I heard about your day. What a nightmare! What can I do?" Luke hadn't planned on seeing Cameron Judge. He certainly hadn't thought of what he would say if he did see him but everything he did now, he did on impulse.

Cameron looked at his old friend. "To be honest, Luke, I don't know what to do now. But, God, it's good to see you – I need you, man. Would you stick around? Surely to God it's time for a drink."

Luke simply nodded.

Wendy and Gillian flocked to Cameron and James Judge's side in support. Tess held back. She had heard what she had needed to hear. That poor woman, Kathleen White, was going to be fine and she was safely deposited in Wicklow General Hospital with her daughter.

Tess didn't dare repeat to Wendy any of what that poor drunk woman had said to her when they were alone in the house earlier that day. It was good to see that Cameron had returned to the Manor too. That meant he wasn't anywhere near Samantha White. Tess said another prayer that the mother and daughter could talk to each other properly. What needed to be said needed to be heard. That was imperative.

Cameron looked pretty dishevelled but James looked utterly crushed and dejected. She almost pitied them, but she knew better. The Judges were survivors. They looked spent and worn out this evening but it wouldn't take them long to rally again and woe betide anyone who crossed a Judge's path.

Tess realised sadly that there was nothing more she could do to support the Whites for the time being. It wasn't clear to everybody yet but having listened to Kathleen White, Tess knew that there was trouble, serious trouble brewing between the Judges and the Whites. Today was just the first day. The battle lines were being drawn and she could feel it in her soul: this was going to be a war.

CHAPTER 9

It was three o'clock in the morning when Samantha woke up to the sounds of her mother's voice.

"Sam, where are you? Are you here?" the older woman asked, her voice high-pitched with panic. She tried to sit up in her hospital bed but was unable to with all her drips.

Sam was quick to wake. "I'm right here, Mum. Don't worry." She came and sat on the side of her mother's bed. "Don't try to move. They've hooked you up to various drips to rehydrate you and God knows what else."

Kathleen saw the needles inserted into the thin skin on the back of both of her hands. When she moved even a fraction the needles jarred and the pain was intense. Then she looked up at her daughter. "Oh, you poor thing! Have you been sitting in that chair all night?"

"Well, I didn't want to leave you. We need to talk, Mum. How are you feeling?"

"Pretty rotten," Kathleen sighed. "I'm very sorry for everything I've put you through, Sam. It's no secret that I've been an appalling mother but I never meant to hurt or embarrass you the way I did today – or was it yesterday?" She looked at her daughter. "What day is it?"

This time it was Samantha's turn to sigh. "Technically it's very early on Sunday morning." She looked at her watch as she rubbed her eyes. "It's coming up on three o'clock, Mum. Look, you have to talk to me about today or yesterday or whatever you want to call it – the wedding. I left the man I love at the altar. I'm not sure that he'll ever forgive me. Could you please tell me what the hell you were playing at? I have to sort this mess out."

Kathleen looked at her beautiful daughter. She should have a happy life, she should have married a fine man – a doctor perhaps or a solicitor and they would have produced beautiful babies. Samantha was intelligent as well as being beautiful. The world should have been her oyster. Why did it all have to go so terribly wrong? Sam could have had her choice of any man. Why did she have to bloody well pick a Judge? The chances of it happening were just too slim. It was definitely some sick twist of fate. Or worse again, could it be the hand of God maybe? Exacting revenge on her for being such a bad mother and wife?

"Mum?" Samantha was impatient and utterly fed up. "Will you explain yourself?"

"Where do you want me to begin?"

"Well, how about the beginning?" Sam's tone was sharp and cross.

Kathleen closed her eyes as if she was trying to gather her strength and then she began.

"My mother was right, of course, but I couldn't see it at the time. She said that Pablo was not the man for me but I didn't believe her. I thought she was out of touch and didn't understand what we were about. Now I realise that she knew everything. She knew how I felt about him. She knew why it wouldn't work, she probably knew more about my future then than I remember about my past."

"Mother, what are you talking about?"

"Pablo."

"Dad?" Samantha asked assertively.

Kathleen raised her eyes to look at her daughter but she ignored the 'dad' reference and continued. "I met him in London in 1968.

I was there to do a beautician's course. My mother had saved up every brass farthing she had in the world to send me there and for that, I really was grateful. I wanted to make something out of my life. Back then I really had plans that I was going to be somebody." Her eyes sparkled for a brief moment but then they went dead again. "Pablo was in London at the same time. He was there to try and get work. Sami, I thought he was the sexiest man I had ever met. He was infinitely better looking than any Irish fella I had ever seen with his dark Spanish skin and his big brown eyes. His hair was jet black and he gelled it back from his face. He was such a handsome man and he seemed to find me attractive too." Kathleen's gaze was distant as she remembered the image of Pablo. "He had such a passion for life. I fell deeply in love with him, very quickly."

Samantha considered interrupting to get her mother back on track and on to the day's theatrics. Then again she had heard so little about her father and mother's courtship she wanted to listen.

"I remember our first date. I took so much time getting ready. I wanted to look my best. I blew my entire weekly allowance and went without food for the week so I could buy a Mary Quant dress. To this day, it's still the prettiest dress I have ever owned. It was a white mini-dress with huge big black polka dots. I thought I looked a million dollars and in fairness so did Pablo, I think." She looked sad for a moment. "He took me for a picnic in Hyde Park. I thought it was so romantic. It never even occurred to me that we were going there because he couldn't afford to take me to any of those fine restaurants. He had made the sandwiches and he had brought along some very nice Spanish wine. Pedro was fantastically proud of the Rioja wines as that was his area and it all sounded so exotic to me. We actually had two bottles of wine! I had never drunk so much and I was really flying. Pablo and I flamencoed together on the grass of Hyde Park. People stopped to watch us and they applauded when we had finished – it was really magical. I had never felt so alive in my entire life, Samantha. Every atom of my body, every hair on my head tingled. That man made me feel electric. He lifted me into the air and spun me around like a child. I remember thinking

I would burst with happiness. Then it started to rain. Oh, Sami, I remember, it was so sudden! One minute it was blue skies and the next it was like a tropical storm. Everybody ran for cover but not Pablo and I. We stood there looking into each other's eyes, oblivious to the rain, oblivious to everything but each other." Kathleen's eyes opened wide as she relived her experiences. "We got soaked through to the skin. My hair was stuck to my back and I remember the drops running down his face, over those magnificent cheekbones. Still we didn't move. We just stared into each other's eyes. The emotion was so powerful – and then he kissed me."

Sam was enraptured by the story.

"*No tienes sangre en tus venas – tienes fuego!*'" Kathleen whispered.

"What?" Samantha didn't speak Spanish.

Kathleen blinked back to the moment in hand. "That's what he said to me – 'You don't have blood in your veins, you have fire!'"

A shiver went down Sam's back. Smooth-talking bastard, she thought.

"So you were madly in love with Dad," she happily concluded.

"I certainly was that day. I did everything in my power to snare that man and snare him I did. He proposed one month later."

Samantha looked at her frail and tired-looking mother, now. It was difficult to imagine her in a Mary Quant creation. "You must have been very happy."

"We were, for a short time, but when I took him home to meet my mother she went crazy. She was furious with me. She called me every name under the sun, saying that she hadn't paid all that money, just for me to fall in love with some Spanish labourer."

"Was he poor?"

"Well, he was a gardener and landscaper and mother had plans for me that involved marrying some London MP."

"Ah."

"But it didn't matter, I was madly in love with Pablo. In my eyes he could do no wrong. He was just the most perfect man on the planet."

"So you married him against your mother's will?" Samantha

asked, genuinely surprised to realise that she had never known this before. If she had, she probably would have ignored her mother in the church and gone ahead and married Cameron. It was as if Kathleen knew what she was thinking, however.

"Yes, but I should have listened to my mum, Sam. It soon became apparent that she was right. I did love Pablo but I also longed for the finer things in life. I wanted a big house and lots of fine clothes. He was happy to live a simple life. He loved me deeply but he was very happy to live in a smaller house with a large garden where he could grow his fruit and vegetables. His only regret was the Irish weather. He always lamented the fact that he couldn't grow vines here. Pablo always said that people should not live where grapes can't grow."

"You moved back to Ireland, to Galway?"

Kathleen ignored her daughter's reference to Galway and she continued. "As soon as Mother kicked us out, we went straight back to London and got married in a registry office so she couldn't split us up. Then we moved back to Dublin. We were determined to stay together back then."

"Well, that obviously changed somewhere along the line." Samantha's tone was sarcastic but Kathleen just nodded.

"It's very sad and I have no doubt it was all my fault. Pablo was a good man and very loving man but he quite simply couldn't make me happy. I didn't understand, when Mother had been trying to break us up, that she could see from the outset that Pablo and I needed different things from life. But we had to learn that for ourselves."

"Mum, if you're trying to tell me that you deliberately broke up our wedding because you feel Cameron and I have different needs and agendas, I assure you we have been through a lot together and we have very good communication skills. I think, with all due respect, he and I are a good deal more mature and clued in going into this marriage than you and Dad were."

"No, Sam. I don't doubt for one second that you and that man have discussed what you want out of life. That's not the problem."

"Then tell me what bloody well is!"

Kathleen bit her lip and her eyes became misty. "Oh, Sami, I'm so so sorry."

"What for?" She was becoming even more exasperated.

"Well, poor Pablo was beginning to feel the strain with me. We had moved back to Dublin because I had a job as a beautician in Brown Thomas. He was trying to get a gardening business started up in Dublin but things were very different then. People didn't spend money on their gardens and he was getting nowhere. I was very frustrated and then one day in the spring of '69, he came home with what he thought was terrific news: he had got himself a job running an entire estate. It was a full-time job."

Samantha felt her stomach begin to churn when she heard the word 'estate'.

"There was a house with the job so we would be living rent-free."

Samantha dug her nails into the bedclothes on her mother's bed.

Kathleen continued as the tears rolled down the sides of her face. "They were very nice people and Pablo really liked the man of the house. It was Dunross, Samantha. Pablo took a job at Dunross."

The young girl jumped up off the bed as if she had been physically burned. "I don't want to hear any more. I've heard enough. You bloody well knew the Judges! Did you have an affair with James Judge? Jesus, Mum, what the hell are you saying? Are you telling me that Pablo isn't my father? Are you saying that James Judge is? This just isn't happening to me. This is shit, shit, shit!"

Kathleen sat up in the bed, ignoring the pain of the needles from the drips as they wrenched at her fine skin. She was crying openly now.

"I am so so sorry. It wasn't an affair. It was an accident. There was just one night. I was very drunk – there was a party in the house. It all happened so fast."

Samantha paced up and down the small hospital room like a caged cat. She was wringing her hands. "Jesus, Mum, do you know what you're saying? Cameron Judge is my – oh God, he's my half-brother!" She put her hands to her mouth and looked around the room manically. There was a bin in the corner. She ran over and began to vomit into it. Her two bottles of Gracias from earlier in the evening came up easily. Eventually in desperation, Kathleen tore the drips from her flesh and climbed down from her hospital bed to help her daughter. She put her arms around Samantha but the girl pushed her back.

"Get away from me," she cried miserably as she leaned over the small bucket. "Do you have any idea what you've done? What *I've* done? Oh, Jesus, it's too sick to think about!" She retched again. "He's my brother – oh, God, this can't be real. Somebody tell me this is a bad dream!"

Kathleen tried again to come close to her daughter but Samantha lashed out.

"Get away from me, woman!" She fell into a heap beside the bin and shook like an injured dog. "Get back into bed," her voice quavered. It didn't sound like her voice to her. It sounded much deeper and more savage. "Tell me exactly what happened. I want to know everything. I *need* to know everything." She stared at the floor, unable to even look at her mother, such was her contempt for her. "Leave nothing out so at least I know just how bad it is."

Kathleen climbed straight back into the bed obediently.

"We moved into the groundkeeper's house in the spring of 1969. I think it was April. Pablo did well there which is just as well because I had to give up my job. I couldn't commute from Wicklow to Dublin because it was too far. Life was OK for a while until we were invited to a party in that godforsaken house. Oh, God, Sam, I'm so sorry."

"Just get on with it," Samantha moaned as she hugged the little bin and propped herself up against the corner.

"I was very excited because I hadn't been to any parties in a long time. I wore my Mary Quant dress and we went to the party."

"Go on."

"Everybody was dancing with everybody and James was a very attractive man. Oh, Sam, please let me stop!"

"*Go on!*"

"Well, I was dancing with him to this new song by the Archies – it was called 'Sugar, Sugar' and he started to call me Sugar. I liked my new nickname. Then I saw Rose. She was dancing with Pablo. The song had changed to the Beatles, 'Get Back'. I remember that bitch. She was singing the words and looking at me – telling me to get back to where I once belonged. She was trying to tell me that I was above my station. Imagine her saying that to me. She was such a snobby bitch, God, I hated her."

"And so you screwed her husband?"

"I didn't mean to, I just wanted to get her jealous. He told me he had just bought a new car. It was brand new silver Aston Martin. I had never seen such an amazing sports car up close before, so we went out to look at it. Pablo had just taken me to the big movie of the summer. It was the James Bond one – George Lazenby in the film *On Her Majesty's Secret Service*. I remember how bitter I was when Pablo kissed me on the cheek and happily announced that we could never be in a car like that. I wanted to drive in fast cars, Sam. I wanted more while Pablo had happily settled into a life of less. Anyway, James and I went out to look at his new toy. Sam, it was James Bond's car." Kathleen's eyes sparkled at the memory. "I got so excited and giddy. This was the closest I had ever got to living the George Lazenby life." She was pleading, trying to make it sound reasonable to her daughter but Samantha's expression was venomous. Kathleen slowed down and composed herself again. "When we were in the car, he put on the radio and there was a new song on. I had never heard it before. It was French and sounded very exotic. It was called '*Je t'aime*'," she explained guiltily.

Samantha groaned.

"I didn't mean for it to happen."

"And so you conceived me in a fucking car listening to '*Je t'aime*'?"

"It all happened so fast. It was a mistake."

"I was a mistake? Well, this just gets better and better. Thanks a lot."

"Oh, no, not you. You're the best thing that's ever happened to me but I am so sorry I haven't told you before."

"Why the hell didn't you warn me years ago when I told you that I was working for Judges' Whiskey?"

"I tried."

"Not hard enough." Another groan from Samantha. "Mum, is there any way in hell that you could be wrong about this? I mean, I could be Pablo's and you got your dates wrong."

"I know when I got pregnant. Pablo had just recovered from a bout of severe flu – he had exhausted himself working on the estate in his first enthusiasm for the new job – and we hadn't had sex for a couple of weeks before the party. Then he and I had a huge row the night of the party. He was flirting with Rose too much and I was jealous. And he was angry with me about James."

"Did he know you had screwed his boss?"

"No. He thought I had just flirted with him. But the fight was so bad and I felt so guilty, we didn't make up for several weeks. By then I should have had my period. I didn't. And there were other symptoms . . . I knew."

Samantha was defeated. The big fat tears ran down her thin face and landed on her jumper. She wiped her nose with her Lynn Marr sleeve. She didn't care at that moment if she lived or died. In fact death was looking pretty attractive.

"Does Papi know now?"

"No."

"Does James know?"

"Yes."

"*What?*"

"Yes, he knows. That's another reason why I thought you wouldn't ever end up with a Judge. I always reckoned that James would put a stop to it if you and his son even looked sideways at each other. In fact, I thought that might have been *why* you got the job in the first place. Maybe he was looking after his own child."

"Holy shit! What kind of a sick animal does that make him? He knows?" She still couldn't accept it. "No, this just doesn't make sense. Something doesn't add up." Then, just like pain, another wave of grief hit Samantha as the reality of her situation sank in. "Oh my God, what have I been doing?" She let the bin slip from her hands and spill out onto the floor. She clutched her stomach in agony as her body convulsed in physical rejection of what her mind was being forced to digest. Then she curled her legs up to her stomach in the foetal position and became very still.

Kathleen stopped talking.

Cameron did what most jilted grooms would have done. He had a few drinks. To his immense relief, most of the wedding guests had had the good sense to leave the Manor, but he still took refuge in the library. Only residents could go in there, so he was able to avoid prying eyes. Gillian had tried to get his attention but to her immense fury he sent her away. It was Luke that Cameron wanted – not her. Well fine, she fumed, two could play that game.

The library was a smaller more intimate room than the larger reception areas of the Manor. Vast leather armchairs circled around the fireplace and, to Cameron's joy, a good fire still blazed in the hearth. On either side of the mantelpiece and on the other three walls, French-polished mahogany bookshelves carried thousands of volumes.

The room made Cameron feel comfortable. He was joined by his brother-in-law, David, and Caroline's boyfriend, Marcus. His best man Vinny and Luke (whom he had smuggled in) were already minding him.

The five men kept the waiter busy for a few hours. At the start they drank heavily and talked nonsense. Anything to avoid the topic of the day.

David Neilson had drunk more than the other men and as such, he was the least sensitive to Cameron's wounded pride so he was the first to approach the taboo subject. "What are you going to do now?" he asked simply.

Thanks to a few Judges' Whiskeys, however, Cam was a little less edgy by that time. "Damned if I know, Dave. I mean, I always knew Sam's mother was estranged but even I didn't realise she was quite so dangerous. Bloody hell, she's a nutter."

"So, there's no truth in what she said?"

"What? David, I can't believe you're even asking that! There's no possible connection." He cast his mind back to what his mother had told him about Pablo and Kathleen Garcia working for them years before either he or Sam were even conceived, let alone born. Cameron made the very firm decision to keep that particular nugget of information out of the public arena. "Trust me, that poor old woman is just deranged."

"So does that mean you and Sam will be getting married after all?"

Cameron looked at his brother-in-law. "Dave, get off my case and order another round of drinks, will you?"

"What you need is a little time out," Marcus offered. "Why don't you take off for a few days and see how you feel about things?"

Cameron smiled gratefully. "Now there's a good idea. Hey, I could head over to Barbados."

"Isn't that where you were meant to be going for the honeymoon?" Vinny asked.

"Yes, only I wasn't going to take her to the villa – we were going to stay in Sandy Lane." Cameron took a large gulp of whiskey. "But I guess there's not much point in forfeiting the entire holiday. I could just go by myself and have a bloody good rest after all of this."

Vinny nodded in agreement. "And if you wanted her to, Sam could go and meet you there after the first week – only if it was cool, that is."

"All I want now is my bed," Cameron sighed.

Luke had been sitting next to him, a silent guardian angel. Cameron could feel his strength and support even though he said nothing. It was reassuring. Luke didn't ask difficult questions. He didn't make stupid remarks like Cameron's drunken brother-in-law. In short he didn't make any demands from Cameron which was very refreshing. Luke was a soft, easygoing sort of guy. He didn't try to say the right thing. He didn't make an effort to plug the gaps in conversation. Cameron made a mental note to work on forging his friendship with Luke again. He was the most solid man that the groom knew. He needed people like him in his life. It felt like everybody around him these days just took from him. Even his bloody fiancée had let him down in the most appalling public manner. For that she would pay . . .

Cameron rose to his feet and clapped his hands together. "Jesus, what a way to spend your birthday! I want to thank you guys for minding me. This wasn't exactly how I figured the day would end but there you go."

The other men stood and each one in turn bear-hugged him.

Vinny was first. "I'm turning in too, but remember, I'm still in Room 9. If you can't sleep and you want to talk, or drink more," he managed a laugh, "phone me, I'll be right over."

Then David hugged him. "Brother, it may have been a lucky escape. Have you thought about that?"

Next it was Marcus. "Sorry, man. If I can do anything, just yell."

Luke bear-hugged Cameron last and, true to form, he didn't say anything – he just held his old friend for a moment longer than the other men. It was enough to make the groom's eyes glass up. He coughed and wiped his face quickly. "Yeah, right, shit," then he shook Luke's hand. "Luke, I really appreciate you being here. I'll phone you over the next few days. Jesus, how did we lose touch?" He looked at his friends. "Thanks for everything, guys. Goodnight." He swept out of the room before he lost any more self-control.

The other four men made small talk for a matter of minutes, just to give Cameron time to leave and then Vinny retired to bed too.

"That was bloody hard work," Dave mumbled.

"Poor bastard," Marcus agreed.

Luke Delaney, as always, kept his opinion to himself. "I'm going to head off now." He nodded goodnight to both Dave and Marcus and left them.

"He's a man of few words," Marcus commented when he reckoned Luke was out of earshot.

Gillian got to him before he got to the door, however. "There you are." She gave one of her most alluring smiles. "I've been looking for you everywhere, Luke."

"Oh, hello," he smiled, delighted that she was still up and about. He hadn't wanted to leave her company earlier but Cameron's need was greater than his own.

"I was wondering," she played with a strand of her hair, hooking it around her finger, her dark auburn mane now perfectly blow-dried, "if we could perhaps have a little walk together. It's been such a long day and I really need to unwind, you see."

Luke looked at the lady of his dreams. This was too good to be true.

"Sure," he agreed. He opened the front door of the Manor and to his immense relief the storm of earlier had blown itself away. It was positively balmy outside.

"What an exquisite night," Gillian enthused. "Do you know the grounds of the Manor at all, Luke?"

"No, I can't say that I do."

"Better again," she smiled at him with dazzling eyes. "We can explore new territory – together."

Cameron was furious when he discovered that Gillian wasn't in his bed in the bridal suite. That had been the arrangement. Where the hell was she? He phoned her room but, when Wendy answered, he had to hang up. Four o'clock in the morning – it was hardly a reasonable time for a groom to be phoning a bridesmaid. Where had she bloody well got to?

It was only when he went into his en suite that he found her note.

Got tired waiting for you, darling. Happy birthday, Love G

CHAPTER 10

It was after 4 am when Stephanie Judge-Neilson looked up and saw her husband walk back into the main bar of Rathnew Manor with Marcus in tow. There were very few people still awake around the Manor.

She stubbed out her cigarette in the V of the upside-down no smoking sign and dumped the butt into an empty glass. Then she took her vodka and orange up again. "So," she said, managing to remove all interest from her voice, "how's Cameron dearest? Will he live?"

"Steph," Caroline, who had been dancing by herself in the middle of the floor, admonished her sister loudly, "Don't talk about your only brother like that."

"Like what?" Stephanie asked aggressively. She was spoiling for a fight. "Caroline, will you sit down, you're driving me crazy."

"Can't you hear the music?" Caroline asked dreamily. "It's beautiful."

"No, I can't, because I'm not high," Stephanie snarled disapprovingly.

David came over and flopped into the seat next to them. Then he stole one of his wife's cigarettes.

"Your brother is going to be fine. He has had a shit day, though, and he does deserve the family's support, if that's not asking too much, Stephanie."

Caroline had tried to engage Marcus in a dance but he managed to gently pull her down into one of the luxuriant armchairs by the fire. For a change, she seemed content to sit on his lap.

Marcus talked to them. "The whole family has been through the mill. It's not very nice having your name dragged about like that. You all need to cut each other a little slack."

Steph eyed up her little sister's newest beau wearily. "We are a little tougher than that, Marcus. There's no truth in it, so why should we give it a moment's concern?"

Caroline sat up on Marcus's lap as if suddenly having a brainwave. "What if it is?" she giggled.

"Don't be disgusting," Steph cut her younger sister off.

"No, seriously. What if the old lush was telling the truth? Maybe she had an illicit affair with Daddy. God knows she wouldn't be the first to have a Judge baby outside the blanket."

"Caroline!"

But, Caro was on a roll. "Or could it be that Mummy carried darling little Samantha White and then gave her away because she wasn't a Judge?"

This time it was David who spoke, "OK, Caroline, now you're really getting carried away."

"Oh, or could it be that our dear brother Cameron isn't our brother at all? Perhaps failing to produce a son and heir Mum and Dad adopted him and –"

"Look, I'm sure it's all crap," David cut across her before she did further damage. "Let's lay low until the press get their mileage out of it and then they'll move on to something else."

Stephanie covered her face with her hands. "Christ, don't mention the press. Those animals are going to have a field day with this. Has anybody seen the Sunday tabloids yet? Surely they're out by now?"

Marcus studied Stephanie. It was amazing to think that she was his girlfriend's older sister. The two girls were like chalk and cheese. Caroline was wild and carefree. Stephanie was dour and permanently miserable, it seemed. Caro was positively skeletal with impossibly white skin, while her older sister was considerably fuller of figure.

Marcus's girlfriend was gorgeous with a long mane of dark brown curly hair and huge Audrey Hepburn eyes, which she was very proficient at using suggestively. Poor Stephanie had mousy brown hair cut somewhere between short and shoulder-length. Even today, her brother's wedding day, she still managed to look frumpy. Marcus reckoned that it must be tough on her. Rose Judge was such a stunner and Caroline had inherited those looks. Stephanie, on the other hand, had her father's big bones but she didn't have his *joie de vivre*. She was no fun to be around. Marcus pitied David Neilson. What ever had he seen in her? Then he remembered what he found most attractive about Caroline – the famous Judge fortune.

One thing Marcus knew for certain, he really didn't want to get into a fight with Stephanie Judge-Neilson at four o'clock in the morning. He gave her a friendly smile. "Yes, Steph," he agreed with whatever it was she had just been disagreeing with.

David rubbed his eyes with his index finger and his thumb. "What are we all doing? I assume it's home tomorrow, after breakfast."

"What else would you suggest?" Caroline laughed as she rolled yet another joint.

Dave looked at the girls. "What about James? Your dad is obviously worried, what with your mother in hospital."

Caroline began to blow circles into the air above her head. "Mum is a force of nature. It would take more than a family scandal to beat her. She'll be fine. Steph, why don't you take Daddy home with you for a few days just until this thing blows away? A change of scenery would do the old man good."

"Me? Why me? Why the hell should we have him? I have the kids. What about you? You have no responsibilities. Christ, you're still bloody well living on the grounds of Dunross. Why don't you move back into the main house for a few weeks to mind your father? Jesus, he's still supporting you. You don't even work."

Because of the amount of grass in Caroline's system, her response was a good deal mellower than it could have been. "Take that back," she argued dreamily. "I work harder than you ever did. I'm an artist – we work twenty-four hours a day for our craft."

Steph snorted, "Oh, pu-lease! You just spend your time getting high or flouncing around with a brush and easel. Caroline, cop on!"

"Me – cop on? That's a laugh. OK, I do a little pot but I also do magnificent work." She waved her arms around in the air expansively. "You, on the other hand? You're a sad middle-aged woman with no life and no future. You've lost your figure, you have no motivation and you have fallen out of love with your husband." She stopped to take another deep drag, oblivious of how tender a nerve she had touched.

Stephanie looked at David and he at her. It was a moment of honesty and clarity between them.

Even through her hazy pot vision, Caroline sensed that maybe she had gone too far. "OK, OK," she giggled skittishly, "I'm sorry. I didn't mean that last bit, about you and Dave." She fell back into her seat and Marcus. He began to massage her shoulders and whispered something into her ear in an effort to distract her.

For Stephanie, however, what had been said could not be unsaid. She rose to her feet and ran out of the room in tears.

"Should I go after her?" Caroline looked at the two men.

Dave answered. "No. You stay where you are, honey. The truth is, in your rather mellow state you hit on something that Steph and I have been dancing around for months now."

"Did somebody say dance?" Caro smiled and jumped to her feet again, pulling Marcus up with her.

Marcus glanced at David, "Are you OK? Sorry about that."

Dave nodded. "I'll go after her," he sighed as he stubbed out his half-smoked cigarette and downed the last of his whiskey. "This conversation has been a long time coming," he sighed as he dragged himself to his feet and slowly followed his wife upstairs.

James Judge was the only person in Rathnew Manor who had had the sense to go to bed early. It didn't help, however. He lay in the bed he had shared with his wife the previous night and stared into the infinite darkness of his room. He had tried to sleep but failed miserably. While it was an enormous shock and he was getting a little old for this kind of surprise, there was little doubt that there could be some truth in it. "Good God," he sighed heavily again. "Samantha White is Katie Garcia's daughter." He might have made some sort of association if Sam still used the Garcia name. Why hadn't she approached him before today? Why had Katie or Kathleen as she called herself today – why had she left it so late to stop the wedding? James's mind span with the same questions again and again like some stupid merry-go-round that he couldn't get off. He climbed out of bed for the umpteenth time and paced the floor.

"From the top," he announced firmly. "Samantha White's mother is Katie Garcia. OK, now. Katie claims Cameron and Sam are brother and sister. Damn it all, that means I got poor Katie pregnant. Why the hell didn't she tell me? I would have looked after her. We Judges always look after our children," he assured himself aloud. James thought about Katie Garcia. She was a lovely little thing, all right. As cute as a button and full of fun and laughter. He still remembered that incredible little black-and-white mini-dress – it was a knock-out all right. Was it possible that the beautiful bubbly Katie Garcia he had once known had turned into that wizened old drunk that he saw in the church today? Surely not.

He climbed back into bed. "Unless, of course, she's just ranting." He was into his circle of arguments again. "She is, after all, an alcoholic and totally untrustworthy." He lay down and pulled up the bedclothes. There was only one possible solution, he realised. He would have to go and see Katie Garcia and have this out with her one on one. How soon could he visit her, he wondered as he looked at his watch. The luminous digits told him that it was heading for 5 am. In another two hours or so he could get up.

David Neilson knocked on his own bedroom door.

"We need to talk, Stephanie," he started as soon as he walked into their suite.

"No, we don't. It's late and I'm tired." She was lying on the bed crying.

"You're always tired."

"Two children are exhausting," she defended herself.

"Stephanie, we haven't had sex since Amy was born."

"Oh, that's just typical. Bring it back to bloody sex. Is that all men ever think about?" she snarled.

"No, but it does cross a man's mind when he hasn't got it in over a year."

She tried to defend herself. "Look, you know as well as I do that these are tough times. The years that the children are young are very tiring on a woman. I know I've lost my figure. I know I'm not as glamorous as that bitch downstairs but I'm doing my best."

David's tone softened. He didn't want a fight. They had had enough of them. "I'm not talking about that. You're figure is fine. I'm talking about us. Stephanie, do you even love me anymore?"

"Don't be stupid, of course I do. You're my husband, aren't you?"

"Only in name."

"We have kids together. Doesn't that stand for something?"

"Why do you even want to be with me anymore? I really feel that you don't care for me at all. Would you rather be free again?"

"You mean you want *your* freedom again," she replied victoriously. "David, have you found someone new? Are you having an affair – oh God!"

He came and sat on the bed but he kept a good distance between them. The gravity of the conversation sobered him sufficiently to speak clearly and calmly. The last thing he wanted was a blazing row. It was way too late for that.

"Stephanie, I am not having an affair. I am not seeing anyone else but I am not happy nor have I been for a long time now. I did seriously question whether we should have had another child after Zoë. Steph, this just isn't working. There's nothing left between us, is there? Tell me if you think I'm wrong or I'm missing something."

He waited and watched her as she sat up against the pillows and blew her nose. His tone was soft and non-threatening. "Steph, you don't really love me anymore, do you?"

"Yes, I do."

"No, you don't."

She sighed. "Oh, OK then, I don't."

He gave a short miserable laugh. "Well, that's it then, isn't it? We don't have a marriage any more. Wow."

"We're pathetic, aren't we?"

"I guess so," David felt lousy. "I guess I should move out."

"Yeah."

"OK, well, I'll get another room for what's left of tonight. I assume there are loads of spare ones because of all the cancellations from the wedding guests. I'll drive you and the kids home tomorrow and pack a small case."

"Don't forget Cathy."

"What?"

"Our nanny, David."

"Oh, yes. Jeez, Cathy. How could I forget?" he said with miserable sarcasm. "I'll move into the apartment in town until we figure out how this is going to work."

"Fine." Stephanie put up no fight. She couldn't look him in the eye.

"Well, that's it then," he repeated and, at a loss for anything else to say, he rose from the bed and walked back out of their suite. He was numb as he walked along the corridor and down the stairs to reception. He worked on autopilot as he booked into another room and picked up his new key. He was oblivious to Caroline and Marcus scampering up the stairs behind him, like teenagers on the promise of another rollicking good romp together.

David Neilson was shown to his new room by a night porter. He stripped down into his boxers and climbed into his new bed. It was cold and lonely like his new life.

"Wait, wait, I have a better idea," Caroline announced as Marcus was getting out of his clothes. "Let's go outside."

"Oh, Caroline, we're here now. All I want to do is shag you into the middle of next week." He looked around the room, desperately searching for excuses to stay where they were. "Look at this cool four-poster bed. Wouldn't you just love to lie down there and let me tie you up?"

"Yes, that would be good," she purred, "later. Now come on."

Caroline was totally naked and utterly uninhibited. Marcus was still in his trousers but he had already removed his shirt. She grabbed him by the hand and pulled him over to the bedroom door which she then opened a few inches. After a little peep either way, she tip-toed out onto the landing, pulling him behind her. They sneaked along the hall to the top of the stairs.

"We're never going to get down there with you looking like that," he whispered nervously.

Caroline swung her head around to look at him in the half-light of the hall. Her eyes blazed at the challenge. "Want to bet?" She smirked and then she ran down the stairs and across the main foyer of Rathnew Manor with the speed and agility of a nymph.

"Oh Christ," Marcus muttered to himself. "Any other girl and I'd go back to bloody bed." He ran after her and just got past the reception desk before the night porter returned from bringing David up to his new single room.

"Isn't this wonderful?" Caroline whispered loudly as she danced on the front lawn of the Manor. The grass was as smooth as a putting green.

"I must admit it has turned into a lovely night – it was lashing earlier," Marcus agreed begrudgingly. He really wanted his bedroom.

"That was ages ago, darling. It's almost sun-up now." She ran over to him and hugged him. "Isn't this much nicer than being inside?" She lay down on the grass. "The ground has even dried off. Feel it." She rolled over onto her tummy.

"It can't be dry, Caroline, not after all that rain – and it should be soaked with dew anyway," said Marcus in irritation. "Let's go back inside."

"It is dry! Feel it!"

117

"It's not the grass I want to feel, Caroline," Marcus squatted down on his hunkers and stroked her perfectly round bottom, "but if you think I'm getting down with you right here on the doorstep of the Manor you can think again." He pulled her up. "Let's at least find somewhere a little more discreet."

They walked hand in hand away from the Manor and through the formal gardens. She was utterly comfortable being naked and not inhibited in the slightest.

"Aren't you nervous about bumping into somebody?" he asked her.

"If I do, I do and if I don't, I don't. And anyway I know I have a beautiful body so why be embarrassed by it?"

"Spoken like a true artist!" He kissed her on the lips and let his hands run over her soft curves and petite frame. "God, you're gorgeous," he mumbled into her long thick curly hair. "I want you, Caro."

"Then take me," she whispered back, returning his kisses passionately.

As she unfastened his trousers and pulled down his fly, Marcus's instincts took over. He let her pull him down onto the soft lawn.

"What the hell," he mumbled. "I'd say everybody else is asleep by now."

"For sure," Caroline agreed breathlessly.

The *al fresco* frolics turned them on enormously. Marcus didn't even get his trousers off properly which was probably a good thing because Gillian and Luke walked past them a few moments later.

Luke hadn't actually seen them; if he had, he would have insisted that they find another path back to the Manor but Gillian knew exactly what she was doing. It was an *opportunity* and God knows, *opportunities* should never be wasted. She took Luke's hand and walked slightly in front of him so she could block his view. That way she was able to guide him right past the two lovers.

Marcus and Caroline were oblivious, Marcus on top while Caroline gazed up at the exquisite vista of stars fading into the early morning sky.

Then bloody Gillian Johnston's head came into view.

"Hi, Caro," she smiled down at Cameron's sister.

"Good morning, Gillian," Caroline replied, utterly unembarrassed by the interruption.

Marcus and Luke were shocked into silence, however. Luke just looked dead ahead as he walked on, pretending the incident hadn't taken place. Marcus, however, froze mid-shag. Preoccupied as he was, he hadn't seen or heard anybody coming.

"Did you just say hello to someone," he whispered into Caroline's hair, praying that his girlfriend was just messing with him.

She stroked his back lovingly, "Yes, it was Gillian Johnston with Luke Delaney. He's an old friend of Cameron's."

Marcus glanced up in time to see the backs of Gilly and Luke heading up towards the Manor.

"Oh fuck," he moaned.

"What? Again?" Caroline asked, deliberately misunderstanding him. "OK."

Luke Delaney was equally embarrassed.

"I can't believe you said hi to that woman. Did you see them? Christ!"

"Well, I didn't see them until we were literally on top of them. If I had, naturally I would have brought you back by another route," she lied comfortably, sounding as appalled as she could.

"But you actually said hi to her!"

"Well, she was looking straight at me. Wouldn't it have been ruder to ignore her?"

"I don't really know," Luke shrugged. "I've never actually been in that position."

Gillian wrapped her arms around his waist. "Haven't you?" she asked, raising one perfectly plucked eyebrow.

She was in a fabulous mood compared with earlier. When Cameron snubbed her she had been furious – that's when she decided to use Luke as her bait. With any luck Caroline would mention it to her brother and that might stir up some good old-fashioned jealousy in Cameron. It was quite clear that Cam had a strong affection for Luke and so he was the perfect candidate to make Cameron mad with jealousy. She hadn't actually planned on having sex with him but he was so intense.

The sand on the glorious beach of Rathnew Manor was soft under her bare feet. The moon was fading as morning approached and hung like a ghost of itself in the sky, its reflection in the totally flat Irish Sea clear on the dead calm water. The atmosphere was so magical Gillian got caught up in her own trap and ended up having wonderful sex with this strange man. It was going to be a thoroughly satisfying affair getting Cameron's jealousy up.

Luke looked deep into Gillian's eyes. Christ, she was gorgeous. "What I meant earlier was —"

She cut him off with a kiss. "What you meant, Luke Delaney —" she kissed him again, "was that you just didn't get caught."

CHAPTER 11

Samantha walked out of her mother's tiny room in the Accident and Emergency ward of Wicklow General Hospital in a zombie-like daze. It was the early hours of the morning and she was thankful that there was nobody around. Her mother was asleep and she was grateful for not having to talk with her. She wasn't sure what time it was but daylight had almost broken and a taxi was sitting just outside the door.

She got in and asked to be taken to Rathnew Manor.

The short and unmemorable journey passed swiftly. Samantha didn't speak, she just sat in the backseat shivering. Even her big chunky jumper couldn't warm her as she wrapped her thin arms around her ribcage for support. The driver had the wisdom to leave the young lady alone.

"That'll be twenty euro, love," he said softly as he pulled up outside the front door of the Manor.

"What?" she came out of her trance.

"Twenty euro, from Wicklow General to here, love."

"Oh, God, I don't know if I have any money," she panicked briefly as she dug down into her jeans pockets. Wendy hadn't thought to give her any cash.

"Ah, Good Jaysus, that's all I need now, love," the taximan groaned. Then he studied her face. He glanced down at the *Sunday World*, which lay on the passenger seat beside him.

"Wait one little minute," he grinned as he snatched up the paper. "Is this you?" He pointed to the photo of a bride running around the side of Fiddler's Point church.

Sam covered her face with her hands.

"You're all right love, I know the whole story. It's all on page seven – here, I'll show you." He began to finger through the paper's pages.

"No, I don't want to see it."

"Ah," he nodded gently. "Well, tell you what, this ride is on me, OK?"

"Thank you!" She stumbled out of the car and rushed into the Manor.

The night porter was still on duty and the lights were dim at the reception desk. It was obviously very much the night time as opposed to the morning by Manor time-keeping.

"Hello, madam." The porter smirked at her. Had he also read the Sunday papers, she wondered nervously. "Can I help you?"

"Yes, my things were to be moved to the, er, bridal suite yesterday. Were they actually moved or are they still in my old room?"

The porter tapped the query into his keyboard and waited for his snoozing computer to respond. It bleeped and whirred as the screen flashed awake and illuminated his face with the answer.

"Your belongings were transferred yesterday, just after you left the Manor, as per your request, madam."

Then she noticed the clock above his head. It was only seven am. Everybody would still be asleep. This was a good time to get to Cameron alone. She raised herself up to her full height, threw back her shoulders and asked with all the conviction that she could muster for the keys to her room.

Cameron didn't hear the door open but he did feel her come and sit on the side of his bed.

"And where the hell have you been all night?" he mumbled into the pillow.

"I told you," Samantha said, "I had to talk to Mummy before we could – well, before anything."

Cameron shot bolt upright in the bed, having assumed it was Gillian. One of the things he liked about Gillian was her deep husky voice probably acquired courtesy of a twenty-cigarette-a-day habit. Sam's voice on the other hand was lively and light. There was no confusing the two women.

"Sam! It's you! Jesus, you scared me half to death!"

"Well, who did you think it was?" She laughed for the first time in ages.

"Sorry." He gave her one of his lopsided grins because they always made her smile. Out of habit he reached out to stroke her face. "How are you? What news from your nutty mother?"

Samantha instantly pulled away from his physical contact and stood up. "You won't believe what I have to tell you, Cameron." She began to walk away from him towards the window.

"No, no, let me guess," Cameron's tone was strong and confident. As he sat in the enormous seven-foot bed of the bridal suite, he rearranged the mountain of pillows so he could lie back against the ocean of white Egyptian cotton. He smirked at her as he clasped his hands behind his head. "Samantha, your mother told you that your father once worked for mine."

She swung around. "How did you know?"

He grinned with a sort of egotistic satisfaction. "Haven't I told you enough times – knowledge is power and I know everything. She told you that she was raped by one of my dad's friends."

"Raped?" Samantha gasped. "Oh, God, no, nothing that bad. No, Cameron, Mum slept with your dad – James." She began to wring her hands. "My mum and your dad – Cam, I am the product of that bloody –" she couldn't finish her sentence.

Cameron jumped out of the bed and rushed to her as she began to weep openly. He tried to take her in his embrace. "You're wrong," he insisted. "I know what happened."

But Samantha backed away from his arms. He always slept naked and this morning was no exception. She couldn't be that close to him. "Please, put something on, Cameron."

He put his hands on his hips and laughed as he threw his head back. Cameron was fanatical about going to the gym at least four times a week, often more. The result was a perfectly sculptured body with highly defined stomach muscles and seriously toned pecks. He was proud of his body because he knew it was in excellent condition. "God, Sam, are you coming over all coy on me?"

"Don't you get it? You're my brother."

"No, I'm not."

"Yes, you are! I think my own mother should have a better idea than you do of who fathered me."

This silenced Cameron for an instant. She had a point. He strolled into the ensuite and returned momentarily wrapped in a brand new ice-white towelling robe. "Better?" he asked, slightly impatiently.

"Thank you," Sam smiled weakly.

"OK," Cameron continued, "Why don't I order us some breakfast and you can tell me what you know and I'll tell you what I know? Sound like a good idea?"

"Thanks."

James Judge didn't wake Paul, the driver. He didn't want anybody to know where he was going. When he phoned reception to order a taxi he was delighted to be informed that there was already one on hand. Within minutes of Sam getting out of the cab, James was in it, heading back up to Wicklow General Hospital.

"Jaysus, this is a popular run this morning," the taximan grumbled. "I hope you have money on you, now, sir. I mean, no disrespect an' all, but I've done me quota of bleedin mercy dashes for one day."

"Yes, I have," James replied absently.

"I don't suppose you're connected to any to this malarkey that's going on with the wedding that was on in Fiddler's Point yesterday?" The taxi driver studied his newest fare.

"Good Lord, no. Who are they? What are you talking about?" James was already nervous about being spotted heading out to the hospital and so he was quite prepared to lie.

"Ah, I just dropped off the poor bride to the Manor. I have to tell you she looked fairly knackered – poor kid." He threw his Sunday paper into the back seat beside James. "Apparently," the driver continued, delighted to have an audience, "the bride's mother stopped the whole hooley on account of the bride and groom being brother an' sister. Can ye' credit tha'?"

But James was reading the story for himself. It was all there in horrible technicolour. On the cover was a picture of poor Samantha, skirts gathered up in her arms as she ran from the church to find her mother. Then on pages six and seven there were loads more photographs. There must have been a photographer with a long-distance lens some way from the church. Splashed across the pages were photographs of Cameron carrying his mother out of the church. In the background were James, Stephanie, Paul and other guests. There was a photograph of Minister Bill Boggan's Merc speeding away from the church. There was also a photograph of the Minister himself, obviously taken much later in what looked like The Fiddler's Rest. He was red-faced and surrounded by pretty young women and he was singing. Mrs Boggan wasn't going to like that one.

"They don't have much actual facts at the moment," the driver interrupted his read. "But they'll get them, mark me words. There's no smoke without fire. I blame the parents meself. I reckon the old dear was having it off with somebody. Either that or the groom's family isn't as precious as they would have us all believe. What do you call them again?"

"The Judges," James mumbled miserably.

"Yeah, that's them. I'm telling you, somebody's going to have to pay, big time."

James couldn't take any more. Nor did he want to be recognised. "Look, could you just let me out here?"

"Here? But the hospital is another two miles."

"I know but I need the exercise."

"Whatever you say, Gov," the taxi driver grumbled. "That'll be twenty euro, please."

Relieved to get away from the constant banter, James began to walk towards the hospital. Was this really happening? he asked himself for the umpteenth time? There was one thing that his tormentor taxi-driver had been right about: somebody was going to have to pay. Whether or not James was Samantha's real father, it was looking pretty inevitable that Katie was going to let the cat out of the bag about their little amorous encounter. What would Rose say? She would kill him. It wasn't the actual infidelity that she would be angry about, it was the public spectacle. Rose didn't *do* humiliation.

Cameron would be furious too. He was such an upstanding young man and he had his father on such a pedestal. Now he, James, had managed to ruin the most important day in his son's life. How had things got so out of hand? He sighed heavily. Then he clung to his one morsel of hope. Maybe Kathleen White was just a nutty old woman trying to ruin the wedding out of envy and spite. He couldn't believe she was the same Katie Garcia he had retained such fond memories of for over thirty years. She certainly didn't look at all the same.

Katie Garcia had been a vibrant, passionate woman without a care in the world. Every man at that party had fancied her, with her shocking black-and-white short dress – what there was of it. He couldn't help smiling at the memory of those huge playful eyes. How could that be the same person as the skeletal lady who halted proceedings in Fiddler's Point church? The two women had nothing in common. And, in fact, that miserable woman from yesterday didn't have any physical resemblance to Samantha either – obviously the bride looked more like her father, whoever he was, James reasoned involuntarily. A shiver went down his back as he walked up to the Hospital. After yesterday's bed-confusion, he knew exactly where Katie's room was, so with any luck he wouldn't meet any medical roadblocks.

Accident and Emergency was mercifully quiet. At seven-thirty on a Sunday morning, most of the Saturday night bumps and bruises had been fixed up and sent home. He knocked gently on Kathleen's door.

"Come in," she said weakly.

He put his head around the door. "Hello, Katie. It's me, James Judge."

"Oh."

"Can I come in?" He clung to the door for moral support.

"Is Samantha about?"

"Eh no, I think she has gone back to Rathnew Manor. I didn't see her but I think she used the same taxi as I did."

"So she's left me. Well, I don't blame her." Kathleen sighed miserably. "Come in if you want. Just don't stand there," she grumbled.

Suddenly he regretted not bringing some flowers or sweets.

"I'm sorry, I haven't brought you anything. I was in such a rush to get here." He pulled up a chair to sit beside her bed.

"Were you, now?" she asked sarcastically as she looked at him straight in the eye.

Looking at this woman now in the calm sterility of the hospital, James knew that it was, in fact, Katie Garcia. There was no doubt about it. The years had not been kind to her and she looked very frail but the huge eyes that gazed upon him stirred something deep within. He recognised the small pouting lips. They were thinner and more lined now but it was definitely the same woman.

"Katie, I think I have to start by saying how truly sorry I am for any pain I may have caused you," he ventured.

"It's a bit late for that now, James, wouldn't you think?" She sounded bitter and resigned, a miserable combination.

"Kathleen —" he whispered breathlessly, not knowing what else to say or where to start.

She dropped her gaze and studied her bedspread. The nurse had obviously plugged her drips back in at some point during the night, she noticed without interest. "I know, I know, you're sorry. Just tell me one thing. How the hell were you able to let them get married? Do you know how many laws of nature that breaks, James?"

"That's just it, woman. I had no idea. In the first place, she called herself White, not Garcia. In the second place, I had no idea you had had my child."

Her head jerked back up to look at his face as her own flooded with panic. "Don't lie to me now, James. I don't think I could be that strong. You've hurt me enough over the years. Why would you hurt me now as well? Haven't I done everything you wanted? Haven't I left you alone all these years?"

"Jesus, Katie, I don't want to hurt you. This is not a lie. I swear to you on my father's grave. I didn't know. I had no idea you were ever pregnant with my child! "

Kathleen began to cry. "You knew! I wrote to you. You wrote back. Why are you being this cruel to me? I can't take this all over again!"

"What are you talking about? When did you write to me?" he asked desperately.

Kathleen looked at him with pleading eyes. "James, for weeks I walked around like a zombie. I was so young and confused. I wanted to tell you but I couldn't say it to your face. I was so shy and scared. Then so help me – I will never forget this. I wrote to you at the end of September. I was over ten weeks pregnant. I had already told Pablo that I was pregnant and he was delighted, assuming that he was the natural father but something inside me was going crazy. The prouder Pablo became, the more desperate I got to tell you. You did, after all, have a right to know. Now with hindsight I'm not sure what I wanted to achieve by telling you but I just had to let you know. I needed to tell you that you were the real father. The secret was getting harder not easier to keep."

"How did you know it – er, she was mine and not Pablo's?"

"Trust me – women know these things. She's yours, James, of that there's no doubt but then you wrote back to me with that horrendous letter. I couldn't believe how nasty you were. I nearly went mad with shock and despair."

"But, Katie, I swear I never got your letter. I never wrote you a letter. This is all some terrible mistake."

Kathleen looked wretched. "Don't lie to me, James. I couldn't take it again. You practically destroyed me the last time. This time you might succeed. Where's my buzzer? You're going to have to go, James." She fumbled around her bed for her nurse-pager and began to press it as if her very life depended on it.

"No, wait," he pleaded. "Don't call for help. Talk to me."

"You told me to go away and I did. I did what you asked. You said I was never to bother you again and I didn't. It was only when I read that Sami was going to marry your son that I had to get involved. And even then I delayed, expecting you to do something to prevent it happening. But you didn't. The wedding was still on! James, I had to stop her marrying her brother!"

"Oh, dear Lord, how did this happen?" James got to his feet. "I don't want to hurt you and I swear I'm not lying to you. In fact, I don't think I've ever lied to you."

"Ha!" she laughed a little manically this time. "There's another one." She pressed her button again.

"When did I ever lie to you?" He looked into her huge sad eyes.

"In your car. In the middle of – well. You told me you would look after me if anything – well, if I got into trouble." She pouted and suddenly she didn't look old any more.

His heart skipped a beat and he was overcome with the desire to put his arms around her, to protect her. "That wasn't a lie, Katie."

"What's all this?" The matron came storming into the room. "Who are you? How did you get in here?" she demanded with authority. Then she looked at her patient crying. "Look what you've done to Mrs Garcia. Really, this is no time for visitors, sir. I'm afraid you'll have to come back at a more appropriate time."

"We have to talk, Katie. We have to get to the bottom of this," he said, as he was matron-handled out of the room.

Katie watched him go. He seemed so sincere. But *of course* he knew. He had *written* to her. He had *replied*. This was just more Judge lies. They had nearly destroyed her once before. She couldn't let him get near to her again. When the matron returned to give her something 'for her nerves', Kathleen asked that she have strictly no visitors. The matron was more than agreeable to that.

She thought about her darling daughter. With any luck she might have saved Sami from the same fate. There was nothing she could do about it now; she had done all she could. It was quite obvious that Sami was utterly disgusted with her mother and with good reason. If the price Kathleen had to pay to save her daughter was Sami's contempt and disgust, so be it. The only thing Katie could do was to leave her in peace. Maybe if she went back to Galway, her children could try to pick up the pieces of their damaged lives. Poor Ricky didn't even know the full extent of his mother's depravity yet and already he hated her. Kathleen decided that it would be better for everybody if she were dead.

The reception area at Rathnew Manor had a very awkward atmosphere by mid-morning. David Neilson was loading up his soon-to-be-ex-wife's things into the car. The children were fighting. The nanny was crying because Stephanie had told her that she and David were finally throwing in the towel. Gillian Johnston was in a thunderous mood when she saw Cameron and Samantha coming out of the bridal suite together. Cameron was equally cross with her for disappearing without permission although with hindsight it was a good thing as Sam had walked in unannounced that morning.

Marcus could hardly speak, he was so physically exhausted from Caroline's amorous demands on the lawn and in the showers of the Manor. Vinny and Wendy were joined in the restaurant by a pretty tired Ricky. He had returned to the Manor in the small wee hours with a lady friend but he had been wise enough to see her off earlier before everybody surfaced. Now he joined the other two for a full Irish breakfast. They were still in the dining-room finishing up their bacon and eggs when Sam came in.

"Please, tell me some good news." Wendy tugged at her friend's sleeve. "It's so sad about David and Stephanie!"

"Well, the good news is that Cameron and I are talking but, no, I'm afraid there'll be no wedding."

"Why not?" Ricky asked, chewing a sausage at the same time.

Samantha looked at her little brother. Was he really that naïve? Surely there could only be one reason for not getting married. The one he himself had heard the previous day in the little church of Fiddler's Point. Cameron still didn't believe her but Samantha knew that her mother had been telling the truth. There was too much pain in her voice. Kathleen simply couldn't have made that up.

She didn't have the entire thing figured out yet – for example, how could James have let the wedding go ahead? Was he really so self-centred that he would rather let his only son walk into a potentially disastrous marriage rather than come clean?

"How's your mum?" Vinny offered.

"Don't know, don't care," Samantha shook herself. "Ricky, could you please give me a lift back to Dublin?" She smiled at him, wondering how she was going to break the truth to him.

"Sure," he replied without even looking up from his full Irish.

Alone in the car, she would do it as softly as possible.

Cameron pulled the porter aside discreetly. "Can you tell me, is my father still here?"

"Yes, sir. He was up and out early but he's back now. He's having breakfast in his room."

Cameron didn't hang about. He headed straight up to James.

Having spoken to his mother he had felt fine but after listening to Samantha for twenty minutes, Cameron wasn't feeling so carefree anymore.

"Well, is it true?" he thundered as soon as his father opened the door to him.

"Yes, son."

"*What?*"

"I'm very sorry but it appears that I am, in fact, Samantha's father. It's true." He stopped for a moment and looked at his shell-shocked son, then took a deep breath and ploughed on. The sooner he got all of this out, the better. "I've been to the hospital myself already this morning to see Samantha's mother and it is definitely true."

"Jesus Christ, Dad. Of all the women in the world you had to screw, you pick my fiancée's mother!"

The older man examined the floor. He couldn't look at his son in the face. "I had no idea. I certainly didn't know of any baby."

"That's not what Sam says."

"Well, you have to believe me."

"How the hell can I believe anything you say, old man? You nearly let me marry my bloody sister! Hell, Dad, how the hell did it happen?"

"Kathleen's husband worked for us a long time ago. It just happened, OK? It was a party. We were all drunk."

"Mummy has it arseways, I hope you know. She thinks Kathleen was raped by one of your friends."

"Good God, where did she get that idea?" James was genuinely shocked.

"If she gets wind of the true facts, it will kill her," said Cameron.

"She'll be even angrier if she hears about it through the papers. God only knows what they may have dredged up – you know what bloodhounds they are."

"Christ, you don't propose telling her?" Cameron looked anxious.

"I don't know what to do. It's all over the Sundays. I don't see how I can keep that from her."

"Oh, dear God!" Cameron was devastated.

"I really am so sorry, Cameron,"

"It's a bit bloody late for that, father," he snarled. "And what about Kathleen White? She was vocal enough yesterday. What's to stop her selling her story to the press? The full story. Jesus, Dad, forget Mum. What about the business?" He began to tug at his hair.

James collapsed into the chair he had been sitting in before Cameron's arrival. "I don't think Katie will talk any more. She only came to the church yesterday to save her daughter. She's not interested in making money out of the story. I don't think she wants revenge either. She's just miserable about the whole thing."

"Well, excuse me if I don't burst out crying just at the moment," Cameron said through gritted teeth. "You can't trust an old bag like that. Maybe we could buy her silence."

"Shut your mouth!" James spoke with more force than Cameron had ever heard him use before. "Katie Garcia won't bother us any more."

Cameron was not appeased. "Jesus, Dad, could you not have used condoms or something? It's bloody careless leaving babies around the place. You know they'll only catch up on you in the long run."

James shrugged.

"Jesus, what bearing will this have on the Judge stock if Samantha is a bloody Judge?" Then Cameron became very still. "Oh dear sweet Lord, I've just had the sickest thought!"

James looked at the child he had thought was his first-born, now relegated to second place. It was quite clear that the penny was only just beginning to drop with Cam about his own *intimate* relationship with Samantha – physically. Cameron's face paled and he stumbled back onto this father's bed.

"She was my sister!"

"It's over now," James tried to soothe him. He went over and placed his hands on his son's shoulders. "Look, don't think about that. She was only your half-sister. Did you know that sort of thing was commonplace in ancient Egypt?"

"Dad, this is not ancient Egypt! We're in Wicklow."

James tried again, "Well, it's not like you had a child or anything."

Cameron stared aggressively into his father's eyes. "No," he snarled, "I wasn't that bloody stupid."

CHAPTER 12

The staff at Dunross were rushed off their feet. Mrs Bumble, who had managed the Judges' home for over forty years, ran the place with the utmost efficiency but even she and the two helpers she had hastily recruited were pushed to the pin of their collars as cars continued to arrive throughout Sunday afternoon.

The day at Dunross had started calmly enough with only Granny Victoria in residence. It was she who had told Mrs Bumble about the catastrophe the day before. "I expect everybody will return back here, Mrs B. Best double the size of tonight's roast."

Mrs Bumble realised that the old woman was right. The family always retreated to Dunross when there was a crisis. This would be no exception.

By mid-morning Caroline and her new boyfriend, Marcus, had moved back to their house on the estate and the surprise at lunchtime was that Stephanie Judge-Neilson along with her two children and the nanny were all moving back into Dunross for 'a while' as she put it. Another three bedrooms were hastily prepared. Her husband was not staying. The next to arrive, looking very worn and tired, was Cameron Judge. Mrs Bumble loved that boy as if he was her own and it broke her heart to see him in this situation. She never let anybody else stay in his old bedroom and so it was easily freshened up for him. The original plan had been that he and his new wife would take over the guest wing as their new permanent residence. Those rooms were left unoccupied.

The mood in the house was sombre and quiet with the exception of an occasional yelp or squeal from one of Stephanie's girls. Without any discussion or instruction, Mrs Bumble prepared two succulent legs of lamb and roast potatoes for the entire house. Things were delayed, however, when James Judge informed her that Rose was in fact leaving hospital. She would be returning to Dunross that evening and dinner should be delayed until she was back.

He had been hoping that his wife might stay in St Vincent's Private for a few days, until things blew over, but Rose would not hear of it. The doctors had told her that she was physically fit and healthy. Fainting was simply a reaction to the events of the day before and she was free to leave.

James had delayed the visit to his wife as long as he dared. By lunch time he decided he had to go to her. En route to the hospital, he took a double shot of whiskey in the car. With Paul driving, he was free with his turbulent thoughts in the back seat. Trying to delay their encounter a little longer, James took a quick detour into the hospital chapel. He walked slowly up the aisle. There were a few other people in prayer but no Mass was on and it was a peaceful place. When he reached the top of the church he stepped into the front pew and sank heavily to his knees. He dropped his head and started to pray. Nurse Emily who was on Rose Judge's ward recognised her patient's husband. She marvelled at how such a giant of a man could look so small and vulnerable. Where she was sitting Emily could see his great broad shoulders stooped and shrunken. From a few pews behind he seemed weighed down by some invisible burden. Well, it certainly wasn't Rose's health that he was worried about – she was in great nick for a woman of her age. Emily's mind wandered off from her prayers. What could a man who has everything be so worried about? she wondered.

"Well, hello," Rose looked up at her husband without approval. "I was beginning to wonder if you had forgotten all about me."

James went to her bedside and kissed her gently on the cheek, as was their habit. "Hello, Rose, I came as soon as I could."

She looked at her watch but said nothing.

"Here are the clothes you asked me to bring." He handed over the small overnight case.

Rose slipped out of the bed and, taking the case, she headed for the ensuite bathroom.

"Mrs Bumble packed it for you. I trust everything's there."

"It's fine, thank you."

"Rose," he started, speaking to her through the slightly open bathroom door, "there are some issues we have to discuss, I'm afraid."

"Oh, James," she called back as she changed, "I have the most frightful headache. Don't let's have discussions this afternoon. There's nothing that can't wait until tomorrow, is there?"

"Actually, there are some things that can't wait, Rose." He tried to be a little firmer. She wasn't going to make this easy. Why should she?

"Well, I don't want to discuss anything with regard to yesterday!" she shouted back emphatically. "Outside of this you have my undivided attention, darling." She was good at this.

Rose walked out of the en suite in a pair of brushed-wool, navy, pleated trousers and a similar-coloured soft angora cowl-neck jumper. Over this she wore a long heavy gold chain with a locket on the end. James knew the heavy locket well. Inside, it had room for four photographs – her three children and a rather flattering old one of him. The oval antique clip-on earrings finished off her outfit. As always, she looked magnificent and more like a forty-five-year-old. She smiled indulgently at her husband as she adjusted her hair.

James just jumped in. "Rose, I think Samantha is my daughter."

Her face flinched but only for a moment. Then it returned to a polite indifferent smile. "Well, that's nonsense." She tried to sound confident but even James could hear that her pitch was higher than she had intended.

Rose pretended to busy herself about the room collecting her belongings. It didn't really work because she had precious little with her. James blocked her way and took her hands in his. "Rose, please stop and listen to me. I'm so so sorry about this but it's not nonsense."

"Well, I simply don't believe it. James, that woman was a tart and a whore thirty-odd years ago and quite clearly she still is. There is no way of knowing that Samantha is yours. She's just after your money."

He fell back onto his wife's bed. "I don't think so, Rose. I think she was telling the truth."

"When was she telling you this truth? Have you spoken to her since church yesterday?" There was a slight panic in her voice.

"I had to."

"Like hell you did! How could you, James? When did you meet that tinker?"

"Rose," he tried, "I had to know if she was telling the truth."

"You silly old fool! It's the oldest trick in the book. When did you see her?"

"I went to her this morning. Nobody saw me if that's what you're worried about."

"That's exactly what I'm worried about. Did you see the papers today?" She gestured to the corner of the room and there, in a neat pile, were what must have been every single paper available on a Sunday.

"Yes, I did. To be honest I stopped looking."

"Oh, James! You're impossible. That's exactly what I'm talking about. You don't want to know and so you simply stop looking. Do you really think that the problem goes away then?"

"But, Rose —" He was thinking that, a few minutes earlier, she had been the one who had tried to ignore the problem, not him.

"Well, it doesn't, James. You're just blind to what's happening around you. It's called the ostrich syndrome. Look, you have to give me your word that you won't talk to that malevolent, interfering cat again."

"But, Rose —"

"Your word, James!"

"How can I?"

She put her hands up to stop him talking. "I will only stand by you over so much, James Judge. I quite understand what you have said, do you hear me? I have heard you – now you have to give me something in return. You must give me your solemn word that you won't attempt to make any contact with that woman again." Suddenly James understood what his wife was saying. She liked to talk in the abstract. What she was saying indirectly was that she knew James had had a small indiscretion with Katie Garcia a long time ago. This was her way of dealing with it. Surely he could grant her that much dignity if he was going to get off the hook so easily?

He looked at her with his most gallant and sincere face. "You have my word as a gentleman, Rose. I won't talk to her again."

She studied his face for a moment and then she nodded. "Very well then, let's go home and put this nasty business behind us."

Traditionally the music room was where the Judges met before Sunday dinner was served. During the week they would convene in the drawing-room but there was something a little special and different about Sundays. The music room was a very large circular room with five enormous floor-to-ceiling windows that could optimise the spectacular view. Dunross Lake was at the back of Dunross Hall and because the back of the house faced west, the sun reflected on the water as it set. The room was large enough to take two Queen Anne armchairs and a sofa. There were also a scattering of upright chairs, presumably for sitting to play music. There was a grand piano that nobody played any more and a cello, locked in its case, that hadn't seen the light of day in years. The room had a cultured ambience that could have inhibited lesser souls but a huge fire crackled and welcomed everyone's arrival. Between the windows hung long thin gilt-framed mirrors, throwing more light back into the room. The walls were painted in the palest turquoise colour and the floor was a dark varnished timber.

Granny Victoria had been sitting quietly enjoying the sunset. The low evening light bounced off the lake's surface and into the music room, drenching it in the most delicious honey warm glow. Then her granddaughter, Stephanie Judge-Neilson, broke into her daydreams.

"Where the hell are Mummy and Daddy?" she asked impatiently. "My girls are famished and Zoë has school tomorrow, I need to get her fed and bedded."

"Why don't you feed them now?" Victoria asked.

"They're part of the family, Granny. Why shouldn't they eat with the rest of us?" she replied indignantly as she stubbed out yet another cigarette into the ashtray on top of the grand piano.

Caroline glided in as Stephanie stomped off.

"She's a little uptight today, Gran," Caro reached her grandmother and kissed the old woman's soft hollowed cheek. "I assume you've heard about her and David?"

"Yes, I'm afraid I did, bloody awful business. I still don't quite understand why, though. I mean nobody was being naughty or anything, were they?"

Caroline laughed. "No, Granny, nobody was naughty. I think they simply fell out of love."

"Such nonsense," Victoria sniffed. "All this fiddle faddle about love. You young things simply have life too easy these days. Nothing a little hardship wouldn't solve, I say."

Sufficiently stoned not to bother arguing with her grandmother, Caroline simply shrugged with indifference. "Don't talk about love now, Gran, here's Cam."

"Where the hell are Mum and Dad? I'm starving!" he grumbled as he walked into the music room with a large whiskey. "Hi, Gran, how's your sherry? Need a top-up?"

Victoria handed him her empty glass by way of answer. Marcus followed in behind Cameron. "I think I see your parents' car coming now," he offered as he crossed the room to admire the sunset.

Everybody fussed over Rose when she arrived and Cameron was relieved to note that he was no longer the centre of attention. What he really wanted was a little space. He needed time to think and yet there had been ample time to reflect that afternoon. Dunross was a very secluded house and as such it was incredibly peaceful. Built on two hundred acres of land, there was enough space for anybody to get lost there. Driving from Fiddler's Point, the road gradually turned away from the sea and it was at this point that Cameron's great-grandfather, James Judge the First had bought the enormous parcel of land. Then he built a home fit for a king. The story had been passed down through the family. James the First wanted to enjoy the spectacular sea views that Fiddler's Point had available to the east. He also wanted to make the most of the sunsets and so he found a place where there were great sea views over the east coast of Ireland but there was also an enormous lake to the west. Cameron's great-grandfather figured that if he could build his mansion between the sea and the lake he could enjoy the best of both worlds. He had the glorious sunrises off the east coast of Ireland in the early morning. Then in the evenings, he had the majestic sunsets as the sun slipped down behind the hills, beyond the lake to the west. It worked.

Cameron loved Dunross. The winding private driveway was almost a mile long. In the spring it was at its best as the enormous rhododendrons bloomed in a cacophony of colour. From a distance it looked as if the road led down to the sea. It was in fact a T-junction. The view from this point was one of Cameron's favourites. The choppy blue expanse of the Irish Sea spread out to the north, south and east, usually accompanied by fresh gusty white clouds. There were no obstructions to this magnificent scene. On very rare occasions the Irish Sea was dead calm. Then it acted as a mirror to the white clouds and the view was truly humbling. James Judge the First had chosen well.

Where the laneway split into a T, the left branch went to the farm and the stables. It was also where Caroline's art studio and love nest was. The right branch turned back up to Dunross hall. The driveway swept up to the magnificent façade of the great house. Built in 1910, James Judge had spared no expense. He invested £15,000 in the building, which was the most spent on any building in Ireland that year according to proud Judge folklore. Four twenty-foot white pillars stood sentry at the front of the building. They were massive and quite imposing as they guarded the two huge Irish Oak doors. The house was a brilliant white and appeared perfectly balanced. There were four large windows to the left of the front door and the same on the right. On the second floor the windows lined up with those below and above the front door was a balcony with double doors to take full advantage of the spectacular scenery.

Cameron had broken away from his family early in the afternoon and walked out onto the estate with no particular destination in mind. Eventually he found himself over in the stables, where the horses were delighted for a bit of attention. The weather hadn't really turned cold yet but he knew the horses could sense that the hunting season was drawing in. They neighed and kicked at their doors impatiently. Cameron knew where Joey, the stable hand, kept the sugar lumps hidden and he gave each animal a cube. It had been years since he had hunted – why was that, he wondered? Then Cameron left the stables behind.

As he walked through the farm, he bumped into Sean, the farmer.

"No rest for the wicked," he explained simply as he tipped his hat at young Master Judge.

"No, indeed," Cameron smiled back weakly. He was thankful that Sean didn't want a conversation about the weather or the state of the harvest. Much of Dunross land was devoted to growing barley for Judge's Whiskey. In truth it was only a tiny proportion of the barley they needed but it made for good marketing. As Cameron headed off in the other direction away from the farm, Barley, one of the Dunross dogs, found him and happily fell into step beside him.

"You're about the only company I'm able for today, Barley," Cameron said as he rubbed the big sheepdog's head.

Cameron and his new companion made their way past the clutch of houses next to the farm. Sean lived in one. Mrs Bumble lived in another. Caroline and Marcus had taken over another and two remained empty for guests. He had assumed that Stephanie with her nanny and two brats would move into one of those but his painful sister didn't even entertain that notion. She marched straight up to the Manor and shacked up there. It would be interesting to see how long that lasted, Cameron smiled to himself. Surely Rose would have other ideas.

A little distance past the farm the path led man and dog to the sea. Subconsciously this was where he had been coming all the time, Cameron realised. It was the only real constant in his life. He walked along the beach on the wet sand just at the water's edge. It was firm and reassuring underfoot. Barley felt the fresh sea air in his nostrils and tore off into the distance.

"Some company you are," Cameron laughed as he watched the dog dash after a low-flying seagull that he had no hope of catching.

The clear air began to fill his lungs and his head. It was good to get out of the house. He walked the mile and a half of private beach that the family owned and then he turned back on his own footsteps. The tide was going out so his old footprints were still clearly marked in the sand. How many times in the past had he walked this beach, he wondered, and yet there was no evidence of it. How many times had his father done the same thing and his father before him? Cameron tried to think about Samantha, but he couldn't. It was just too rotten. He tried to focus on the business and how this would affect Judges' Distilleries but again, he couldn't do it. Would he need legal advice? Would she fight for a larger shareholding now that it looked like she was a Judge? Where the fuck did Gillian get to last night? The last thing he needed was two uptight bitches in his life. He swung his head around and yelled for the dog who was still holding sentry for seagulls.

"Barley," he bellowed and the sheepdog came bounding over obediently.

"What'll I do, dog?" he asked his walking companion. "What will I do?"

Rose took her habitual place at the top of the table. Quickly she took command again.

"I want my son on my right-hand side and, Marcus, why don't you sit on my left?" She beamed at her daughter's boyfriend.

Caroline quickly sat down beside Marcus. Trust her bloody mother to sit between the two young men. Granny Vic ignored her daughter-in-law's efforts at taking control of the seating plan and took her usual place next to her own son, James. He sat at the bottom of the table directly opposite Rose. Zoë plonked down beside her Uncle Cameron and Stephanie sat next to her at her mother's request.

"Perhaps, that way, you'll be able to control her," Rose said bitchily.

This left only two places. To James's right sat Cathy the nanny with baby Amy precariously strapped onto the Chippendale.

"Do you really think that the baby is ready to eat with us in the dining-room, Stephanie?" Rose looked doubtful.

Her daughter's lower lip began to quiver. "Well, what else was I going to do with her? I can hardly leave her out in the kitchen alone."

Sensing an imminent outburst and not really able for it, Rose let the matter drop.

"Well," she smiled a little too brightly, "this is nice. It's not very often that I have all my children gathered together, now is it?"

"We were all together yesterday too," Zoë answered her forgetful grandmother.

"I mean back at Dunross, child." Rose gave the girl a cool stare – when would she learn to hold her tongue? Then she looked at her elder daughter. "Do you think you'll be staying long, Stephanie?"

"I have no idea." Again the lower lip wobbled.

Victoria decided it was time to speak. "She should stay as long as she likes – this is her home, isn't it?" Then she turned to Stephanie. "You should take over one of the houses down by the farm, though. That way your energetic children won't drive us around the bend and visa versa."

"Can't I stay at Dunross? This is my home, not one of the outhouses," Stephanie sniffed.

"I'm only saying it for your own sanity, child," Victoria explained, continuing to cut her roast lamb. "I see Zoë has been at my chocolate stash already and you've only just moved in."

Stephanie cut a how-could-you look at her seven-year-old and Zoë gave a guilty-as-charged look back.

"I'm sure the children will want to make noise and run about. That's what young girls do these days. It only seems sensible," Victoria concluded.

Rose pushed her roast lamb around the plate. "Victoria is right, darling. For your girls' sake."

Stephanie knew she had no choice. They may have wrapped it in velvet but the elder ladies packed a punch. She couldn't fight both of them. The message was clear: *You can come back as long as you stay in one of the farmhouses.* What the heck? It was free and she and the kids could eat in the Manor.

"Only for my girls' sake," she conceded, smiling at the two Mrs Judges.

"Now, Cameron . . ." Rose straightened her back and managed to look down at her son which was no mean feat as he was considerably taller than her. Sitting at the top of the table, however, she was chairing this meeting. "How are you bearing up, darling?"

Oh Christ, here we go, he thought miserably. He forced a smile and looked at his mother. "I'll survive."

She squeezed his hand reassuringly. "While we are all together," she addressed the family at large, "your father and I would like to reassure each and every one of you that there is absolutely no truth in what that madwoman said yesterday. Isn't that right, James?" Her tone was particularly strong and authoritative.

James was not expecting this little speech but she seemed to know what she was doing. Perhaps she was trying to protect the girls and Victoria.

James nodded mutely under the pressure of her stare.

Rose was satisfied and so she continued. "Doubtless we will have a few difficult weeks ahead of us with the gossip and tittle tattle."

144

Zoë giggled at the strange words but her mother pinched her. She recoiled sharply and grasped her arm where it hurt.

"As I was saying. The next few weeks will be a little difficult but it will pass and then life will return to normal. Cameron, you and you alone can decide if you can have a future with Samantha White but rest assured her mother is talking sheer nonsense."

James gaped at Rose, his mouth open wide in shock. What the hell was she saying? She certainly wasn't making any sense! There was no way that Cameron had a future with Samantha – they were brother and sister.

Cameron was equally perplexed but he was marginally better at hiding it than his father was. He smiled reassuringly at his mother and nodded as if in contemplation. In reality he was wondering what his mother was banging on about. He glanced toward his father for assistance – no help there. Poor pathetic James looked even more lost than usual. This annoyed Cam but he didn't show it.

Who was telling the bloody truth in this house? he fumed silently.

"Son, do you hear me? You must just let this blow over." Rose was squeezing his hand again.

That much he understood. He would love if it bloody well blew away to oblivion. He nodded in agreement with her.

"Good," Rose continued. "With this in mind I think that you should go to Barbados tomorrow, Cameron."

"What?"

"Well, don't sound so surprised. You were meant to be going anyway. The flight is booked and paid for and you need a break, after all that you've been through. Why not?" Then she looked up at her husband again. "What do you think, James? Isn't it a good idea for Cameron to get away for a while?"

"Whatever you think is best," James agreed. "But wouldn't he be a little cut off over there? It's not a good time for him to be alone." Then he addressed his son. "Cameron, is there a buddy you could phone who could go with you at this short notice? Perhaps Vinny?"

Rose lifted her hands to stop her husband talking. "That won't be necessary."

"Why not?" Cameron looked at his mother.

"Because I'm coming with you."

CHAPTER 13

Tess Delaney had never seen her son so happy. He was positively buoyant. It worried and excited her at the same time. Mathew and Mark were supremely normal young men – they were always out looking for trouble and they found plenty because they were strong and handsome. But Luke was different from his elder brothers. He was such a deep and reserved young man, he didn't let go easily. In truth, that was an understatement, Tess realised. He had never let go.

She had heard him return home from Rathnew Manor in the wee small hours of Sunday morning. His brothers regularly disappeared from Saturday night right through to Sunday evening, but Luke wasn't like that. She hadn't dared enquire where he had been all night, much less what he had been up to, but he actually volunteered the information himself late on Sunday evening.

Mathew and Mark were in the front room with their dad watching the news. It was a house that went to bed early and rose very early for fishing. Luke sat at the small table in the back kitchen and read the *Sunday Tribune* while his mother turned a full loaf of bread into sandwiches for the men to take on the boat the next day.

"I think I've met the woman I'm going to marry," he said simply without looking up from the newspaper.

Tess's body froze. She didn't dare swing around and scream with joy. She was scared to move a muscle in case she somehow broke this incredible moment with her son.

"Oh?" she asked as lightly as she could without turning around.

"Yes. It's Gillian, Mam – you met her yesterday. She's a lovely girl, and I'm in love with her."

Tess remembered the cool and particularly sophisticated young bridesmaid with the husky, sexy voice. She was not the kind of woman she thought her darling boy would go for or indeed end up with. She wiped her hands slowly and deliberately with the tea towel next to the bread bin and then she came and sat at the table.

"Would this be the Gillian that was bridesmaid to Samantha White?"

"It would," he looked up from his newspaper and at his mother. His face was bursting with excitement and full of joy. There was no uncertainty in his eyes, no seeking reassurance.

"Have you come to know her, Luke?" she asked gently.

"I know enough. I know I've never met anyone like her, Mam. She's an angel on this earth. Christ, I've fallen head over heels in love." He slapped his leg incredulously and laughed.

The door burst open.

"I'm off to bed," Matt announced as he barged into the room and kissed his mother goodnight. Tess jumped to her feet guiltily. She didn't want Matt to overhear anything. She hugged her eldest and, after he'd gone, came back to the table.

"Luke," she asked nervously. "Does she feel the same way? I mean you can hardly know each other that well just yet, if you only met yesterday."

He shook his head as if he didn't believe it himself and laughed. "I know, it sounds crazy but that's the way it is. I just wanted to tell you."

"Thank you for that, son. The only bit of motherly advice I could give you is to take it slowly with her. She may not have realised it yet that she has the best man in Ireland."

Luke couldn't help himself. He looked up at his mother and

grinned like a schoolboy. It made Tess's heart sink. He was hopelessly in love. When a man was that much in love he was a fool and did foolish things. It was written all over his face. She could only hope that Gillian would feel the same way.

When she had finished making the sandwiches, Tess headed off up to bed.

Luke, however, couldn't sleep – he was as restless as a stallion near a mare. Eventually, feeling caged in, he went for a walk into Fiddler's Point and up along the promenade. The village was quiet, it being late on a Sunday night. There were a few locals just coming out of The Fiddler's Rest. He kept his head down and lost himself in his thoughts.

Luke hadn't been looking for love. Such things didn't really bother him. He liked his life well enough. The sea was his friend. He loved nothing better than to spend the day out there with his brothers and his father. The gentle rock of the boat was as familiar to him as his own heartbeat. The rhythm of the sea was the rhythm of his life. He was used to getting up early and he found the actual activity of fishing very rewarding. You could physically see the fruit of your labour from day to day. To be stuck in an office would be Luke's idea of hell. He hadn't liked school. It had made him claustrophobic although he did love English and Art and he still read vociferously. He found it amusing that so many people now worked at a feverish rate only to earn more money in order to drive bigger cars which they could crash all the faster. Why? He chuckled to himself. He had all that he wanted. His was physical but rewarding work. Not financially rewarding, of course.

He laughed as he remembered watching the mix of emotions dance across Gillian's face the night before when he explained that he was not a wealthy man. Gillian's beautiful serene face. God, he had never seen such a beautiful woman! From the first instant he saw her, he was wildly attracted to her. Her strong confident eyes, the beautiful curvaceous shape of her body, the swing of her hips, her full rounded lips. Luke felt himself becoming aroused again. He took a few deep breaths of the cold night air in an effort to shake the feeling away. The fresh salty taste soothed him as mother's milk would a baby.

Fiddler's Point was his home and he had no intention of leaving it. He dug his hands down into the pockets of his winter jacket and began to walk faster. Gillian would get used to the slower pace. In fact it would be good for her. He looked about his beloved little village. She would come to love it here.

One thing he was particularly happy about was that she knew he was not a wealthy man. She knew he was a fisherman and his life was a simple one. With all this information she had made the first move. She had no misconceptions about him being rich or a city type or anything he wasn't, and that meant she was attracted to him for himself.

He went down along the short promenade of the village and up towards the Anchor Hotel. The soft light of the lounge pub beckoned him in. A whiskey would be nice, he thought. The least he could do was drink a Judges', by way of thanks to the family for introducing him to Gillian.

Safely ensconced in a little snug where he could barely be seen, he nursed his whiskey.

The image of her floated back into his mind. She had the grace of a swan and the spirit of a salmon, that girl. Seeing her for the first time was like a light getting switched on inside his soul. It was not something he had ever felt before, nor was it something that he had missed in the past but now that he had met her she was the most fundamental part of his existence.

Cameron's arrival back to the Manor the night before had been unfortunate in that Luke and Gillian had only just met – but of course Luke was honour bound to support his old friend. That was, of course, *before*. Luke stared into nothingness. Now Gillian and he were lovers, she was his top priority. In truth, he would do anything for her now.

Luke had little choice but to spend most of Saturday night with Cameron. They had been good friends when they were kids and it was the least he could do. He quietly supported Cameron just by being there for him. He wasn't a big talker but that was because he didn't feel much need to rant and rave about anything in particular. If he had something to say, Luke said it. If not, he simply said nothing. He had been disappointed to see that the women did not join them when they went into the library. He had really given up on meeting Gillian again that evening, although he had plans of coming up to the Manor the next day to see if he could see her again.

She was way ahead of him, however. Luke grinned at the memory of how she had appeared out of the shadows as he left the Manor, and shook his head as if in disbelief at his own good fortune. He took a drink of his whiskey.

His mind flashed back to the more intimate parts of their time together. Obviously she felt the same way as he did. To end up making love on the beach on the first evening of their relationship was surely a sign that they were made for each other. Her feelings had to be as strong as his were. He had, at last, met a woman who felt, as he did, that words were unnecessary. They'd walked in silence, hand in hand, to the beach. She'd led him along the shore. It was Gillian who took her shoes off first and paddled in the shallow water. Still they didn't speak, he simply followed her lead. He took off his shoes and rolled up his jeans. The cool and confident woman he had met earlier in the evening was gone, however. Now, she looked up nervously at him, and gently bit her lower lip. Luke's desire was like a tidal wave washing over him. He swept her up in his arms and carried her up onto the dry, warm sand. Luke hadn't planned on having sex with her. He simply wanted to hold her and kiss her. With her help, he might have had the willpower to be a gentleman. But she wanted him. She guided him with her hands and her lips. She willed it so he certainly wasn't going to stop it.

Luke drank some more as he remembered what she had felt like. Her skin was so soft it terrified him. He worried that his coarse hands would feel like sandpaper on her smooth ribcage. His skin was rough from the nets and ropes on the boat. Her hands were tiny and nymph-like. He thought he might hurt her, she seemed so small under his large frame but she smiled at him and wrapped her legs around his, willing him closer. When she eased his manhood out of his boxers, he assumed it was passion that was getting the better of her. He never thought for a moment that she would take it inside her own body so quickly and enthusiastically.

"We can wait," he had offered breathlessly. It was his one last valiant stab at maintaining her honour.

"No, we bloody well can't!" she murmured as she grasped him. "You're magnificent, Luke!" She smiled brightly as she led him into her body.

He made it last. He desperately wanted to let go inside this goddess but Luke knew his responsibilities. Firstly he had to please her. He so wanted it to be a good experience for her. Gillian thankfully was not inhibited in the least. She moved with him and kissed him every bit as hungrily as he did her. The poor angel was obviously not very experienced as she screamed out so loud she doubtless didn't quite know what was happening . . . he smiled with deep satisfaction at the memory.

"Shh," he'd laughed as he gently put his hand over her mouth. "You'll scare the fish."

She looked into his eyes and laughed, nodding mutely.

Luke himself wouldn't come. He had more sense. This night was not planned and so they were not using protection. Now that he had found the creature of his dreams, he certainly wasn't going to ruin it all by getting her pregnant on their first date. Luke kept it all inside – literally. Bless her, she didn't even seem to notice. She was probably innocent about such matters, he realised. God, she may even have been a virgin. He had tried to ask her if she was all right as they walked back up to the Manor but she had insisted that everything was fine.

"Are you OK about this? It's all been so sudden, Gillian," he had offered.

"Yes, Luke. It was really marvellous."

"You know you are OK? I didn't do anything that will get you into trouble."

Gillian had stopped to collect her shoes. "Luke," she smiled, "you are a gentleman."

He wrapped his arm around her shoulders. "Yes, Gillian, that I am. Can I call you later?"

"Err, today won't be good, Luke. I'm going to be minding Samantha all day. It might upset her if she knew that I was talking with one of Cameron's best friends."

"You could tell her I was somebody else," he tried.

"She's no fool, Luke. No, she really will need my attention and comforting. Her marriage has just broken up, for God's sake."

He looked crestfallen. "I'm sorry. I am being selfish. It's just that now that I've found you I don't want to let you go."

"You really are a romantic, aren't you?" she said, hugging him.

"I'll call you later if I can but if not, I'll call on Monday, OK?"

"OK," he gave in unwillingly.

For that reason he shouldn't have been surprised that she hadn't called all day Sunday. She'd said that it would be very difficult but still it saddened him. It did, however, make him even more in love with her. She would call tomorrow, he convinced himself. She would call on Monday.

Gillian and Wendy had got back to their apartment around lunch time Sunday. Samantha arrived back soon after them. She then moved straight back into her old bedroom. Ironically she hadn't really moved much stuff out so it was relatively easy to settle back in.

Wendy had ordered their habitual Sunday night Chinese which went down well. It was the first time in two days that Samantha had actually eaten.

She came clean with the girls as soon as they got back to the flat. Detail by gory detail, she told them what her mother had told her. There was no way out: Cameron was her half-brother. The bridesmaids soothed her and pointed out all the obvious.

"Wasn't it just as well she stepped in when she did?" Wendy suggested.

"You're really only half siblings," Gillian clarified. "Byron, the world's greatest poet, had a long-term relationship with his half sister."

That actually made Samantha cry again.

"Wine – that will make all of us all feel better." Wendy rushed off to get a bottle of white from the fridge.

Then Gillian told them about her wicked indiscretion the previous night.

"Well, well, Gilly. I think that's another first. I don't think you ever did it with a fisherman before, did you?" Wendy teased.

"No, you're right there. That was a first and I have to say a last. God, he was so intense."

"He seemed nice to me," Wendy said.

"Ah, he was grand but only for one night. Jesus, he barely talked but as it happened that suited me. I wasn't bothered with making small talk. It's not like we had anything in common. No, I just needed a service!" She laughed wickedly. "Poor guy! You know I have the coil in but, bless him, he held back to protect my honour."

"What honour?" Wendy snorted. "Why didn't you tell him he was in safe territory – poor guy?"

"What and tarnish my good name?" Gillian pretended to look shocked. "No, I decided to leave him with his perfect image of the virgin on the beach."

"'Virgin' on the ridiculous," Samantha scoffed. "Are you sure there's no future with him, Gill? I've seen him around Fiddler's Point – he's a bloody good-looking guy."

"Do I look like a fisherman's wife?" demanded Gilly. She stood up and did twirl in her Donna Karen black wool dress.

"Hardly," Sam smiled. "Well, you must have liked him to go with him in the first place, I assume."

"Well, I was just trying to –" she stopped herself. She could hardly explain that she was trying to get the gorgeous Cameron jealous and so she changed tack. "You know what they say. If you have one man you can get loads more – well, that's why I went with him."

"Poor guy. Does he know that you were only in it for the night?" Wendy asked.

"Er . . ."

"Gillian!" both Sam and Wendy chorused together.

But Gilly was in great form and laughed off their disapproval. She was in terrific sprits because she now knew that Samantha and Cameron were definitely over for ever. Despite all Cameron's arguments to the contrary, she did believe that he had some feelings for Samantha. Surely no man would get married purely for business reasons? Deep down, Gillian believed that he could have loved Samantha – well, not any more. Sleeping with his half sister? How sick was that? Now that was all over, her path was clear. Cameron would soon be hers.

They were just finishing their Chinese takeaway when Wendy got her nerve up.

"What are you going to do tomorrow, Sam?" she asked shyly.

"Jesus, what am I going to do for the rest of my life?" Samantha responded and buried her face in a cushion.

"Well, how about one day at a time?" Wendy was a little firmer. "Are you going to go to work or do you think you would like to take a few days off? It's just that I have a few days holidays long overdue and if you liked, I could go away with you somewhere. Spain, maybe, or Italy? The weather should still be pretty good there and I can bloody well feel winter creeping into my bones here. What do you think?

"I think you're a dote to offer, Wendy, but I have to face the music sooner or later. The later I leave it the worse it's going to get. I have to go back to work."

Both Gillian and Wendy made sounds of protest.

"Surely it's too soon," Wendy offered.

"They won't welcome you," Gillian warned. "Perhaps you should think about changing jobs," she offered tentatively. "You know – a good clean break and a fresh start."

Samantha looked appalled. "It's my job. What's more, Gracias is my baby. I won't let them take that away from me." She sat up aggressively.

"Sorry, it was just a suggestion." Gillian smiled weakly as she looked at her old friend. If Cameron thought he could get regain control of Gracias just by marrying Sam he was a fool. If, on the other hand, he was marrying her because he really did love her then she, Gillian, was the fool.

CHAPTER 14

Samantha didn't even have to get out of bed to know that it was a miserable Monday morning. She could hear the rain beating against her window-pane with the ferocity of a jilted lover. She tried to roll over and snuggle down again but her mind was already alert and ready for action. Excluding the terrible weather, what sort of day was it going to be, she wondered.

Samantha knew that she would have a good deal of sympathy to deal with at the office. They were a small team in the Gracias department but a large part of the business overlapped with Judges' Whiskey and obviously she would have to meet all those members of staff too. On balance she had a terrific relationship with everybody she worked with but what she really wanted to do was bury her head in her work and ignore the events of the weekend.

On Monday morning, as was usual, Sam was up earlier than her flatmates. This was because she commuted from Dublin to Wicklow each day. Gillian was a complete city girl. One of the reasons she chose to work for the Marketing Company she was in was because of its location. Wendy, on the other hand, spent most of her time on the road driving between her various beauty salons. She had an office in Monkstown above her salon there.

Samantha was driving out of Donnybrook, on the road to Wicklow, before eight o'clock. It was considerably darker than it had been at the same time the previous week, she realised. Was that because of the rain or was it just that her perspective had darkened? It was October, she realised, and autumn had finally taken a grip. Dark days ahead, she thought miserably. If things had turned out differently, she would have been catching the red eye to Gatwick and then she and Cameron would have been flying on to Barbados.

"What the hell am I going to do?" she wailed aloud in the car. She wondered if Cameron would be in the office later. With any luck he would be taking some time out. She needed space away from him while she got her head around her new status in life. Then she realised with a start what she really needed was to talk to James Judge. Jesus, he was her father! It was still too big to grasp. As Samantha drove through Rathnew Village and past the Manor where she was meant to have had her wedding party, she wondered if she was wise to go into work that day. Equally firmly, however, she convinced herself that she was. It was all Samantha knew. When things got tough, she worked. That was what she had always done and it was what she would do now.

She parked her BMW in its usual spot and took a deep breath as she crossed the courtyard of the distillery. There weren't many people in yet and so the carpark was quiet. The usual sign greeted her. It read *Welcome to Judges' Distillery, the home of Irish whiskey for over a hundred years.* This morning, quite suddenly, it irked her. There was no reference to Gracias anywhere on the building. OK, they were selling it into the market as a Latin American drink but it did deserve a mention. She would have it out with Cameron later. Then she caught herself. How could she have that discussion with him now? Everything had changed so utterly. He must hate her.

Jean the receptionist looked up when she heard the automatic doors glide open.

"Oh, Samantha, er, hi . . ." She couldn't hide her surprise.

Sam held her head high and marched across the large reception area over to Jean's highly polished oakwood desk. The Liscannor stone click-clacked under the high heels of her shoes. The strong aroma of malted barley from the distilleries assailed her senses. It felt familiar and reassuring. That made her feel good.

"Good morning, Jean. How are you today?" she asked as she always did.

"Fine. Thanks. Yeah, great. You're the first in as usual."

They were straight back into their familiar pitter-patter.

"Any post?"

The girl handed over a small bundle. "Nothing that looks too urgent. Er, Samantha, I'm sorry to hear about your weekend."

Sam looked at the receptionist. "Yes, quite a shock to say the least. Look, Jean, to be honest I just want to put it behind me and get back to work, so if you get any phone calls or bloody journalists in here today, can you get rid of them for me?"

"You got it. They won't get past me!" Jean puffed out her chest proudly.

"Good woman." Sam forced a smile and headed up the stairs to her office. "Work," she commanded herself in a quiet whisper, "work."

As the morning wore on various people from various departments stuck their heads around her office door. It was quite clear that the word was out. Samantha was back to work. To her enormous relief, Cameron never arrived into the office. It was lunch time before she got the nerve up to ask her own PA if there had been any word from him. When she heard that he had gone to Barbados, she felt like crying. Why didn't she bloody well go to the Caribbean and leave him back in Wicklow? Why was he the one who always had the good time while she worked like a demon? Why had her life turned out so shitty? She barely heard the knock on the door but she recognised the voice instantly.

"Samantha, may I come in?" James Judge stood at her office door.

"Oh God, James – yes, come in, sit down – I didn't know that you were in today," she babbled.

"Well, to be honest I came in to check that the company was

still ticking over and then I heard that you were at your desk. Hardly surprising, really, Samantha. You're such a workaholic."

"That's me!" She clapped her hands together and smiled like an imbecile. Cop on, she tried to command herself, but she suddenly realised how terrified of meeting James she actually was.

"Look, do you mind if I close the door, Samantha? I think we need to have a small talk."

To her utter horror and surprise, Samantha burst out crying. She had to bury her face in her hands. James quickly closed the door and pulled down the blind that furnished a window between her office and the inner corridor. They were totally private now. He rushed to her and put his arms around her. She gladly took his support.

"I am so, so sorry, Samantha. You have to believe me, I had no idea, ever. Your mother and I – well, that was a very, very long time ago. I had no notion that you were related to Katie Garcia."

"I just hope you realise you've ruined my life!"

James felt his own eyes water up too. "Believe me, if there was anything I could do to change the situation . . . Jesus, it's just too outlandish." He stroked her back. "You're such a beautiful, intelligent woman, I couldn't believe that Cameron had had the wisdom and talent to catch you."

She laughed through her tears. "We fell for each other."

"Perhaps, but Cameron was usually such a poor judge of character. I was delighted when you and he got together. Little did I know –" he didn't finish his sentence.

"Well, it appears that everybody knows now." She began to recompose herself slightly and so she pulled away from his arms. "Sit down, James. Would you like a coffee?"

"Hang that, I thought we might both need a whiskey – that is, if it's alright with you," he added tentatively.

She smiled. He was absolutely right, of course. They both needed a drink and it was the afternoon, just about.

"A drink sounds like a great idea," she said. "After all, it isn't every day that you sit down with a man you've just discovered is your father."

James winked at her and disappeared out the door for a moment, returning with two glasses and a bottle of Royal Judge twenty.

"Going for the good stuff, are we?" She raised an eyebrow.

"Nothing but the best for my new daughter."

"Eh, yeah. James, this is really going to take some getting used to, isn't it?"

"Take as long as you want to, Samantha."

"It's not you being my father that's the problem, James. It's the fact that you fathered both me and Cameron. Do you realise the implications of that?" She looked at him manically.

"Ah," he sighed. "Yes. That is a pretty horrendous coincidence and one best put behind you."

"I can't just ignore what I've been doing for the last two years, James!"

"Well, dwelling on it isn't too prudent either, is it, girl?" Then he forced a laugh. "Did you know that Byron, probably the greatest poet the world has ever seen, had a long standing relationship with his sis–"

"Yes, yes, I already heard," Samantha cut him off.

James continued. "Try to think of it this way: I was going to be your father-in-law and now I'm simply your father."

This quietened Sam for a moment. "But I feel very disloyal to Pablo, even though I haven't seen him for years."

He handed her a rudely full glass of amber whiskey, then poured himself an equally generous measure. "Do you think that perhaps he knows?"

Samantha looked horrified. "Christ, do you think that's why they broke up. Was it my fault?"

James reached across the table and took her hand. "No way, Samantha, darling. It was certainly not your fault. If that was the reason and I'm not saying it was, then surely the fault would lie firmly at your mother's and my door."

"Mom," Samantha said vacantly. "I don't even know where she is now."

"I expect she's gone home if I know your mother."

"You did know her pretty well," Sam said bitchily, unable to stop herself.

James sighed and accepted the remark. "Yes, I did. To be honest, Samantha, your mother was some stunner and she was what I would call a free spirit. I was utterly infatuated with the woman. Had been from the first moment I clapped eyes on her. A man would have to have been blind not to, and I must admit that when I got my chance I took it. I was quite hopeful of a long affair with her but then she suddenly disappeared with Pablo. Believe me, if I had known about you, things would have been different."

"How?"

"Well," he scratched his head, "I can't really say now. It was all so long ago but I do remember I was utterly infatuated with her and, don't forget, Rose and I had no children at that stage. Who knows what might have happened?"

"But I assume you were in love with your wife? How could you have been so disloyal so early in your marriage, James?"

James looked sheepishly at Samantha. "I'm genetically flawed, I'm afraid."

"What?"

"It's a famous or rather an infamous familial trait. The Judge Infidelity Gene." Then he sat up straight to reassure her. "Oh, I'm sure Cameron doesn't have it. He was always more Rose's son than mine."

"What a strange thing to say. What do you mean by that?"

"You'll know what I mean when you have your own children." James winced at the awkward turn the conversation had taken. Then he went back to talking about the Judge family. "Neither I nor my father, Edward — that's Victoria's late husband — nor his father James the First were capable of staying faithful. We called it The Judge Infidelity Gene. It's a family thing."

"It's a load of bullshit if you ask me!" Samantha spoke frankly as the whiskey soothed her rattled nerves. "It's just a cop-out."

He shrugged.

"Christ, James, you could only have been married a short while if you had no kids. Wasn't that a bit soon to be starting the affairs?"

"Well, to be honest, Rose had been a little bold herself."

"*What?*"

"Oh, no I don't mean playing around. No, that's not her style – at least not to the best of my knowledge. No, it's something else. I'm not sure if you've noticed yet but Rose can be just a little manipulative."

"A little?" Samantha laughed aloud.

"Well, OK, quite manipulative."

"What did she do to you, James?" To her surprise, Samantha realised that she was starting to enjoy their chat. He was a straight talker and an all-round nice man. She could do worse as fathers go.

"Rose told me she was pregnant before we married. In fact, that's rather *why* we did get married."

"I don't believe you!"

"You must never tell anyone, Samantha. Her own children don't even know that. That has to be our little secret."

"Mum's the word, James." She winked at him. "So the old wagon tricked you into marriage?"

"Well, in a nutshell, yes."

"Oh God, was that Cameron?"

"Eh, no. That particular baby never arrived. She told me that she miscarried on our honeymoon."

"Do you think there really was a baby, James?"

James looked at Samantha and raised a bushy eyebrow. "What do you think, girl? You know the woman as well as most by now."

Samantha decided not to say what she thought Rose was capable of. "That was a hell of a way to start a marriage."

"Yes, well, it was just off the back of that when I met your mother. Now I have to admit Pablo was a really decent skin. But your mother? She would knock the common sense out of any man."

"Have you talked to her since – since –"

"Yes, I went to her yesterday. I had to clear this up and that's actually one of my problems, Samantha."

She cocked her head as if she was trying to listen more carefully.

"Your mother insists that she told me about you thirty-five years ago, child, and I have to tell you she didn't. She told me that she wrote to me and that I wrote back – but that just didn't happen. I don't know if her mind is playing tricks on her or if she's just been through too much but I assure you there was no letter-writing. If she did, I would never have let her go or I certainly would have made some sort of effort at supporting her."

Samantha nodded.

"I just don't want her poisoning your head with stories about me. That's why I wanted to talk to you alone."

"Mum has always been a little confused. I never know what to believe or not believe from her, to be honest. Thanks for the frank talk, James."

"Samantha," he stared at her beautiful face for a long moment as if weighing up whether to say something or not, "I hope we have many talks together over the next thirty-odd years."

She smiled at him. "Thanks."

The mood was interrupted by his mobile phone. It was Rose. There was some problem with the fact that first-class, transatlantic seats were booked in Samantha's name and not hers. Could he fix it? He couldn't. This meant that Rose had to travel in economy while Cameron sat alone up in first-class. When he hung up both he and Samantha had a good laugh at her expense. Secretly, however, Sam was jealous that Rose had taken her place so quickly and selfishly.

They both took another whiskey.

"Now, girl, we have to talk about business."

She looked nervous. Was he going to fire her?

"I think, as one of my four children, that I should give you a larger shareholding in Judges' Distilleries."

She tried to stop him. "Oh, James, I don't think we should talk about such things now. This situation is so new. Let's let the dust settle first."

"No," he held his hands up to stop her talking. "I think there'll be holy war if I try to dilute the Judges' Whiskey shareholding. Get it, dilute – whiskey?" He laughed.

Samantha laughed, noticing that between them they had downed nearly three quarters of the bottle.

James continued. "No, seriously, I've been thinking about this. What I plan to do is to give you my 10% shareholding in Gracias. That way, if there's any trouble between you and, er, Cameron, you can work in separate areas and not have to be too close to each other." He stared at her. "What do you think?"

"I think it's too generous and not at all necessary, James."

"Well, the Judge family, not counting you, holds a 30% share in Gracias. I don't really think that's fair considering it's your creation. I just want to return my shareholding to its rightful owner, if you know what I mean. Rose, Cameron and the girls still hold a 20% stake so they can't complain."

"And don't forget the bloody VCs," she answered more miserably than she meant.

"Yes, well, we'll get the venture capitalists off your back with time. It's a wonderful product, Samantha. It's moving so fast. I tell you it's a regular goldmine you have there. Hang onto it."

She patted the long-neck bottle of Gracias that sat on her desk as a decoration. "I'm very proud of it," she agreed. "And I have huge plans for it. I was even thinking of rolling out a sister product and calling it Fiesta. What do you think?"

James clapped his hands in approval. "There you go. Of course, it all makes perfect sense now."

"What does?"

"Well, your role in the distillery, of course, Samantha. Perhaps even the fact you were drawn to apply for a job here in the first place! I had just thought you were a good businesswoman but, the truth is, it's in your blood."

"I'm not so sure."

"I'm talking about the genes, girl. No wonder you're so good in the booze business. You're a Judge!"

"It's funny," she laughed as the whiskey finally caught up with her. "This time last week I thought I would be a Judge by today. Not because I was born one but because I had married one."

"There you are now," James grinned inanely. "Different path but the same result," he added with great satisfaction.

Samantha looked at her ex-father-in-law-now-father and thought about the other Judge women. There was Rose the manipulator, Caroline the nutter, Stephanie the moaner. Was she now to be counted among them? It was very unsettling. To *marry* a Judge was one thing, but to *be* one? Now that was another matter altogether.

The storm that battered the east coast of Ireland all day had a detrimental effect on the fishing too. The going was rough and they had to turn for home early. Luke was in a dark and sombre mood by the time he got back to his house on Monday afternoon. He didn't have a mobile but he had given Gillian Matt's number to call. It was the first time in his life that he regretted not having a mobile phone. He had also given her the house number. When there was no word on his brother's phone all morning, he assumed that she had phoned the house instead but that was not the case. Luke had hoped that Gillian would phone early in the day because he was becoming desperate to see her again. He really wanted to meet her that evening. Surely she would be at the office all day and as such easily capable of phoning. What was wrong with her? Was she ill? The one thing that never even entered his mind was the possibility that she might not want to see him again. They had made love, damn it. They were serious about each other. If she didn't call that day, he would go to her.

CHAPTER 15

"Thank God for Barbados!" Cameron sighed as he watched yet another huge sailing yacht cruise by, out to sea. Even the boats had a look of serene indifference in this part of the world. Nobody hurried in Barbados – that was its magic. Well, that along with its incredible climate, outstanding beaches and particularly friendly residents. "I should move here," he mumbled as he applied some more oil to his already darkening torso. Having been on the island for almost twenty-four hours, he was relaxing considerably and beginning to forget about his problems back in Ireland. It was easily done when the biggest decision of the day involved deciding between a rum cocktail or a daiquiri.

The beach he relaxed on was called Sandy Beach. The hotel behind him, the world famous Sandy Lane. It was snugly situated at the centre of a small natural bay whose golden sand swept along the entire length of the beach. The strip of sand was quite narrow, only about forty feet, which meant that it was never much of a walk to get wet. To make things even better, the Caribbean Sea had negligible tides so there was never a time when one was forced to walk miles out to have a swim. Running along the back of the strand was a lush tropical woodland so the effect was turquoise water next to white sand next to deep green foliage – an artist's dream.

Cameron thought of his little sister. Caroline should spend more time here and less at Dunross he decided as he gazed out on the water. The sea was an intoxicating aquamarine blue. Behind him, the majestic hotel nestled in amongst its palm trees and exotic plants. It was situated a stone's throw from the strand and so he only had metres to walk from his luxurious suite to the sun lounger. What made the place even more appealing was the fact that the Sandy Lane staff kept it spotless. The sand was constantly raked over and smoothed. All beach towels and glasses were regularly freshened or replaced. The real genius, in Cameron's opinion, was that the drinks were not too strong. It meant that one could happily sip Barbados cocktails from dawn till dusk without feeling anything more than pleasantly sedated.

He caught Frank's eye. Frank was one of the Sandy Lane beach attendants. Cameron had met him the day before and tipped him heavily. He always tipped at the start of a holiday as well as at the end so he could enjoy good service during his stay. Frank was dressed in a startling white jacket and he wore black trousers. Despite the five-star tailoring and excellent beachside manner, Frank's Barbadian good humour shone through the formality.

He was by Cameron's side in an instant. He spoke slowly with that soft benign Caribbean laughter bubbling just under the surface. "How you doin', dis fine afternoon, Cameron?"

"I'm doing good, Frank, thanks. I wonder could you book me a table in The Cliff tonight?"

Frank raised his eyebrows playfully and displayed a set of teeth that made his jacket look dull. "You goin' in real style tonight, boss. I am tinkin' you gonna have kadooment!" Frank's eyes opened even wider as he stressed the 'oo'.

Cameron laughed. "I don't quite understand what kadooment is, Frank, but I have to tell you that I'm taking my mother so I don't think it's the kind of night you're implying."

"What? Why you takin' your Ma to De Cliff? You wanna be

takin' some fine woman der. You doin' Dixie in De Cliff, man!"
The soft lilting tones which always reminded Cameron of the
Cavan accent cheered him enormously. The Barbadians had a way
of laughing while they talked. It really cheered the soul and everything
rotated around either sex or drink. In fact, usually everything rotated
around sex *and* drink! Was it any wonder he loved this place?

"Do you know any fine women I could take to The Cliff,
Frank?"

"Look around you, man. Dey everywhere! Dis is Barbados –
island of beautiful women!" Frank beamed. His eyes were bright
and highly intelligent. If Cameron wanted a woman, he could get
one himself. That was the message but the way Frank presented it
was so friendly, Cameron just laughed again.

"To be honest, I'm here with my mother to get away from
women just for a while."

"No woman?" Frank gasped as his eyebrows arched. "What
good is life with no woman?" He didn't wait for a reply. "No good,
I tell you. A man needs a woman to be rumbustous!"

Cameron laughed again. "I'll take your word for it, Frank, but I
just want to have a little rest, away from them."

"Ah, I know your problem, man. You been doin' *too much* Dixie!
Dat mean you exhausted, boy," he nodded sagely. "Too many
women?" he asked conspiratorially.

"I think that's it, Frank. Now I just want to sleep and lie in the
sun."

"Well, you come to de right place so. I will book De Cliff for
you now and you be limein'."

This was one bit or Barbadian dialect that Cameron did recognise.
"Yes, I'll be limeing." He knew it meant he would be chilling out.

He flopped down into his deeply padded sun lounger. The towel
that covered his blue and white striped cushions had been replaced
since his morning visit and he noticed with satisfaction that his
small table had been cleaned. The sun umbrella had also been
moved marginally to keep his bed out of the direct sunlight. What
the hell, he thought, as he realised he was lying in the shade, I'll

sunbathe later. Cameron had slipped into the Barbados way of life. "No hurry," he whispered as he closed his eyes.

One evening meal alone with his mother had been enough to remind him how little he enjoyed her company when she was in bad form. The previous day she had complained bitterly in the limo from the airport all the way to the hotel and she continued to complain through their evening meal. It was hardly his fault that she couldn't use Samantha's first-class seat. Rose was obliged to buy a new one in economy as there was a queue for first-class. Cameron argued that there was really little point in his giving up his first-class ticket just to keep her company. And so he remained where he was alone but arrived in Barbados relaxed and refreshed while she was tired and aching with cramps from eight hours in the impossibly small seats.

"You should see the size of the chairs they use, down there," she grumbled. "And as for the service! Well, there actually is none. You have to get up and out of your chair just to get a glass of water. I mean, really, it is most disagreeable."

"Yes, Mother, but it's over now so why don't we just forget about it and try to get on with enjoying ourselves. Isn't it a nice change to be staying in a hotel as opposed to the villa?" Cameron tried to distract her out of her foul form. It worked to a certain extent. Nobody could ignore the splendour of Sandy Lane. There were two restaurants to choose from, one formal and one not so formal. In view of their exhaustion and general bad mood, they chose the less auspicious but found the food simply outstanding. Half of the tables were actually out on the sand of the beach but they were formally set with bright white linen tablecloths, and candelabra on each table to illuminate them. There was soft music emanating from the indoor part of the restaurant and a gentle yellow glow shone out from the lights within. The atmosphere was formal yet soothing and intimate.

On the beach where Cameron and Rose chose to sit, despite the music, the predominant sound was that of gentle waves lapping on the shore. The night sky was very dark and the sea was not actually visible except for the fact that the hotel had a single enormously strong blue light shining out along the water's surface. Occasionally in the distance a pleasure craft would sail silently by, noticeable only by its lights. There were also the tour boats which were a little more garish. The sound of loud music and party revellers sometimes carried to the strand if the waves were momentarily silent.

Rose cheered up as the meal went on and she approached something nearing charm by dessert.

"I must say, it is a real treat to be staying here," she finally agreed. "Thank you for bringing me with you, Cam."

"Mother, I can safely tell you that there is no other woman I would rather spend a holiday with at the moment." He refilled her wine glass.

"Cameron, you must use this time to try and recover from that ghastly day. Put it behind you. We'll both become stronger out here and we'll head home fit and in fighting form again. OK?"

"That sounds like a good plan, mother."

She reached out across the table and tapped his hand maternally. "I've booked myself into the spa tomorrow. I thought I could use one of their stress-buster massages and I need a pedicure before I grace any beach." Rose didn't mention that she was also booked in for a full body wax at the same time. That was more than her son needed to know.

"I'm just going to relax on the beach," he added.

"I was thinking that I might pop up to the villa too just to make sure that Patrick and Roisin are behaving themselves." Rose was referring to the two Barbadians who had managed their villa for the past thirty years. They lived in the small coach-house on the land of the villa. Like so many residents of Barbados, they had Irish names even though they quite obviously had no connection with Ireland other than their employers.

"It might be polite to phone first, Mother. That way they don't think you're trying to spy on them."

171

"But that's exactly what I am doing." she replied indignantly.

Cam pushed his mother out of his head and focused on the carnal pleasure of where he was at that precise moment. Barbados was a second home to him. James had bought the large villa just after Barbados gained its independence in the late sixties, as his wedding present to Rose. It was to be the family's bolthole. Cameron spent nearly all his Christmases as well as many long hot summers there. He knew Bridgetown, the capital of Barbados, like the back of his hand. The island had always been a safe place for adults and kids alike. When he was young, he and his sisters had had the run of the place. The beaches were safe and Cameron knew a lot of the locals around their villa which was a little further up the coast, just north of Hole Town. Island life was a wonderful life.

The Cliff was his favourite restaurant in the whole world and so he thought treating his mother to a meal there might lift her spirits after her appalling flight. He had dined in Sandy Lane a few times previously but he had never actually stayed there before and so he had thought it would be a nice place for his honeymoon. Little did he realise that he would be spending his honeymoon with his bloody mother. Sandy Lane had quickly and effortlessly changed the honeymoon suite to a large executive one with two separate bedrooms overlooking the Caribbean Sea.

Cameron sat up in his lounger now in an attempt to get Samantha out of his mind. The water was absolutely clear and he could see the occasional flying fish jump right out of the water further out to sea. Sandy Beach was on the westerly side of the island and as such, the waters were "ciam", as Frank would say. The easterly side of the island was the Atlantic side and the winds were considerably stronger, although still gloriously warm. It was mid-afternoon and the sun was just beginning to meander down towards the horizon. There were still a few hours of unbroken sunshine left in the day, however. Watching the sun go down over the Caribbean Sea was a national pastime, Cameron remembered with relish as he considered which cocktail he would have as his sundowner.

Involuntarily, his mind went back to the other conversation he had had with his mother the previous evening.

Rose's voice was soft. "Cameron, have you given any thought to Samantha?"

"Well, actually I'm doing my best to avoid all thoughts that involve her."

"Son, she was your fiancée up until two days ago. I assume you still have feelings for her."

"Mother, I would rather not have this conversation, if you don't mind," he mumbled as he looked around to see if they could be overheard. The large candlelit, open-air restaurant was peaceful, however. The tables were well spaced out and the huge, black night sky absorbed private conversations effortlessly, he noticed with relief. The only real noise was the subtle but incessant sea.

Rose persisted. "Well, you were going to marry Samantha two days ago. I assume that means you loved her."

"Of course I loved her," he snapped.

"Well, why should that change, just because you've heard some appalling lies?"

"Mother," he stopped himself. How could he tell her that they weren't lies? She would go crazy if she knew about James's affair.

"What's the matter, son?"

"Oh, it's nothing. How's your food?"

"My food is divine, darling. This restaurant is wonderful. But I am not worried about such things. What I am concerned about is your future." She smiled maternally at him, again reaching for his hand.

"Look, Mum, after all that's happened, I'm not sure that I care for Samantha any more."

"Well, that's ridiculous."

"No, it's not. I'm being serious." He studied his seared dolphin.

"Cameron, you can't just stop loving somebody you were planning to spend the rest of your life with – just like that."

"Yes, I can and I think I have."

Rose, who ate very little at the best of times, put her knife and fork together in indignation. She had barely touched her food.

"How was the blue marlin? It looked terrific," he asked.

"Fine. I've just lost my appetite."

"Oh, Mother. Please don't keep this up for the entire holiday. I'm a big boy now, you know. I'll sort out my own love life, thank you very much."

Rose went for the jugular. "But what about all our conversations? Cameron, she was a perfect match for you for more reasons than one."

"Please, I don't want to discuss this now – or ever to be honest." He also gave up on his food at this point. As soon as he put his knife and fork together, the silver-spoon staff descended upon the table like a school of sharks and cleared everything away with a smile. For such a relaxed and happy people, the English influence was still heavy upon Barbados culture. The meals were formal and the dress code particularly smart.

"Would you like to see the dessert menu?" Their waitress smiled at them.

"No, thank you. I'm no longer hungry," Rose sniffed.

Cameron looked apologetically at the young girl who was serving them. "I'll have an Irish coffee, please. Mother?"

"Well, that might be a good idea. I'll have an Irish coffee too, but make sure they make it with Judges' Whiskey – I don't want any inferior whiskeys, thank you very much."

As the waitress departed, guaranteeing Judges' whiskey, Cameron tried to change the subject.

"Would you like to go to Oistins on Friday night? When was the last time you were at the fish fry?" He referred to the biggest party in Barbados. Every Friday night most people of all ages descended upon the fishing village of Oistins, just next to Bridgetown, the capital, to enjoy music, loads of freshly fried fish and of course a little Barbados rum or beer.

"That might be a good idea." Rose made an effort to be nice.

"How about this? If you let this whole Samantha thing drop, I'll take you to The Cliff tomorrow night?"

Rose positively glowed. "Not another word," she smiled coquettishly. "Not another word."

Lying on the beach now, Cameron wondered if she would keep her promise.

The sun was beginning to hang heavily in the sky as he ordered his first cocktail of the evening. He had another hour of relaxing and enjoying the sunset before he went and got changed for his promised night out with his mother. He knew just how strict the dress code was in the evenings, even by the water. Swimming trunks and bikinis were welcome during the day but once the sun set, smart dress was essential to even get served. He smiled to himself. It would never work in the west of Ireland.

"*Cameron, yoo-hoo!*" His mother appeared at the beach gate. Her rather gauche call to him was to attract the attention of the other bathers and not just Cameron. He knew her games. She had been with the beautician for the best part of the day and now she was ready to hit the beach. Cameron watched his mother teeter over to where he lay and in fairness, she did look good for a woman of her age. She certainly knew how to dress for the beach. Rose wore a dark one-piece with a matching sarong that stopped just below her knees. Her calves were good so she showed them off. She wore little beach sandals but, even on the strand, she wore a slight heel. Cameron often heard her tell his sisters that every inch up took four pounds off the hips. It wasn't as if she needed to look any skinnier than she actually was. Rose was a thin woman so she had always been very comfortable in beach wear. As usual, she wore a ridiculously wide-brimmed hat and her obligatory Jackie Onassis sunglasses which ironically were making a comeback in fashion. Rose had maintained the same image for the last forty years and it had always worked for her, but as luck would have it this year she looked particularly trendy, he realised with mild amusement. Her large beach bag matched her Chanel swimsuit. Cameron liked women's fashion. He particularly liked the woman in his life to be well dressed and his mother had never let him down. He knew she was wearing about five thousand euros worth of beach wear and he reckoned it was money well spent as he saw the looks of admiration she was getting from the other men on the beach, some as young as himself.

"Mother," he beamed as she reached his sun lounger, making sure he said it loud enough for the ooglers to know that he wasn't dating a woman old enough to be his mother.

"Have you been here all day?" she asked.

"I have and it's been most enjoyable. How was your day in the spa? You look wonderful."

"Simply divine. I'm totally relaxed at this stage and looking forward to our evening together."

Frank began to hover, to see if there was a possible drink order with Rose's arrival.

"Great," Cameron gestured to the sun lounger next to his. "Will you have a drink and watch the sun go down with me?"

"That would be exquisite." She smiled at the waiter. "I'll have a strawberry daiquiri, please."

"Sure. What about the big man?" He looked at Cameron.

"I'll have another rum cocktail, please, Frank."

After he was out of earshot, Rose teased her son. "You know the staff by name already? That's my boy."

Cameron lay back on his bed and closed his eyes against the soft late-afternoon sun. It was now low enough to shine on him under his sun umbrella. "He's my minder for this week, Mother. His name is Frank and he has booked The Cliff for us for nine. OK?"

"Simply splendid, Cam." Rose looked at her magnificent boy as the sun caressed his perfectly toned body.

He was a fine specimen of a man. She knew he could have any woman he wanted. Cameron had it all: the body, the looks, the intelligence and of course, the Judge fortune. That was the problem, really. He didn't realise how much he had to offer and as such he didn't know how many women would be after him for all the wrong reasons. Rose knew, however. Damn it, the truth be told, she was one of those women a generation ago. Competition had been stiff for James Judge but she saw the others off and James was none the wiser. She would not let Cameron fall victim to the same fate.

Rose could see her son's golden chest rise and fall with each relaxed breath. It was only a moment ago he was a tiny baby in her arms – well, in his nanny's arms – but it did really feel like a brief moment in time.

"I phoned home a few hours ago," Rose said.

"How is everything?" Cameron asked without showing too much genuine interest.

"Fine, no news. It's raining of course."

"Ha!" Cameron laughed and opened his eyes. "That's always good to hear."

Frank returned with their cocktails as the sun perched itself on the horizon. A large pleasure boat sailed by at just the right moment to use the huge round ball of light as a perfect backdrop.

Cameron sat up and raised his drink to clink with his mother's.

"To your good health, Mother, and to a restful holiday!"

"To your good health, Cameron, and to your happiness!"

He thought about it for a moment as the sun slipped down below the horizon and the boat sailed on. Then he nodded happily. "I'll drink to that, certainly."

CHAPTER 16

It had been teatime at Dunross when a jubilant Rose Judge phoned from the Caribbean. She had just had her late breakfast on her private patio and she was heading off for a day with the resident beautician.

Stephanie had answered the phone.

"What time is it with you, anyway?" she asked jealously.

"Oh, I think it's just after midday," Rose had replied. "How are things there? Is Daddy OK? He's not missing us too terribly, is he?"

"Not in the slightest. He got pissed yesterday afternoon with Samantha White and he had to go to bed at teatime. He didn't even go in to the distillery today." Stephanie was deliberately trying to goad her mother. Why should she have all the bloody fun while, she, Steph was stuck back in bloody Wicklow with two screaming brats?

"Oh, I'm so pleased," Rose tittered. "It's important that they stay together – business-wise, I mean."

That was not the reaction Stephanie had been expecting. She changed tack. "I'm missing you, Mummy," she whined. She did not sound like her thirty years.

"I'm sorry, darling. How are you? Any word from David?"

"He's coming over at the weekend to take the girls for the night but the children are being dreadfully behaved as usual. Cathy has no control over them. I really don't know how she got her nanny exams."

"There, there, darling. Why don't you phone David? Perhaps he could cheer you up."

"Not bloody likely."

"Well, somebody has to make the first move." The tone had become cooler across the Atlantic.

"I don't see why. We've separated, mother. If I never speak to him again it will be too soon."

"But think of the children, Stephanie."

"I am thinking of the children," Steph lied.

"Well, don't get too upset, I'll be home soon."

"When are you coming home, actually, Mummy?"

"I don't quite know. I have to talk to the tour operator. There was a most appalling situation coming over and I had to travel in lower class."

Stephanie laughed. "That was a first. How did you survive?"

"I don't know but I promise I will never ever do it again. It was quite beastly. Look, darling, I must dash. Pedicure appointment in five minutes. Love to everybody, OK? Bye."

Stephanie hung up feeling even worse, if that was possible. Two miserable days into her single life and things were utterly wretched. She, the nanny and the girls had moved into one of the old farm workers' houses down by the stables the previous day. Next to the farm were a small clutch of houses that had once been occupied by farm hands. Now the land was harvested by large machinery and Sean the farmer did most of it himself, hiring casual labour when he needed it. The result was that the cute little two-story stone-cut dwellings were, for the most part uninhabited. Sean lived in one. Caroline and Marcus lived in another. Naturally, Caroline had gutted hers and made the entire top floor into an art studio. Downstairs she had a small bedroom and a large living and dining area.

Stephanie chose to move into the largest of the remaining houses, claiming that each of her two daughters needed her own room because of the great age difference. It was a four-bedroom house with a large living-room and kitchen. There was also a small study and utility room. The farmhouse had a delightful Aga. It was very comforting to Steph to rest against it but she didn't use it for cooking. Theirs was a microwave family and, anyway, now that she was home, she and the children came up to Dunross to eat. Mrs Bumble did not comment on the development – she just increased her larder contents to hold such goodies as petit filous and Frosties. Stephanie gave her a full list of requirements and Mrs Bumble duly went out and purchased them. It was as much for the social engagement as anything else that Stephanie went up to the house but the truth was there wasn't anyone there. Mrs B, she noticed, made herself scarce as soon as they descended upon the kitchen and her father was usually reading in the library. Caroline kept the most ridiculous hours, explaining that as an artist she had to work when the mood hit her. James had explained that she often went for days without making an appearance. Marcus was the same. He worked in Dublin and commuted so he could be with Caroline. He usually got home late at night and left early in the morning. Stephanie had tried to suggest that he could take Zoë to school in the mornings but he had been quick to argue that he left too early.

Steph turned her attention to her nanny. "Cathy, I have to talk to Daddy with regard to some business Mummy phoned about. Feed the girls, would you?"

The nanny simply nodded. This job was nose-diving quickly. It was bad enough when she lived in Dublin but this Wicklow thing was not her cup of tea at all, she fumed silently.

Stephanie walked out without waiting for a response and, seeing her go, Zoë pinched Amy. Anarchy broke out as the baby screamed and Cathy yelled at Zoë who pleaded innocence and promptly burst out crying. Stephanie ignored the pandemonium behind her and headed to the library. She had had enough of mothering. She went to the drinks cabinet and poured herself a double gin and tonic.

"Do you want anything, Dad?" she asked.

"No, thank you, Stephanie. I think I'll have a dry day."

"How's the head?"

"It's been better but I think I've slept most of it off," he muttered with embarrassment.

Stephanie came over to the deep armchair next to his. The fire was warm and welcoming. The library was not a room that had interested Stephanie much when she was growing up at Dunross but now she saw its appeal. She surveyed the laden shelves. Some of the books were very old and some were practically new. There was everything from the complete works of Shakespeare to anything Robert Ludlum had written. James was an absolute bookworm and, now in retirement, he spent most of his days here. Rose had her shelves too. She favoured autobiographies but she had also gathered the complete works of Cathy Kelly and Jilly Cooper.

This evening it was James's sanctuary. As October had rolled in, the temperature had plummeted. The trees seemed to have lost their leaves in one day and suddenly winter was upon them. The glow of the fire and the deep red colour of the walls, what little you could see above the bookshelves, all served to welcome and warm the reader. This evening, James was reading the new Tom Clancy, Stephanie noticed.

"Mummy just phoned."

"Oh, I should have spoken to her." He looked up.

"No, she seemed quite happy to speak to me, Daddy," Stephanie shot back. "Having a ball by all accounts."

"Well, that's good." James nodded inanely.

"Aren't you in the least bit jealous, Daddy? Why didn't you go too?"

"I think she wanted to be alone with Cameron. That doesn't really bother me. They've had a hellish few days."

"So have you."

"Yes, well. I don't mind." James tried to get back to his book but Stephanie had other plans.

"You were as much maligned if not more so than Mother,

Daddy. You seem to be taking all of this very much in your stride."
He looked at her and tried to decide what to say. It was quite clear
that she had chosen not to believe any of Katie Garcia's claims.
James wondered if he should tell her the truth, that Samantha was
in fact her half-sister. Or would that upset her too much? Stephanie
was the most easily upset of the Judge children, he reasoned. She
had enough on her plate for the time being.

"How is the farm house? Warm enough, I hope?" he asked.

"Oh, yes it's fine. A little cramped but beggars can't be choosers."

"No, I suppose not. Look, Stephanie, I am most dreadfully sorry
about you and David. Is there any hope of reconciliation?"

She took a large gulp of gin. "I don't think so, Daddy. We're
finished."

"It is a dreadful business when marriages break up. What are you
going to do?"

"What about?"

"Have you considered your future and that of the girls?"

Stephanie looked surprised. "What do you mean? What is there
to consider? Life will just go on, only without David."

"Well, Stephanie, you are of course welcome to stay here
indefinitely. It is, after all, your home but you're a beautiful young
woman. Your life isn't over yet. Surely you'll want to return to
some sort of social life at some point, perhaps even a job?" he
suggested gently. James was far too gallant to mention the increased
food and electric bill he was incurring thanks to the return of his
two fully-grown daughters and now there were grand-daughters
too. But he did think that a job might at least pay for some of her
clothing bills. "Will David continue to support you?" he risked.

"He bloody well better," Stephanie snarled. "There's no way I'm
using my trust fund to dress his brats."

The door bell rang at Dunross. Oblivious to James's horror at her
comment, Stephanie rose to answer it. Some tiny flicker of hope
licked around her heart that it might be David.

Luke Delaney stood at the door, looking dark and menacing.

"God, Luke, long time no see," Stephanie drawled. She knew

the Delaney boys from her youth. They had spent a lot of time at Dunross playing with Cameron when they were young. "Hey, are you OK?" she asked as she noticed his sombre face.

"I need to speak to Cameron," he explained, his usual succinct self.

"Well, I'm afraid he's in Barbados so that might be a little difficult. What's wrong? Got to say, Luke, you don't look the best." She clinked the ice in her gin and tonic. "Can I offer you a drink?"

He barely nodded but he followed her back into the library.

"Dad, you remember Luke Delaney, don't you?"

"Hello, sir. Please don't get up. I didn't mean to intrude."

James was on his feet. "You? Intrude? What gave you that idea, lad? Good to see you, Luke. How have you been keeping? How's the family?" As they shook hands, James could smell the alcohol emanating from his guest. He noticed the creased jeans and the unshaved face. Luke Delaney was definitely a little the worse for wear.

"Whiskey?" Stephanie offered from the drinks cabinet. He looked at her. "I just wanted to speak to Cameron."

"It sounds very intriguing," she teased. "Can we help, in any way?"

He hovered as if weighing up the situation.

"Well, you might. I'm looking for Gillian Johnston's phone number."

Stephanie gasped ostentatiously. "Luke Delaney, has somebody got to you at last?" she taunted.

His eyes were cold as he looked at her. He obviously didn't appreciate her humour. "I just want to speak to her."

Stephanie handed him the whiskey he hadn't said he wanted. She didn't offer him water as it was considered sacrilege to add water to Judges' Whiskey at Dunross.

James could see that he was in a bad way. "Look here, she's one of Sam's friends, isn't she?"

Luke nodded at him. "A bridesmaid."

"Ha, I have the number you need," James smiled, delighted to be able to help. "I'll have it in my phone book in the study," he explained as he headed towards the door.

"Daddy, what are you doing with that pretty young thing's number?"

"No, it's not as bad as it sounds. She lives with Sam whose number I do have. That should get her." He was happy to see Luke's face light up with gratitude.

"What are you doing with Samantha White's home phone number, Daddy?" Stephanie continued to tease but this time there was a slight edge to her voice. She was still furious with her would-be sister-in-law for embarrassing the family so badly.

"We work together, remember?" he said as he left the room.

"You're meant to be retired," she grumbled into her glass. Then she turned her attention to the guest.

"So, do you have the hots for Gillian Johnston, Luke? She looked like a foxy one to me."

He didn't answer. He just gave her a long cool stare as he took a large gulp of whiskey.

"What's the matter? Have you gone all shy on me now? Don't worry, I won't tell a soul. Good luck to you."

Still he said nothing so Stephanie fixed herself another drink. It was making her feel a little better. "You know David and I have separated?"

"I'm sorry. I didn't hear that."

"Yeah, well. Shit happens." She shrugged but then she looked at Luke again as if having a new idea. "That said," she crossed over to where he was, "I am single again." She smirked as she stood directly in front of him. He didn't move a muscle. Stephanie stroked his cheek with the palm of her hand and his stubble bristled against her skin. "You really are a fine-looking man in a rugged sort of way, Luke." She kept her hand on his cheek. "If you and Gillian don't get it together, you could perhaps take me out for a drink and cheer me up a little?"

He didn't find her at all attractive but she was good at flirting. "Gillian and I are already together," he explained as he gently removed her hand from his face.

Stephanie took the rebuke badly. She walked away and sat down in one of the deep armchairs next to the fire. "Doesn't sound like it if you don't have her bloody phone number."

James walked back into the library. "Here we are, son. As I say, this is Samantha's home phone number but I know she shares a flat with those two bridesmaids. You should be able to get her there."

Luke downed the last of his whiskey and then the two men walked out to the front door together. James was a tall man and matched Luke's height. He put his arm around the boy's shoulders and glanced behind to ensure that Stephanie was out of earshot. Then he whispered, "I also took the liberty of writing down the address, in case you wanted to pay her a little visit at some point."

For the first time in his life James Judge saw Luke Delaney smile, a big broad open smile. He obviously had it bad.

Granny Victoria shuffled into the library, where Steph was sitting alone. The second walking stick she had recently started to use made her look a great deal older quite suddenly, thought Steph. Then again, she was almost ninety-five.

"Are you all right there, Gran?" Stephanie asked.

"Would you get me a sherry, child?"

Steph did as requested.

Then, with considerable effort, Victoria settled herself down into her seat. She placed a blanket over her legs and she looked at Steph. "Now," she said, "tell me what's bothering you? Why have you and David split up?"

"Oh Gran, I don't know. We've just fallen out of love."

"What nonsense! People don't just fall out of love. Was he having an affair, child?"

Stephanie was shocked at her grandmother's bluntness. She shouldn't have been because Granny Vic was always blunt.

"God, no. I don't think he's having an affair. There's no way I would stay with him if he was having an affair.

Victoria laughed. "You're still so naïve, child. Do you think there's a rich man in Ireland who stays faithful?" She looked at Steph incredulously as she took a medicinal sip of sherry. "It's the law of the jungle, child. The richer they are, the more unfaithful they are – it's just like the lions in Burma really," she explained lightly. "The strongest beast gets the biggest pride of lionesses. You should be happy. You're the Queen Bee. Isn't that enough for you?"

"He's not having an affair, Gran."

"Ah – denial. That can be a problem."

"I'm not in denial and, anyway, I should be able to give David everything he wants."

Victoria's tone changed to that of a patient schoolteacher. "No woman can give a man everything he wants, because what a man wants is variety. Believe me, I know. Edward was out of Dunross every second night."

"Granny Vic!" Stephanie was aghast. She had never heard that before.

"Oh, yes," Victoria went on. "I'm not sure if half of Fiddler's Point aren't Judges. He was a right bounder, your grandfather." Then the old woman laughed as if she were quite proud of the fact.

"I had no idea," was all Stephanie could manage.

"How would you? It was long before your time." Victoria smiled with resignation. "Well, is it the sex then, child?"

"Sorry?"

"Don't say 'sorry', say 'pardon'. I asked, are you and your husband having enough sex?"

"Grandma, I'm not sure that this is really a conversation I should be having with you."

"Well, I can't very well see you having it with your mother," said Victoria with a chuckle. "The only reason a man doesn't want to have sex is if he's just had it! Is he still looking for sex? That's the only sure way to know if he's having an affair or not."

Much to Stephanie's relief, James walked back into the room so Victoria dropped the subject.

"Now," she addressed her grand-daughter again as she held up her drained glass, "I think I'm ready for the other half of that sherry, child."

CHAPTER 17

"You know, you really need to cut down on that stuff," Marcus remarked when he heard Caroline take another long deep snort of the feather-light powder. He had been reading *The Irish Times* as he unwound from another tough day at the office. Business was not going well for him. He stopped to look at her from over the corner of his newspaper. Marcus had kicked off his shoes and had his feet up on the same table Caroline was snorting her cocaine from.

"I can handle it." Her reply was the same as it always was. She threw her head back and her magnificent long dark curly mane shimmered as it settled back into place. "And anyway, it helps me with my work."

"What are you working on now?" he asked, trying to sound interested. Marcus was not a great appreciator of art, especially Caroline's kind. While not totally abstract, there was a lot of swirling colours involved. It was possible to make out faces and objects but they usually had disfigured bodies almost as if they were ghosts. He had tried to tease her about it once. "Is that how you see people?" he had asked and to his surprise she had nodded, "Yes, it's exactly how I see them." That was the first time he had successfully seduced her. Poor Caroline genuinely believed that he understood her and even more incredibly, her art. All Marcus really understood was her bank balance. Caro, precious little Caroline, was a Judge. His life was going to be charmed. Marcus saw a life of whiskey, free living and most importantly, money ahead of him. She had fallen for him and now all he had to do was to hang in with her for a few months and then propose. To do it too soon might risk unsettling the family. They would become suspicious. Marcus was moving as fast as he dared and it was all working out perfectly, he thought smugly as he watched her now.

"You know," he said, "you really are very sexy when you throw your head back like that."

"Am I?" Her big brown eyes opened even wider. "Should I do it again?" She bit her lip coquettishly.

"No, not if it means more shit up your nose. Caroline, I'm serious about you cutting back."

"What you gonna do about it?" She tilted her head as she threw him the challenge. "What will you do if I'm bold? Will you spank me?" She turned her back to him and pushed her bum out.

"Jesus, Caroline, where do you get your energy?" he laughed realising where this was going.

"Is it me or is it hot in here?" she asked as she pulled her shocking-pink, long-sleeved, cotton T-shirt up and over her head. Naturally, she wasn't wearing a bra. She didn't need to. Caroline's breasts were particularly small and didn't need support. She herself was quite small and impossibly thin, probably because she did too many drugs and not much food. She also seemed to use up a great deal of energy painting and, of course, shagging for which she had a voracious appetite. Even standing in the middle of their little living-room topless wasn't getting his attention so she took off the rest of her clothes. "Yep, it's just too hot." She turned and smiled at him. "What about you? Aren't you even a little warm?"

"Well, I must admit, I'm beginning to feel the heat," he smirked as he stood up and took her into his arms. He began to kiss her, softly at first. "You know you really are a very demanding little brat," he said through kisses.

"Yes, I am and I command you to make love to me now!" She was pulling at his clothes. His shirt slipped out of his navy trousers easily. Marcus was slim and in pretty good shape. He didn't work out but he watched what he ate and the cigarettes helped. Caroline began to fumble with his zipper.

"What am I? Your bloody sex slave?" he laughed as he started to help her.

"That's exactly what you are," she agreed as she crouched down to pull his trousers off. "Hello, tiger," she kissed him.

"Well," he pulled her up so he could kiss her on the mouth, "the slaves are breaking free and we're exacting revenge!"

"You don't scare me," she snarled playfully as she kissed him back hungrily and grabbed him in her hand.

"No?"

"No."

"We'll see about that!" He flipped her over and took her from behind.

"You're not hurting me," she taunted him.

"No?" He held her pelvic bones as he thrust into her but as his hand slipped he accidentally broke their union and Caroline skipped away.

"Hey, where are you going? I wasn't finished with you." He ran after her.

Caroline skipped into the kitchen giggling but there was nowhere to run. The room was small and made even smaller by the kitchen table in the centre. She turned and squealed, half in fear, half in delight as she saw him standing in the doorframe.

"Come here, my love!" He put his hand out lovingly and tenderly.

Had the rules of the game changed, she wondered, or was this a trick? She didn't know. Tentatively she stretched her hand out and into his.

Then he grabbed it savagely. Caroline screamed in rapturous terror as he pushed her down on the kitchen floor. It was cold and hard under her body. The living-room floor was wood but the kitchen had rough quarry tiles. The surface was abrasive on her skin. He plunged into her again.

"Don't," *plunge,* "you," *plunge* "ever," *plunge,* "run," *plunge,* "away again," *plunge, plunge, plunge!*

She screamed as she came in a sky-high wave of colours and aggression. When she was sated, Marcus came. He was sweating and exhausted as he pulled himself away and sat up.

"You are a wonderful sex slave, Marcus."

"Thanks."

"Let's do it again."

"Jesus, Caro. I'm wrecked." He got up and went back into the living-room to get his trousers. As soon as he was dressed he flopped down and returned to his paper. Caroline, on the other hand, was quite happy to wander around the room naked.

When there was a knock on the door they both looked at each other in mild surprise. The house was small and didn't have a doorbell.

"I'd better get it," Marcus sighed as he put his paper down. He was never going to get it read, he thought, mildly irritated.

Stephanie was at the door.

"The next time you two feel like fucking when there are children still up can you do me the great favour of drawing the curtains?" she barked.

"Jeez," Marcus slapped his forehead as he realised what she was saying. Caroline came to the door when she heard her sister's complaints.

"We were only doing what comes naturally," Caroline snapped at her sister.

"What? Getting it up the rear from your boyfriend? That hardly constitutes a normal teatime exercise!" Stephanie was outraged.

"It does in this house!" Caroline refused to be reprimanded.

"Try explaining that to my seven-year-old."

"Oh, shit, sorry," Marcus was mortified.

"Well, I'm not. Sex is a perfectly natural, happy part of life and if Zoë saw us, it may help her to understand what goes on in *healthy* relationships."

The remark hurt Stephanie. The implication was obvious. Hers and David's had not been a 'healthy relationship'.

"Bitch!" was all she managed as she ran back to her own house in tears.

"That was a really shitty thing to say, Caro." Marcus came in and picked up his paper again.

"Well, she is a prude and she's breeding real little bitches over there. They need to learn to be free and to love life."

"All in good time," Marcus suggested, realising that there was no point in talking to her when she was high.

"I'm going to paint," she said after a little more naked dancing around the room. "Unless, that is, you want to play again."

"Paint," he growled from behind the paper. As she pranced up the stairs to her studio on the balls of her feet, singing lightly to herself, Marcus breathed a sigh of relief. She really was a handful but she was a very very rich handful.

By Thursday, Luke thought he was going mad. For the first time in his life he told his father that he was sick and couldn't go out to fish that day. Frank Delaney had tried talking to his son. Mathew and Mark had given it a go too but to no avail. Tess was the only person he would talk to and even then he kept her at a distance. The euphoria quickly turned to misery as it slowly dawned on Luke that Gillian was not going to return his calls. He had phoned more times than he knew. He had spoken to Wendy and Samantha many times and both had promised to pass on his messages. In subsequent phone calls, both girls had claimed that they had spoken to Gillian and told her about his calls and no, they didn't know where she was or when she would be back. He knew that they were covering for her. She was probably there in the apartment and laughing at him. Why would she do that? How could she have done such a U-turn so fast? What had changed? It just didn't make sense. Luke hadn't eaten for days but he wasn't in the least bit hungry. He couldn't think of anything but Gillian. She haunted his mind by day and tortured his dreams by night. Her face kept sailing into his thoughts, only now it had a mocking, leering expression. Why had she been so cruel to him? She had actively sought him out that night. They had been so good together. It was so real and so special. How could she just throw it away? He couldn't get her out of his head. Now it had got so bad he couldn't even work. Fishing was his life; for him not to be able to fish was like not being able to breathe. He knew that he was going crazy. His only option was to go to her apartment and simply wait for her to return. He had to have it out with her. He didn't really care about her motives any more and he certainly didn't mind looking like an idiot. He just had to understand what had happened? How could she have changed so fast?

Getting into the complex where she lived wasn't so difficult even with its enormous security gates. There were cars coming and going regularly so he simply waited until one unassuming driver blipped them open and he strolled up to her block. With James Judge's help, he had the full address. The apartment was on Eglington Road in Donnybrook, not particularly difficult to find. The complex was clearly marked. She was Apartment 16, Block C. The development was very nice, Luke noticed, with excellently manicured lawns and shrubs.

He didn't expect any of the girls to be home because it was early afternoon when he got there. A friendly neighbour let him into the building, however, so after he had checked that there was no-one in the apartment, he was able to wait in the warmth and comfort of block C. There were two chairs decoratively placed beside the large window at one end of the corridor. The girls' apartment was at the other end. Luke sat down to wait. The carpets that ran through the halls were a pale brown. Tall plants stood in chrome buckets every ten feet or so, to soften the lines of the long corridors. There were four apartments to each floor. Gillian's was on the fourth floor. He imagined that her views of the gardens would be quite pleasant.

Luke wasn't nervous or anxious waiting for her return. He was calm and composed – dangerously so.

When the lift bell chimed to indicate that it was stopping on his floor, he didn't jump to his feet. He just sat and waited some more. Gillian walked out of the lift. His heart did a flip. She turned right as she got out of the lift and headed straight for her front door. She hadn't even seen him so he rose and walked after her.

"Hello, Gillian."

She jumped and swung around, obviously very startled. "Jesus Christ, you scared me half to death. Luke, hi. Eh, how did you get in?"

"A neighbour let me in."

"Oh, great. Look, sorry about not getting back to you. Things have been a little hectic in the office." She fumbled with her keys and eventually opened the door.

He didn't speak, he just stared into her eyes. When she met his stare, it unnerved her.

"Why don't you come in and I can fix us a drink. I could use it after the day I've had."

Still he didn't speak. He just followed her into the apartment. Walking in the front door, Luke found himself in a very large living area. One entire wall was made of glass and there was a balcony outside. He saw an open door to the kitchen on his right.

"Have a seat," she called over her shoulder as she walked away from him. "I just need to drop my stuff in my room." She walked out another door on the left which obviously led to the bedrooms. When she returned she found him gazing out of the window.

"Nice view, isn't it?"

"You can't see the sea."

"What? Oh, no. God, I never thought of that."

"I couldn't live any place where I couldn't see the sea."

His voice was low and slightly creepy and Gillian was not in the least bit happy to see him. "Look, Luke, I really am sorry about not getting back to you, but as I said life has been crazy and –"

"*Life?*" He swung around quite suddenly and she could see

193

he was furious. "Your *life* has been crazy. I've been in *hell*, Gillian!"

"What?"

"*Hell!* That's where I've been. At first I thought you might have lost my number, and then I thought you might have been killed in an accident, then I didn't know what in the world was wrong with you." His fists were clenched and his eyes were wide with anger. "At last, the penny dropped, Gillian. I was the one who was ill, not you. I was the gobshite who thought we had something really real and special. Something worth hanging onto for dear life." He didn't realise that as he said this, he had grabbed her by the arms.

"Ow, you're hurting me, Luke! Please let go!"

Luke suddenly saw his own two hands clutching her arms and released her instantly.

"Why did you do it, Gillian? Why did you come near me? Help me here. I'm out of my mind."

"Luke. I really am sorry."

"Did you not feel what I felt?"

"I did, well, I do, I mean – Luke, you're a very nice guy and all but I'm not really ready to get serious yet."

He laughed at this but it was a manic sort of laugh. "And did you think I was? Jesus, Gillian, I wasn't looking for bloody love or pain for that matter the day I met you. It just happened. It hit me like a deep-sea trawler. Dear sweet Jesus!" He began to sob.

Oh, hell, Gillian thought to herself. This guy's a nutter.

"I'm getting us a drink," she said succinctly and walked into the kitchen. She buried her head in the fridge, praying that they had tonic water – she didn't even care if it wasn't slimline this was such an emergency. As she closed the fridge door, she stood up and turned around and he was standing there looking at her. "Shit, can you stop doing that? You scared me half to death – again."

For the second time, he grabbed her. This time by the biceps. "Gillian, maybe you can feel what I feel. You just need to listen to your heart. Believe me, it's so strong it can't just be me. If we just give it a go! Come back to Fiddler's Point with me now. You said yourself that work was hell. Come home, and live a different life.

We'll be happy." Gillian was listening to him so he continued. "When we were together on the beach, it was the most wonderful beautiful experience of my life. I want to do it again. I want to be with you for ever, Gillian. You and me, what do you say? Will you marry me? Say yes." His eyes were desperate as he searched her face for a flicker of acceptance but her expression was unreadable.

Then slowly she smiled. It started as a small grin. Next it broadened out and then she began to laugh.

He laughed too. "Will you come with me, Gillian?"

"Luke, that's the sweetest thing anyone has ever said to me, really it is." She tried to stop herself from more laughter. "You really are such a romantic, at heart. But you've got the wrong girl. I am not your life partner, really."

It was then that Luke realised that she was laughing at him and not with him. He tried to kiss her but she pulled away. He tried harder.

"Stop, Luke, I don't want this."

"You do." He pinned her against the fridge as his hands moved in under her blouse. He quickly found her breasts and began to squeeze them as he forced his tongue into her mouth.

"Stop this, Luke! Stop!"

"I'll love you enough for the both of us. I'll teach you to love me the way I love you." He was totally aroused as he pushed his groin into hers. The fridge jerked back against their collective body weight.

"*Luke, no!*" she shouted as best she could under his mouth.

"*She said no!*" Samantha was standing behind him.

He stopped instantly when he heard the new voice and swung around. He looked at Sam in openmouthed shock. Then he turned back to look at Gillian. He had managed to rip her blouse open and she looked scared. "Jesus, what was I doing?" he asked, his voice shaking.

"Do you want me to call the police, Gill?"

Luke stared at his own two hands as if he didn't know what they were doing at the end of his arms. He looked utterly shellshocked.

Gillian felt sorry for him. "No," she sighed. "It's partly my fault." She addressed Luke directly. "I think you'd better go, now. I'm sorry if you got the wrong idea after last weekend. It was just, you know — one of those things."

He nodded mutely, the vacant look still in his eyes.

"No hard feelings?" she asked as she walked him to the door with Samantha.

"No," he whispered. "Bye." And he was gone.

When they closed and bolted it, Gillian slowly slid down against the front door and plonked onto the floor.

"Jesus, Sam, thanks for coming when you did."

"That looked serious, Gillian. You've got be more careful in future."

"Ah, he wouldn't have got much further. I could have always grabbed the rolling pin."

"We have a rolling pin?"

Gillian laughed. "Actually it was kind of horny. I was just beginning to enjoy myself."

Samantha slapped her forehead. "You're incorrigible, girl. But seriously, you've got to get more selective about the men you let into your life."

"I intend to, Samantha. I swear, from now on, no trash. Only high-calibre men," she smiled wickedly at Samantha's back. "That I promise you."

CHAPTER 18

Because Samantha was up and out so early each day, she was usually gone before the post arrived. For this reason, it was Friday evening when she opened the letter with the Galway postmark.

"Three guesses who this is from," she said, her voice heavy with resignation. The week had ticked by slowly but steadily and Samantha had, as planned, buried herself in her work. Those around her ignored the scandal of the previous weekend. It was also considerably easier because Cameron wasn't in the office. She didn't let herself think about his return.

Wendy was home from work too. She looked at Samantha with the letter.

"If you think she's going to have another go at you, why don't you just not bother reading it?" she suggested as she brought two plates of chicken chasseur to the table. "Any word from Gillian? I've cooked for her too and there's still no sign of her. It'll be ruined soon."

Samantha was distracted from her letter as the aroma of the roasted onions and chicken hit her. "Wendy, you're a star. This smells terrific. How did you get new potatoes in October?" She speared one of the tiny spuds, no bigger than a sprout, in delight.

"Oh, it's easy if you buy the genetically modified ones," Wendy laughed. "You can have any food in any season and they'll last for months without going off. Who says GM foods are a bad thing?"

"Don't get me started," Samantha warned.

They ate in silence for a while, then Samantha asked, "Have you checked your voice-mail messages to see if Gillian called?"

"Good thinking, Sam," Wendy went off in search of her handbag and her phone while Samantha turned her attention back to her letter from Galway.

Impatiently, she ripped the envelope open and pulled out the contents. The first letter was a short, handwritten note from her mother. The writing was shaky and weak. Samantha's first instinct was that her mother was probably drunk when she was writing it. Some things would never change, she thought. "*Dear Samantha, I do not want to intrude upon your life as I know you don't want me in it.*" Despite her best efforts, Sam felt the guilt. "*I just felt that I had to send you a copy of the enclosed letter so you would know that I have been telling the truth.*" What the hell is she on about now, Samantha wondered with a slight sense of panic. She couldn't possibly have another bombshell. The letter continued, "*Contrary to what you think, I do love you and I miss you terribly. I have joined AA here in Salthill, Love Mum.*"

"Hey, that's a first," Sam said aloud.

"What is?" Wendy called from her room.

"Mum has joined AA."

"Wow, is it possible she could stop drinking after all these years?"

"No."

"I can't find my bloody phone, I must have left it in the car," Wendy complained as she returned to their large living-room. "Back in a jiff," she said and headed out of the apartment.

"Your food will be cold!" Sam shouted after her. She took a forkful of her chicken and another little potato from her plate and then she began to read the second letter from her mother. It was quite obviously a photocopy. The first thing that she noticed was the address. It was: *Dunross, Fiddler's Point, Co Wicklow.*

The letter was from James Judge.

"Jesus," Sam whispered to herself as she began to read. "*Dear Mrs Garcia, With reference to your recent letter, I have to inform you that I do not have any idea what you are talking about. As I have never had any physical contact with you, it is quite impossible that you are carrying my child. Any suggestion to the contrary will force me to sue for slander and defamation of character. Can I suggest that if you are unhappy with being pregnant, you consider a termination in England but please do not address me in this matter ever again. Yours, without prejudice, James Judge 2nd*

Samantha felt sick. Having worked with James for several years before he retired, she knew his handwritten signature well enough and there was little doubt that it was he who had signed the letter. Was this her father speaking? Was this the man who had been so nice to her just last Monday?

He did know all about her after all and he had tried to cover it up.

"She's not coming home – again," Wendy snarled as she slammed the front door behind her. "Can you believe it? She left me a bloody message on the phone. If she had made the damn effort to tell me properly, I wouldn't have gone to so much trouble." Wendy crossed the large living-room to where Sam was sitting. "Girl, are you OK? You've gone all pale on me again."

Samantha handed over the letter. "He knew," she said simply.

"Who knew?" Wendy scanned the letter. "What?"

"James Judge the fucking Second. He bloody knew that Kathleen Garcia – Mum was pregnant. He swore to me that he didn't. Jesus, Wendy –" Sam began to cry, "he's such a bastard! He wanted Mum to have an abortion. What is the date on the letter?"

"September 30th 1969. Christ, your mother has had it all this time."

"You don't think it's a forgery, do you? Would Mum go that far?"

"To be honest, with your mum, Sam, who knows? Obviously it's a photocopy but I have to tell you it looks authentic enough to me. But bear in mind he didn't know that you were a Garcia before the wedding – he thought you were a White. He had no idea you were connected to what was obviously a pretty dark period in his life. Jesus, what a letter though. He is some bastard."

"He's not my father."

"Sam? Just because he denied it back then isn't going to change what you've discovered to be true over the last few days. Both he and your mom have come out and told you that he is in fact your natural father," Wendy urged gently. "Look, this was written ages ago. Who knows what was going through his head? Why don't you have it out with him? Confront him on his lies – the shit. Jesus, men! Are they all assholes?"

"No, what I mean is even if he is the man who got mum pregnant, even if I am made up of his shitty genes, he's still not my father. I don't want a man who asked my mother to have an abortion to suddenly adopt me now that I'm all grown up. That's so callous. Now that I'm older and self-sufficient, he's happy to claim me as his own – whoopdeedoo. That bastard even wanted to give me his shares in Gracias. I see it now, he was trying to buy me off. It was his guilt gift."

"Don't cut off your nose to spite your face. It was a nice guilt gift. Take his money and run," Wendy whispered but Samantha glared at her.

"Are you mad? Screw that bastard. He got my mum pregnant and then tried to get her to have an abortion. That was me, Wendy. I could have been aborted if he had his way. Then when all that failed and I ended up back in his life, he came on all hard-done-by and acting like the bewildered victim. Wendy, he sat down with me last Monday and got drunk with me. He's a cold conniving –"

"OK, OK, I get the picture. What do you want to do about it?"

"I'm going to find my real dad."

"Samantha?" Wendy thought her dear friend had finally snapped.

"I'm talking about the man who bounced me on his knee, the one who taught me to count and sing ABC. He may not be in my life any more but I'm talking about the guy who checked under my bed for monsters and took me to my first day at school. Mum was drunk."

Wendy looked at her flatmate. She sometimes forgot how much Samantha had been through. It was so true, you just never knew what other people had to deal with. "What do you want to do?"

Samantha looked at her best friend with eyes ablaze.

"I'm going to find Pablo Garcia, Wendy. I'm going to Spain."

Gillian got home after two that Friday night. She was totally sober because she hadn't been drinking. The night had been a chronic bore as far as she was concerned but it was part of her job to be there and look interested. She had been involved in the launch of yet another low-fat butter. Christ, why couldn't her clients be more inventive? Lovely Low had shifted double its projected target for the month of September thanks to a quirky back-to-school campaign that Gillian had spearheaded. The result was that her company had to take the fat cat management of Lovely Low out to dinner to celebrate. Naturally they had all got disgustingly drunk and made passes at her and her team. As usual, the girls had to act all coy and flattered and even vaguely interested if it weren't for their fictitious boyfriends. There were all the predictable jokes. They hoped that the butter in the restaurant was Lovely Low. Of course it wasn't. As the night progressed, the jokes about being easy to spread came out. Gillian sighed heavily. She was getting too old for this bloody game. The only good thing about Lovely Low as far as she was concerned was the whopping bonus she got for shifting so much stock. A cool ten grand in the back pocket, thank you very much. The thought did cheer her.

When she got into the apartment she read Wendy's note first. *Your dinner is in the dog. Next time you're not coming home, talk to me. Don't leave a message on my phone, please. Actually your dinner is in the microwave if you're still hungry and don't forget you're on kitchen duty next Friday and I don't want another take-away — you're cooking.* Gillian laughed. Wendy was a natural homemaker. She also loved to cook. To the best of her memory, Gillian had never actually cooked in the kitchen although she had bought some very good meals and hidden the foil wrappers to fool her friends. The new one in Dalkey would do just fine for next Friday, she decided. Then she picked up Samantha's note. *Hi Gill, By the time you get this, I'll be in Spain. My flight leaves in two hours – 10pm, so I have to rush. Don't know when I'm coming back. Wendy will explain. Love Sam.* Gillian read it again and again. What the hell was she doing in Spain? Barbados, she could understand, but Spain! She wandered into the kitchen to examine the contents of the microwave. That was where she found the photocopied letter from James Judge to Kathleen Garcia. She sat down and studied it. Really, it was quite clear. James Judge was emphatically denying all possibility of being Sam's father.

"Holy, fuck," Gillian whispered to herself as she lit up. She pulled out the Sancerre from the fridge. If James wasn't Samantha's father, the wedding could still go ahead. "That bloody family," she fumed as she tried to figure out all the possibilities. Perhaps Samantha was catching a flight to Madrid and then on to bloody Barbados. She had to get to Cameron before Sam did. All thoughts of playing hard to get were out the window. Cameron didn't even know about her and Luke – some jealousy trick that had turned out to be, she fumed. What was the point in her staying at home bonking Luke bloody Delaney in an effort to get Cameron jealous if he was happily making whoopee in Barbados with Sam? Gillian reached for the phone. It was remarkably easy to track him down. International enquiries got the number for Sandy Lane, Barbados, effortlessly. They even put her through. She asked to speak to Cameron Judge and the polite telephonist asked her to please hold. Suddenly she was speaking to him.

"Cam. Wow, that was easy. Hi, it's Gillian," she said a little uncertainly.

"Gill, darling," he drawled, "how are you?"

"Great," she answered a little shyly. Calling him broke all the rules of boy/girl chasing but the bloody rules didn't seem to be working and he sounded happy enough to hear from her. "I was just wondering how you are?"

"Things are terrific. I'm about to go into dinner now. It's just

after 9pm. Jesus, I can't believe the first week is almost over already."
The line was incredibly clear.

"How's your Mum?"

"Well, she's not the happiest. She's going home tomorrow."

"Why?"

"I'm afraid my mother will only fly first-class and there are no first-class seats available on the flight on Monday week but there is one available on the Virgin flight tomorrow."

"What about Samantha's?"

"It's already been resold. As soon as she didn't show for the outgoing flight, the computer picked up on it and resold the seat. Rose was positively furious." He laughed.

"You don't sound too upset."

"To be honest, Gilly, she's doing my head in." Then he paused for a moment. "I'd much rather your company," he suggested lightly.

"Well, it's funny you should say that." Gillian began to play with her hair. "I do have some free time owing to me. Are you quite sure you're going to be all alone out there?"

"Hell, yeah. Are you serious? Could you really get over here?"

"What's the weather like in Barbados?"

"Heavenly."

"I may have to travel economy class," she pretended to moan.

"I could make it up to you when you got out here."

"Expect me sometime tomorrow or the next day," she laughed.

"Anyway, there's a small matter of my birthday present," Cameron teased. "Where did you get to that night?"

"It's a long story, darling," she dodged his question. "But I am looking forward to giving you your very personal birthday present."

Wendy hovered in the hall. Was she hearing things? She had heard Gillian come in and eventually managed to drag herself out of bed. She wanted to tell her all about the evening's events and explain why Samantha was in Spain. She hadn't heard all of Gillian's conversation but she knew that she was talking to a man and she had mentioned Barbados and Samantha. Could it possibly be Cameron? That just didn't make sense. Whoever it was, she definitely called him 'darling'. Wendy decided to slip back to bed. She could have her chat with Gillian in the morning.

When James Judge woke on Saturday morning, it took him a few moments to recall why he was in such a foul mood. Then all too suddenly he remembered. Like Samantha, he hadn't managed to get around to all his post until later on Friday afternoon. He had also received a note from Kathleen Garcia or White or whatever she wanted to call herself these days. He would always think of her as Katie Garcia. Her note to him had not been as polite or loving as the one she wrote to Samantha. *Dear James*, it said. *You claimed to remember nothing of our encounter some thirty-six years ago. How can that be when I wrote to you and told you I was carrying your child? I know that you got my note because I enclose a copy of the letter you sent back. As I said to you when we met recently, I did not mean to re-enter your life but I had no choice. I will not make any further attempt to contact you. Yours sincerely, Katie Garcia.*

She had used the name he remembered and loved her by.

Then he took out and read the photocopied letter. Quickly and with mounting horror, he scanned the words. They seemed to move about on the sheet of paper. The address was definitely his, but the words – *I do not have any idea of what you are talking about* – he hadn't written this! He scanned down the page: it certainly looked like his signature. He rescanned the letter – *quite impossible that you are carrying my child* – he began to tremble – *slander, defamation* – he would never have written this sort of letter and he would certainly never have forgotten writing such an appalling and menacing message – *termination*. James collapsed into the seat next to his bureau. Who would say such a thing to a pretty young woman carrying her first child? James rose only to fix himself a treble whiskey. Then he sat down and read the letter again. His first instinct was to phone Katie but he realised miserably that he didn't have a contact phone number for her. He thought about phoning Samantha but he didn't have the strength.

Again he read the letter, this time in more detail. He cast his mind back to the events of 1969. They were all pretty hazy at this stage. He remembered the big party and he certainly remembered Katie with her big Bambi eyes that worked so well with the heavy eye make-up all the girls used back then. He remembered showing her the new car he was so proud of. One thing had simply led to another. No one was happier than he. A little extra-marital affair never hurt anyone. As long as they were discreet and he didn't flaunt it in front of Rose or Pablo, what harm? James knew that his father had done it before him and so had his grandfather. It was a proud Judge family tradition. The women rarely knew about it and he certainly had no intention of hurting Rose. She need never have known.

Then, equally suddenly, Katie turned cold on him. He clearly remembered meeting her the day after the party. She had been a little shy until he managed to squeeze her hand and wink at her. Suddenly her face lit up and she smiled at him. He still remembered how good it made him feel. Rose never looked at him like that, ever. Rose managed life with an air of disapproval and she frowned a lot. Katie looked up to James with a gaze bordering on awe. She certainly gave him a hero complex which was a first for him and he thoroughly enjoyed it. He had thought and even dared to hope that their relationship might continue for a while but that was not to be as quite suddenly Katie turned cold. It seemed like she was avoiding him and when they did meet she was positively hostile.

Then he cast his mind back to their conversation in the hospital. It was probably around the end of September when she became cool and aloof. Katie had said that she wrote to him around that time and he in turn had written back. At least it explained her change of heart. At the time it had made no sense. He never got the chance to discuss it with her because Katie managed to avoid him for the next few weeks and then just before Christmas she and

Pablo left Dunross. She would have been five or six months pregnant but being so petite he didn't notice and Pablo already assumed that it was his child.

He read the letter again. Now, at least he understood why she was so angry with him. James thought about what she must have felt like. She was so young back then, probably under twenty, he realised with horror. Damn it, they were all practically children with little idea about the ways of the world. He felt wretched. Who would put her through such a thing? Who would write such a horrendous note? He asked the question of himself but he already knew the answer. There was only one person who could. There was only one person who could intercept his mail as had obviously been done, only one person who could easily forge his bloody signature. James felt his blood begin to boil. He rarely got angry but he was positively livid as the logical conclusion formed in his mind now. Nobody had ever invaded his privacy so maliciously before. Nobody had ever lied so overtly and cheated him so horrendously. This was positively barbaric.

Only one person on the planet could have been in a position to do this.

It was Rose.

CHAPTER 19

"Spain? What the hell is she doing in Spain?" Ricky asked in surprise as Wendy prepared him a coffee in her kitchen.

"It all happened very suddenly," she explained. "She got that note from your mother and then she decided that she wanted to meet Pablo, the man she considered to be her real dad."

Ricky then read the letter that Wendy had handed him a moment earlier. "What the hell does this mean? He has already admitted to her that he is her father. The bastard obviously put the screws into Mom back then."

Wendy handed him the freshly brewed coffee with a splash of milk, just as he liked it, and then she sat down gently. Samantha had been through a hell of a week but, on reflection, it couldn't have been easy for Ricky either.

"Ricky," she started gently, "James swore to Samantha that he knew nothing about her existence and then she got this letter from Galway, making it perfectly clear that he did. She's furious and very hurt. She's in shock really and this is a kind of a knee-jerk reaction, but she decided that Pablo was more of a father to her than James ever was and now she wants to catch up with him."

"I don't believe it. If I had known I might have gone with her.

After all, he is my father – I think. Jesus, what a mess! God, maybe Pablo isn't my father either."

"I'm so sorry about all of this."

"Why should you be sorry? It's hardly your fault." He grinned up at her through his bad mood.

"Well, no. I wasn't even born." Wendy ventured delicately, "Ricky, do you think you should talk to your mother? She could tell you everything you might need to know."

"She's the bloody reason we're all in this mess now."

Wendy held her tongue.

"Why didn't she just tell us sooner? This time last week poor Sam nearly married her half-brother. Mom really has a lot to answer for."

"Ricky, you have to talk to Kathleen."

He looked at her as he sipped his coffee. "Yeah, I know," he finally agreed. Then he looked around the apartment. "Gillian still in bed?"

"I think so – she got in very late last night. I think her bloody dinner is still in the microwave."

"No, it's not, nor am I in bed." Gillian strode into the room. "Hi, Ricky. Good morning, Wendy. I'm really sorry about last night's dinner. I did phone your mobile and when I got no reply, I texted you. It was just crazy in work. I had to take the Lovely Low louts out."

Wendy smiled at Gillian. "Don't worry, I'm getting used to it."

"Hey, where has Samantha gone so suddenly?" Gillian asked brightly.

"That's just what we were discussing," Wendy looked at Ricky. "Sam has gone over to Spain to meet up with Pablo. She suddenly decided that she wanted to see him again. It's just that, with a little notice, Ricky might have gone with her," Wendy explained.

Gillian tussled Ricky's gorgeous dark straight hair. "You could always follow her out."

"Nah, I think I need to talk to Mom first."

Wendy tried to change the subject. "You seem very fresh for –"

she looked at her watch, "eleven o'clock in the morning. What has you up and out so early on a Saturday?"

Gillian beamed. "Well, actually, my boss has given me a special bonus because we did so well on the Lovely Low account."

"What sort of bonus, Gill?" Ricky asked, his voice heavy with sarcasm.

"He's given me the keys to his Bermuda villa for a couple of weeks."

"Get out!" Wendy cried.

"Nice work if you can get it," Ricky agreed.

"Hey, I worked my ass off for that account and I've made the company a small fortune. The least they can do is dish out a few perks now and again."

Ricky spoke. "Earlier this week, Sam told me that Cameron is in Barbados. It's a pity your boss's villa isn't there. I mean, you are in the Caribbean and all. You could cheer him up."

Gillian's face froze for an instant but Wendy spotted it. Then Gillian smiled broadly. "To be honest, all I want to do is sunbathe with a few good novels and loads of cocktails."

Could she really be going out to Cameron, Wendy wondered with a profound feeling of dread. On the phone, she had definitely heard Barbados and not Bermuda. Wendy convinced herself that it just wasn't possible. She was half asleep last night, she probably got it all mixed up. "Yeah, and he's with his mother anyway. Best to leave them alone," Wendy agreed. "Anyway, what would Samantha think?" She sounded horrified. "If she heard that Gillian was down in Barbados with Cameron, she would be devastated, wouldn't she?"

"I'm not suggesting Gilly and Cam get it on, Wendy," Ricky laughed at the ridiculous idea. "I did mean just as friends."

"Still, it would really upset Samantha, I'm sure." Wendy looked straight into her flatmate's eyes.

Gillian caught Wendy's eye for an instant. Was it possible? Could Wendy know? No way. How? She pasted on her best corporate smile and laughed. "Well, it's all academic because I'm going to Bermuda not Barbados, remember?"

"When are you going?" Wendy asked.

Gillian looked at her watch. "Right now, actually. Must dash. I have an evening flight to London but I need a full body treatment first, waxing and all that." She blew them both a kiss. "See you in a few weeks." And she was gone out the door.

Why is she so worried about having a body beautiful if she's going to be all alone? Wendy pondered with mounting dread but she kept it to herself.

"Jesus, that was fast," Ricky sniffed. "Are you dashing off somewhere too?"

"No, I'm afraid not. I don't even have anything planned for the weekend."

"I don't suppose you fancy keeping me company in Galway."

"Are you going to talk with your mother?" she asked gently.

"I think I had better," he said without much conviction.

"Daaaaaddddeeeee!" The shouts of sheer delight would have gladdened any heart, except that of Stephanie Judge. As was agreed, David came to Dunross on Saturday lunch time, to take the children for the weekend. Zoë was thrilled to see him and rushed straight into his embrace. He wrapped his arms around her and lifted her into the air.

"How is my little princess?" he asked her as he planted a paternal kiss on her nose.

"Dreadful, I hate it here, Daddy. Why can't we come home with you?"

"You can today, for one night, darling," he said softly as he nuzzled into her hair. He had missed her terribly during the week.

Stephanie appeared a moment later. "Hello, David," she said coolly. "Cathy is just getting Amy ready for you now. Are you sure you know all her feeds and creams or do you want to go over them one more time with Cathy?"

"I know all I need to know, Steph," he said, trying to hold his patience. He was always very hands-on with the kids. If the truth be known, even with his full-time job in Dublin, he probably saw more of the girls than Steph did, between her girls' lunches and golf outings. He suppressed the annoyance he felt at being asked that question and looked at his wife.

"How are you keeping, Steph? You OK?"

She forced herself to stand tall. "Yes, I'm absolutely fine. Things are great here," she lied.

"If you'd rather live in the house, I could move into the flat."

"We're fine here, thank you very much."

"No, we're not," Zoë interrupted. "We don't live up here in Dunross, we live down in the servant's house. It's horrible."

David looked at Steph and smirked. Despite her best efforts, Steph laughed. "It's not that bad, Zoë. I think Mum wasn't too keen on the joys of young children around here so she asked us to move into one of the farmhouses."

David looked at his daughter. "But they're lovely, Zoë. You can play with the farm animals."

"Well, I do like horse-riding and I've been able to do that every day now."

"I hope you're riding with your hard hat on," he said in a warning voice.

Zoë began to wriggle to be let down. "Of course, Daaaaad," she replied, as indignant as any fifteen-year-old. "Can we go now? Will you take us to Eddy Rocket's? Does Amy have to come?"

As if on cue Cathy arrived with the baby in her arms and two large baby bags full of toys, nappies and bottles.

"Could you give Cathy a lift back up to Dublin? She's having car trouble. Sean is going to fix it over the weekend for her," asked Stephanie.

"Sure," David grinned at the nanny. She smiled back. Cathy had always liked David more than she liked super-spoilt Steph.

Stephanie saw them exchange the smiles and felt the icy stab of jealousy.

"OK, off you go. See you sometime tomorrow evening, girls." She gave them both a perfunctory kiss on the top of the head and walked away, leaving them to sort themselves out, getting into David's car. He watched her walk away in dismay. She didn't even say goodbye to him. He had secretly been hoping that she might like to come with him, even if it was just to Eddy Rocket's. It was quite clear that she was happy in her new single life and she no longer needed or wanted him in it. It was hardly surprising, he thought miserably. He was stuck in a boring rut in his job and they lived a very average life with little or no excitement. It was only when he came back to Dunross that he remembered what a dynasty she came from. How could she possibly be happy with him?

Stephanie secretly watched the car drive away from behind the kitchen blinds. In that car was her life – her soon-to-be-ex-husband, her two beautiful daughters and of course, her sanity, Cathy. As they drove back down the lane, away from Dunross and away from her, she wondered why she was so hostile to all the people she loved so much. She felt even more miserable than she had done all week.

"Is that David I saw driving away?" James Judge had finally surfaced.

"Good morning, Daddy," Steph greeted her father, "although, technically it's the afternoon now but, yes, David has taken the girls for the weekend."

"Very good. Well, what are you going to do with your new-found freedom?" He busied himself putting a great big heavy pan on top of the Aga.

"I have no idea," she answered miserably.

James heard the tone of her voice and stopped preparing his fry. He crossed over to where she sat at the kitchen table. "My dear, dear child," he crooned as he put his arm around her shoulders.

"Oh, Daddy! How did it get this bad? I'm thirty years old with a husband who doesn't love me, two children who hate me, and no life to speak of. How did it all get so mixed up?"

"There, there," he soothed as he rocked her gently. "I rather think the problem is that you don't know what you want, dear girl," he said simply.

"Well, even if that was the problem what can I do about it?"

"You've got to figure it out, Steph," he suggested gently. Then he said suddenly, "I say, would you like to come to work at Judges'?"

Steph broke away from her father's embrace and looked at him. "Me?"

"Yes, you. Why not? Would you like to?"

"Well, what about the children?"

"Isn't that what the nanny is for?"

"What would I do? I'd be like a square peg in a round hole."

"Nonsense, you'd be a square peg in a square hole. You're a Judge, damn it. As for what you'd do, I don't really know. What would you like to do?"

"I have no idea," but she was smiling.

"Tell you what, next Monday why don't you come in with me? I'll walk you around the plant and show you how everything works and you can see if any particular department appeals to you. Administration might suit you. You're very good at details. And Marketing still has a gap since we lost Samantha to Gracias."

Stephanie's face darkened at the mere mention of Samantha's name and James saw it. "Steph, you're going to have to accept Sam into your heart. Look, she was going to be your sister-in-law, so what if she actually did end up being your half-sister? There isn't that much of a difference, is there?"

"Yes, there bloody well is!" Stephanie looked horrified. "Daddy, you're not suggesting that there's any truth to what that old bitch said?"

"Please don't call Kathleen Garcia a bitch. You don't know the woman."

"Do you?"

"Steph, you're getting all excited about absolutely nothing and, to be honest, I rather think you have enough on your plate without worrying about other peoples' problems too. Now if you would give some thought to what sort of work you would find appealing in Judges' Distilleries, perhaps I could make some calls."

Stephanie didn't reply but James saw her eyes soften. She was listening, that was enough for now. He didn't tell Stephanie that the job was actually Granny Vic's idea. She had taken James aside and suggested that what her granddaughter needed was some good old-fashioned hard work. That would distract her.

Tess Delaney was beside herself with worry. She didn't usually go to Mass on a Saturday. She preferred to worship on a Sunday but she did today and she would go again tomorrow. As she came out and went for a short walk along the little promenade of Fiddler's Point to clear her head, she saw David Neilson drive past with his two children – Rose Judge's grandchildren – in his car. She also saw that the woman in the passenger seat was not young Stephanie Judge. Tess had heard from Mrs Bumble that Stephanie and her husband had split up. "What's the world coming to?" she sighed. "And how the dickens can a man like David Neilson move on to a new woman so fast when my poor Luke is in such a bad way after just one date?" She talked to herself as she watched the waves lap on the beach.

For the last week there had been no talking to Luke. He was usually a quiet lad but Tess understood him and usually knew what was going on in his mind. These days, however, she was at a loss. He refused food. He had even stopped reading which was unheard of for Luke. Instead he just sat in his room and stared into space. It was as if he had been through some sort of deep trauma. She hadn't phoned a doctor yet, but Tess was seriously thinking about it. If he didn't snap out of it soon she would have to take drastic measures.

The straw that broke the camel's back, however, was the previous Thursday when Luke refused to get out of bed in the morning. Usually he was the first up and out. She would make the breakfast for the men and then they all went out together. On Thursday morning, however, there was no sign of Luke. She eventually went up to his room where she found him wide awake but not moving in the bed.

"Why aren't you up at this stage?" she had asked him.

"I don't want to fish," he said simply.

It was only five little words but it shattered Tess's world. For that boy not to want to fish was like a painter not painting, a sculptor not sculpting, a lover not loving. And that of course is where all this trouble began. Poor poor Luke was heartbroken. He was suffering from unrequited love but unlike most men who would get back up and dust themselves off Luke had shut himself away from the world. He was getting more and more depressed with each passing day and she could see no way out. Tess always knew that Luke was different from other people. He was more intense, calmer than the average person and he felt things at a spiritual level. At one point she hoped he might become a priest but that didn't happen on account of the fact that he had no faith. She had reached the end of the promenade and the end of her tether so she had to turn around and head back to her house.

Despite her understanding of her son and the situation, however, she was at a complete loss as to what to do about it. Gillian was hardly going to change her mind about her feelings for Tess's son and there seemed little chance of him changing his feelings for her. She had tried to talk to Frank but he just shrugged helplessly. Tess pulled her old winter coat around her body. The winter was definitely upon them. She quickened her step towards her house, towards her family and her favourite son. Luke needed help, that was certain. She just didn't know where to look. Just then the church bell chimed and she thought of God. She looked towards the heavens. "Maybe you could send us a little miracle from above," she whispered.

Granny Victoria sounded surprised when Stephanie told her over lunch that she was going to work at Judge's.

"What a clever idea," she enthused.

For the first time in ages Stephanie's voice was light and her mood upbeat. "Of course, I have no idea what I'm going to be doing yet, but Dad is sure that they can find me something interesting."

215

"Smashing. That should keep Cameron on his feet and concentrating on work. Does he know about it yet?"

"No, I don't suppose he does. We only talked about it this morning," Steph explained.

James spoke. "I'm sure he won't mind, Mum."

"Not at all, he should be delighted to have more help. The more family in the business, the better," Victoria added, looking straight at James.

He blinked back at his mother. Was it possible that she knew about Samantha?

Victoria continued, "When is that boy coming home, anyway? I thought he was running the family business now. Haven't you retired, James?"

"Well, yes, but Rose rather thought he needed a break and so I was happy to step into the driving seat just for a while."

"When are they coming home?" Victoria asked, unable to hide the disapproval in her voice.

"Cameron has another week," James answered. "Rose is in the air as we speak. Then she is catching a connecting flight to Dublin. I'll collect her from the airport later this afternoon."

"Daddy, why don't you let Paul collect Mum? That way you can have a rest, especially if you are back in the office on Monday," Stephanie suggested.

"Paul will drive, naturally, but I want to meet her there." James was very firm. "There are some matters I wish to discuss with your mother sooner rather than later."

Victoria and Stephanie exchanged curious glances.

With considerable effort, the old woman lifted up the china teapot and asked, "More tea anyone?"

CHAPTER 20

Getting a flight to Madrid was easy as was booking a room in the airport Hilton for what little remained of the night. Samantha had rented the car online before leaving her Dublin apartment so no problems there either. What she found difficult was phoning her mother. Sam didn't particularly want to speak to her but how else would she know where to start looking for Pablo Garcia – her dad?

Samantha knew deep down that Pablo wasn't her father but the more she thought about it, the more she was convinced that she had to see him. He was the man who had minded her when she was a baby. He was the guy who chased away the scary monsters she dreamt up when she was small, but most importantly he *believed* himself to be her father. It was time to heal the rift.

Samantha had delayed the call as much as possible. She was now sitting in her small Ford in the huge carpark of the rental company. Using her mobile, she dialled her mother's house in Galway. Despite the infrequency with which she used that phone number, it was annoyingly ingrained in her memory.

"Hello," a weak voice answered.

"Mum, it's Samantha. How are you?" she couldn't help herself from asking.

"Oh, Sami, it's good to hear your voice. I'm good. Did you get my letter? I hope it didn't upset you too much. I just needed to be sure you knew that I wasn't lying."

"Yes, Mum, look, don't worry about that. I'm actually in Spain. It's, er, business but I will be in the Rioja region of Spain," she lied. She hadn't planned on being deceitful but why hurt the old lady any more than was necessary. "I thought it might be nice to look up Pablo. Do you have an address for him?"

Kathleen was silent.

"Mum?"

"Samantha, you know that he still believes himself to be your natural father. You won't tell him, will you?"

Sam sighed. Was it always this exhausting talking to one's mother, she wondered? "No, Mom, I won't tell him at this stage. Look, do you have an address for him?"

"No, I'm afraid I don't. It was a long time ago – when I was very sick –" She stalled.

"Mum?"

"Well, I threw almost everything away one particularly bad night."

"What do you mean?"

"You know, all Papi's letters, Christmas cards to you two and his contact information. I hadn't heard from him for ages at that stage so I didn't think I would ever need it again. It was all just a painful reminder." Samantha wondered why she hadn't bothered to throw out James Judge's letter too but she didn't dare ask.

Kathleen continued. "I'm sorry, Sam. Look, the area isn't as big as you would think. I'm pretty sure if you go to Haro – that's the town he lives in or at least he used to – if you ask around, you'll find him pretty quickly."

"Great."

"Sorry I can't help more. Try Haro," Kathleen offered again with a little more conviction.

Samantha looked around the carpark. There was nobody around, just rows of little cars and two *salida* signs. "Where in tarnation is Haro?" she asked miserably.

"Where are you right now?"

"I'm in a car rental, not far from the airport."

"Well, that's a help. Madrid's airport is at the north of the city and you're heading north, so you needn't go into the capital at all. Just take the main road to the north of Spain. I think you head for Burgos and then take a right for Haro."

"Bloody hell, well done, Mum."

Kathleen chuckled. "It's funny the things you remember. I couldn't tell you what I had for breakfast but I know how to get to Haro."

"When was the last time you were over here?"

Kathleen didn't answer immediately. Then she just sighed sadly. "It was a very very long time ago."

"Mum, is *salida* the Spanish for exit?"

"Yes, drive safely, my love, and tell Pablo −" She stopped herself. "Well, just drive safely."

Samantha headed off, shakily at first. She was used to driving on the left-hand side of the road and it took a few surprised motorists and a couple of blasts from irate car horns before she got the gist of driving on the right-hand side. Thankfully the roads around Madrid airport were very well signposted and she saw the one for Burgos easily. The busy traffic around the north of the city and the airport slowly fell away and the motorway became somewhat calmer. Alone in the car she was able to marvel at the great stretches of countryside that swept by her on either side. As autumn crept over the Spanish landscape, the fields had a patchwork-quilt look about them − many still carried their autumn crop while others had been stripped bare. In some fields, farmers worked the land with huge tractors, tilling the rich, dark-brown earth. How simple and stress-free their lives seemed to Samantha as she drove along! "Perhaps this is where I should be," she said to herself. "It could be a clean start," she sighed. She could certainly do with a bit of that.

As the kilometres flew by, Samantha fantasised about living in

Spain with Pablo. He would be a good deal older than she remembered him, of course, but she knew that he lived off the land, or at least he had done. He had always enjoyed the simpler things in life. Perhaps his attitudes could wear off on her a little.

The motorway was gloriously straight and smooth so the journey was relatively easy on her. With just the vista of beautiful, autumnal countryside, she found the morning altogether pleasant. The chocolate-brown fields blended beautifully with the honey-gold leaves of the trees she passed. There were deep crimson forests and bright yellow pockets of sunlight streaming through branches as they slowly shed their summer mantle, leaf by lovely leaf. It was a wonderful drive and cheered her up enormously.

She stopped in one of the Repsol stations that punctuated the motorway for a chorizo sandwich and a cola lite. She tried to check with the girl behind the counter that she was on the right road for Burgos but Samantha had no Spanish and the young girl had no English so they concluded by nodding at each other and pointing in the direction Samantha was already driving in and saying "Burgos".

By lunchtime she had reached the outskirts of the town and signposts were beginning to appear for the Rioja region. She took the Burgos bypass and so she missed any tourist attractions that it had to offer. The only things she did see, which were stunning, were the huge church spires that dominated the skyline above the city.

Then she took her exit from the motorway. Quite suddenly, the roads were like the west of Ireland. They were narrow and very bendy. Twice she stopped to ask if she was on the right road. About an hour later, the small town of Haro came into sight. She drove past what looked like a medium-size factory, but her trained eyes spotted the pipes and ventilation that meant it had to be a distillery of some sort. *Bodega de Marques de Riscal*, it said. Of course, she remembered. A bodega was a winery. "That would be one of the posher ones," she laughed aloud as she remembered James's weakness for *Marques de Riscal* wine. "Mmm, I wonder if I could get it any cheaper here than at home," she said to herself. Then she recalled how much she hated James and resolved to buy some just for herself. Quite suddenly, the road turned a sharp left and crossed over a little river. A huge signpost on her right listed off about fifteen different bodegas, all obviously local. Samantha drove on.

The streets were very narrow and she had to pull in a number of times to let oncoming traffic pass her. With all the cars parked along the street, there wasn't enough room for two-way traffic. "Same problems, different location," she said to herself as she nodded at the driver of the other car. Eventually she found what she was looking for – a big tourist information sign. Her first enquiry was easily handled. The young girl in the tourist office was quick to recommend a hotel in the town. Her English was good but she had never heard of a man called Pablo Garcia. Samantha was deflated. Was she going to have to go around the town asking people in the street? That would be quite embarrassing.

Just as she was about to head out of the office, an older woman walked in.

"*Mama, conoces a un tal, Pablo Garcia, que vive aqui, en Haro?*"

All Samantha understood was Mama, Pablo and Haro but the woman looked at her up and down and then nodded slowly.

Using her daughter as interpreter, Samantha understood that Pablo lived a little way out of the town, the lady didn't know exactly where but just like all the other bodega workers, surely he would be at "*La Herradura*," for lunch.

"What's *La Herradura*?" Samantha asked helplessly.

"Eet's a horseshoe, I sink," the young girl translated as best she could.

"Pablo is in a pub called The Horseshoe?" Samantha was still confused.

"No, *La Herradura* is a place. It is, how you say, the old town." The tourist information girl took Sam by the hand and guided her to the door. Then she pointed the way down one of the streets Samantha had driven up earlier. "There are a few restaurants zere. Ze men from the bodegas and vineyards eat and drink zere for a few hours during the middle of ze day. He will be in one of zem, my mozer says." Then she shrugged and smiled shyly as if to say that was the best she could do.

"*Muchos gracias!*" Samantha shook her hand and headed off. After quickly checking into the recommended hotel and dropping her case into her new room, she went in search of the *Herradura*, whatever it was. To her relief, as Haro was a small town, it had been easy to find. Finding her father was not so easy.

The first bar she tried was actually closed and so she went on to the next. After five bars and five sets of blank of faces, Samantha began to despair. What if this was a wild-goose chase? Her father could have left the area years ago for all she knew.

Without much hope she persevered. The last pub she tried looked a little busier and as a result it was more inhibiting than the others. It was only when she opened the door that she became a little shy. Was this really such a good idea? Would the bodega workers even be there on a Saturday? Was anybody inside going to be able to speak bloody English? Maybe she hadn't thought this through really well. Tentatively she pushed the door open further. It was an old-fashioned pub inside. The floor was covered in a pretty awful cream and brown lino and, overhead, a single bulb hung down by way of lighting. The windows were frosted, dark-green glass so the place looked quite dark and in Samantha's opinion, quite uninviting. The tables were basic black Formica units with standard black stools and chairs. The bar's counter dominated one entire wall of the room. It was about fifteen feet long. She had, of course, been spotted as soon as she opened the door so she knew that she had to keep going. The place was quite busy so it took a few moments of standing there before she could get the girl's attention. It was during these first few, nervous moments that Sam realised she was in fact the only woman in the pub outside of the bar girl. Oh, shit, she thought, I'm in a men's only bar.

"*Digame?*" the bar girl threw her a challenging glance.

"Pablo Garcia?" Samantha spoke clearly and slowly, but the girl leered at her and raised one side of her lip.

"Heh?" she asked with something definitely bordering on contempt.

"Pablo Garcia?" Sam tried again.

"*Que queires? Mujer, no te entiendo.*" She sniffed as she turned her attention to another patron and quite obviously discussed Samantha with him. He looked at their new visitor and winked.

"*Hola, guapa,*" he said.

Samantha didn't understand but she got the gist and she didn't like it. "Pablo Garcia," she said it louder this time, so everyone in the pub turned around to examine her, most of them lecherously. "Jesus, does nobody in this town know of a man by the name of Pablo Garcia?" she shouted in desperation.

The room went quiet, for a moment, shocked by this melodramatic outburst. Then, behind Sam's back, between her and the door, she heard footsteps and a chair being pushed aside. She saw the not-so-friendly bar girl glance at the new arrival.

"I know who you speak of," a dark warm voice replied.

Samantha swung around. Her first reaction was to blush. She had been shouting like a bloody banshee and here was this cool calm *hombre* who could help her. He wore a long navy wax coat and a broad-brimmed cowboy hat of the same material. On any guy in Ireland, it would have looked utterly ridiculous but on this man it seemed right. His hobnail boots clanked on the floor noisily.

"Oh, great, eh, thanks," she stuttered. "Sorry, I was getting a little frustrated."

But he didn't appear to be listening. "Maria," he called to the girl behind the bar. She swung around instantly, hair flicking and eyelashes batting. Sam listened to him speak to the bar girl at what seemed like a million miles an hour. Maria nodded with the flicker of a smile on her lips.

"Come, seet," he gestured to the table nearest him. He sat down without waiting for her. Samantha looked at him. Good-looking he might be but he certainly wasn't a gentleman. She took the other chair at his table and sat down a little awkwardly. Almost ignoring her, he pulled out his bag of tobacco and cigarette papers and began to roll himself a cigarette. Sam waited for as long as she could, which wasn't very long.

"Look, if you could just tell me where I could find Pablo, I'll be off," she offered.

Maria arrived with what looked like a large stew of artichokes, asparagus, peppers, tomatoes and broad beans. For good measure there were potatoes and some fresh bread on the side. Then she returned with a bottle of wine and a glass. She plonked them down unceremoniously in front of him.

"God, that was fast," Samantha smiled.

He looked up at Maria and winked, and then as if noticing something, he called her back. *"Eh, dos vasos!"*

Samantha didn't understand the language but she knew a dirty look when she got one from Maria. The young girl stomped off and returned with a second small glass. This time he smacked her bum as she walked away. She shrieked and giggled happily at him.

Caveman, Sam thought sullenly. She was beginning to dislike him intensely.

Without speaking, he poured out two glasses of deep red wine and offered one to Samantha. Then he took his hat off and placed it on the table beside him.

"Thank you very much. I don't even know your name –"

"Pedro," he said without looking up from his stew. He was forking it through as if looking for something.

"Hello, Pedro. I really don't want to intrude upon your meal or your time," she explained. "If you could just tell me where Pablo is, I really need to speak with him as soon as I can."

He leaned over his food, almost as if he was protecting it from possible predators, both elbows firmly planted on the table. His boorish nature irked Sam.

"Why do you need to speak to Pablo?" he asked, still studying his lunch.

"Well, to be honest, that's really a matter for him and me."

Pedro shrugged and pushed his stool back as if he were just about to leave the table.

"Please," Samantha put her hand on his arm. The skin was warm to her touch and she noticed that his wrist was very wide. He looked up at her. "I'm sorry but I'm not sure that he would want me to say who I am. I just need to see him. It's – well, it's been a long time."

Pedro's eyes bored into hers. He waited for maybe fifteen seconds but she was a confident girl and not easily scared off so she forced herself to match his stare, not that it was too difficult. If he was coarse and vulgar, his redemption was his most hypnotic eyes. They were a rich, deep dark brown, rarely seen in Ireland but common enough in Spain. Jet-black eyelashes framed them above and below. The effect was almost feminine were it not for his black and heavy-set eyebrows. His face was angular but the look was softened because his hair grew long and straight, well below his shoulders. He had a centre split which didn't work very well. Without his hat to hold it back, his hair kept falling down onto his face. He wasn't at all Samantha's type of man but he was, none the less, very attractive – in an earthy sort of way.

Pedro eventually spoke. "Will he know you?"

"I don't think he will recognise me. As I said it's been a long time, but he should remember me from long ago."

"Will it upset him to meet you?" Pedro asked.

This annoyed her slightly. What the hell was it to this guy? Pablo hardly needed a bodyguard. She forced a smile.

"No, I promise I won't hurt him. In fact, I'm hoping he will be happy to see me."

Pedro remained unconvinced. "Pablo is an old man. I don't want him getting any nasty surprises." This surprised Sam. Surely he wasn't much older than Kathleen. If he was in his sixties, there should be plenty of life in him yet.

"What ees your name?" Pedro cut into her thoughts.

"Samantha, Samantha White," she said looking straight at him. She could hardly plunge in and say she was Sam Garcia. Two and two did equal four.

Pedro continued to study her while he ate. She found his table manners uncouth and unpleasant. Throughout the meal he kept his elbows on the table and he never actually managed to put the fork down. Until that moment, Samantha hadn't realised how much she valued good table manners. Stop it, she thought to herself, it's just a different culture!

"Drink," he said gruffly, gesturing with his fork at the full glass of wine he had poured for her. Neither he nor anybody else in the bar used wine glasses, she noticed. They all used small tumbler types. It was kind of nice, actually. She sipped the wine and then sipped it again. It was the nicest wine she had ever tasted.

"My God, that is delicious," she gasped as she tried to look at the wine label. "Is this locally produced and can I buy it?"

He laughed and threw his head back as he did so. With his laughter, his entire face lit up and his body language changed utterly. He suddenly became alive and animated. His posture was open and welcoming as his hair fell back from his face. Was it the wine he consumed with such gusto that had suddenly lifted his spirits or had she said something to please him, she wondered? Pedro refilled his own glass and gestured for her to drink more so he could do the same to hers.

"It should be good wine," he smiled broadly. "It is Pablo's!"

Samantha's heart soared. She was drinking her father's wine! As her eyes lit up, so too did Pedro's. It was as if he had decided that she wasn't in fact an axe murderer. Perhaps he would tell her what she needed to know now.

Only a few minutes later Pedro excused himself. Sam assumed he was going to the toilet because he hadn't gone out the front door of the pub. He had in fact gone to the back of the room and climbed a set of stairs there. The wine had soothed her and she no longer felt threatened by the dagger looks she was still getting from Maria the barmaid. Nor was she bothered by any more unwanted advances from the other men in the pub. As soon as she sat down with Pedro, the other suitors had respectfully retreated.

Soon Pedro returned. "Come wiz me," he said as he turned again on his heel.

Samantha scrambled to her feet and grabbed her bag. She had to run to catch up with him as he marched back up the stairs at the end of the room. To her surprise, it was a great deal more pleasant up there. The windows were large and looked out over the old town square, which she now gathered was called *La Herradura*. The tables had pristine white linen napkins and an altogether nicer clientele were dining up here. Samantha also noted with relief that there were a few women scattered among the diners but, while not quite as bad as downstairs, it was still 90 per cent male occupancy. Where are all the women, Samantha wondered as she rushed to catch up with Pedro. He was now hovering over a dining-table by the window.

He turned as she reached his side.

"Samantha, thees is Pablo Garcia," he said, nodding at the man seated at the table.

Suddenly, everything went still. "Pablo?" she whispered, feeling five years old again. "It's me, Samantha."

The man who stared up at her was not what she was expecting. Here sat a man who looked like he was well into his seventies and frail at that.

"Sami?" he asked as the confusion cleared from his eyes. "My Sami?" he demanded again as she nodded gently. Pablo may have looked old and weak but his eyes were bright. He had to work to get to his feet and his chair nearly fell over but Pedro grabbed it and pulled it out of the way. Pablo stretched out his arms. "Is it really you? My little Sami?"

She rushed to hug him. "Yes, Papi, it is me." Samantha started to cry gentle tears.

"I cannot beleef you have come to see me, my *cosa guapa*." He was choking on emotion too. "My little Sami! It is so good to see you. I thought I would never see you again, my angel. Let me look at you!" He pulled her back and studied her face. He stroked her long curly blond hair and her high cheekbones. Then he admired her slowly from head to toe as Samantha squirmed slightly under his proud paternal eye. "You are a beautiful woman. But then of course you were always beautiful," he smiled through his tears of joy.

Samantha laughed and cried simultaneously too. She hadn't realised how much emotion this would dredge up for her but she was glad she had come. This felt right. So what if he hadn't aged as well as James Judge! It was only then that she realised that Pablo was in fact dining with another man of almost equal maturity and for that matter the entire restaurant was now looking at them with great curiosity.

Pablo spoke to Pedro for a brief moment. The younger man tried to argue but Pablo simply ignored the protests. He used Pedro's arm to help him climb onto his dining-chair. It quite obviously was an enormous effort for him and Pedro was most anxious in case he might fall. Pablo, although shaking with the physical effort, seemed less concerned. Once up, he turned to face the other diners. Then he clapped his hands together to get their attention even though he had it already. He spoke in a mixture of English and Spanish, presumably for Sam's benefit.

"*Amigos mios, os quiero presentar a todos a —*" and then he stopped and reverted to English, "My friends, I want you all to meet my daughter, *mi hija*, Sammiii!" There were gasps and guffaws from various tables around the small restaurant and then everybody applauded and raised their glasses. Samantha went a deep shade of Rioja rose but she managed an awkward smile at her benevolent audience.

With Pedro's help, Pablo struggled back down from his perch and hugged her again. "Seet, seet, you must talk with me and my friend here and you have met Pedro already."

Samantha smiled at the only other person she knew in all of Spain.

Still standing, the old man put one arm around Pedro and the other one around Sam.

"Pedro," Pablo explained as he smiled at Samantha, "is your brozer!"

The younger man looked at her awkwardly.

Oh, Christ, she thought in anguish, not another one!

CHAPTER 21

James Judge was surprised to see the airport so busy on a Saturday evening.

"I thought all the summer holiday traffic would be over by October, Paul. Where are all these people coming from?" he asked his driver as they pulled up in the set-down-only area.

"It's like this all the time, these days, Mr Judge. There's never a quiet time in Dublin Airport."

The driver noticed as he held James's car door open for him that his boss was looking particularly tired. "Are you all right, sir? Would you like me to come with you?"

"No, no, Paul," James forced himself to smile, "I'm quite all right by myself. But you might try to be back here to pick us up, so we don't have to walk to those confounded carparks."

"Fine, sir. I'll be here."

"Good man, thank you." He placed his hand on his chauffeur's shoulder. "Where would I be without you?"

Paul smiled. Cameron might be a pain in the butt but James was a good man. As long as James was at the head of the family he would stay with the Judges.

James glanced at his watch as he walked into the airport. He was almost an hour early for Rose's flight and it was almost teatime. That explained why he was a little peckish. He headed to the nearest newsagent's to buy himself a bar of chocolate. As he fumbled through the vast array of confectionary he heard the husky voice of a woman asking the sales assistant for a packet of cigarettes. The girl had a particularly throaty and rather sexy voice and James recognised it instantly.

"Gillian, I say, is that you?" he asked in surprise.

"Oh hello, Mr Judge. Fancy meeting you here."

"Please call me James."

"James," she purred demurely as she batted her long eyelashes at him. Men like him were easy to charm.

"What are you doing in the airport?" he asked.

"I'm – well, actually I'm taking a few days' holiday. What about you? Are you off somewhere nice?" She knew full well that he was there to collect the old bag.

"No. Rose, my wife, is flying back in from Barbados this morning. I've come to collect her."

"James, you are too kind. Does she know how lucky she is to have a man like you?"

He warmed to her charm. "How very sweet of you to think so, Gillian. Tell me, did Luke Delaney manage to get hold of you last week? He was most keen to."

"He got hold of me all right. I'm afraid Luke Delaney, while he is a very nice young man . . . well, let's just say he's not the man for me. It was all rather awkward to be honest."

"Good God, Gillian. I'm most desperately sorry. You see, I'm the old fool who gave him your address. He came up to Dunross – oh, I don't know, about a week ago. He was looking for Cameron in order to get your phone number." James's eyes were full of regret. "Cameron is away, you see, and I was trying to help."

Gillian put her hand on his arm. "Don't worry. No harm done. It's not your fault." Then she slipped her arm inside his so they could walk together closely. "But if any more men come looking for my address from you, put the dogs on them!" She smiled indulgently.

"Quite right. So so sorry. I say, can I buy a drink by way of apology?"

Gillian spotted another opportunity. "Well, that's most generous of you, James, although I think there is something you should do first."

He was preoccupied with her and delighted to have quite suddenly found himself in such charming company. "What?" he asked, smiling at her as they crossed the floor.

"Should you perhaps go back to the shop and pay for that chocolate?" she laughed.

He rushed back into the shop, dropping the bars on the first shelf he saw. Gillian stood where she was and waited for him. He was obviously thrilled with her company. Old men were so much easier to charm, she thought as she watched him rush back to her side. It was then that a particularly evil idea occurred to her. Why was she bothering with Cameron when James was the real prize? Of course he was considerably older but then he would probably die sooner. She could be a very very rich young widow. If she could seduce James away from Rose, she could acquire a significantly larger proportion of Judge's stocks and shares than if she ended up with Cameron. Surely when James died his inheritance would be split between his wife and children, so Cameron would get just a slice of the cake. Yes, she suddenly realised. Financially speaking, James was a much better catch than Cameron Judge.

"Everything OK?" she asked brightly.

"No problem. They didn't even see me or if they did, they didn't care. I had no idea that stealing was so easy," he chuckled.

Gillian laughed heartily. "Oh, James, you are funny!" she enthused. "I'd say you were just too fast for them. They didn't see you, that's all."

"Gillian, I'm not too fast any more, I'm afraid."

Again she snaked her arm in around his so they could walk arm in arm. This time she hugged in snugly. "You know, James," she whispered, "we ladies don't like fast men. A man who moves at a slower pace is infinitely more attractive." She squeezed into his arm, pressing her body against his.

He looked at her in delighted shock. "Quite," he agreed. "Now where can we get a drink?"

Within minutes they were settled into a snug in the Sky Bar on the top floor of Dublin Airport. He hadn't planned to, but James found himself ordering a bottle of Dom Perignon. She clapped her hands enthusiastically when he returned to the table with the loaded ice bucket and two champagne glasses.

"Oh, James, you are clever! This is the best possible way to start a holiday. How did you know? DP is my very favourite champagne." Gillian tapped the sofa beside her, beckoning him to sit next to her as opposed to opposite her. He did as he was bid.

"Thank you for being so nice to me," she sighed as she kissed him on the cheek.

He shrugged. "It's the least I could do, having told Luke where you live. Really, Gillian, I am so sorry. I never thought about it as private information. It won't happen again."

Then she put on a sad face. "Don't worry. It's not like a lot of guys come looking for my address," she sighed.

James took a large gulp of Dom Perignon. "Now, just wait one minute there. I'm sure that's not true. You're a real corker. There must be lots of lads who would give their right hand to be where I am right now." He beamed. "Now if I was only a few years younger . . ."

"I don't think you're old. I think you're a more mature man and you know I prefer that. Is it so awful if I have a preference for men of experience?"

"No, not at all," he agreed with delight as he refilled their glasses and Gillian nipped to the ladies'.

Upon her return they shared a very pleasant further twenty minutes together. When he glanced at his watch, he was surprised at how fast the time had zoomed by.

"Damn, I have to go," he grumbled as he threw a glass of champagne into himself and stood up reluctantly. It wasn't every day his company was as utterly charming as Gillian Johnston.

"Perhaps we'll meet again," she suggested as she gazed up at him demurely.

"That would be very nice," he nodded enthusiastically, unwilling to leave her but now again very conscious of the coming showdown with his wife.

"Thank you for the champagne, James."

"Not at all, a pleasure." Then with just the slightest hesitation, he leaned down and kissed her cheek.

To her utmost satisfaction, the kiss lingered just beyond the limits of politeness. Yes, he was hooked.

"Until the next time, James," she said huskily.

"Yes, until the next time," he echoed as he headed off.

Gillian watched him go. This was really too easy. He was actually a very sweet man and not altogether unattractive. She could probably drive him mad without even the need for seduction. How much easier was he than his son? Gilly sat back and luxuriated in the notion of becoming James's wife . . . It would certainly take the wind out of a few sails around her – Samantha, Rose and not least Cameron. She sipped her champagne. Yes, she decided this idea was worth pursuing.

James was thoroughly fed up when he got back down to Arrivals. Rose's plane had been delayed by a further half hour. That was thirty exquisite minutes that he could have spent with Gillian. What a smashing young lady! Of course there was no future in it but she really was delightful company. He let his imagination run away with him. Was it really possible that she could find him that attractive? God knows, he found her utterly adorable.

James hadn't had an affair for years. There had been a brief encounter with one of Rose's flower-arranging friends but it was short-lived and not particularly exciting. A girl like Gillian, however – now, that was something. She was a real stunner. He had watched her walk to the ladies', and he was aware that he wasn't the only man watching. Gillian was wearing a pair of tight light blue jeans that flared out over her high stiletto boots. She had a white fitted cotton shirt on which accentuated her glorious curves. Her bottom was round and pert. She really was a dish. This thought invigorated him. Of course it was all in the realms of fantasy, he reminded himself – or was it, his mind teased him equally quickly. A new woman would certainly put the life back into his loins.

Gillian Johnston felt equally good. Why hadn't she thought of it earlier? James was such easy prey while Cameron was a lot of bloody work. She was sure she could wrap James around her little finger with little or no effort. He would do anything for her. She was pretty certain that she could make him leave his wife – probably glad for the excuse in fairness. Rose Judge was an absolute bitch. It was quite clear that he was a doormat by virtue of the fact that he had stayed with her for so long. Well, now James Judge the Second could be *her* doormat. It was then that Gillian realised where her real fight lay. Getting James to fall in love with her would be the easy part. Making Rose let go of him – that was where the work was. This was going to take some careful consideration, Gillian decided. They called her flight as she thought about her situation. Whatever way you looked at it, she had acquired another good card. There were any number of ways that she could play her hand. She had the next week to try and seduce Cameron Judge into marriage. If she was successful, she was quite sure that she could use her relationship with James to manipulate him into supporting the union. If she was unsuccessful, she would just settle for James. Either way she was determined to end up Gillian Judge.

James's good humour deflated instantly when Rose walked through the sliding doors of arrivals. She smiled and waved at him.

"Hello, James." She offered him her cheek to kiss. "What a beastly journey. Where's Paul?"

"Welcome home, Rose. The car is outside but I want to talk to you first."

Rose had left her luggage trolley beside James and started to walk towards the exit of the airport but he didn't move. She had gone ten paces before she realised that he wasn't following her.

"Well, come along, James. You're causing a traffic jam," she said impatiently.

"We have to talk," he repeated, moving the trolley out of the way.

"We can talk in the car."

"I'm not getting in the car until I've sorted this out."

Rose huffed loudly. "Really, James, you are being very tiresome. What is so urgent that it can't wait until I'm sitting down?"

"If you want to sit down we can sit, but I'm not leaving this airport until we talk."

Rose looked around, her face looking pained with enforced tolerance. She pointed to the seats beside the Arrivals entrance. The back row was empty.

"There?" she asked with mock concern. "Will that do you?"

He nodded by way of assent and pushed the trolley over to the seats. Then he sat down next to her. From out of his pocket he took the letter that Katie Garcia had sent him. He handed it to his wife, making sure to study her face as she looked at it.

"What's all this about, James?" she said, sounding annoyed as she opened the letter. "What is it?" she asked again impatiently as she scanned the contents.

"You know what it is, Rose. You wrote it."

She pointed at the letter, glaring at him. "*I* wrote it? That's *your* signature!"

"Rose, I didn't write it. And we both know you are well able to forge my signature."

"And am I the *only* person capable of doing so? What nonsense! Where in heaven's name did you get this? Have you been talking to *her* again? You gave me your word."

"You wrote it and you sent it to her thirty-five odd years ago, didn't you?"

"James, you're behaving like a child. I don't know what you're talking about." Rose scanned the letter again. "Oh God, you think

I sent her away?" Rose looked at her husband in horror. "James, are you that naïve? She wrote this! Can't you see that she's up to her old tricks again? She's deceiving you. She's trying to get back into your life and it's working, God help me!" Rose began to cry. "I leave you for one week, only because I think my son needs me on the other side of the world and when I get back here I discover that you've been back in touch with your old flame – because that's what she is, isn't she?" Rose stood up, her voice rising too. "She's poisoning your mind against me. This can't be happening."

Mothers nearby were covering children's ears and giving James dagger looks as he tried to placate his wife.

"Please sit down, Rose. People are staring." He took her hand and pulled her back into her seat. "Look, what you're saying could make sense," he offered.

"Do you honestly think that I would have just sat back and done nothing if I discovered that you had got another girl pregnant? I would have come straight to you, James. We would have fought like alley cats. I certainly wouldn't have let it go for – how long has it been?" She looked at the date of the letter. "1969. Dear Lord, we were newly-weds! Is that when you had your first affair, James?" Rose was practically shouting again.

He shook his head. "It's all in the past. I'm sorry. I shouldn't have shown it to you." He paused, at a loss as to how to proceed. "You're sure that you've never seen this letter before?"

"Of course I'm sure. What do you think?"

He said nothing but just shook his head.

"Well, it's obvious to me if not to you, James. She wrote it – probably in the last week or so and she has you eating out of her hand again. That's the bit that really upsets me."

"Don't be upset, Rose. I haven't spoken to her. This came in the post."

Rose searched her handbag for a tissue and, as she did so, she slipped the letter into her bag. "I haven't got a tissue. Do you?" she sobbed.

"No, sorry." James felt wretched for upsetting her so much. He obviously hadn't thought this through properly. "Come on out to the car," he suggested. "I'm sure Paul has some tissues."

"Yes," Rose sniffed as she got to her feet. "You're absolutely right, Paul will have tissues." She closed her bag tightly and placed it firmly under her arm.

CHAPTER 22

Samantha was relieved when Pablo insisted that she come and stay in their house. "Their" meaning his and Pedro's. Pablo explained that they lived together in a small house just a few kilometres outside Haro. He had also insisted that Pedro travel in her car so she didn't get lost.

She had to go back to the hotel to collect her bags and check out. The receptionist tried to charge her for having occupied the room for a few hours but Pedro fought her corner and no money changed hands.

"Thank you for that," Samantha said shyly as she opened her car door. He shrugged indifferently as he threw her case into the boot of the car and slammed it shut. It made her jump. She was a little shy around him. When he got in, he gestured for her to turn the car around. They were facing the wrong way. She nodded that she understood and then set about trying to manoeuvre the car in the tiny street. Somebody blasting their horn at her made her jump again just as she was in the middle of the road.

"*Ayeee!*" Pedro waved at the other driver. "This road, eets – how you say – you have to go zis way." He gestured in the direction that Sam had been pointing to begin with.

"You mean it's one-way?" she asked nervously. "Bloody brilliant! I'm trying to do a U-turn in a one-way road? Just bloody brilliant!" After a lot of gear-crunching and one stall, they were able to move off. He did that on purpose, Sam thought miserably to herself. He doesn't like me and, in fairness, who can blame him? I've come in and staked a claim on his father – my God, *his* father. Then she reminded herself that she had no real blood connection to Pablo. She was so conditioned to thinking of him as her father, albeit a distant father, that it was difficult to let go of the deeply engrained belief. The harsh reality was that there was no connection between the old man, Pablo Garcia, and her other than the fact that he had *acted* like a father to her for the first few years of her life. We weren't even related, she thought miserably as she drove along and waited to be told where to go.

"OK, you must turn zis way," he said pointing to the right. His voice was deep and without any warmth or friendliness. As they turned, Sam realised that they were obviously on the ring road around the little town of Haro.

The town centre was clearly very old with its impossibly narrow streets. The medieval-looking buildings that towered overhead seemed to compete for what little space there was. Now, however, the road was wide and open. They had turned onto a beautiful tree-lined avenue and it was not –

"Watch out, woman!" Pedro yelled, crashing into her thoughts as he grabbed the steering wheel and yanked it towards him in order to swerve the car back onto the right-hand side of the road. "Ziz is a two-way road," he explained.

She hadn't even seen the car coming towards them, she was so absorbed in her surroundings.

"I'm sorry, I completely forgot. When I turned right, I just pulled on to the left-hand side of the road through habit. Driving up here from Madrid was easy because the roads were motorway." She looked at Pedro, expecting to see a pensive scowl but he was grinning at her.

"Foolish woman," he said but he smirked as he said it. "Maybe I can drive, if you like. You are tired, yes?"

"Yes."

Delighted for someone to take the reins from her, she hopped out of the car and ran around the front to take his place in the passenger seat. He did the same only he walked around the back of the car. It struck her that he was avoiding her. Yep, this was a bad idea. She was severely intruding upon his life as well as nearly killing him, of course – thanks to her dangerous driving.

The rest of the journey was uneventful. Some minutes outside the town, Pedro took a left turn up a dirt track and eventually, after about a mile, he came to a gate. It was open but there was a letterbox next to it that said *Casa Garcia*. She pointed to the name.

"That means 'the house of Garcia'?" she asked.

He gave her a sort of a half nod where his face just jerked up but didn't come back down again. It appeared hostile to her but she took it for a begrudging yes.

The dirt lane they drove up was carved deep into the land. There were high banks of earth on either side of the road inhibiting her view of the landscape. On the top of the banks, however, she could see that vines grew on every spare inch of land. The narrow little lane wound around to the right but still she couldn't see what was ahead of them.

"Grapes," she announced gleefully in an effort to make conversation. She pointed up to the vines growing on the banks. He didn't react or respond to her in any way. It had probably been an incredibly stupid thing to say. Of course there were grapes everywhere. She knew that Pedro lived on a vineyard.

"When will these vines be harvested?" she asked, trying to sound a little more knowledgeable.

"Soon," he answered unhelpfully.

The man was boorish and not worth her effort, she decided, as the car bumped very severely over the potholes in the little lane. Within minutes they rounded another corner and the steep banks fell away as the land levelled off. There in front of her was an exquisite country house. It had not been what she was expecting at all.

The dirt track spread out in front of the building into a sort of parking area although it was really just scorched earth. The ground was an orange colour, she noticed with interest, which actually matched the house because the bright tiles on the roof were of a similar colour. It was larger than she anticipated too and altogether prettier. The walls were constructed with brown granite stonework and the woodwork around the window frames was painted deep green. There was no garden per se, just dried-out tufts of grass growing haphazardly around the parking area. There were a number of large fir trees offering something in the way of protection but as she got out of the car she realised that in every direction as far as the eye could see, there were vines – beautiful lush, full, ripe vines.

Pablo came out to greet them.

"What took you so long? You didn't get lost, my *cosa guapa?*"

Samantha smiled shyly at the man who thought he was her father. "What does '*cosa guapa*' mean?"

He winked at her. "Pretty thing," he said.

She blushed, "I was making such a mess of driving that Pedro took over. I'm finding it difficult to remember what side of the road I should be on." Pablo laughed as he walked towards her. "You will learn, Sami. You will learn." He hugged and kissed her again. "Welcome to our home. Come in, I will show you where you are sleeping. Are you tired? Do you want to have a small rest now?" She looked anxiously at Pedro who was removing her case from the boot.

"I hope I'm not putting anybody out by being here. I don't want to get in the way."

Pablo followed her gaze and called to Pedro. "We are happy to see Sami, are we not?" He spoke with authority. It was more of a challenge than a question.

Pedro looked up and forced an incredibly pained smile onto his face. *"Seguro que si,"* he said and he walked into the house with the case.

"That's a yes," Pablo whispered as they began to follow Pedro. When the younger man had gone inside, Pablo placed his arm around Sam's shoulders in a paternal manner and continued, "You must forgive him – he is not used to company. We lead a quiet life here and rarely have visitors." Then he laughed. "In fact you are the first visitor I think we have ever had. Pedro was an only child and his mother died when he was a baby so he is especially unused to female company. You will have to give him time."

Samantha thought about how comfortable that same young man had been with the girl in the bar back in Haro but decided to keep that to herself. If Pablo had a slightly rose-tinted view of Pedro, who was she to tarnish it?

"Your home is beautiful, Pablo. The vines look great."

"Great?" he asked with astonishment, his eyebrows getting lost somewhere under the baseball cap he wore. "Great?" he repeated incredulously. "These vines are not great. They are *perfecto, lucido* – how would you say, magnificent. Zey are without equal. Everybody in all of Rioja knows that Pablo Garcia," he slapped his own chest proudly, "*yo* – me – Pablo grows the most wonderful, sweet," he pursed his lips, "lushest vines in all of Spain."

Samantha bit her lip nervously. "Sorry, I'm sure they're the best grapes, er, vines anywhere."

He studied her face for a moment and then he laughed. "Don't worry, my leetle one. I will teach you the difference between a good and a bad vine over the next few weeks. You will know why and how your father grows such good wine before we are finished with you."

Weeks, she thought silently. She couldn't possibly take that much time away from work. She wasn't sure how long she was going to be around but she was pretty sure it wasn't going to be that long.

On entering the house she had to blink to get used to the darkness of the area. It was an open-plan arrangement. The floor was covered with dark red tiles. To the left, steps led down to a sitting area where a huge fireplace dominated one entire wall. A single sofa and two old armchairs furnished the place and in the centre was a low coffee table made of very dark wood. Beyond the seating area was a set of stairs leading to the bedrooms presumably

242

but it was to the right and down a corridor that Pablo walked. He gestured for her to follow him.

"This is where you will sleep," he explained as he guided her through a door.

It was a small, perfectly adequate room. The walls were painted a dull cream. They were bare but clean. She saw that there was a narrow wardrobe to the right and a bedside locker with a lamp. She had a single bed upon which Pedro had thrown her case. There was a window overlooking the side of the house. Her view was of huge fir trees beyond which she could see yet more vines. They were simply everywhere.

She turned to the old man. "This is more than I expected, Pablo," she enthused.

His eyes looked a little hurt then. "Why you not call me Papi?" he whispered.

It took Sam by surprise. She didn't realise that she had even made the change from Papi to Pablo. It felt strange, wrong even to call him Papi now that she knew he wasn't really her father. But she couldn't explain that to him. "I'm sorry, it's just been such a long time," she lied.

"I understand," he nodded a little sadly. "Perhaps with time, I can earn the name again." He looked at her hopefully.

It was at that exact moment that Samantha realised she could never ever tell him the truth. He was a good man and now an old man with his memories both sweet and sour. She would not take away one of his best memories with something as small and insignificant as the truth.

Pedro entered the room. "You will need these," he said, offering her bedsheets.

"Oh, thank you, Pedro," she smiled as she took them from him.

He gave her that half-nod again and left them.

"OK, we'll leave you to unpack and get comfortable," Pablo said as he clapped his hands together. "It's time for my walk. Every evening and every morning I have to walk around my vines to see how they are. Perhaps you can come with me tomorrow?"

"I would love that," she agreed.

"Good. I will walk now and you relax. We will eat around ten this evening if you like."

Samantha looked at her watch. It was after six already. "That sounds great," she agreed, happy to have some time to unpack properly and perhaps rest for an hour or so. She hadn't slept much the previous night in the Madrid hotel and she knew that the lovely lunch-time wine had only added to her exhaustion.

Pablo kissed her lightly on the cheek and took his leave.

Left alone, Sam looked around her little room again. She went over to her window and threw it open. She inhaled the fresh, pine-scented air deep into her lungs. If was better than champagne. It tasted cool, clean and invigorating. She admired the huge trees that towered over her, just some twenty feet away from her. Beyond them she could see the vines winding their way into the distance. The land slipped downwards then into a valley, the bottom of which she couldn't see. Her bedroom was at ground level and as such she didn't have the advantage of height from her position. "Later," she sighed contently. "Later, I'll explore." She felt like a little girl in a new playground. It was so beautiful and so different to anywhere she had ever been before. The best thing about it, she realised, was the fact that she was a lifetime away from Fiddler's Point and all that involved. Perhaps coming here was a good idea, she thought to herself, and hump Pedro Garcia.

She returned to her bed and pulled her case off. It dropped to the floor with a thud. Then she flopped onto the soft mattress herself. She looked at the ceiling and wondered what the next few days would bring. Then she fell asleep.

Rose Judge was exhausted by the time she got back to her beloved Dunross. The transatlantic flight hadn't been too tiresome because she was in first-class and she was adequately treated. It was her Oscar-winning performance with her husband that had taken it out of her.

She sat down at her dressing-table. The truth was she had been waiting for that particular boot to fall ever since Kathleen bloody Garcia had re-entered their lives. You didn't have to be a brain surgeon to figure it out. That greedy little money-grabbing slut was going to do anything in her power to get her nails back into James Judge. The surprise for Rose was actually *seeing* her letter again. Damn it, she had forged that note some thirty-five years ago. Would her past never let her go? Who the hell kept a letter for thirty-five years? It was just preposterous.

Rose studied her face in the gilt-edged mirror on her dressing-table. She reapplied her make-up and powdered her face. There were more lines showing than normal. Even after a glorious week in Barbados, the strain of her performance in front of James had taken it out of her. Next she tended to her hair. As the soft bristles spruced up her small curls, she thought about Cameron. The poor boy would be alone for the second week of his honeymoon. How dreadful was that? Well, there was nothing she could do about it now.

Rose was far more concerned about how close she had come to being discovered by her husband. If he realised she had written that letter, there was no telling what he would do. What she needed was a distraction. She stroked her hairbrush pensively as she let her mind wander. The antique silver brush and mirror set had been a birthday present from Granny Vic many decades previously.

Then she had a flash of inspiration. It was such a good idea she burst out laughing at her own brilliance.

"I know how to get this family back on track," she said to her own reflection. "I can sort out Cameron and James in one stroke and perhaps even redeem this family's reputation."

James joined his mother in the drawing-room for a pre-dinner drink while he let Rose get settled in again. Neither of his daughters had appeared yet which gave him some much-appreciated quiet time. Victoria was sitting next to the fire, contentedly sipping her sherry.

"Welcome home, James. I trust Rose is home and in one piece."

"Yes, yes, quite so. Everything is fine," he answered absently as he studied the bright orange flames dance up the chimney.

"Why so distracted, then?"

James looked at his mother. "Oh, Mum, you were always so good at reading peoples' minds."

She raised her eyebrows and spoke quietly. "Yours was always pretty easy to read, darling. What's the matter, James?"

"It's this ruddy letter I got last week."

"More inheritance tax problems?"

"No, no nothing like that. It was an old letter, very old as a matter of fact, about thirty-five years old to be exact and, well, the problem is — it's my signature on the bottom of it but I know I didn't write it, Mother. I just know I didn't."

"What is it about?"

James regarded his mother pensively. "I don't think I'm really at liberty to say just yet, Mum. It is rather personal."

She shrugged indifferently. "Not another illegitimate?" she sighed.

James looked at her sharply. "No, no, not quite that bad. It's just that I didn't write this bloody letter but it certainly looks like my signature."

"Well, if you didn't, who did?"

"That's just it. I rather assumed it was Rose. I had it out with her this evening at the airport and she quite clearly didn't write it. In fact, I really upset her with the accusation. Ruddy awful thing to do really, now that I think about it."

"Well, if it wasn't Rose, who else could have written it?"

"Mother, I'm damned if I know. It was so long ago, I barely remember who else was in our lives back then. Rose, I'm afraid, was the most likely candidate."

"Is it possible she was lying?"

"What? No. If you saw how upset she was!"

"Where is the letter now?"

James looked at his mother again. "She has it."

"Oh."

"Mother, you don't think she could have done it, surely?"

"Why don't you get the letter back and get it checked for fingerprints?"

"Good Lord, this isn't Hawaii 5 – 0!"

"Do you want to know or not?"

"Yes, of course I want to know. Somebody slandered me very badly and I would like to know who it was."

"Well, the first thing you'd better do is get that letter back." With that, Rose swept into the room. "Victoria, I've had the most splendid idea," she said. "Why don't we throw you a big party for your 95th? It's only next month so we need to make plans now. Wouldn't it be a wonderful way to cheer everybody up?"

Victoria looked at her daughter-in-law and smiled. "That sounds like great fun." Then she looked at James as if willing him to speak.

"Rose," he said, "that letter I showed you earlier, where is it? I need it."

"Oh, darling, I threw it in the fire. I didn't think you'd want it. I certainly don't want it anywhere near me." She shuddered as she readdressed Victoria. "It was such a beastly letter." Then she smiled. "Now, Victoria, let's make a list!"

CHAPTER 23

Before she was even fully awake, Sam was a little confused. The odd noise in her room was that of birds chirping. It was morning. Then she heard muffled voices. Two men were speaking in Spanish. She sat up in the bed suddenly as she remembered that she was in Spain, in Pablo's house.

Samantha threw off the blanket which covered her. She didn't remember pulling it over herself the previous evening. Pablo must have come into her room, perhaps trying to wake her for dinner. Or worse, Pedro may have been in her room. She blushed profusely at the thought. How embarrassing, she fumed to herself as she went to look out her window. The reason the birds were so loud was because she had slept with the windows wide open all night.

She couldn't believe she had slept so long. At what time had she fallen asleep? It had been ridiculously early. She glanced at her watch. It was eight o'clock in the morning. The view from her window had changed somewhat from the evening before but it was equally breathtaking. The sun had only peeped over the hills to the east but its beams managed to shine in through the low trunks of the great pines. The birds that had woken her were noisily fighting over grains and seed that were scattered on the ground between the thick trees. Something moving up in one of the pines caught her eye. It was a delightful little brown squirrel scampering up the trunk. "This place is magical," she whispered to herself.

Just then Pedro walked past her bedroom window.

"Good morning," he said sullenly.

"Hello," she answered shyly. "I'm sorry I slept so much."

He shrugged and was about to move on when she spoke again.

"Pedro, I'm sorry. I was wondering if you could tell me where the bathroom is. I mean, could I use the shower?"

Another shrug. "If you want. I will show you." He walked away. Sam found him very disconcerting. She wasn't sure but assumed that he was coming around to her bedroom door. A few moments later he arrived with Pablo in tow.

"Good morning, my little Sami! You were tired, no? Poor little thing." He kissed her on both cheeks and Pedro hovered behind. Pablo looked at them. "Well," he laughed. "Aren't you going to say hello to each other?"

"Hi, Pedro," Sammy forced herself to be chirpy.

"Ah, no," Pablo explained, "here we kiss hello and goodbye. It is so much more friendly and respectful."

Oh shit, Sam thought as she forced a smile. She stepped up to her would-be half-brother and kissed him on the cheek. He kissed her other cheek.

"Now, that's better," Pablo announced. "You had a fantastic sleep. Perhaps you want to go to the bathroom?" He shuffled off, obviously expecting her to follow.

Samantha risked a glance at Pedro. He looked positively mutinous. Christ, he hates me, she thought again.

After her shower and a change of clothes, Samantha went in search of Pablo. He was in the kitchen fixing a feast for her.

"Surely, you are hungry," he offered, smiling broadly at her.

Samantha noticed that he was wearing the same clothes as the day before. He had dark brown boot-type shoes that were caked in dry mud and a pair of faded black trousers with a black round-neck jumper. Under this he had a light blue, possibly denim shirt. Even in the house he still wore his baseball cap. It was also black with some sort of cigarette brand advertised on the front.

It was Pablo's face that Samantha was most struck by, however. Because she didn't remember him except through the eyes of a child, she hadn't really known what to expect. Obviously, it was the face of an older man than she had expected. But he looked a good twenty years older than James Judge, she realised. Surely they were more or less the same age? Pablo was in his sixties but he looked like he was approaching eighty. It was probably the outdoor life, she reasoned with herself. Pablo also had a definite grey tint under his olive skin. Was he ill? she wondered.

"Come, sit," he interrupted her thoughts. He had obviously gone to a lot of effort for her. The round table had been laid with a white tablecloth and he had laid out a fresh loaf of bread with meats and cheeses. How could she tell him that she was just a black-coffee-in-the-morning type of girl?

He came and sat with her, bringing with him a plate of small cakes and a large pot of strong black coffee.

"That smells great!" she said.

"Good. Drink." He filled the mug beside her with steaming freshly-brewed coffee. "You see, I have some very fine chorizo here for you. Iberian ham. You know eet is the best in the world!" Again he slapped his chest proudly. Samantha nodded and took a tiny morsel of meat.

Pablo looked aghast at her. "What is this? You must eat more. Zat is nozing."

Samantha looked at him and laughed. For an instant she was whisked back to Salthill when this same man was trying to get her to eat a fish finger. She suddenly remembered it very vividly. "This reminds me of when I was young," she explained but he already understood as he laughed too.

"Eet is so good to see you, my little Sami. I thought I would never see you again . . ." his voice trailed off as he reached over and tucked a stray strand of hair back behind her ear.

"And Enrique? How is my little son?" he asked with a mixture of pride and regret that wrenched at Samantha's heart.

"He's very good, Pablo," she smiled. "He's so big now. Bigger than Pedro, even. You know he is a gardener?"

"No! My boy, a gardener?" He removed his cap and combed his hand through his hair.

"Well, they call themselves landscape artists now so they can charge more money but basically it's the same thing. He loves it and I have to tell you he's very popular. I think he's pretty good at what he does."

"And what about you, my *cosa guapa*? What are you doing with your life? You are so beautiful and I see in your eyes how clever you are. Is your life full of love?"

The question caught her by surprise. Samantha had resolved on the plane journey over to Spain that she would *not* burden this man with her problems from home. She would not mention her fiasco of a wedding, the Judges, the state her mother was in – none of it. Who was she to bring that much grief into his life? She was a big girl now. That said, when he asked her about love she blinked at him, biting her lower lip. He opened his arms to hug her as she collapsed into tears and gratefully accepted his hug.

"Oh, Pablo, you can't imagine what a fool I am! Life is so complicated, it's horrible. I can't begin to tell you how bad it is," she gushed as if a floodgate had been opened.

"Eet's not necessary," he sighed as he stroked her beautiful long blonde curls. "I see it in your eyes, *chica*. I see your heart in your eyes."

On Sunday evening, Stephanie Judge was as giddy as a schoolgirl before her first date. She had tried on five different outfits, three of which were new, in preparation for the next day. It was going to be her first day at work – ever. She had scraped through her arts degree in UCD a million years earlier but then she had met David Neilson, got married and produced Zoë nine months later and that was that.

Her life had rotated around shopping really. This was something new. She had heard a lot of the mothers up in Zoë's school talking about going back to work just to keep their minds active. Perhaps that's what she needed, she reasoned. A little extra-curricular activity was just what the doctor ordered.

When David returned with the girls in the late afternoon she was more civil than usual. She offered him a pot of tea which to her amazement he accepted. They kept the conversation light and the choices of topic safe. David commented on Amy's progress.

"She seems to be growing up so fast. It's incredible, Steph, I'd swear she said 'Dada'."

Stephanie laughed at him. "No way, that's just wishful thinking," she teased. "You'll have to wait a little longer before she can talk."

"I'll wait for ever," he whispered but when Steph looked at him to figure if he was trying to say something to her, she saw that he was staring at the baby. David had always loved Amy more than herself or Zoë, she realised bitterly.

"Well, I'm starting a new job tomorrow," she finally announced.

You could have knocked David off the chair with a feather. "You're what?" he gasped.

"Yep, Dad offered me a job in the distillery. I really need to find something to occupy my days, David. Who knows, it might even lighten the financial burden on you eventually but don't hold your breath just yet. I'll probably be fired after the first week."

"No way, Steph. There are a million things you could do in that company. I think it's a great idea. I just didn't realise that you were considering it."

"I wasn't. Like I said, it was an offer out of the blue." She smiled weakly. "I may not be able to do anything in there. That's my greatest fear at the moment."

"Hey," David became animated, "who is it that knows exactly what department in BTs is shifting stock and when? *You* know if they change their prices even by the tiniest of margins. Stephanie, you can actually tell when they've changed their buyers," he said vehemently. "Remember the time you told me that you had sussed they had a new buyer in and she was making a shambles with her orders? You predicted that all her stock would have to be sold in sale. Well, were you right or were you right?"

Stephanie laughed and nodded. "But what good is that in a bloody distillery? Sure I know when paisley's in and faux-fur is out but I know nothing about whiskey!"

"You'd be amazed how much you really do know," he argued, "and anyway it's the tools of talent I'm talking about. You're good at details and I'm talking about minute details. You're a stickler for things."

Steph shot him a glare. It was one of things they often fought about – her obsession with the smaller details.

"You used to call me pernickety or picky," she said more harshly than she meant.

"And you called me vague and thick," he cut back equally acerbically. The truth was his laid-back, *laissez faire* attitude used to drive her nuts, as she thought it was lazy and haphazard.

They couldn't look at each other. The mellow and friendly vibe between them was lost and in its place the familiar chill of animosity had returned. It was what they were most used to these days.

"I'd better be going," he said, clapping his hands together in a subconscious effort to break the negative atmosphere.

"Thanks for the coffee," he added brightly as he kissed both his daughters goodbye.

"It was tea," Stephanie said sullenly. Would he ever notice anything?

"Oh yeah, right. Thanks for the tea, then." Would she ever chill on the small stuff?

David got into his car and waved at the three Neilson women. Stephanie held Amy and Zoë stood next to her in the little doorway of the farmhouse. He hadn't had the courage or strength to try to kiss Stephanie on the cheek. She wouldn't be a Neilson for much longer, anyway, he realised miserably as he started the car and waved one last time. She was really hell bent on the divorce. He forced himself to smile for the sake of his girls.

It was becoming clear to him now, anyway. She was simply a higher achiever than he. A brief week of separation and she was back out to work. Stephanie was too bright to sit on the sidelines and watch her life tick by. She was getting out there and doing something. Their lives had drifted apart and now they were most definitely heading in very different directions. He was going downhill and she was going up.

As he drove out the vast gates of Dunross, David had never felt so alone in all his life

Tess Delaney usually managed the household and Frank was happy to go along with that but this time she begged him to have a word with Luke. Something had to be done. The boy hadn't eaten in a week and he was becoming bony-looking. He was always a fair boy but now he had a hue of grey to his skin. The brothers had tried to have a go at him too, cajoling him into drink or a night out but Luke had been very harsh with them. Ordinarily they would have fought back but it was so out of character for Luke to be overtly hostile that both brothers backed off and left him alone. Frank was the only one left.

Mathew, Mark and the parents discussed it openly at the dinner table. It was just another meal which Luke wanted no part in.

"This can't go on," Tess fussed. "He has to eat."

"He has to bloody work," Mathew grumbled. The work load on the boat was the same no matter how many men were aboard so naturally it was easier when there were four instead of three.

"He's lovesick, but Jaysus, he has it bad," Mark agreed as he chomped on a succulent bit of hake.

"Frank, it's up to you now," Tess had said.

"Me? Sure I wouldn't know what to say."

"Well, we've all tried so you have to now," Tess explained.

He looked at her and at his other two sons who were collectively willing him to give it a go.

"You've nothing to lose," Mathew laughed.

"This is serious, Matty," his mother scolded him. Then she looked back at her husband and her tone softened again. "I need you, Frank. Will you do this for me? Will you try to reach our son?"

He nodded and put his knife and fork together, leaving them to their dinner in peace. The sooner he gave it a go, the better.

Frank knocked on the bedroom door. There was no reply. He peeped around the door and saw that Luke was lying on the bed, staring at the ceiling, and his hands clasped behind his head.

"Luke, son, can I have a word?"

No reply.

Tentatively, he came over and sat on the edge of Luke's bed. The room was cramped by the fact that it had to house three single beds. How the boys still put up with it Frank didn't know. Perhaps it was just what they were used to.

"Son, you have to try to snap out of this," he began.

Luke's eyes didn't even blink.

"I know you've been burnt badly. It must hurt you like hell but you have to go on living." Still no reaction. "You have your mother worried sick." Nothing.

"Your brothers miss you, especially on the boat."

Luke ignored him.

"You'll find another girl, eventually, if you look." Frank was running out of gems of wisdom. "I know you might not believe me now but it will get easier. It always does. I'm not saying it will go away altogether but I have to tell you, Luke, the best way to get over one love is to find another. Gillian was a fine –"

He stopped short as Luke sat bolt upright on the bed.

"Don't," he said menacingly, "don't even mention her name to me. You hear, Dad? Don't even utter a syllable of it. I never want to hear that – that woman's name again."

Frank was startled not only by the speed of his son's reactions but also by the violence. Luke was a peaceful sort, never given to tantrums in his childhood or even in his adolescence. And so Frank sighed deeply and didn't take it personally.

"Right so, I'm sorry, I didn't mean to upset you. It's just that we need you back, boy. Your mother, myself, your brothers. We want you back with us."

He waited for some more reaction but Luke had lain back down on the bed again and resumed his position with his hands behind his head.

"Look, will you at least come back to work? The boat needs four pairs of hands. It's very hard without you."

Luke knew this to be true.

"Tomorrow," he said. "I'll come back to work tomorrow."

This was more than Frank had hoped for.

"You'll need food if you're going to work. I have no room for sickness aboard the *The Ashling*."

Luke didn't answer; he just studied the ceiling.

"If I send sandwiches up to you, will you eat them? You have to eat if you're going to work," he repeated.

Nothing.

Frank took this for acceptance. He got up and walked to the bedroom door. But he turned back to his son before he left.

"It will get easier, Luke," he repeated himself softly. Then he closed the door gently.

Left alone again, Luke felt his heart aching even more. The pain was so intense he actually thought he was having a heart attack the first time it happened. That was just after he had walked out of Gillian's apartment and out of her life. Now he knew what that searing agony was. He simply had a broken heart – nothing more, nothing less. He knew his father was wrong about it becoming easier. Once something was broken in two, literally torn down the centre, it didn't just 'get better'. It didn't slowly heal and re-sew itself back up. All his love and possible happiness had bled away. There was nothing left inside him except the broken carcass of what used to be his heart. How it thumped into life on first seeing her! How it awoke with a mighty flash and now that was gone forever!

He didn't care about his mother's concerns and he cared less about his brothers. He was broken inside, in his very core, and nothing would ever fix him. Not now, not ever.

CHAPTER 24

"Welcome to Barbados!" Cameron walked towards Gillian, his arms outstretched.

She nearly fainted with desire. He was looking absolutely stunning after a week in the Caribbean sun. He wore a cream linen suit and the softest light-brown, suede moccasins. His skin colour was that of rich honey and his eyes and teeth looked all the more white because of the tan. She embraced him eagerly.

The airport was small and informal. Customs had been casual but strict enough. There was a ferocious racket as they walked out into the main parking lot.

"Sorry about this, darling. They've been extending this airport for as long as I can remember." He took her by the hand and waved to a car that was obviously waiting for his signal. A long shiny jet-black Merc purred up to them.

God, I love this man, Gillian thought. How could I possibly have been thinking about seducing his father when I could have him? He's worth the extra effort. So what if it's only thirty million and not one hundred?

Their driver appeared and took Gillian's cases from her, then she and Cameron settled themselves in the back of the car.

"Do you remember the last time we were in the back of a Merc together, darling?" Gillian teased.

Judging by Cameron's blank expression he obviously had no idea what she was talking about.

"Bill Boggan's car. Remember?"

He laughed and threw his head back. "Ah yes, now that was a pleasant ride! God, I've missed you!" He sighed as he let his eyes wander all over her body.

"Well, I'm here now. We have a whole week to enjoy each other." She squeezed his thigh and began to stroke his groin.

Cameron laughed. "Eh, not just yet." He watched the driver get back into the car. "We'll be at the hotel soon enough."

Although thrilled to see Cameron, Gillian was also utterly captivated by the Barbadian scenery.

After they passed through the bright and active little town of Bridgetown, the roads quickly became small and winding. The island was surprisingly hilly as they wound their way across it and some of the old houses were positively palatial.

"There was obviously landed gentry here a few hundred years ago," she said, admiring a particularly imposing-looking mansion.

"Oh yes," Cameron nodded. "The two big businesses to come out of Barbados are sugar and rum. They used Irish slaves for the sugar fields."

"No way!"

"Yes. You'll find more Murphys and Flanagans here than in Ireland."

"When was that?"

"The sixteen hundreds, I think," Cameron answered.

After watching miles and miles of the same vegetation, Gillian asked what the crop was.

"That's the sugar," he explained.

"It's beautiful – very green."

Cameron laughed. "If an American said that to you in Ireland you would think he was stating the obvious."

"That's not what I meant," she elbowed him gently. "I mean it's actually lime green. A very vibrant colour."

"That's probably how the Americans see Ireland. If you think it looks good now, you should see it just before it's harvested – bloody huge – about fifteen feet tall. It looks more like a forest than a crop. But the area that interests me most is their other large export."

"What, the rum?" she enquired.

He nodded. "Barbados rum is drunk the world over. I swear you can taste the sunshine in it, Gilly, and as luck would have it, there's a very interesting little distillery for sale at the moment."

She groaned loudly. "Don't tell me I've crossed halfway around the world only to be deserted by the pool while you go off to put some bloody business deal together, Cam?"

He laughed at her mock histrionics. "No, darling. It won't take up much of my time and it could interest you too, I'm sure. Come on, wouldn't it be fun to buy a distillery while we're out here?"

"Only if you're buying it for me," she said, smiling coquettishly at him.

Cameron kissed her nose and winked at her. Over my dead body, he thought, as he kept his face passive, over my dead body.

The Sandy Lane Hotel was all that she had hoped it would be. Security was tight at the huge black gates. Upon entering the building, she was descended upon by the concierge and two luggage-handlers who whisked her cases off to her suite without even bothering her.

Cameron excused himself to make a phone call regarding the distillery for sale so she grabbed a moment to look around her. The door she had walked in was obviously the main front entrance. A small group of attendants hovered nearby, ready to jump at her sideways glance but she studiously ignored them. She crossed the large bright reception area to a long balcony in front of her. On both her right and left, massive white marble staircases swept around and down to the lower area. There, seating was available in the form of enormous white-leather sofas and chairs. The highly-polished glass drinks tables glistened in the sunlight. The entire two-storey wall at the back of the hotel was made of glass. It made Gillian catch her breath for there, some fifty metres away, just beyond a small patio area was the most aquamarine, sparkling water she had ever seen. The sand was the palest brown colour and dark blue parasols gently flapped in the soft onshore sea breeze. "Truly, this is paradise," she sighed to herself.

Having travelled halfway around the world, Gillian hadn't expected to hear a soft Irish accent greet her. "Good afternoon, and welcome to Sandy Lane."

She swung around to see who had greeted her.

"My name is Deirdre. I am the day manager. If there is any way I can make your stay with us more comfortable, please don't hesitate to let me know."

"You're Irish," Gillian looked at the small, pert blonde who had addressed her.

"That I am," she beamed back. "Shannon School of Catering and proud of it! There are a lot of Irish working here, you'll find."

Gillian thought about this. Of course, the hotel was Irish-owned. They probably had a preference for Irish staff.

"Do you have many Irish guests?" she enquired.

"Oh, yes," Deirdre nodded. "A large percentage of our residents would be Irish and English but they really come from all over the world."

"Do you have many Irish here at the moment?" she asked, wondering how likely her hitherto private affair with Cameron was to hit the Irish gossip columns.

The day manager laughed. "No. Things are pretty quiet just now what with it being the hurricane season."

"The *what*?" Gillian dropped her Gucci handbag to the cool marble floor.

"Oh, yes. I'm afraid it's the hurricane season."

"But the weather is wonderful!" Gill protested.

Deirdre nodded in agreement. "It has been terrific for the last two weeks but the forecast isn't too good, I'm afraid. I gather we're due a bit of a blow later this afternoon."

"Oh, that's just great. I've come all this way for sunshine and you're telling me there's a 'blow' on the way!"

"They don't last long, madam. We call the rain here liquid sunshine. It usually downpours for a while and then the sun comes out again. It's great for the vegetation."

"I'm not here for the bloody vegetation. I was here for the dry kind of sunshine. We get enough of the wet stuff back in dear old Ireland."

Deirdre tried to cheer her newest guest. "Don't worry, they rarely last long."

"Are you telling me that a hurricane will pass quickly?"

"Oh, God, no. A hurricane will last for a day or so, maybe more. I was talking about the rainstorms. They only last for a few minutes."

Cameron returned. "Everything OK?"

Deirdre flashed another bright smile. "Here are your new keys, Mr Judge, and all your belongings have been transferred to your new suite as you requested."

"Thanks, Dee," he gave her one of his mouth-wateringly fine smiles.

Then he winked at Gillian. "I have a little surprise for you. We're in the honeymoon suite."

But Gillian was not for cheering up. "Wonderful," she said flatly. "It's bloody marvellous that we have a lovely room because there's a hurricane coming. We won't be doing much sunbathing."

"What?" he asked incredulously.

"You heard me. There's a hurricane coming."

Deirdre coughed lightly to interrupt. "It's not actually a hurricane, just a small storm. It'll pass soon enough," she tried.

But Gillian was not for consoling. "You never told me that it was the blooming hurricane season, Cameron!"

"Of course I didn't. If I told you that, you mightn't have come," he laughed as he squeezed her waist. As he led her away he added softly, "Now come on and remind me why I've missed you so much."

Samantha had spent a lovely day with her father, reminiscing about their time together in Galway and she filled him in on both Enrique and Kathleen. She saw the hurt in his eyes when he talked about Sam's mother. It looked very much to her like Pablo still had strong feelings for Katie Garcia. Would that be so strange, she wondered. Sam didn't have the nerve to ask him why he had left or why he had lost touch. It was too soon for that. Pedro had been absent for most of the day. Pablo explained that he was helping a neighbouring vineyard bring in their grape stock.

"Even on a Sunday? Do you guys never rest?"

The old man laughed. "The vines are a way of life here. They don't fit into a Monday to Friday lifestyle. When the grapes are ready, they are ready," he said simply. "Mine will be ready soon and when they need to be picked we will pick them, no matter what time of the day or what day of the week."

"Bloody demanding fruit," Samantha laughed. When she looked up at Pablo he was studying her face silently.

"You are very beautiful," he said quietly.

Samantha felt awkward. "Thanks," she murmured.

Then he slapped his leg loudly. "Come," he announced. "Eet is time you met my beauties, the great love of my life – my grapes." Then just as Pablo got to the door he stumbled slightly and almost fell over. He caught himself before he fell but Samantha had seen him and it gave her a start.

"Pablo, sit down." She put her arm around him and guided him back to the armchair that he had just risen from. "Are you dizzy?" He closed his eyes and breathed deeply for a moment but he shook his head at her by way of response.

"I'll get you a glass of water." She ran off into the kitchen and came back seconds later.

He had begun to compose himself, however. "Eet's all right, child. I'm fine now."

"What happened? Do you think you can walk?"

Pablo forced a smile. "I'm absolutely fine. I just stumbled on the carpet or something." He gestured to the perfectly flat mat that lay on the floor.

Samantha didn't believe it. "I don't think so, Pedro. Are you dizzy?"

He looked at her. "What are you now, a doctor?" he asked sharply. She felt like she had been summarily slapped on the wrist.

"Sorry," she whispered.

The old man's face softened as he nodded. "It's OK, *bonita*. I shouldn't have snapped at you but I don't need any doctor." Slowly Pablo rose to his feet but Samantha could see the effort it was costing him. Then he made himself smile at his daughter. "Come, we must see to the vines."

Dressed in jeans and a sweater, Sam was perfectly comfortable walking among the grapes with Pablo. She knew she was coming to a vineyard and as such she had brought her old boots. Much to her delight the climate was still considerably warmer than Ireland although not quite warm enough for a T-shirt.

Pablo explained how the region of the Rioja was broken into three areas: the Alta, the Alavesa and the Baja. They were in the Alta which was the highest part of the Rioja region and, as such, the last to be harvested. The other two Rioja areas had already, for the most part, had their harvests taken in. The word in the region was that this year's wine would be good. The summer had been long and hot and the grapes had grown well. Equally important, however, Pablo had explained, the previous winter had been very cold. Evidently this was good.

"Eef the winter is cold, the roots of the vine must fight for important nutrients," Pablo explained excitedly. He clenched his fists as if trying to capture the nutrients in his hands. "Eef the roots *fight* well," his eyes sparkled at the idea, "they become strong. Then the fruit will be good with very many flavour."

Samantha nodded, genuinely fascinated to learn about the vineyards. His enthusiasm was infectious.

Pablo glanced at her. "Eet's a little like life, I suppose. If you have to fight for something, eet is all the sweeter. No?"

She gave a half-grin, wondering if he was trying to tell her more than he was actually saying.

"Those mountains," he pointed to the distance, "they are the Sierra de Cantabira mountain range. They protect the vines from the winds and the rain of the Atlantic."

"Lucky vines," Samantha laughed but Pablo shrugged.

"Well, they protect us from the same winds. If you are here you are safe, my little one."

Samantha knew that it wouldn't take much to make her cry again but he was a wonderful source of comfort in her otherwise crazy world. She slipped her hand into his.

"Thanks, Pablo. I am very happy to be here. Thanks for taking me in so readily."

"For what?" His eyebrows disappeared somewhere under his cap again. "You are my daughter. I am so happy that you are here!" He kissed her on the forehead. "Now, come and meet my angels." From his back pocket, he retrieved something that looked like a secateurs. "Ziz is *corquetes*. Eet is what we use to cut the grapes off the vine. The wood is very strong." He took Samantha's hand and looked at her palm. Then he shook his head morosely. "I do not think you will be any help with the harvest," he sighed. "Skin like milk," he scoffed with mock disgust.

She laughed at the insult which she took as a compliment. "I could wear gloves!"

"We will see," he winked at her. "Now the lesson begins." He approached one of his vines and spoke to it softly in Spanish. He positively crooned to the plant as he tenderly turned over some of its leaves and examined them. He handled the large ripe bunches of grapes almost as if they were part of a woman's body and then he took out his *corquetes* and cut off a small bunch. Samantha was certain she heard him thank the plant before he left it. "This is a

Tempranillo," he held up the bunch. "See how dark the grapes are."
He plucked one off. "Taste," he commanded.

The sunkissed grape was bursting with flavour.

Pablo continued, "The Tempranillo is the main grape of the
Rioja region. It's a bold brave grape," he said proudly, "and makes
a good young wine. In fact, it makes even better wine with age,"
he shrugged happily, "maybe like me."

Samantha tried to remember all the details. They walked along
between the vines, occasionally stopping for Pablo to converse with
a particular plant or tend to its leaves. He explained how he and
many other small *bodegueros* – winemakers – supplied the larger
bodegas with their grape stock. He did not actually make wine on
the premises. That was a little too ambitious for him. Pablo's
interest was in being with the vines. He confided to his daughter
that he loved them as if they were his children. Plus, everybody
knew that Pablo Garcia's vines were the best in all of Rioja. Having
walked up and down several rows of vines, he stopped again. "You
see this is a different vine?"

Samantha was temporarily nonplussed. They were still red grapes
and, if the truth be known, they looked pretty darn similar to the
last set he had shown her. She nodded all the same.

"Ziz is the Mazuelo grape." He cut off another brunch. "Eet
produces very good tannins. Eet's a slightly wilder grape – how you
say – untamed. She is unpredictable, like a woman!" He laughed at
his own joke as he handed some grapes to Samantha. She tasted
them and to her surprise they did taste quite different. She also
noticed that the grapes were a slightly smaller size and definitely
blacker in colour.

"I see the difference," she enthused.

"Yes, but you must also taste and smell the difference." He held
the entire bunch to his nose and inhaled sharply, sniffing the aroma.
It was a little off-putting to Samantha but she did the same when
he handed her the bunch.

"These grapes are nearly ready for harvest," he said almost to
himself. "Soon."

"Won't you need to organise help?"

"I have Pedro. We will only need two or three more."

"It strikes me as a lot of grapes for only five people," Sam said with concern.

Pablo looked at her and laughed. "Eet is," he agreed. A further twenty minutes of talking to each other and the vines and Pablo introduced Samantha to his last type of vine. "Zis is ze Graciano," he smiled. "You see now that she is light in colour and fatter." He cut off another bunch of dark red grapes. "She is like ze mozer of the vines because these vines have been here for longer than me."

"How long have you been here?"

"Over thirty years."

Samantha's heart skipped a beat. He's been here since he left us, she realised with a jolt, but Pablo continued talking.

"The Graciano is producing a bright red must, going acidic. She has a very good bouquet. In fact she is the most fragrant of all my vines, the Graciano."

But Sam's mind had wandered. This was where Pablo had been all her life. Ever since leaving their home in Galway, he had been here. For some reason she had pictured him gallivanting off around the world or around Spain at least, but no, he had been in this incredibly peaceful corner of the world, tending to the same plants again and again, year in year out. How was it he could give so much love to plants and not to his own children, she wondered painfully. What did the grapes have that she didn't? Was it Pedro's mother? There were no photographs of her around the house – at least none that she had seen yet. Why did Pablo leave Galway? she wondered for the hundredth time that day.

As if reading her mind he gently wrapped his arm around her shoulders as they walked along side by side. This wasn't easily done as she was actually slightly taller than him.

"I know you have questions, Sami, and I will answer all of them for you as honestly as I can. But like the grapes, this will only happen in the fullness of time. You cannot ask the question before you are ready and the vine cannot produce the grape without the

266

passing of the seasons." He stopped walking and looked into his daughter's eyes. "Give it time, my *cosa guapa,* and everything will come good. Just give it time."

Samantha looked into his chocolate-brown eyes. The millions of lines on his face etched his features into a permanent smile. She forced herself to nod but she wasn't able to keep eye contact. Sam could ask all the questions she liked but that wouldn't help her sort out the horrible truth. She had been sleeping with her half-brother for the past few years and this wonderful man standing in front of her was not in fact, any blood relation of hers, much as she now wished he was. No, she realised miserably, nothing could help her not even Pablo.

CHAPTER 25

The atmosphere was extremely peaceful that evening at Casa Garcia and Samantha loved it like that. She hadn't even noticed until that night that Pablo had neither a radio nor a television. The day seemed to have raced by and yet Samantha wasn't sure how she had filled her time other than walking through the vines. That said, her legs were beginning to throb so she realised that she may have done more walking than she had thought.

"Do you not miss following the news?" she asked him, referring to the absence of a television.

"I spend most of my time out with the vines," he explained. "In the winter when they sleep, so do I," he laughed.

"You can't possibly sleep all winter," Samantha argued.

"No, zis is true. I like to read or I meet my friends in Haro. We have long lunches and talk about the old days," he explained.

Unlike the daytime, the evening had become quite a bit cooler and, after supper, at Pablo's suggestion she lit the fire. They both settled down with a bottle of red wine that had been produced with Pablo's grapes and they watched the flames grow strong and high as the evening began to close in.

It was easy for them to sit in companionable silence. She didn't feel the need to fill the air with hollow pointless chat. Nor, it appeared, did he. Samantha liked that. It was some time before she realised that he had in fact fallen asleep. Having finished her wine, she quietly got up and went to phone Wendy. It was only fair to keep her friend up to date on her movements. To avoid waking Pablo, she grabbed her Lainey Keogh wool jumper and headed out to the front of the house to phone her flatmate.

Wendy answered immediately.

"How the hell are you, girl?" she asked.

"Hi, Wendy. I'm fine, better than fine, actually."

"Where are you?"

"I'm in the most exquisite little vineyard in the north-east of Spain. I'm in a place called the Rioja. The evening is just closing in and it's getting dusky but I can still see pretty clearly. It's so beautiful, Wendy." Samantha wandered down the lane and away from the house as she spoke on the phone so Pablo would not hear her and awaken. The tall banks on either side of her gave her a feeling of privacy while she talked.

"Lucky you, it's bloody dark here already – the joys of living in dear old Ireland. Who are you with? Have you found Pablo?"

"Yes. He's in the house. I've come outside so I wouldn't wake him. He nodded off." She giggled despite herself.

"What time is it with you?"

Samantha looked at her watch. "It's only seven o'clock but we had a glass of wine and he nodded off."

"Are you pissed?" Wendy asked irreverently.

"Thanks a bunch. No, I'm not jarred. It's just been a heck of a couple of days. I have to tell you, it's lovely over here – really lovely. Pablo is absolutely adorable. He's a real wise old owl, if you know what I mean. I like him a lot."

"Any explanations why he bloody well walked out on you when you were a baby, then?" Wendy snapped.

That stung Samantha and so she didn't comment.

"Oh, Jesus, sorry, Sammy. That was really tactless of me. It's just that, well – I've been to Salthill."

"What? Do you mean you saw Mum? When you were there?"

"Well, see, Ricky came to visit yesterday morning. When he heard that you had gone out to Spain, he decided that he wanted to have another go at your mum. He dragged me along for moral support. I hope you don't mind."

Sam did mind. What the hell was Wendy doing visiting her mother? "Mind? Why should I mind? It's a free world. Did he get what he wanted – not that I can imagine what she can offer him at this stage?"

"She was in good shape, Sam." Wendy tried to sound upbeat. The reality was that Katie Garcia looked a thousand years old but she was sober. That was a really big deal. "She's still on the dry, Samantha."

"That won't last."

"She swears it will. She says she hasn't had a drop since that day in the church at your wedding and she's still in AA."

"What about Ricky? Did he check up on who his father is?" She immediately felt ashamed of her snide tone.

"Sam, Katie was absolutely adamant. Ricky is Pablo's son. You were the only – er –"

"Mistake," Sam finished Wendy's sentence for her.

"Samantha, she really wants to make up with you. I have to tell you her heart is broken over this whole thing."

"Well, excuse me if I don't shed a tear." Samantha was distracted by the distant sound of drumming hooves. As the little lane of Casa Garcia had many sharp bends, it was not possible to see what was coming down the track.

"Ricky does seem a lot better after his visit."

"Good for him," Samantha said but she was getting more distracted by the hoofbeats which were getting louder. The lane was very narrow. She glanced at the tall banks of earth on either side of the road. There was no chance of her climbing them they were so steep. "Look, Wendy, I have to go. Will you phone my office tomorrow, please? Tell them I'm on my mobile but I'm going to stay here for another week or so."

"Sure. We miss you, Sam. If there's anything I can do, just call me."

Samantha wasn't listening, however, for Pedro had just rounded the corner in front of her. He was galloping up the little dirt track on the most magnificent beast she had ever seen. The horse was a huge white animal, ears tight back against its head, steam visibly coming off its body. Pedro's coat billowed out behind him like a sail as he galloped towards her. His hat was pulled down fast on his head and the wide brim hid his eyes in its shadow. The thundering hooves now filled the air and terrified her. Manically she looked left and right. The banks on either side of her were just too steep to climb.

Like a deer in the headlights, Samantha froze. It was all happening so quickly.

"Sam!" Wendy called into her mobile.

Samantha couldn't move – literally to save her life. She shut her eyes and waited for impact – this was gonna hurt.

"Sammy?" Wendy called down the phone from Dublin.

In that instant, she heard the grinding of hooves and scraping on the dirt track. Her eyes flew open again to see Pedro standing up in the stirrups, using all his body strength to pull the mighty horse back into a sudden stop. The poor animal dug its front hooves into the dry mud and skidded as its enormous rear quarters struggled to maintain balance, halting all but on top of Samantha. She felt the warmth of the horse's breath steaming down on top of her head.

"What you doing? You crazy woman!" Pedro stormed as he dismounted in one fluid leap. "You want to get yourself killed?"

Samantha stared at him mutely.

"Why did you not move? Stand back?" he asked, genuinely amazed at her stupidity. Then he turned his attention to his horse. He crooned to it in soft, Spanish lilting tones and then he gently rubbed his hands down along the length of its front leg. The horse shuddered at his touch. Pedro soothed the animal with whispers. Then he examined the rear legs, again rubbing down from the massive hind quarters to the hooves. Sam guessed that he was

271

checking for injuries. After a moment he stood up and looked at Samantha once more, his face a mixture of incredulity and annoyance. "Crazy woman," he sighed as he shook his head and walked around her and off towards the house with his horse.

It was only then that she heard the distant voice on her phone.

"Sa-man-tha!"

"Yeah."

"What the hell is going on there? Are you OK?"

"I have to go now, Wendy. Just tell everybody I'm fine and I'll be home in about a week," she answered but her voice sounded vacant.

"Who were you talking to? Don't hang up. Are you OK? Is somebody with you?"

"Yeah. No. Pedro."

"Pedro? Who the hell is Pedro?"

Samantha hung up.

She followed the same path that Pedro and the horse had taken around the back of the house. She watched from a distance as they walked beyond the vines, to a small set of outbuildings that she had not even seen during her day of exploring with Pablo. As she approached, she could hear him talking to the horse. It whinnied in reply. She stopped before turning the corner that presumably would lead her into the yard and listened intently. Judging by the sound effects, Pedro had taken off the horse's saddle and was brushing the animal down. If only she could speak bloody Spanish, she thought in exasperation. She listened to his strong deep baritone voice. When he spoke to Sam, his voice was monotone and without much life. Now, however, the language sounded magical as his words rose and cascaded like a piece of music. Even though his voice was still deep it was warm and friendly. He must be smiling, she realised. Then the tone changed again. Pedro was obviously apologising to the horse for what had just happened to them. She didn't understand the words but the sentiment was coming through loud and clear. Something he had said to his animal made him laugh. She couldn't listen any more. She came around the corner and into his line of vision. As she had guessed he was brushing the horse down.

Pedro glared at her.

"I just wanted to say how truly sorry I am. That was a really stupid thing I did just there. I should have got out of the way. I – I froze."

Pedro stopped and looked at her for a moment. Then he granted her one of his half nods by way of accepting her apology.

"Anyway, I thought when you were being charged," she went on, determined to keep him talking, "you were meant to stand still as a statue."

This made Pedro laugh. "Where did you hear that?"

"I don't know. I think I read it somewhere."

"Is this for a bull too?" he asked but his eyes were smiling. He was laughing at her ignorance.

Samantha shrugged.

"I sink if something is charging at you – horse, bull, car – you get out of the way!" he said.

Samantha felt incredibly stupid. "Why were you going at such a pace?" she asked defensively.

He returned to the horse. "He likes it," he explained simply. "He knows we are almost home and he likes to gallop the last few hundred metres. The road is always deserted. We know it is safe – until now, that is." He began to brush the horse again.

Samantha was at a loss because she knew she was being dismissed and yet she didn't want to go.

"Can I help?" she offered.

"You know anything about horses?"

"I used to ride in Galway, when I was a little girl but it's been a long time."

He shrugged. "How can you help then?"

A little nervously, Samantha approached the massive animal. It towered over her. "She's a beauty."

Pedro smiled. "She's a he," he explained as he handed Sam the reins and continued to brush the horse down.

"Oh, sorry. What's his name?"

"Trueno."

"What?"

"Trueno," Pedro repeated. "It means, how do you say, the big noise in a bad storm. There eez a flash of light and zen a big sound."

"Thunder," Samantha realised, delighted to have figured out what he was talking about. "His name is Thunder."

"No, his name is Trueno. He will not understand that you are calling him if you say Zunder."

Samantha tried to get her mouth around Trueno which Pedro found very amusing. The 'r' sound was difficult. Pedro stopped brushing and concentrated on Samantha's face and particularly her lips.

"Tru," he said softly, encouraging her to purse her lips as he was doing.

She puckered up. "Tru."

"Eno," he said softly.

"Eno," she repeated. Then she tried again. "Trueno," she said, staring into the most captivating eyes she had ever seen in her life. The horse whinnied loudly and nuzzled her shoulder.

"You have it," Pedro smiled. "He understands you so your pronunciation is not so bad."

Samantha smiled broadly. At least she had won the horse over.

"He's a beautiful animal, Pedro. Have you had him long?"

"About five years now. He's an Andalusian – the best horses in the world."

"Of course," Samantha agreed, slightly tongue-in-cheek. "Spanish horses and Spanish wines are both the best in the world."

He had the good grace to smile bashfully. "Well, we think so. I am more interested in the horses than in the vines, to be true."

"I can see why. I don't think I have ever seen such a beautiful animal," Samantha admitted as she stroked the nose of the gentle giant. When she glanced at Pedro he was watching her intently.

"Neither have I," he agreed.

She felt a little awkward. He was talking about the horse, wasn't he? Then he turned away to fetch a horse blanket for Trueno. He threw it over the horse's back and tied the buckles to secure it. Then he took the reins from Samantha.

"Come," he said as he gestured for her to follow. Leading Trueno, they left the courtyard behind them and walked even further away from the main house. Darkness was beginning to fill the air but their eyes had become accustomed to it. The lane was narrow but there was just enough room for her and Pedro to walk side by side with Trueno between them. The horse was obviously tired as his head drooped down to their level. Samantha stroked his ear and massive cheekbone as she walked. Still the vines snaked along beside them.

Pedro looked at Samantha and then explained. "I want to breed Andalusians. That is what I would like to do with my life."

"What an amazing thing to do!" Samantha enthused.

"But I need more space. Eet is not possible to do it with these vines. They take up every inch of land around here." He waved his arm over his head as if to chase away an annoying fly. Samantha was surprised. She had assumed everybody in the region felt as passionately about the vines as Pedro did. How wrong could she be?

"Could you move away?" she suggested softly. "Perhaps go to Andalusia?"

He looked at her severely. "I cannot leave the farm. I cannot leave Pedro."

"That's not fair," Samantha became indignant. "He's a grown man and so are you. He can't expect you to mind him. You have to live your life and he his."

He stared at her for a moment as if weighing up the situation. Then he shrugged. "Perhaps in the future," he sighed just as the little laneway came to an abrupt end at a gate. Trueno's ears pricked up at the sight of the gate.

"This is what I took you down to see," Pedro explained as a second, slightly smaller Andalusian came galloping across the field to greet them. In the dusk, Samantha could see its glorious long mane flying back as it moved and the tail thrashing high in the air like a whip.

"Oh, Pedro, he's even more beautiful than Trueno. What an exquisite animal!"

Pedro laughed again. "That is Centella, only this time he's a she," he explained.

CHAPTER 26

James Judge was saddened but not very surprised to hear that Samantha was taking another week off work. He didn't blame her. If he was Sam, he might never come back. She had had to deal with quite a lot and a few days or indeed weeks off was just what she needed.

With Cameron still away, James was back at the helm of Judges' Distillery and he liked it. Ever since his retirement he had been at a loss to fill his days. A man needed a purpose and James didn't have one when he was away from Judges' Whiskey.

His greatest surprise of the week had been Stephanie's interest in and subsequent aptitude for the business. He took her through the entire company from the barley yard right through to the bottling plant. He personally walked her through the factory step by proud step.

"This is where the barley is malted," he began, as if talking to a tourist.

"But not smoked," she had teased him. "Dad, it may have been quite a while since my last visit but I do know how the company runs. I *am* your daughter," she laughed.

Every Judge was brainwashed from the age they could talk to

believe that smoking the barley was *wrong*. That was what the Scots did and the Irish most definitely did not. Moving on, Stephanie had been most impressed by the huge oak casks that guarded their precious nectar until it matured. She knew that the legal age of maturation in Ireland was three years but that some of Judges' Whiskeys matured for ten and twenty years, making it one of Ireland's most exclusive and refined whiskeys.

Having had the tour, Stephanie expressed an interest in seeing the offices. James took her through their substantial accounts department. There was a staff of ninety in the factory alone. So that involved a large cheque run as well as much book-keeping and administration. The marketing department, such as it was, involved only one girl. She had been Sam's secretary. Now she managed Judges' PR.

But, for some reason, the area Stephanie was most drawn to was Operations. She seemed intrigued by the actual nuts and bolts of the working of the company – how much barley was ordered, the sourcing and purchasing of the all-important water. Even budgeting for the gas to heat the company attracted her attention.

"It's all in the details," she explained simply to her father. "I just love details."

James couldn't believe it. Details had never bothered him much. He was more of a big-picture person himself. But Stephanie was hooked and that was good. Not only did it give her the lift she needed, it was also one department where it was a definite plus to have a Judge.

He looked at his calendar. It was Wednesday – three days since he had seen Gillian Johnston. He sighed. Three short days and three very long nights. He knew that he was behaving like a love-sick fool but if there was any way in hell of getting together with her he was going to jump at it with both hands. Of course nothing she had said gave him reason to believe that she would be interested in an actual relationship with him but he was damned if he wasn't going to at least try.

James got up and walked around his study. It had become dark outside and he had his office light on, so he was able to examine his reflection in his office window. He was not an unattractive chap. His figure was still trim when he stood tall. He knew that in his youth he had been a very attractive man. All you had to do was look at Cameron to see that but now even James had to concede that the grey hair was making him look older. He thought about those hair-darkening products that were on the market. Would it be wise to get rid of some of the grey? Surely a little help wouldn't be a bad idea? Damn it, women did it all the time, why shouldn't he give nature a helping hand?

"Dad?" Stephanie knocked on his door. "Are you busy?"

He swung around and came back to the moment in hand with a thud.

"No, darling. I was just thinking about heading home, actually. It's gone five o'clock."

"Is it that late?" Stephanie looked at her watch. "I had no idea. I have to get home. I promised Zoë I would help her with her homework. Look, there's just one thing I wanted to ask you about. Do you put your barley order out to tender yearly?"

"Good Lord, no." James looked horrified. "Obviously we use our own barley from Dunross but for the bulk of our needs we've been working with the same co-op of farmers for years, since Pa's day. Sometimes the suppliers change within the co-op but that's not our problem which is rather convenient."

"Eh, yeah, right, Dad. It's just that I made a few phone calls today anonymously and I found prices up to 40 per cent lower than what we're paying."

"As much as that? That's preposterous. I would assume the barley is seriously lacking in comparison to the stock we use," he said proudly.

"Daddy, it was the same farmers." She paused. "The very same barley."

"*What?* The robbing bastards!" James gazed at his daughter. "Well done, Steph. You've just earned your first year's salary. Good girl."

"Do I have your permission to take the co-op on tomorrow?"

"You certainly do."

"Great," she kissed her father on the cheek. "Now I really must dash. The girls will be expecting me."

James watched his daughter fly out the door. She was hardly recognisable as the miserable daughter he was used to seeing moping around Dunross. He had assumed he was going to give her a small back office from which she could call her friends and file her nails. It never occurred to him that Stephanie could be an actual asset to the company. Granny Victoria really was a wise old owl.

He returned to examining his reflection in his office window. It had got even darker and he could see himself quite clearly. He wondered what his mother would think if she knew that he was attempting to get involved with one of Samantha's bridesmaids.

"You bold boy, James," he said to his reflection, trying to mimic his mother's voice. "You bold, bold boy."

Like Stephanie, Marcus Haywood was also driving home to Dunross. Only, for him, things were getting more and more difficult at work. He knew that he was running out of time. He had been given a second written warning. Next time he failed to reach his targets, he would be fired. It was hardly his bloody fault, he fumed as he lit up another cigarette. The entire real-estate business was on its ass in the last six months. Marcus's sector was top-of-the-range commercial real estate and everybody knew that that was the first area to hurt when the economy slowed down a little. The really annoying part was that the other two agents had reached their targets. "Lucky bastards," he said aloud. He knew that real-estate was actually 90 per cent luck and 10 per cent talking the talk. He could sell as well as any of them – it was just that he had been given a list of bum leads for the last few weeks. That could hardly be classified as his fault.

The sooner he got married to Caroline the better. With her money he could set up his own real-estate company. He had it all figured out already.

"Haywood Homes," he said aloud. He even knew that the two Hs would have little roofs on them to make them look like houses. Everybody knew that the easy money was in residential and that's what he would specialise in. He wasn't just going to sell *houses*, he was going to sell *homes*. The profit margins were bigger. He could keep it ticking it over with the minimal amount of work. The rest of the time it was going to be easy street for Marcus Haywood. All he had to do was get Caroline to marry him. Recently he was getting more desperate and so after a particularly energetic romp with her the previous evening he had begun to talk about getting a little more serious. She had laughed at him. The bitch had actually laughed.

"Jesus, let's not worry about that for a few more years, Marcus," she said.

"I thought you would be pleased that I'm thinking this way, Caro. Most girls have to march their men up the aisle. I'm not proposing or anything like that!" He forced himself to laugh. "No, I was just wondering if you're taking this relationship as seriously as I am."

"No rush," she said. "Now, let's do that again."

It was always the same with Caroline. She just really wanted him for the sex. She was using him every bit as much as he was using her. "The bitch," he fumed to himself in the car.

He thought about asking her properly. What woman refuses a guy down on one knee with a cute little diamond in his hand? Marcus knew he could turn on the charm when he had to. Naturally he didn't have enough cash for a ring just at the moment. Perhaps if he could swipe something small belonging to Rose Judge? The old dear would hardly notice, she had so much bloody gold. If he could just get his hands on something insignificant and then hock it for a ring for Caroline. Then once they were married, the pressure would be off his bloody bank balance. The idea made Marcus feel a little better.

He pressed the button on his dashboard and the car filled with music. It was Dido, singing that she would go down with the ship.

281

Marcus pushed another button. "Not me!" he muttered, laughing bitterly. "I am not going down, not with any ship, sunshine!" The next station on his car radio blasted out a golden oldie about some woman having some guy's baby – barf. Again he moved the station on. "I don't think so," he laughed as he flicked onto a news station but then he began to think. He flicked back again to the crooner who was going on about what a wonderful way it was of her saying how much she loved him – double barf. But the idea really had merit.

"Why not?" he thought aloud. It would get her to slow down on the bloody drugs. It might tame her slightly and if she suddenly discovered she was pregnant, she might be more inclined towards matrimony. Marcus threw his cigarette out his car window and turned the song up. He tried to imagine Caroline pregnant. She was so thin it would probably suit her down to the ground. It would just look like she had swallowed a basketball. Of course a baby would mean another mouth to feed but then again it would be a Judge. "Jesus," he laughed aloud as he thought about Zoë and Amy. "The baby would get a trust fund, from Grandma and Grandpa. Why didn't I think of this earlier?" He switched the nauseating golden-oldie off. He also closed his car window because it was getting colder outside. Marcus pressed the accelerator to get home faster. If Caroline had an insatiable appetite for sex, he would give it to her morning, noon and night. All he had to do was puncture a few holes in her diaphragm. How hard was that? She would think she was perfectly safe but it would only be a matter of time before she became pregnant. Naturally Marcus would then do the honourable thing and take her as his wife and then he would take her for all she had.

"Marcus," he said to himself, "you're a genius."

Caroline Judge was delirious. She couldn't believe that she had, at last, finished her collection of paintings. It had been a long time coming but it was worth the wait. She was dying for Marcus to come home so she could show them to him. He would understand.

He was one of the few people who understood her work. Now that the collection of three was finished it also meant that she was well on her way to her first exhibition. She had spoken to the owner of The Blue Leaf Gallery in Dublin and they had provisionally invited her to be part of a 'New Talent' exhibition just before Christmas. That was provided she had six pieces of work to furnish them with. She was halfway there, already. She opened a bottle of champagne to celebrate. Then she took a line of coke, again just because it was a celebration. She knew that her boyfriend was right, she would have to think about cutting back – but not today.

Thankfully Marcus got home soon after.

"Darling, come upstairs!" she called from her studio. "I'm finished and I want to know what you think!"

He braced himself. He had never really been able to make head or tail out of her work and so he had to psych himself up for a large amount of bullshit now.

He mounted the steps to her private room. She didn't like him to come up there uninvited and that suited him perfectly as he had no real desire to go anywhere near her weird art.

"Great," he enthused. "Now, you'll have to talk me through it. You know I'm a mere mortal and I need your spin on it."

"Well, firstly it's a collection of three paintings. You have to look at them in a certain order."

"Whatever you say," he smiled and kissed her hello. It cheered him to see her animated. Caroline's eyes danced with so much excitement that she looked like a little girl.

She took him by the hand and guided him to sit down. He did as he was bid. It was the only chair in the studio and he noticed that it had been painted white since his last visit. The wood-panelled flooring and the walls were also painted white so the room was very bright but severe too. There were two sets of windows on each of the two walls which meant an enormous amount of light streamed in during the day, especially since Caroline had ripped down the Laura Ashley curtains that her mother had had made especially for the room.

About fifteen feet in front of him were three large canvases measuring about four foot by four each. Caroline had obviously turned then around so he could only see the backs.

"You have to look at them in the correct order for this to work properly. OK?"

"Whatever you say, angel." Marcus was in particularly good form since he had come up with his new master plan. After he had humoured her sufficiently here, he would go to the bathroom and pierce a few holes in her diaphragm. Life was going to be just tickety-boo.

Caroline turned her first painting around.

"I call this Shepherd's Delight," she explained.

Marcus stared at it for a moment – unblinking. It was probably the most beautiful painting of a sunset he had ever seen. The top of the picture was a deep crimson red and ever so gradually, almost imperceptibly, it transmuted into a fiery orange which in turn faded into a translucent yellow. "My God, Caroline . . ." He tried to stand.

"No, no, you have to stay sitting. I haven't finished yet."

Marcus sat back down again. "But that is quite simply amazing. It's gorgeous, Caro. The colours, the warmth. You've really captured the moment. It looks like a photograph only I've never really seen a sunset that beautiful."

For once, he was being genuinely honest with her about her work. Somehow Caroline had managed to create a sunset even more vibrant and stunning than the real thing. It had more impact than a photograph and was more colourful than a genuine sunset. It was a little like a sunset on speed he realised. It probably was.

"What did you say it was called again?"

"Well, you see, that's the point. It's called Shepherd's Delight because of the old saying. You must have heard it: *Red sky at night – shepherd's delight*. It's superstition – people say if the sky is red at night, the next day will have good weather."

"You and your superstition," Marcus laughed. "Now let me see the next one – it couldn't be more beautiful than that."

Caroline giggled. "I call this one Shepherd's Warning," she explained as she turned the second canvas around.

Marcus studied it for a moment and then he looked at her, confusion across his face.

"What the hell's going on? It's a mirror image of the last one. Are you taking the piss?"

"No," she explained. "That's just the point. The image is identical but now it's Shepherd's Warning because the expression has a second part. As I told you – *Red sky at night is the shepherd's delight, but red sky in the morning is the shepherd's warning.* It means if you see a red sky in the morning the weather's going to be awful." Caroline stopped and looked at her boyfriend, willing him to understand. "Do you get it?" She asked impatiently. "What I'm trying to get at is the fact that the same thing can look brilliant at one time and dreadful at another. It just depends on where you, the viewer, are – you know, were you're at in your head and in the universe."

Marcus tried to look convinced. "Oh, yeah, right. Cool. It's still an amazing painting, Caro. Jesus, the colours!" He knew he was repeating himself, but he didn't know what else to say. "How did you get the two paintings to look so bloody alike?"

"That was easy. I just painted one long canvas and then I cut it in two."

Marcus winced. "Brave girl. I wouldn't fancy cutting up any of your art. It's amazing, Caroline. You really have something here. Let me see number three."

She turned around her last canvas. "I call this one Shepherd's Pie," she said and waited for Marcus's reaction. He had to squint to see what was in the centre of the canvas because it was very small, but there it was – a small packet of Knorr Shepherd's Pie mix. Around it Caroline had painted borders of all the colours of the rainbow.

"OK, now you really are taking the piss, Caro. You've stuck a supermarket packet of Shepherd's Pie onto a canvas. You hardly think anyone is going to call that art?" he asked incredulously.

"Philistine!" she snarled. "You're not looking at it in the context of the other two paintings. I'm trying to show the unpredictability of life – its uncertainty." She tired to explain by waving her arms in the air manically. "You see Shepherd's Delight, then you see

Shepherd's Warning and you're thinking 'shepherd's' but you're also thinking the elements and nature but it actually ends up being one of the most dependable and staple family dinners in the country – Shepherd's Pie." Caroline raised her hands in the air as if her explanation made perfect sense.

Marcus plastered on a broad smile. One thing he was certain of, his girlfriend was either a raving lunatic who should be locked up or else he was going out with the next big thing in the art world.

CHAPTER 27

Samantha spent the next few days working harder than she had ever done in her life before. When she got back to Casa Garcia on the Thursday evening, she was absolutely exhausted. This was not the kind of 'exercising all day' or the 'shop till you drop' fatigue that she had suffered from in the past. It was a deep-down mental and physical thing, one so profound that she genuinely wondered if she would ever feel good again. If Pablo hadn't said it was time to stop when he did, she really thought she might have collapsed. Samantha flopped down onto one of the armchairs by the fire. For three days now she had helped them bring in the harvest.

It was Monday evening when Pablo had said that the time was right. The grapes were ready. Naturally she had offered to help in any way that she could. Little did she know what she had let herself in for. For the last three mornings Pablo had rapped on her bedroom door at six o'clock. They were in the fields before seven and the work had been gruelling. Pablo had hired a few other farmhands to help them out but it was quite clear to Samantha that Pablo and Pedro were doing the lion's share. She had wanted to prove herself to them. She wanted to show them just how hard she could work. Samantha knew that she could be tough and knuckle down when the need arose but she now realised that she had no concept of hard work until that week.

On the first morning she had great difficulty with the *corquetes*. They felt awkward and clumsy in her hands. She kept nicking her own skin with them as she tried to cut the surprisingly tough vines. Pedro had tried to help her. Sam was quietly cursing to herself as she tried to get a particular bunch of grapes off the bloody vine. She didn't hear him coming up behind her. Pedro placed his hand on hers to show her how to use the instrument properly but Sam jumped in surprise and accidentally banged her head into his chin.

"Oh God, I'm sorry!" She rubbed her head as he rubbed his chin.

"Eet's OK. I shouldn't have crept up on you like that," he smiled.

Was it her imagination or was he warming to her slightly, she wondered. Perhaps it was because she was making an effort to get involved and help out?

"I can't quite get the hang of this bloody yoke," she explained, examining the *corquetes* as if that was going to make it easier to understand.

Pedro had gently turned her around again to face the vine. He stretched his arm over her shoulder and along the length of her own arm. Samantha knew it was utterly ridiculous but she found it very exhilarating to be so close to him. He smelt of ozone and fresh air – clean and invigorating. She could feel the warmth of his body even though there was still a nip in the air and she herself was wrapped up in a fleece. Pedro put his hand on top of hers and guided her to a large bunch of ripe grapes.

"You must know where to cut the stalk," he explained. He brought his other hand around her body and gently took her left hand. He guided her to softly hold the bunch so they wouldn't fall when separated from the vine.

Wrapped in his arms, however, Samantha was definitely not concentrating as much as she should have been on the vines.

"Cut." Pedro appeared to effortlessly snip the stalk and the huge bunch of grapes plopped into his and her left hand. She turned to look at his face which was inches away from hers. He glanced at her and smiled. It was a friendly, boy-next-door smile. It was quite clear that he was not feeling the same electricity that she did.

But, then, how could he when he thought she was his sister?

"Easy," he explained as he pulled back from her and tossed the grapes gently into the wicker basket next to them.

"Easy for you perhaps," she sniffed, angry with herself for her own immaturity.

Pedro laughed. "Well, what did you expect? It is only your first day. I have been doing this for all my life. It will take you a few years to become a master harvester."

"Ha," she commented as she examined his neat cut on the vine, "I don't think I'll be around here that long, Pedro. I wouldn't have the patience." She turned to look at him as she spoke but his face had soured and then he walked away.

As she looked at the unlit fire now she felt her muscles solidify in protest against the amount of physical labour she was making them do. She wondered about that first morning. Had he taken offence at her comment that she wouldn't be hanging around? Or did he just not like her? Why was she so bloody bothered anyway? she silently raged at herself. She rose to light the fire as the men walked into the house.

"Sami, I think we will be finished tomorrow. That is good news, no?" Pablo asked with a twinkle in his eye. Pedro walked on through to the kitchen without even acknowledging her. He was either cross with her or totally oblivious to her existence.

Samantha looked at the man who thought he was her father.

"To be honest, it is good news, Pablo. I had no idea how much work it was. You are obviously a very fit bunch. I'm whacked." She set a match to the fire.

Pablo began to laugh at her but suddenly, in doing so, he swayed and to her horror stumbled and fell. There was an almighty clatter as he took a small coffee table with him.

Pedro came running back into the room. He lifted the old man up and placed him gently onto a seat.

"Pablo, are you OK?" Sam asked, despite the fact he was clearly anything but OK.

Pedro spoke to him urgently but in soothing tones in Spanish.

"*Agua,*" Pablo grumbled as he caught his breath.

Samantha rushed to the kitchen, all thoughts of fatigue truly vanquished. This was ridiculous, she thought. That man shouldn't be in the fields and he definitely needs to see a doctor. His balance was most certainly off and he was looking weak. In an instant she was back. Pedro had got the old man settled into the armchair. He wrapped his strong young arms around Pablo as if trying to placate him.

"Look, I really think you need to see a doctor, Pablo," Samantha said, a little more sharply than she intended.

Pablo was focusing on his breathing but he still managed to look up at her and give her a withering stare. It was the most aggressive gesture she had ever seen him make. It made her shiver. Obviously he wasn't into doctors. Pedro spoke in rapid Spanish to Pablo but the old man just shook his head vehemently and glanced again at Samantha. They're arguing about me, she realised.

"What are you saying? I know it's got to do with me."

Pedro looked at her. Again there was a rushed conversation between the two men in fluent and fast Spanish.

"Eet is over. I am fine – see?" Pablo forced a smile.

"Eet is most certainly not over," Pedro snapped as he stood up and left the room.

Samantha stared at the old man, wanting to believe him, but her gut instinct told her that Pablo was holding back.

"Why won't you tell me? What can be so bad?" she asked but Pablo had regained his self-composure and was smiling reassuringly at her.

"I am a tired old man, Sami, and I hate doctors. Is that so bad?"

She came and sat on the arm of his chair. "No, Papi, that is not so bad but I do think maybe you need medicine."

The old man looked up at her with a broad smile and watery eyes. "You called me Papi," he whispered.

Samantha was as surprised as he was. She leaned over to give him a hug. "So I did, Papi. I don't know why. It just felt right."

It was some minutes later when Pedro stormed back into the room with his long coat on. The hob-nail boots click-clacked on the tiles. "I am going out," he said simply as he pulled his hat on. Pablo nodded in resignation and there the conversation ended as Pedro stomped out the door.

Samantha was horrified. They had worked so amiably together side by side all day. Pedro kept the fact that he didn't really like the vines totally to himself. He worked hard and appeared to be as happy on the land as the old man was. They didn't look particularly similar but both men had the same olive skin and broad smile. She had become very fond of Pablo. Pedro was a slightly different and confusing matter.

Samantha went off to prepare the evening meal. The house seemed quieter without Pedro about. That in itself was strange because he wasn't exactly a huge conversationalist.

"Let us eat by the fire, tonight," Pablo suggested when she came in to tell him that their dinner was ready.

Soon they were both sitting down by a lovely big fire with their plates of chicken stew and spuds on their laps.

"Pedro is cross with me," Pablo said eventually.

"I know. It's because you won't go to a doctor."

"Why can't an old man be left in peace?" Pablo grumbled.

Again Sam was struck by how tired and weathered he looked. She decided to change the subject.

"Tell me about his mother," she said gently.

"Lydia?" Pablo smiled. "Oh, she was a wonderful woman."

Samantha felt a tide of jealousy rise within. "Did you meet her after you came back here?"

Pablo looked puzzled. "No, I knew her long before that!"

"Before Mum?"

"Why, of course, all my life! Lydia lived here and Pedro was born here."

"But Pablo, what are you saying?" Samantha looked appalled. "Do you mean that you had Pedro before you met with Mum?"

Pablo looked confused and then a dawning realisation set upon his face. "Oh, my *cosa guapa*," he laughed. "Pedro is not my son. Bueno, he is, but not by blood. Actually he is my blood but he is not my actual son."

"What the heck are you saying, Papi?"

"Pedro is the son of my sister and brother-in-law. But I have taken care of him since he was little so he has always been like a son to me."

"But you told me he was my brother!" She was indignant.

"Did I?" Pablo looked shocked. "Ah, that was the day I met you in Haro! Sami, I hadn't spoken English in thirty years. Also I was so excited at seeing you. Pedro is your cousin not your brother but my English was so rusty I must have used the wrong word." Pablo shrugged. "But surely you see him like a brother now?"

"Yes, no. God, I don't know, but Papi you cannot just go around saying people are my half-brothers when they're actually my cousins." Then a thought struck her. "So what is his name then?"

"Pedro Martinez Garcia!"

"What?" Sam was confused. "His name is Garcia, like yours?"

Pablo nodded. "Yes – but not exactly – in Spain a child is given two family names, first the father's, then the mother's! My full name is Pablo Garcia Lopez but of course in Ireland, because of your custom there, I only used one – my father's name – Garcia."

"So, by Spanish custom, I should be called Samantha Garcia White?"

"That is correct."

Samantha sighed. "I feel I don't know who I am any more."

"You are my little Sami! Come, let's have more wine!"

As Samantha filled their glasses with a full-bodied red that had warmed by the fire, Pablo broached another subject.

"Sami, I am so happy that you have come to see me and I must say you are welcome to stay here for as long as you like but I have to wonder in my *curazon*, in my heart," he made a fist of his hand and gently hit his chest, "are you OK, my *cosa guapa*? Is there something I can help with you?"

She looked at him. He was a lovely old man but he couldn't help her.

"Life had just become a little crazy in Ireland, Papi. I have been working so hard and striving for what I thought I wanted but I am not happy so I had to get away and try and regain my perspective. Does that make sense?"

He laughed, "But of course. It makes perfect sense. You know, if you want to be happy," he leaned forward to stress his point, "travel light through life."

"What?"

"If you want to fly, girl, travel light through life. Everybody spends so much time working in order to have more possessions. It is zeez possessions that make them sad. Then you are worried about how to keep everything safe. All that matters is your heart and your happiness. Travel light through life and you will be OK."

Samantha thought about her precious BMW sitting in the long-term carpark in Dublin. Doubtless it was racking up a horrendous debt in parking fees. She thought about her extensive designer wardrobe and her essential D4 address. It was all very well to sit there in the heart of the Rioja and agree about the madness of materialism but it was a different story in dear old Dublin. She thought about her friend Gillian's favourite expression: "Anything but Jimmy Choo, just won't do." It made Sam smile.

"I hear you, Papi, but life can get a little more complicated than that."

Pablo shrugged. "It needn't," he said simply. "Look at Pedro."

"Yes," she agreed but of course she knew that he wasn't happy. Pablo didn't know about his deep wish to breed Andalusians.

"I know about the horses," Papi said with a raised eyebrow as if reading her mind. His eyes sparkled as he looked at Samantha "And I am thinking you know too."

"Gosh, eh," she stuttered, unwilling to say too much.

"Eet's OK − he has told me all about them. Every man must follow his dream. We have talked about it, Pedro and me."

"What will he do?"

"When I am gone, he will sell the vineyard and move to Andalusia with his horses."

"What do you mean when you are gone? Sure you'll be around for years and years yet, Papi? Why don't you just let him go now?"

Pablo stared at her for an instant, then he continued. "You don't understand. This is his house and land. I lived with my sister and little Pedro when he was a baby because I had no money and nowhere to live when I returned from Ireland."

Samantha felt a terrible wave of guilt. It had never occurred to her that he could be broke. Jesus, she hadn't even offered to pay her way since she arrived!

"It never occurred to me that it wasn't yours," she said. "Especially as it's called Casa Garcia."

"My brother-in-law named it after my sister when he bought it. He loved her very much. Then he died the year before I returned, just after his son was born."

"How did he die so young?"

A shadow crossed Pablo's face. "It was a stupid car accident – so unnecessary."

"I'm sorry," Samantha murmured.

For the second time since Sam had met Pablo, she witnessed him take off his cap. His hair seemed very thin on top but still he combed what little there was back with his hand. She knew it was a nervous reaction. Perhaps this conversation was too stressful for him to have, she realised, but he continued of his own accord. "Lydia needed help with the vines. I needed a place to stay and so it made sense. Actually you are in my old room," he chuckled as his mood began to lift again. "Anyway, when Lydia became sick it was the obvious solution that I would stay and mind Pedro as my own. We would live here together but it has always been in his name. I just stay here as his guest."

"I think you're a little more than that, Papi." Then she continued softly. "How did Lydia die? She must have been very young." Pablo looked at the floor miserably. "She was far too young but she had a broken heart. The doctors say it was cancer, but I think it was a broken heart."

Samantha hated to see Pablo so sad. "Papi, you have been like a father to Pedro. He's lucky to have had you."

"Well, the fact remains that he wants to breed horses. He is being kind to me, letting me keep the vines."

"Gosh, I see the problem."

Pablo sighed a deep melancholy sigh. "Eet's not a big problem, Sami. You see I am not well."

"What?"

"I am sick, Sami," he said softly but the words punched her in the face. It wasn't what he had said as much as how he had said it that made her realise the significance. Pablo was more than sick. Four little words and her body began to tremble. Now she knew why he didn't want a doctor. Now she knew why he had a slightly grey pallor. Now she knew why Pedro wouldn't leave him to go and breed horses in Andalusia.

"What is it?" she whispered.

"What does it matter?" he shrugged but then he looked at her and saw the piercing pain in her eyes. Samantha needed answers. For too long she had been denied that.

"Last year I have a stroke."

"Ohmigod, Papi!"

He raised his hands in the air to stop her fussing.

"Eet's OK. Look at me, I am alive. I am lucky. Many men my age have strokes and they cannot walk or talk after. I can still live life!" Then the old man sighed and his shoulders sank a little more. "But Pedro thinks I do too much."

Samantha became indignant. "He's right. My God, when I think of the days you have been putting in. Papi, you should be resting."

"Now zat would be stupid, I say. You must *live* when you are alive," he argued. "But when I get tired, I slip a little."

"You mean you lose your balance?"

Pablo shrugged. "I just want to live my life as I choose."

"Are you on medication?" she asked, her voice full of concern but again Pablo waved her talk away with an impatient hand.

Then he reached for his cigarettes and lit up. "What is life with all medicine and no wine or cigarettes? Eet's like you are dead already," he grumbled.

Samantha realised that he was very much on borrowed time. She clenched her fists. Suddenly it all made perfect sense. A stroke would explain why he had aged so drastically. In the next instant, the tears were freefalling down Samantha's face as she rushed to hug him.

"I don't believe this. I have only found you and now you are telling me that you are ill, Papi. There must be something we can do. There has to be a way to help you."

As she knelt at his feet, Pablo hugged Samantha but his voice was firm and stronger now. "This is life, my *cosa guapa*, and you must understand that I am not going to spend my old age searching like some crazy man for a miracle. I am going to enjoy the time I have left until God calls me and that is that but hopefully not for some years yet!"

"Why didn't you tell me sooner?"

"I did not even want to tell you now, but Pedro has made me. He told me that if I did not tell you tonight, he was going to tell you when he came home."

"Is that why he has gone out?"

"Yes. He thinks you have earned the right to know. I was hoping that maybe I could send you back to Ireland happy with your time here and perhaps you wouldn't have discovered for a few years."

"But how could that have happened, Papi? Do you think I am just going leave you again and not even bother to stay in touch? I would phone regularly and write and come and visit you again and again."

Pablo looked at his daughter. "Life is funny. Eet is very good that you are here but maybe when you go back to Ireland your life goes fast again and you forget about us."

"How could I forget about you?" Then a new wave of tears

assaulted her. "But I can't believe you mightn't be here! Oh, Papi, this is too big to take in. We have to tell Ricky and Mum."

"No," Pablo's voice was strong again. "I do not want to suddenly start meeting people who I do not even know. Let them get on with their lives. They are not part of mine."

"Nor was I up until this week."

"But you came of your own accord, not because you were told that I was ill," he explained reasonably. "Now you are part of my life. I am still sad that I had to tell you but maybe it is better this way."

Sam became indignant. "Pedro was absolutely right. If you had not told me and I went back to Ireland ignorant, think how crushed I would have been to discover after —" she couldn't finish her sentence. "I still can't believe this."

He cupped her face in his hands. "Sami, I must ask you one thing."

"Of course, anything."

Pablo continued. "Even if you do not stay here, can you please keep an eye on Pedro for me? I think he will follow his heart and sell the farm so he can move to Andalusia with his horses. That is good and I am glad that he is following his dream but can you look out for him because, after I am gone, you will be the only family he has."

Samantha nodded mutely. She couldn't tell him the truth even though he was dying. Surely it would destroy him to discover that she was not in fact his daughter. The dreadful sad truth was that after Pablo died, Pedro would have no family.

CHAPTER 28

Even if Pablo had wanted to keep it a secret he couldn't have because once the grapes were in, he had another minor stroke. It was almost as if his body was hanging on till then before he finally gave in. Finally a doctor was permitted into Casa Garcia. He claimed that it was the physical exertion of the actual harvest that had affected Pablo so badly.

The old man simply laughed. "Zat is what I was living for. It would have been stupid to sit back and watch the others do it."

Eventually Samantha was obliged to phone the office. She had to talk to James. She didn't really want to speak to the man who she now saw as her fake father but she didn't have any choice.

"Take as long as you want," James said. "You deserve a little time out." Delighted to hear from her, he proceeded to fill her in on life at Judges'. Cameron was due back to the office in a matter of days, Steph was the discovery of the year and Gracias was, as always, booming, practically selling itself. As per Sam's request, her second in command had moved into the role of general manager in her absence. Gracias was running smoothly in her absence. Samantha listened politely but in reality she didn't care about what he was saying.

Then, quite suddenly, James tried to broach an entirely different matter.

"Samantha, there is something I need to discuss with you." He paused. "Your mother has sent me a copy of the letter she claims I wrote."

"Yes. I got it too. Certainly puts an interesting slant on everything you've been filling my head with – Dad." She spat out the 'dad' with venom.

"You have to believe me that I never in my life saw that letter before. I certainly didn't write it," he pleaded with her.

"Look, James, none of that really matters much to me any more. I'll tell you one thing though, it wasn't Mum who wrote it. I know it wasn't – so go figure. Now if you'll excuse me, I have to go." Samantha didn't want to be drawn back into the mess that she had left behind her in Ireland. It was hardly her mess anyway. That letter had been written before she was even born so it certainly wasn't her doing. All her concerns now rested with Pablo. She could be contacted on her mobile if there were any serious problems and other than that she wanted to be left alone for the foreseeable future.

James caved. There was no talking to his daughter. She may have been his child but the dogged determination had to be a trait of her mother's – Katie. She had always been a strong personality and Samantha had inherited that, he thought proudly. For the hundredth time that day, James's mind rested on Katie Garcia. If only he hadn't given Rose his word to stay away from her! If he could just talk to her, maybe he could sort this whole mess out.

As the days slipped by into weeks, the atmosphere at Casa Garcia took on a more peaceful tone. Pablo finally agreed to rest more and in a strange way life became happier than it had been before. Ever so slowly the old man regained his strength again, although to look at him he had aged yet another decade.

Pedro calmed considerably once he realised that Samantha knew about Pablo's condition. The manic workload was over too, now that the harvest was in. Not surprisingly, for the tenth consecutive year Pablo was told that his grapes were the best in the region. They had had a tremendous party that night and Sami had got quite squiffy with her cousin. She now insisted on calling him 'coz' much to his amusement. Samantha's grasp of the Spanish language was starting to improve too. With the exception of the horrendous cloud of death hanging over the house, the three of them were content in each others' company.

Pedro had even reintroduced Samantha to horse-riding. She got back into it as if she had never stopped. They went for long treks over the Rioja countryside together, sometimes galloping, sometimes walking, and talking for hours. Samantha was getting to know the locals and nodded to them as they bid her and Pedro good day. She did not know how she and Pedro looked to an outsider, however. She didn't realise what a handsome couple they made, he huge and broad with a dark mane of long straight hair that ran well beyond his shoulders, she with her soft blonde curls dancing down her back. Both of them rode the same startling white Andalusian horses, hers a little smaller than his. The horses were mates, why not the riders – a stranger might think? Samantha didn't think like that. She refused to. Sam had certainly grown very very fond of the man she once thought boorish. She now understood that he had grown up in a home without any feminine influence. All things considered, he was in fact very soft and sensitive. His horses adored him and he really had a natural affinity with them. Calling him 'coz' reminded her of how Haro saw them, however. They were related in the eyes of the little town and she had to keep remembering that. Pablo was her top priority. That was why she was still in Spain. Getting on so well with Pedro was good for Pablo's health. It quite obviously cheered him enormously and so she was doubly happy to spend time with 'her cousin'.

When she came in one day, she was surprised to find a message on her mobile from Mrs Judge. It wasn't the old bat, Rose Judge. It was Granny Vic. Considerably more favourably disposed to the elder of the two Mrs Judges, she phoned straight back.

"Samantha, how good to hear from you," the old woman enthused.

Sam felt the same way. She had always liked Granny Vic and to hear her voice again after what felt like a lifetime was nice. It also brought home to her how frail Pablo had become. There was considerably more energy and life in the ninety-four-year-old's voice than there was in his and he had to be almost thirty years younger.

"Look, dear, the reason I'm phoning is to ask you a big favour."

"Sure, what can I do?"

"Well, Rose has taken it upon herself to throw a bloody big birthday party for me at the end of November and I was wondering if you would come."

"Victoria, I'm in Spain," Samantha tried to explain.

"I know, my love, but it's just that I would so like you to be there. You are my grand-daughter after all and it is my ninety-fifth. Can you believe it? Where does the time go?" She chuckled good-naturedly.

Good God, thought Sam, had James told the entire family the truth – that she really was his daughter? Well, Victoria was certainly on her side. She longed to question Victoria further but somehow she couldn't get herself to discuss it casually on the phone. In fact, the party would be a good opportunity to see how the land lay.

Besides, she loved that old woman and it wasn't really that big a deal to leave Pablo for just one week. He was getting stronger by the day.

"Don't worry about the family. They are all on their honour to be on their best behaviour. I'll see to that, girl."

"I'm not sure that they all know the truth yet, Victoria, and –" Sam suddenly realised something much more significant. "I haven't seen Cameron since the day after our wedding. This is going to be really awkward. I don't think I'm up to it."

"Of course you are, my dear. I'll be looking out for you. You are my guest and of course James will be minding you too."

Sam wasn't convinced by a long shot. "Don't get me started on him. I know he's your son but we still have a few unresolved issues to be honest, Gran."

Victoria remembered the letter but said nothing about it. "Look, pet, why don't you bring a friend?"

She thought about this. She had spoken to Wendy regularly on the phone and Sam reckoned that her old friend would be glad to have another go at Paul, the Judges' driver. "If I could bring Wendy along it might be easier," she conceded. Sam was also thinking that it might be an opportunity to gently encourage Ricky to come to Spain. She didn't have to say that Pablo was actually ill. She could just give him a little nudge into visiting.

"Oh marvellous, that's settled then. Last Saturday in November. At Dunross, of course."

"OK," Sam agreed.

Victoria hung up as Rose entered the room. She looked her daughter-in-law in the face.

"Well, Rose, I just called Samantha. She will come. But I don't know why you're so hell bent on this."

Rose smiled at the old woman. "I just thought it was a perfect opportunity to bring her back into the family and try to repair the breach. We all want to leave that mess behind us, do we not? I'm sure you feel the same way."

Rose was being too smooth and sickly-sweet. Victoria knew that she was up to something but she didn't know what. One thing that had come out of the phone call was that it served to remind Victoria about that very odd letter. She resolved to talk to James about it again.

It took a week before Samantha got the nerve up to tell Pablo and Pedro that she would have to leave them for a while. She knew they would be crestfallen. She had slipped into their lives so easily. Samantha now cooked and cleaned for them, something she vowed that she would never do for any man. What really amazed her, however, was how rewarding she found it. Her corporate life seemed like somebody else's existence. She loved the slower pace and the elegant simplicity of her life in Casa Garcia. They all rose early. Pablo walked among his freshly-cut vines and Pedro saw to his horses. Sam tended to the house and the men. Sometimes when she caught sight of her reflection in a mirror or window she laughed at the change. If Wendy and Gillian could only see her now! She had started baking and she had even tried a bit of home decorating, something she had taken no interest in before. Wendy looked after all the furniture in their apartment in Dublin. Samantha had never been remotely involved in anything to do with homemaking and yet here she was running the house and loving it.

When she told them over lunch one day that she must go to Ireland, the men reacted predictably – they sulked.

"How long will you be gone for?" Pablo had asked.

"I don't know – not long."

"When will you come back?" Pedro asked looking hurt that she was going at all.

"Soon," she tried to reassure them.

After the meal, Pablo decided to go out to the vines yet again. It was clear that he was upset she was leaving. Pedro headed for the stables in an equally unsavoury mood. When she had finished tidying, Sam followed him down to the horses. She knew it was dreadfully wrong but Samantha still loved to surreptitiously listen to him talk to his animals. The way the path and stables were designed, it was possible to stand by the wall, just before the corner, and eavesdrop. It was only a matter of metres from where he tethered the horses. Samantha held her breath and listened. She didn't understand too much of what he said but more of it was beginning to make sense. She heard her name, she heard *guapa* – pretty, she understood that Pedro was asking his horse what he would do without her. Samantha gasped with pleasure and, a second later, his face popped around the corner.

"What are you doing there?" he asked in annoyance.

"I was just coming down to see if I could help," she lied.

"I'm going out for a ride. Do you want to come?"

"Yes, please."

"Centella is in the field. Do you want to go and saddle her up?"

"Fine." Sam tried to look composed. It was quite clear that he thought she had been listening to his conversation with Trueno. As if!

She went to fetch Centella. She had learned that, just as Trueno was the Spanish for thunder, Centella meant lightning. They were a match made in heaven but still no foals.

Within ten minutes Pedro and Sam were out on the horses, moving side by side through the country lanes.

"I am sad to be going," she ventured eventually.

"You will go back to your old life and forget us."

"No, I won't," she defended herself.

He looked at her from under his dark heavy eyelashes. His good looks were almost boyish when he looked as insecure as he was obviously feeling now.

"Will you really come back?" he asked quietly.

"Do you want me to?"

"Yes, I do."

"I will come back."

Pedro's face broke out into a broad smile that illuminated his entire face and made his eyes shine brightly. "Good," he nodded in satisfaction and then he squeezed Trueno hard. "*Venga, vamos!*" he yelled as the mighty beast broke into a spontaneous gallop and tore off into the distance. Both Samantha and her horse, Centella, were taken by surprise and clambered to catch up with the boys. They rode hard for a good fifteen minutes, exhausting both humans and horses. It was only when it started to rain lightly that Pedro slowed down. He laughed at Samantha's inability to catch up with him.

"You had a head-start and Trueno's legs are longer than poor Centella's."

"Perhaps but she had a lighter load to carry. I think we were evenly matched. No, we won. Eet's the truth." He patted Trueno's huge neck in thanks for the effort the horse had put in. He looked at the sky. "Sami, I sink there is a rainstorm coming. We must find shelter or the horses will catch a cold."

"Will we make it back to Casa Garcia in time?"

He looked around. "No. But I know of a good place." Pedro nudged his horse. "Come on," he smiled at her as he tore off in the direction of the hills.

Sam didn't need to be asked twice.

The land became hillier and as the rain began to hit them, he pulled Trueno up at what looked like a small mountain.

"What's this?" Sam asked as she caught up a moment later.

"Eet's a magic place. You will see," he answered as he dismounted and took his horse by the reins.

Samantha copied him. He seemed to be searching for something in the thick vegetation that grew alongside them.

"I have not been here for a very long time," he explained as he walked and searched.

"What are you looking for?"

"You will see."

At last he gasped with pleasure.

"Here, take Trueno," he commanded as he handed Samantha the reins and began to trample down the long overgrown weeds and brambles. Then she saw what he had been looking for. It was a large hole in the orange rock face – the entrance to a cave, obscured by fallen branches and small tree-trunks.

"Surely you're not suggesting we go in there. It looks creepy and the horses won't fit."

"Si, si, they will. I have done it many times before." He began to drag the branches away. "We always used these fallen trees to hide the entrance."

"Who?"

He didn't answer as he took Trueno's reins back and led the way.

The rain was getting harder so Sam didn't have much choice as she followed Pedro and Trueno into the narrow crack in the mountain.

Now that the tree-trunks were cleared away, the opening was easily large enough for the horses to walk through. Inside, the cave opened into a large area of about thirty feet in diameter.

"My God, this is like a big hall!" It was surprisingly light for a cave. "How is it so bright?"

Pedro pointed to the cracks in the roof. "Zey are like windows. No?"

Samantha looked over her head. "Oh, yes, I see."

"I used to play here when I was small. It was our headquarters for our gang. That was a long time ago. Look!" He pointed to a small circle of stones, the traces of a campfire. "It is still there – that was where we lit our fires."

"What an amazing gang-hut! It must be very old – thousands of years."

"I think millions. It is from the glaciers."

Samantha tried to make out the rock walls. It was bright enough to see that they were the same shade of orange as the earth outside was but there were dark shadows too where nothing could be seen.

Centella whinnied and showed the whites of her eyes. "I think she's a little spooked by the shadows," Samantha suggested.

"I will make a fire," Pedro said as he tethered his horse to a large boulder on the ground. "I will get some wood outside – let us hope it is not too wet."

"There are some sticks scattered around in here too," said Sam.

Minutes later with the aid of some dry sticks and his lighter, he had a small camp fire crackling away. The smoke obediently wandered up and curled out the would-be chimney-holes in the roof.

"You're a regular boy scout, aren't you?" Sam teased.

Pedro smiled sheepishly. "We always lit fires here."

She tethered her horse next to Trueno and came to sit at the fire next to Pedro. "This is really nice," she smiled at him. "Was it a fun place to grow up?"

Pedro's eyes clouded over. He was obviously thinking about his mother but he didn't mention her by name. "Pablo was good to me."

Samantha sensed his pain.

Quite suddenly there was a whirring sound about ten feet above their heads which scared Sam.

"Ah," Pedro glanced up. "The smoke has annoyed the bats."

"Bats?" she shrieked as she jumped to her feet.

"Sit, woman. If you jump around you will scare them more and they might fly into your hair."

Samantha began to screech and jump from foot to foot. "You never told me that there were bats in here. I'm terrified of bats! Come on, let's go!" But Pedro grabbed her by the hand and pulled her down onto the soft earth. "If you sit still they will fly away. Stay low and they won't come near you. They don't like the fire and believe it or not they don't actually want to get caught in your hair." He slipped his coat off and put it over both of their heads, gently drawing her close to his side.

Samantha would not be appeased, however. "Pedro, I really hate bats," she whispered.

His face was inches from hers as he watched the flames from his little camp fire dance across her face. "You are very beautiful when you are scared," he smiled. "Really eet's OK. They are flying out of the cave now. They don't like the smoke. They prefer the rain."

She stared into his eyes. "They're going?"

"They're going," he stared back.

They froze in that position for what felt like an age, snuggled under his coat, sitting at the little fire, luxuriating in each other's gaze.

Pedro was the first to glance away. "They're gone."

"Who?" she whispered.

"Ze bats," he grinned at her confusion.

"Pedro, I –" She stalled as he looked at her, willing her to say something or nothing – she didn't know what. "I'm not your cousin," she blurted.

"What?"

"It's a long story and you mustn't tell Pablo because he doesn't know but I'm not actually related to you. You see, he's not my father –"

No more explanations were necessary as Pedro stopped her from talking by bringing his lips to hers.

The coat fell away as he took her face in both his hands and kissed her so tenderly and softly she was scared to breathe.

Then he broke away and searched her eyes. "How long have you known?"

"Not long," she answered breathlessly. "Everything has been so upside-down —"

He cut her off by kissing her again but this time there was no tenderness as he pushed her down onto the wax coat that had slipped off them just a few moments earlier.

Pedro kissed her with the passion and tension that he had been trying to ignore or at least suppress for the last month. Every day, every night, every move she made, he had ached to touch her, longed for her so desperately it had almost driven him mad. Now, suddenly the floodgates opened. They were not family.

It took an instant for Samantha to respond. She felt him kiss her and it was glorious. It had been something she had fantasised about but she never permitted the dream to go anywhere. She kissed him back with equal urgency. His strong warm hands moved in under her slightly damp blouse. They only stopped kissing to peel their clothes off as fast as possible.

"I thought you hated me," she whispered in the half light of the camp fire.

"I did, because you were my cousin. I thought we were family," he smiled as he showered her with more kisses. His body was even better than she had imagined. He was toned and had a thick mat of dark hair on his chest.

He broke away from her embrace for an instant to ensure that the horses were well tethered.

"*Lo siento*, Centella," he smiled at Samantha as he apologised to his horse, "but I don't want any interruptions."

He laid his long wax coat on the dry cave floor and then he threw a few more sticks on the fire. It flared up nicely thanks to the new wood. Next, he took Samantha's hand and gently pulled her down onto the soft warm lining of his coat.

He stroked her cheek. "You are so beautiful," he whispered as his eyes searched every millimetre of her face.

She shivered – only not with cold but with pleasure. Sam was deliriously happy. Deep down, she knew that she had been playing mind games on herself since her arrival in Spain. The real truth was that she had been wildly attracted to him from that first meeting in the café in Haro. She wouldn't let herself think about Pedro in that way, however, because they were supposedly siblings and after her recent experiences the mere thought gave her the horrors. Then by the time she discovered that they were not, she was so accustomed to his hostility and indifference, she had forced herself to believe that she felt the same way. But she didn't. Her dreams about him were positively blue and now here he was – loving her.

At first it was mad and passionate. They began to kiss and explore each other, hungry to make up for all the lost time. The misunderstanding had robbed them of their first few weeks together. Pedro loved her, bringing her along, knowing exactly what he was doing. In a mad moment, Sam remembered how Pablo had said that Pedro wasn't used to female company. How wrong could he be! Samantha devoured his love and he gave her everything he had. She screamed out but neither Trueno nor Centella were remotely concerned.

The stress and tension that had knotted Pedro and her together over the previous month now miraculously moulded them into one.

Afterwards she lay in the crook of his arm, warm and ridiculously happy. Where only a brief while earlier she had felt threatened and scared by the bats, now she loved their warm little cave as the fire made some shadows bounce along the uneven walls. It was better than any sex she had ever had before.

"I really thought you didn't like me," she sighed.

Pedro turned his face down towards her. "You are right – I hated you!"

She laughed and poked him in the ribs. He pretended to recoil in pain and so she kissed it better. "I thought you did! You seemed to leave a room when I entered it!"

"From the moment I saw you in Haro, I knew I wanted you, but when I discovered you were my cousin I thought my life was over." He stroked her gently. "I have been living in hell since then, Sami. My feelings for you —" he kissed her again, "my desire for you sickened me. What kind of animal would I be to want my cousin? A cousin is like a sister. I fought with myself every day and as for the nights," he slapped his forehead, "oh my God!"

Samantha smiled and kissed him back. "Good, because I felt the same way."

"But now you must explain to me how it is that Pedro thinks that he is your father if it is not the case. How is that?"

The mood changed instantly and Sam bit her lip. She knew that she had to tell him the truth. It was the only way. If she wasn't completely honest with him at this early stage, what hope did their relationship have?

"Eet's OK," he assured her, seeing her hesitation. "Zer is nozing you could say that will change my feelings for you."

She took a deep breath and began her sorry tale. If she was going to tell him anything, she might as well tell him everything.

Inevitably it resulted in them being wrapped around each other again. He stroked her and spoke to her in Spanish. She only half understood what he was saying but she thoroughly understood what he meant.

This was a journey of discovery, a rite of passage, something she had never experienced before. He spoke to her and loved her slowly and deliberately, watching her all the time, ensuring her happiness. Sam was shy and uncomfortable being studied so intently but he allayed her worries with gentle confident hands. He may have been a genuine horse-whisperer but Samantha reckoned she had found herself the first *bone fide* woman-whisperer!

"Well, Trueno and Centella are really having a good lesson in love," Samantha smiled at her new lover.

The horses whinnied, as if in agreement.

When their little fire at last began to die, they managed to get up and back into their clothes.

Pedro still couldn't keep his hands off her. "How am I going to be able to stop myself from kissing you in front of Pablo?"

She pushed him away and looked at him as severely as she could. "Pedro, you must promise me. Not a word of this to Papi. It would kill him." As soon as she said it, she put her hands to her mouth, "Oh, I don't believe I just said that. Oh, Pedro, I can't believe he's really so ill. Life is just so cruel!"

"I know," Pedro said as he took her in his arms again and stroked her hair. "I do not know how a heart can carry so much joy as mine does now – because I have found you. Yet it is also full of sorrow because I am going to lose Pablo."

Pedro and Samantha stood and clung to each other as they cried over the inevitable loss of their father.

CHAPTER 29

As November wrapped its chilling fingers around Dunross, Gillian worked hard on wrapping hers around Cameron. Their holiday had been bliss. The dreaded storms had come but it only served to keep them in bed which is exactly where she had wanted to be. When the sunshine came back out, everything dried in a matter of hours and it was back to being a paradise island. No hurricanes hit during their week in Barbados.

Towards the end of their stay, Cameron took her on a private yacht. He was a keen sailor and she learnt fast. They sailed the beautiful sixty-footer up and down the west coast of the island. Being the Caribbean side, the weather was a good deal more clement than on the Atlantic coast. The most memorable part of her sail however had to be when they went skin-diving off the boat after their lunch. Fish the size of dinner plates came up to them, looking for bread or bits to eat. At first Gillian had been scared but Cameron showed her how to feed them and she became comfortable in the water. There were electric blue and canary yellow fish. There were striped fish, dotted fish and one with funny spikes sticking out every which way. Cam kept assuring her that she was in no danger and so, somewhat appeased, she swam around close to the water's surface following after the truly incredible creatures. Then she caught her breath as a family of turtles swam up from the slightly sandy depths below her. It was quite obvious which one was the mother turtle. She was eagerly followed by about six babies – miniature versions of herself. Slowly and gracefully the mother swam around Gillian and her bread rolls before letting her little ones follow suit. As she thought about it now in her dreary Dublin office, it all seemed like another wonderful world, somebody else's magical life. She would have happily given everything up to get back there with Cameron. He hadn't phoned her since they got back. Gill had called him twice and he'd been loving and attentive but she did wish that he would do a bit more chasing. When Wendy told her about the party at Dunross to which Samantha had been invited, Gillian was positively mutinous. She had to be at that party. It was her place, they were going to be her people. Subconsciously she rubbed her stomach. It was still too early to tell whether or not she was pregnant, but with a little luck her time in Barbados might have given her the necessary weapon to become Mrs Judge. Then Gillian thought of the other Mr Judge. If Cameron wasn't going to invite her to the party, his father certainly would.

Naturally Luke Delaney had heard talk of Victoria Judge's ninety-fifth birthday party. It was impossible to live in Fiddler's Point and not hear about it. He hadn't been invited nor would he expect to be but Luke couldn't help wondering whether *she* would be there. It had been over five weeks since he had seen Gillian and he was still as sick as a parrot. The thought of her made him break out in a sweat. He was back to work but his heart wasn't in it. Frank and the boys left him alone to his thoughts most of the time now because they only got their heads bitten off if they went near him. Tess was at Mass up to three times a week but it wasn't helping. She began to wonder if perhaps a change of scenery was what he needed. Tess didn't want to see any of her boys leave Wicklow but what if Luke was in another country for a few months? Perhaps being removed from where it all happened would help. There were a lot of fishing boats off the coast of Spain and Portugal. She resolved to look into it.

The horrible day came when Samantha had to leave the Rioja. She didn't want to go. Her short visit had turned out to last over a month and she had been utterly seduced by its charm. Sam had come to know the locals in Haro. She loved the simpler life and the amount of free time she suddenly seemed to have. In Dublin, she spent all her days rushing from meetings to promotions for Gracias and then off to the gym. Around these obligations, she fitted the rest of her life. In Spain, there was none of that: there was simply her life, her father and Pedro. There was enough time for everything – love, life and laughter. Now Dublin held no attraction for her, so why go back? Then, of course, there was the not so small matter of Pablo's health.

"This is crazy, Papi. I can phone Victoria and tell her you are not well and I can't travel."

But he wouldn't hear of it. "Eet is good that you are going back home, Sami."

"No, this is my home now. I want to stay here with you and Pedro."

"But what about your job and your friends?"

"I don't want my job any more." She had said the words before she realised what she was saying. Pablo looked at her face as it flooded with confusion. "My God, that job was my life," she whispered as she tried to rationalise her thoughts and figure out her priorities.

Pablo nodded sagely. "This is why you must go home. We love you, Sami, but you came over for a visit and you must go home before you decide where your future is."

She nodded mutely. The one big factor which she couldn't discuss with him was the fact that she and Pedro were now practically inseparable. She wanted to be with him and that was all she knew for certain.

Pedro was taking her trip to Ireland very hard. She swore that she would return but he reminded her how she had only planned to come to Spain for a few days and how that had changed. Perhaps the same would happen to her when she went back to Dublin. A trip that was meant to last only a matter of weeks could turn out to be a long-term affair. She might see things differently once she was back on Irish soil. No matter how Samantha tried to convince him that she would return, he would not believe her. For this reason, Sam had her last meal at Casa Garcia with only Pablo for company.

"You must forgive him, *bonita*. He has become very fond of you and he will miss you," Pablo explained.

She nodded miserably.

"You feel sad now but still I think you are leaving us with a lighter heart than when you arrived, Sami?" Pablo asked gently.

"Thank you for everything, Papi. I was a mess when I arrived and just being here cured me. I know it was running away but suddenly the problems at home don't seem so big any more. Getting away helps you see things in their true perspective. There's nothing in Ireland that I can't handle."

As they ate their lunch, he reached over and squeezed her hand. "Good girl. You are strong and I know you will win." He smiled at her and then he continued gently, "Will you see your mother?"

"I don't plan to."

This time he didn't speak, he just studied the stew that Samantha had made for him.

"Do you want me to speak with her, about you I mean, Papi?"

"No, my love. It is not necessary at this point." Then he looked at his daughter lovingly. "But I am worried that you have questions that you still have not found answers for."

Sam met his gaze and she knew that he was giving her the chance to ask.

"Why did you leave us, Papi?" Her eyes glassed up. "You are such a lovely man and I have come to love you so much. Why did you go away?"

Pablo pushed his food away and reached to his daughter who did

315

the same. She fell on the floor at his feet and put her head on his lap as she wept. Pablo stroked her mass of long blonde curls and tried to soothe her as his own eyes filled with tears. "I am so so sorry, my little Sami. To see you now is to make me very happy but it breaks my heart to think of all the years I have missed. *Lo siento,*" he repeated.

Samantha looked up at him. "Then why did you leave?" she asked again.

Pablo wept openly now, unable to hide it from his daughter. "She kicked me out. She made me go and so I eventually gave up fighting with her. I should have fought harder to stay with her but she told me she hated me. She told me that you hated me; it was bad for children to be surrounded by so much fighting. I eventually gave up," he explained with a miserable shrug. "I am not a fighter, Sami. I couldn't keep up the struggle."

At last, horrible though it was, Samantha had her answer. Kathleen and her bloody drink had pushed Pablo away. There was no sinister subplot. She herself hadn't been a bad little girl. It was the same as it always was: the bloody drink.

"I hate her," Samantha whispered bitterly but Pablo put his finger on her lips.

"You cannot say that about your mozer. We are mere mortals and both of us made mistakes. I have my share of shame in my life too – things that I regret, but –" he stopped himself from continuing and then he gave his habitual shrug.

They stayed and talked for another hour before Pedro returned. He looked surprised to see Samantha sitting at Pablo's feet but as usual he didn't comment. When he had passed through the room, Pablo turned to Sam. "You will mind him for me, won't you?"

"You know I will. Papi, you're speaking like I won't see you again. I plan on flying back in a few days, a week at the outside."

He closed his eyes for an instant. "Who ever knows what the future holds. I just want you to know how much these last few weeks have meant to me and how happy I am that you re-entered my life."

"Well, I'll be back soon." She forced herself to laugh lightly as she stood up and dusted herself down.

"Pedro will drive you to the airport. I am too tired, my love." Weakly, Pablo rose to his feet.

"I could have got my little rental back. It's a long way for Pedro to come."

"He wants to," Pablo winked at Samantha. "You know, it's a pity you two are so closely related. If you weren't, I think you would have made a wonderful couple."

She nearly got whiplash as she turned to see Pablo's expression but he had turned away and was walking towards the stairs. As he got to the bottom step he grabbed the banisters for support and then he looked back at Samantha.

"Come and give your tired old father one last hug, my wonderful Sami."

She rushed into his arms with such emotion she almost winded the poor man. "Remember," he whispered into her ear as she bear-hugged him. "Always follow your heart and you will be OK."

"I know, Papi, and travel light through life."

Pablo laughed as he pulled away from her. "Aha, so you were listening," his eyes danced. "Safe voyage, my little Sami!" He spoke barely above a whisper as he turned from her and slowly mounted the steps to his room.

As she watched him go, a chill went down her neck and spine. She got the most horrible feeling that she would never see him again.

CHAPTER 30

"What in God's name have you done to your hair?" Rose Judge looked at her husband incredulously.

"What's wrong with it?" he asked defensively even though he already knew. The picture on the packet had been of a young man with rich glossy brown hair. The instructions were perfectly clear about building up the colour *slowly*. He was meant to do it over a matter of weeks to reach the required level of darkness but there hadn't been time. Gillian had only phoned the previous night. Apparently Samantha had flown home a few days earlier and Gillian had heard about the party. The clever girl had suggested that it would be a good time for them to catch up. James believed that Rose would think Gillian was there to support Sam while she was really there for a secret rendezvous with him. Things really were moving up a gear. It wasn't just his imagination! Brilliant, he thought. Just brilliant.

That's when he readdressed the issue of his hair. He had meant to try out the hair-darkener a few days before the party but it had been too hectic. Now, the evening of the actual party, hectic had ramped up to downright manic. There were caterers everywhere. A DJ had taken up residency in the drawing-room, balloon-blowers were filling the den and the library was a no-go zone. It was like a jungle – bursting with orchids, lilies and birds of paradise. Caught up in the excitement of the evening, James decided to go for broke on the hair colouring and he used the whole bottle for twenty minutes longer than the recommended time.

"James, your hair is orange! You'll have to do something," she snapped at him impatiently.

"Guests will be arriving in about an hour. What the hell do you suggest I do, Rose?"

"What about a hat?"

"How can I wear a hat? That would look ridiculous."

"No, James, you look ridiculous now. Believe me, a hat would be a serious improvement."

"I'm not wearing a bloody hat and that's final, Rose."

"Well, you're not going to ruin the night for me by making us the laughing-stock of society. Really, James, you're such an idiot!"

For the first time in his life, James squared up to his wife. "That's really what you believe, isn't it? You think I'm such a sad old fool without a clue what's going on. Well, you're wrong, Rose, I know exactly what's going on and I know you're up to no good tonight. This whole charade is for poor old Mum when all she really wants is a bottle of sherry and a video of *Only Fools and Horses*. Why are you even throwing this bloody party? I'm sure that you're manipulating everybody to your own ends. You know, Rose, I've really had enough."

"How dare you!" Rose turned purple with indignation. "I've never done anything improper in my life," she snapped. "I have always stood by you and your little follies, your lack of initiative and general social ineptness. James, you've been lucky to have me, I tell you."

His normally cool blood was boiling now. Knowing that he was going to be with Gillian before the night was out added fuel to his fire. At this point he didn't care if he had to walk out on Rose.

"What about that bloody letter you wrote? The one you denied writing when I showed it to you in the airport."

"James, I had never seen that letter before."

"Ha! More lies. I fingerprinted it. I know it was you."

"How could you? I burnt it."

"No, Rose, you burnt a copy of the letter. Your fingerprints are all over the original. Explain your way out of that!" He was lying but it didn't matter any more.

"You underhanded brute," she screeched. "How could you not take me at my word? After all I've done for you?"

It took an instant for the realisation to sink in with him that she was actually admitting to writing the letter. He was incredulous.

"My God, what kind of woman could write a letter like that? Jesus, Rose, I have to ask, do I even know you?"

She laughed a little hysterically. "No, you don't, James. You see, you don't have a clue what goes on all around you. You never have." Feeling at last like she had the upper hand, she continued her tirade. "You go around with your head in the clouds and I have to live in the real world, cleaning up your mess. Yes, I wrote that bloody letter and I'd do it again in a flash. She was the manipulating little witch and she needed sorting out. I saw her drop her note up to this house, the one she wrote to you telling you that she was pregnant by you. I knew she was up to no good when I saw it was addressed to you." Rose's eyes opened wide. "She thought she would steal you from right under my nose – poor little fool – but I got her all right. I got her stupid pathetic note and I read it – pregnant by you, my foot! Little tart!"

James was speechless with shock as Rose ranted on. "Well, I took control of the situation and sorted her out pretty sharply." Rose smiled with satisfaction. "You have to keep staff in their place and that's not in your bed, James Judge! She got the message when she got the letter. She wasn't going to get you that easily." Rose's eyes rolled. "Oh no, she had been a stupid girl and her punishment was to be sent away and off she went, suitably chastised. I've been cleaning up after you for decades, you fool, and the least you can do is show some sort of gratitude. Now put on a bloody hat!"

James collapsed onto the bed, defeated. She was right of course and he knew it. Rose had always worn the pants in their relationship. He was pretty certain that she knew he messed around occasionally but he rather understood that she didn't mind much.

Rose marched to the door, indignant and utterly certain that she had the moral high ground. "Well," she asked as she opened their bedroom door, "do you have anything to say for yourself?"

He looked at her feeling two inches tall. How could he defend a life of infidelity and stupidity? "*No man is an island,*" he said meekly but she laughed at him.

"No," she agreed as her eyes turned to ice and she glared at him, "But every woman is."

Samantha couldn't believe how nervous she was as she walked in the front door of Dunross with Wendy in tow. Damn it, she was a guest at her grandmother's party.

Then of course, there was the matter of resigning from her job. She had no idea of how that was going to turn out. Who would run Gracias when she left? Would they let her go? Was there any chance that she could realise her stock options? There was a great deal to sort out.

"Samantha! Welcome, darling. You look absolutely wonderful," Rose Judge gushed as she descended upon her newest guest with the enthusiasm of a famished vulture. "Wendy, you're welcome too," she added as an afterthought. Rose took Samantha by the arm and guided her into the library, where Granny Vic was greeting her guests.

Thankfully, thought Samantha, the house was already fairly busy with party people, so there was the reassuring buzz of conversation all about her. It was very suspicious how friendly Rose Judge was being but there was nothing odd about Victoria's welcome. She struggled to her feet with the aid of a nurse who stood next to her chair and gave Sam a warm, if weak hug.

"Very good of you to come, my child," she whispered into her hair. "And remember I'm on your side in this battle." She looked at her grandchild and winked conspiratorially.

Samantha smiled meekly. Was there going to be a fight tonight? She really hoped not.

Victoria accepted gifts from Wendy and Sam and then sent them into the bar to get a drink.

That's where Sam first caught sight of Cameron. Seeing him again gave her a serious jolt. He and she had been practically living together in the run-up to the wedding. She saw him every day at work and practically every evening afterwards. They worked out in the same gym. They went to movies together. They took long weekends together and of course they slept together. She felt her stomach muscles constrict. This was not a good place to barf. What really tore at her was how incredibly striking he was. Cameron stood a few inches taller than most. He was wearing a cream linen suit with a bright pink shirt. On most Irish men it would have looked prattish but with his Barbados tan still deep and rich, he looked like a Hollywood heart-throb. What Samantha didn't realise was he was experiencing the same reaction on seeing her. She had a colour in her cheeks and a vitality about her that he hadn't seen before. Having spent the last month either in the vineyards or on horseback, Sam was indeed the picture of good health. Pedro's love had only added to her inner glow. She was as strong and beautiful as he had ever seen her. Samantha looked like an angel.

"Sam, it's good to see you," he closed the distance between them.

People were watching.

She turned her face away from him so he ended up kissing her ear. Samantha couldn't look him in the eye. "Cameron," she murmured, studying the floor.

He put his finger under her chin to lift her face up towards his. "Can't we at least talk to each other?" He gave her one of his most charming rogue smiles. It still worked on her. She turned to Wendy who was hovering nearby with the attitude and intent of a Rottweiler. "It's OK, Wendy. Really, I'm OK. Thanks." Not looking at all convinced, Wendy backed off and headed for the bar as the other two wandered into the slightly quieter dining-room to talk.

"How have you been?" he asked as they sat down next to each other on the chaise-longue by the window.

"It's been a hell of a month, that much I will say." She relaxed a little. He seemed quite calm and not at all cross. She continued, "You? I heard you went to Barbados. Did you have a good time?"

"I just had to get away, Sam. It got so crazy here. I've been back for two weeks now, though, and I've just thrown myself into work."

"God, Cameron, how did it get this bad?" She looked up at him and met his eyes. He was looking at her strangely – intently. "Cameron?" she asked, trying to figure out his mood but it was getting clearer by the nanosecond. He looked like he was going to kiss her. She pulled back as he moved fractionally closer. "Cameron?" she asked again, this time with a little more urgency. "What are you doing?"

But he was holding her arm now. "Samantha, you know we were meant to be together. You know as well as me that you're not my half-sister. It was just wishful thinking on your mother's part. My mother has explained it all to me. She talked sense into me in Barbados. She's really keen that you and I get together again. In fact, Sam, it was she who begged Granny Vic to invite you tonight. Sam, Kathleen White is seriously delusional and my poor father will believe anything he's told. Seriously," he laughed, "talk to Rose, she knows what really went on." He spoke with so much certainty that he scared Sam. She backed further away. It was rapidly becoming clear to her that Cameron was the one who was delusional, thanks to his mother's brainwashing.

As for Rose Judge, her behaviour was inexplicable. How could she be so sure of her facts that she was still urging her son to marry a woman accused of being his half-sister?

Gillian roared her car up the front drive of Dunross. Listening to Samantha and Wendy prepare for the party was nauseating but she decided against telling them that she was actually going too. Gillian knew that she would need Cameron by her side when

Samantha found out. Having let them go first, however, Gillian was now anxious to get to Dunross before Sam and Cameron got too friendly again. What if they got back together before she had time to intervene? She ran in the front door of the grand house and straight into Wendy.

"Gillian, what are you doing here?" her flatmate asked.

James was walking down the stairs at just that moment. He saw his would-be new friend.

"Wendy, where's Sam?" Gillian asked desperately.

"She's in the drawing-room with Cameron. I don't think it's a good time to go in there, Gill. They're having a good chat."

"Gill," James whispered to her urgently.

She glanced at him for an instant and then did a double-take and stared at his head. "My God, James what have you done to your hair?" She looked appalled. Then equally quickly she shrugged as she lost interest and looked back towards the library.

Rose saw the newest arrival. "What the hell is she doing here?" the older woman sniffed to herself as she stalked over to greet her gatecrasher. Before Rose or James made it to her, however, Gillian was off to the dining-room.

"Cameron!" she shrieked as she walked in and saw him trying to engage with Sam.

"Gillian!" both Cam and Samantha chorused together.

"What are you doing here?" Cam jumped to his feet guiltily.

"I invited her," James announced proudly from where he and Rose were standing at the door.

Cameron, Gillian and Sam looked up at him. "Jesus, Dad, what did you do to your hair?" Cameron was momentarily sidetracked.

"I said you should have worn a hat," Rose spat through clenched teeth.

"Cameron?" Gillian's eyes were dangerously wild. "Don't you think it's time that we told everybody?"

"Gillian?" James tried to get her attention again but she ignored him.

Cameron looked from Sam to Gill. "Me? Tell them what?

324

There's nothing to tell," he added quickly. "Look, let's all go and get a drink, shall we?"

"No," Gillian practically shouted. "Aren't you going to tell Samantha and your parents? Don't you think it's time they knew the truth?"

Wendy was hovering behind James and Rose. She had just spotted Paul the driver arrive but she figured that something messy was unravelling.

"Cameron," Gillian said again as she wrung her hands and trembled slightly, "I'm carrying your child."

"What?"

James, Rose, Sam, Wendy and Cameron all gasped in unison.

Samantha jumped to her feet and stared at her old friend. "You and Cam? How long has this been going on?"

"Years," Gillian answered desperately hoping Cameron would come and stand beside her. "Cameron?"

But Samantha's attention was completely on Gillian. "I don't believe this, Gill. You're one of my best friends. All along – when I got engaged? In the run-up to the wedding? At the hen party? All this time?" she asked incredulously. Only then did she look at Cameron. "And you? You've been – been with *her*?" She blinked from one to the other disbelievingly. "I don't believe this. Why did you bloody well ask me to marry you?"

"It was because of the business," Gillian answered for him. "You're too powerful in the company, Sam. He needed your shares."

Samantha became very still. She didn't look at Cameron. She just addressed him as she studied the sanded and highly-polished floorboards of the dining-room.

"Is this true, Cameron?" she asked, and her tone was clear and icy cold.

"No, of course not," he grasped at straws.

"Yes, it's true," Gillian interrupted. He says that Gracias is the baby of Judges' Whiskey and somehow you've ended up with a huge shareholding."

Samantha's head snapped up and she studied Cameron's panic-stricken features.

"Is that what you said?" she asked. "And what do you think I should have had? Perhaps a nice little bonus for favours rendered? Or would a golden clock have been more fitting?"

Rose Judge tried to intervene. "Look, Samantha, I really think this is private family business – can we at least withdraw to the library?"

Many of the guests had now abandoned all pretence of surreptitiously eavesdropping and they were openly watching the Judge saga unfold in front of them.

"No way," Samantha laughed. "I want to hear this and I'm quite sure a great many people gathered here do too. So he thinks Gracias is his business, Gillian? And tell me, do you agree with him?"

"Well, what makes it yours?" she asked defensively.

"Oh nothing – other than the fact that I invented the damn drink. It's my ingredients, my logo, and my concept. Damn it, it's my name!"

At last Cameron rose to the bait. "Sam, it's not that simple. I was with you every step of the way. We came up with the logo and the product description together. We jointly decided how and where we were going to place it in the market."

"Oh yeah? Well, tell me then, Cameron, where did you come up with the name? *When* did you decide on Gracias? In fact, *why* did you decide on Gracias?"

He looked at his father as if for inspiration. "Well, it was just a buzz word. I mean we all know it's the Spanish for 'thank you' and it was just a good name for a Latin type of drink."

Samantha applauded him in a mocking sort of way. "So that's it, is it? Your great marketing plan was based on the premise that it's a good name for a Latin type of drink? Well, that's not quite right, Cameron." She looked around at all the enthralled guests. "And ladies and gents of the jury, I ask you to decide. You see Gracias is mine in more ways than one. I chose the name Gracias because I am Samantha Garcia – S Garcia. *Gracias* is an anagram for *S Garcia*. So you see, the drink really is me and I am it!" Then she looked back at Cameron and addressed him in a withering tone. "You didn't even know that, did you? You pathetic little creature!" Then

Samantha looked at Gillian. "You might have taken Cameron from right under my nose but rest assured nobody will take Gracias away from me against my will because it is mine!"

There was absolute silence from the crowds who had gathered at the two sets of large double doors that led to the dining-room. The entire party had ceased as everybody watched.

Cameron was utterly stunned. He had never noticed the S Garcia/Gracias thing. Then again he had always thought Sam's surname was White. He tried to regain her favour. "Samantha, all of this – it's just not true. I can explain!" He reached to take her hands but she backed away towards one of the doors.

"No, not this time, Cameron, you're just as bad as your father!" Samantha's fury was being overtaken by a wave of shock and bitter humiliation. "You're all the same," she began to cry. "You're a shower of no-good bastards and I never want to see you again!"

Then she rushed from the room, fighting her way through the throngs who had gathered at the door. Gillian looked up and caught James's eye by accident. He looked at her miserably. She simply shrugged and turned away from him. James left the room and climbed the stairs to his bedroom. It was time to pack.

Zoë, at the ripe old age of eight, was now considered big enough to come and go from the big house on her own without adult supervision. She bounded through the door into the kitchen of their little farmhouse to where her father and mother were having a civil glass of wine together.

"You won't believe what's happened up at Granny Vic's party," she gushed.

"Calm down," Steph answered a little too sharply. She had been having such a lovely conversation with her soon-to-be-ex-husband, she didn't want the intrusion.

"Samantha's bridesmaid Gillian has Cameron's baby in her tummy and now Sam is really cross! And Grandpa's hair is orange!" Both parents looked at their daughter in shock.

"Are you positive about the baby?" Steph stood up.

"Yeah, Rose is crying and Sam ran away. Cameron and Gillian are screaming at each other. It's brilliant."

"David, I think we'd better head up to the house – this sounds serious."

"Sure," he agreed as he jumped to his feet. "Let's go." No more than Stephanie did he want to leave the comfort and warmth that they had created in the kitchen.

David hadn't expected an invitation to Granny Vic's party and when it did come he fully intended to refuse but the old lady was very persuasive. From Granny Vic's perspective, the fact of the matter was David was her grand-daughter's husband and she wanted him there. The huge surprise for him was his visit to Steph before the party. As soon as he accepted the invitation from Victoria, he phoned Stephanie to warn her that he was expected to be there. She seemed genuinely glad to hear from him and delighted that he was coming. They agreed to meet for a drink in Steph's house before the party, just to see each other. Cathy the nanny had let him in when he arrived. She explained that Steph was putting Amy to bed. They exchanged equally surprised glances. Steph had never put the girls to bed when David lived with them.

"It's because she's out at work all day," Cathy explained. "Now when she's here, she can't get enough of them. Why don't you go up and give her a kiss?"

David looked at her sharply but she had already spotted her blunder.

"I meant give Amy a kiss. Sorry," she winced.

He tiptoed up the stairs for fear of unsettling the baby. Sure enough as he was getting to the top step he could hear Stephanie's soft voice serenading his baby: *"Hush little baby, don't you cry – Mama's gonna sing you a lullaby."* David was overcome by emotion listening to Amy gurgling contentedly. His wife's voice was so loving and warm, he just wanted to lie down on the steps and rest, listening to the enchanting sound.

"David," she whispered as she walked out of the bedroom. "I'm sorry, I didn't know you were here. She's just nodded off. Do you want a peep?" And she smiled at him.

He was too choked to speak, such was the atmosphere of domestic bliss. He simply nodded and crept into the baby's room with Steph in tow. "Isn't she gorgeous?" Stephanie whispered.

"She's just perfect," he agreed.

It was only when they got back down to the bright lights and noise of the kitchen that he was able to compose himself again. The first thing that he noticed was how good Steph was looking. The job obviously agreed with her 100 per cent. She had dropped about two dress sizes, not that he was ever particularly into thin women. He actually preferred the shape she was before, but Steph seemed delighted with her new size.

"The weight really fell off when I started working because I wasn't hanging around the kitchen all day," she explained simply. Stephanie had been effusive about her job. "I love it there, David. I had no idea that work could be so fulfilling and rewarding. And the house runs so much more smoothly now. I gave Cathy a whopping big bonus out of my first pay cheque and she seems happier and the girls are less of headache too. Because I'm away most of the day, I'm dying to see them when I get home. I really don't know why I didn't do this years ago."

What Steph didn't realise, however, was that with every joyful declaration she was making, David's conviction was growing that he had been the poison in her life. Things were just getting better and better since he'd left. Perhaps she could see it too and she was just being too nice to say it.

Now, as they arrived up at Dunross, James came back down to the large reception hall with a small case. Marcus Haywood on the other hand spotted his golden opportunity to sneak upstairs. He had hoped that the evening would provide an opportunity to investigate Rose's jewellery collection but never in his wildest dreams had he reckoned on a chance like this. He was up the stairs in a flash.

When she saw her husband, case in hand, Rose was panic-stricken.

"What in the name of God are you playing at, James?" she asked but her voice was a lot more taut than she had meant it to be.

"Isn't it obvious? I'm doing something I should have done a long time ago," he sighed. There was no venom or hatred in his voice. He was utterly resigned to his fate.

"Father? What are you thinking of? Tonight of all nights." Cameron put his hand on James's arm in a subtle attempt to stop him. "Look, this business with Gillian – it's just a bloody baby. I can deal with it," he whispered.

James stopped and eyeballed his boy. "For your information, Gillian has played me for a song over the past few days too. Just thought you should know that. To be honest, Cameron, I think she would have settled for either one of us. What was it you once said to me? *"Babies catch up on you in the long run"* – that was it. Well, boy, it looks like you just got caught." He glared at Cameron as he pulled his sleeve away. "I'm ashamed to call you my son," he whispered and then he walked off to find Victoria.

"Mother, I have to go away for some time. I'll phone you in a day or two."

The old woman nodded with understanding. "Wise decision," she whispered into his ear as he bent down to kiss her. "Surprised it took you this long," she added.

James blinked at her in surprise but her eyes twinkled.

"This is turning out to be a very eventful birthday," she smirked. "But, James, please do something about your hair."

Despite himself he laughed. "I promise, Mum." He kissed her again and walked out past all the guests about whom he didn't give two figs.

Rose was standing at the front door, looking ten years older than she had half an hour earlier.

"James, you can't be serious," she spoke breathlessly.

"Rose, I've never been more serious in my life."

"But what about the business, the family? What about us and what people will say?"

"For the first time in my life, I can safely say, Rose, I couldn't give a fuck."

"James!" Old habits die hard and she couldn't stop herself from chastising him for his language.

"Lady, you have lied to me, ridiculed me, used and abused me and, to put it simply, I've had enough. It's time we broke up."

"But, James, I love you and you love me."

"Don't make me laugh, Rose. I'm not sure if you ever loved me and, come to think of it, I don't really know if I ever loved you. You loved this house, God help me, and you loved the Judge dynasty. But me, Rose? I don't think so." He spoke without any anger or resentment. It was as if they were discussing a shrub in the garden and whether it should be removed or left where it was. James leaned over and kissed her indifferently on the cheek, much as he had done for the last thirty-five years.

"I'll be on my mobile if there are any further family emergencies but only if it's a genuine emergency."

And with that James Judge walked out of the party, out of Dunross Hall and out of Rose's life.

CHAPTER 31

"What the hell are you doing here?" Rose had dashed to her room for refuge and the last person she expected to meet was bloody Marcus Haywood.

He had been having difficulty finding where she kept her jewels and this whole theft bit was taking longer than he anticipated.

"Rose, hi. I came up to see if you were OK. I mean, I saw James with his case. Good God, is everything all right?"

Rose collapsed into tears and so he was obliged to act concerned.

"He's left me, Marcus. Can you believe it? In the middle of a big party. This was meant to be the party to prove how we had recovered from the fiasco that was Cameron's wedding and now we're in even more shame. How can I ever show my face in polite society again?"

"There, there, Rose. I'm sure he'll come back. It's just a silly misunderstanding. You two have been together through thick and thin. He'll come back in a few days."

Rose calmed slightly. "Did you really come up here to see if I was OK?" she asked looking into his eyes, somewhat comforted by the proximity of a strong young man.

"Yes," he assured her earnestly. "I knocked on your door and I thought I heard you say enter so I walked in. You literally came straight up behind me. Jesus, Rose, I assure I wouldn't have come in if I didn't think you had invited me."

"No," she said. "It's not polite to enter a woman's room uninvited. Marcus, do you have a cigarette?" she asked a little boldly.

"Sure. I didn't know you smoked."

"I don't but it's not every day that your husband walks out on you."

"No." he agreed. "Here, I'll light it for you." He put the cigarette between his lips and looked at her flirtatiously. She was a miserable old prude but a little gentle flirting might just help his cause with Caroline. Having dragged heavily on the cigarette, he placed it between her lips. She responded well.

"I'm not unattractive, am I, Marcus?" she asked, showing considerably more feminine charm than he had ever seen her use before.

"No, you certainly are not. You're still a very beautiful woman, Rose. Believe me, James would be mad to stay away from you for too long. Some other man will snap you up."

Rose preened as she listened to him. "James had taken another young lover, you know."

"No."

"Yes, Gillian Johnston. She was one of Samantha's bridesmaids. Trouble is she's already pregnant by Cameron. Christ, this bloody family!" She shook her head wearily as she crossed the floor of her bedroom to her dressing-table. She stubbed out the cigarette in an empty little trinkets saucer.

Marcus was stunned at the developments of the last five minutes. The biggest shock was that there would be another Judge baby in the not too distant future. That was competition for the Judge fortune.

"Perhaps I should take a lover too," Rose turned and looked directly at Marcus. "What do you think?"

He was assailed by a mild panic. Surely she wasn't suggesting *him?* "Rose, I think you're in shock at the moment. You need to let the dust settle on tonight's events first of all," he tried to reason as she walked back towards him.

"You said I was attractive, Marcus. You said that I still have what it takes." She wound her arms around his neck.

"Rose, please, I'm in love with your daughter."

"Good, well, if you give me what I want right now, I'll give you my daughter."

"What?"

"You heard me," she whispered.

Despite his horror at her advances, she had his attention. Rose could give him the one thing he wanted – Caroline. What harm would a little mild flirtation do?

"I need this," Rose said. "No, I need you. If you do this for me, Marcus, I will see to it that Caroline marries you within the year."

"This is madness!" He looked at her desperately and then she kissed him.

Caroline wasn't concerned about her boyfriend's whereabouts. Doubtless he was enjoying some of the exquisite food or perhaps he was at the bar. When she heard that James had left with a suitcase her thoughts went instantly to her mother, however. Both she and Steph, who had just got up to the house, searched the reception rooms and the kitchen. Next they checked the library, the den and the various other rooms on the ground floor of the house. Then they both rushed up to look in her room. Caroline had never knocked on her mother's door and she wasn't about to start now. She barged straight in with Stephanie and David right behind her. Thankfully, Zoë had been distracted by the strawberry roulade that had just appeared on the dining-room table, because there – in full view for the whole family to see, was Rose Judge being devoured by Marcus Haywood.

"Caroline!" Rose shrieked when she saw her two daughters and son-in-law standing in utter and appalled shock at her bedroom door. "It's not what you think!" The older woman pulled away from her daughter's boyfriend and attempted to straighten her hair.

Marcus pulled back from his future mother-in-law, looking guilty as sin. "Caro," he whispered but she was gone.

As with many November nights in Wicklow it was raining hard and it had become bitterly cold but Samantha couldn't feel it. She was so wretched in her heart and soul that she couldn't feel anything but her misery. She had rushed out of Dunross and had just begun to run. She didn't know where she was going and it was too dark to tell anyway. Poor Wendy had tried to follow her but Samantha had screamed at her to leave her alone.

"I just want to mind you," Wendy explained. "Please let me come with you!"

But Samantha was in no mood for company.

Then, when she was truly alone, Sam cried. She cried like she had never done before. She wept for the betrayal of her fiancé, the bitter and sickening embarrassment of discovering that he was in fact her half-brother. She wept for the loss of her ex-best-friend, Gillian. Samantha had trusted that girl more than anybody else in the world, with the exception of Wendy. How could she really have done that? If she couldn't trust Gillian, could she ever trust anybody on the planet? She already knew to her own bitter experience that you certainly couldn't rely on family. Her mother had destroyed her life – firstly by conceiving her with the wrong man, secondly by pushing Pablo – the right man – out of her life! Now, to top it all, even poor Pablo, the one parent she actually loved and respected was going to leave her alone too. Was there anything else that could possibly go wrong with her life, she wondered as her huge utterly miserable tears mixed with the cutting rain? The Karen Millen dress she wore offered her no heat or protection against the elements. Her ridiculously high heels were badly water-marked and covered in muck. She saw the outline of a man up ahead, standing very still. It was pitch black and Samantha had no idea of where she was. She knew that the sea was behind her and she had crossed a little road in the dark but that was the height of it. As she drew closer, Samantha realised that the man was the Dancing Fiddler – the gift that the Judges had given to the village of Fiddler's Point as a token of good will. She remembered the last time she had noticed him. It was when she was going the church to marry Cameron. When she reached the fiddler she saw the rain lashing at the contours of his bronze face. His light smile and jaunty stance only highlighted her misery. It made her cry even harder. She sat at his feet with the bronze dog next to her and curled up in a little ball.

As the rain pelted down she thought about her life in Ireland. It was an utter shambles and there was nothing to stay for. The man she thought she loved had never really loved her. He just wanted her for her shares in his company. Her friends weren't really her friends and her mother was a raving alcoholic. She hated them all. Samantha resolved to head straight back to Spain. The sooner she got back to Pedro and Pablo the better. With this decision made, she tried to stand but the driving wind was too strong. Samantha slipped and went over on her ankle. A searing pain shot though her entire leg. "Oh, bloody marvellous! That's all I fecking well need now," she howled, "to injure myself out here in the middle of nowhere."

Despite the pain, she made herself stand and half-limp, half-hop to the side of the road just past the Dancing Fiddler. Perhaps she could wave down a passing car. The petrol station beyond had long ago closed for the night. Slowly she pulled herself to the side of the road. It was only a matter of minutes before a car driving towards Fiddler's Point approached. Because it was so dark, Samantha had dragged herself right onto the road. There was, of course, the slight chance that she would be run over but that was infinitely preferable to being left on the side of the road. As headlights shone brightly on her, she waved frantically and the car stopped a safe distance away. The driver door opened and a lone figure climbed out. Samantha tried to stand tall on one leg but she looked the picture of misery, soaked through and covered in a mix of mud and running mascara. With the lights of the car on full beam, she could only see the outline of the driver as he walked towards her but it was one she recognised. She knew the click-clack of the hobnail boots as they started to get closer. She moved her eyes up to see the familiar swing of a shoulder – one she had come to love. The long wax coat pitter-pattered the heavy rain off effortlessly but it was the wide-brimmed wax hat that left her in no doubt. She tried to move towards him but she stumbled on her sore ankle.

He ran and scooped her up in his arms. "*Bonita,* what are you doing out here?" he asked, horrified to see her in such a condition.

"Oh, Pedro," she whispered with relief as she collapsed in his arms.

He carried her back to the rental car and lay her down on the back seat, covering her with his coat. Then he got in next to her and held her while he whispered soft Spanish words in her ear until she was calm.

"My *cosa guapa*, what happened?" he asked as soon as her eyes opened.

"My foot," she winced.

"But why are you out here in this rain?" Pedro handled Samantha's ankle with the same care and attention that she had seen him exercise on Trueno the day he nearly ran her down and now she realised why his horses adored him so much. He stroked her leg with the lightest touch, probing it so gently she was actually enjoying it until he hit the sore bit.

"*Ow!*" she yelped.

He looked at her and smiled. "You'll live. It's just a light sprain you have because of zees crazy shoes you wear, woman."

Samantha reached over and kissed him on the lips. "Thanks for saving me."

"What is going on?" he asked again.

"Oh Pedro, I have just discovered how one of my best friends – well, she's not a friend at all it would appear – has been having an affair for years with Cameron, the man I nearly married! I ran out of the party and then I lost my bearings.

"Ziz Cameron? Again? Where eez he? I will kill him!" Pedro's entire body tensed as he spoke.

Samantha looked at him in shock and then she laughed which felt wonderful. "Oh Pedro, you really are my knight in shining armour," she smiled as she cuddled into him. This softened his fury as he embraced her to keep her warm.

It didn't take her long to ask the inevitable. "Tell me though, happy as I am to see you, what are you doing here? I only gave you my contact details for an emergency." She saw the sudden sombre look on his face. The sorrow in his eyes was unmistakeable.

"It's Pablo," she whispered as she watched his eyes fill up with an ocean of tears and regret. "Is he – is he –?" she couldn't finish her sentence. Instead it was Pedro who collapsed into tears. She realised in a flash that her trials and tribulations were nothing compared to his grief. "He's gone, Samantha," Pedro wept, "Papi is gone."

CHAPTER 32

The next day Dunross was not a pleasant place. Rose wouldn't come out of her room. Gillian Johnston, who had refused to leave the night before, was hiding in the guest suite. Granny Victoria had insisted that she stay as long as she needed to. If she was carrying a Judge, she had to be minded.

Thus, it was Cameron and Victoria alone at breakfast.

"So, James is taking a sabbatical?" she said as she spread a superthin layer of butter on her bread.

"It might be a little longer than that, Grandma," Cameron said as he studied his black coffee.

"And what about you, young man? Have you given any thought to your situation?"

"No, Gran. I'm really doing my best not to think about it."

"Well, that's a little foolhardy," she shrugged. "I would have thought the solution is quite clear really. You have a young lady up in the guest wing who is rather desperately in love with you. She also happens to be carrying your child and as far as I can see her biggest advantage at this point is that she's not actually related to you. Don't you think you could just do the decent thing and marry the poor girl?"

"Jesus, Gran, it's not that simple. She bloody tricked me into that pregnancy."

"I dare say you know about the birds and the bees, Cameron. You knew what you were doing."

"Yes, but I thought she was being careful."

"Just like your father."

"What?"

"Oh nothing. Look, you need a bride. She needs you. Will you at least think about it?"

Cameron nodded indifferently. "I'm not sure that the Judges are destined to find love. Look at Caroline and Marcus and what about Stephanie and David?"

"What about Steph and David?" Stephanie walked into the large kitchen and tussled her little brother's hair. "Good morning, Grandma!" She reached over and kissed the old woman on the cheek.

David walked in behind her with the two girls.

"David, thank you for staying last night and helping out. It was very good of you," Victoria said, looking at her grandson-in-law. He beamed at her as did Stephanie. Then she noticed them glancing at each other and smiling. She may have been an old lady but Victoria recognised young fresh love when she saw it. She didn't dare say anything but she knew that, with any luck, that rift was healing.

"What about Caroline?" she asked. "Has anyone seen her this morning?"

Stephanie answered. "I popped my head into her house and she's pretty upset. She kicked Marcus out last night and he has gone, lock stock and barrel. She's hopping mad with him but she's even more furious with Mother. What the hell was Rose thinking?" Steph shook her head incredulously.

Victoria spoke. "I'm not for one second condoning it but I think your mother was in total shock. She's been married to James for almost forty years now and he had just walked out. She ran to her room for refuge and there was a nice young man offering her solace. Can't say I blame her."

"Still," Cameron snapped, "she's old enough to be his mother."

And James was old enough to be Gillian's father, Victoria thought but she didn't say it. The less said about that, the better.

"Is Paul around? I want to head up to Dublin," Cameron asked trying to change the subject.

"Paul has the weekend off. He asked me for some time off last night and I said he could," Victoria answered.

"Jesus, Gran, what did you do that for?" Cameron snarled.

"Neither your father nor your mother was here so I was well within my rights, young man. If you're so desperate to get to Dublin, you can drive yourself. What a novel idea, but you'd better take that young girl upstairs with you. I'm too old for another day of histrionics."

It was almost lunch by the time Cameron had got the pilot up and out. Why the hell should he drive when they had a company chopper? Gillian had begged him to stay with her but he refused. He made her return to Dublin in her own car but he did promise that he would call to her later in the day. What he hadn't told anybody was that he was having an urgent meeting with his solicitors about the whole Gracias business. He couldn't get over the shock of the Gracias/S Garcia thing and it made him very nervous.

Caroline appeared around mid-morning and told Cameron that she wanted a lift to Dublin. She was meeting a gallery owner or something. He agreed instantly. Privately Cameron thought it was a good idea to keep an eye on her for a few days just to make sure that she was over the whole Marcus debacle.

The chopper was a Jet Ranger, a massive beast, but Cameron was well used to it. He sat up front with their pilot while Caroline strapped herself in and sat quietly in a window seat behind. They took off from the heli-pad at Dunross and turned out to sea in a due north course. The pilot had already submitted their flight plan, the same one they used practically every time they were going to the city so there was nothing unexpected there. What neither Cameron nor the pilot had anticipated, though, was the sudden wind-rush of the back door opening. In a flash, Caroline had jumped from the chopper, narrowly escaping breaking her back on the landing skid. Down, down she fell.

Surely death would be instant and relatively painless, she thought, as she felt herself freefall. Caroline watched the amazing view of the helicopter she had just been sitting in get smaller as she fell further and further down towards the sea. The thought flashed through her brain: if she hadn't been about to die, it would have made an interesting painting. As she dropped, time seemed to go into slow motion. If the fall didn't kill her, she would drown in the freezing Irish Sea very quickly anyway. With a mighty crash, her back hit the water first. As she plunged deep through the icy water her mind was still working clinically. OK, I'm not dead so the fall didn't bloody well kill me. Damn it, I should have waited until we were over the Stillorgan dual carriageway! There was a sharp pain as I hit the water but I don't think my back is broken. The cold made her gasp, her mouth opened involuntarily and the water poured into her mouth and lungs. She began to choke. Oh God, she thought manically, I hope this is fast. Goodbye Marcus, Goodbye Mother! Her mind began to cloud.

Up in the air, the chopper had taken a nosedive in an attempt to see where she was but it was too slow. Caroline was already out of sight and under the water.

Somebody who had seen the entire event unfold however was Luke Delaney. He and his brothers had stopped momentarily to salute the chopper as it flew overhead. It didn't happen every day and so it was enough of a novelty to get an acknowledgement. Then, as they gazed up, they saw the back door of the chopper open and, to their absolute horror, they saw a woman jump from the height and plummet down into the freezing green sea.

Luke's reaction was instant. He didn't think about what he was doing, he didn't even look to his father or brothers to see if they knew that he was jumping. He ran to the side of *The Ashling* and dived into the icy water. His skin reacted as if it had been given an electric shock. Every nerve-end screamed at the contact with the freezing water but he ignored it as he ploughed through the waves. Unlike his brothers who never learnt to swim, Luke was a strong swimmer thanks to summers spent in the Judges' pool.

By the time he got to where he reckoned she had hit the water there was no sign of her. He dived once but found nothing. Then he dived a second time even deeper but still no woman. The third time, he knew it was his last chance. If he didn't get her up his time, she would be dead. Luke dived down into the murky water. Visibility was next to nothing and his lungs began to burn for want of fresh air. Still he went down and still there was no sign. As he was about to give up in sheer desperation his fingers tipped something – it was the woman's hand. He grabbed it and pulled her up as he kicked hard to get back up to the surface. Breaking the surface, and pulling a huge barrelful of oxygen into his screaming lungs, he yanked her up and into the air. "Breathe!" he yelled at the lifeless body. "Come on, cough," he spluttered. "You can breathe now, please breathe!"

His father's boat pulled up alongside. The chopper was hovering above it.

Cameron and the pilot watched as Mark and Mathew Delaney pulled his sister's lifeless body over the side of their boat and Frank Delaney helped Luke out of the water.

Luke quickly got to work with mouth-to-mouth. He was the only one who had done the life-rescue course and he had never been so grateful for that lesson. After what felt like much too long, Caroline began to cough and spit up sea water. As she did, Frank Delaney blessed himself and gave the thumbs-up to the chopper.

Cameron, much to his amazement but not to his embarrassment, burst out crying.

Caroline opened her eyes and looked at Luke. She squinted slightly because of the sun behind his head. "Are you God?" she spluttered.

Luke's heart exploded.

It had been late when Pedro and Samantha got back to her Dublin apartment and so it was late when they awoke. Her first reaction was that she had to get out of there.

"I don't want to meet Gillian. She lives here too and if she comes home this morning I'll die." There was no sign of Wendy either. Pedro tried to soothe Samantha but they were packed and out of the building in no time at all. He managed to talk her into breakfast in The Four Seasons nearby and there he told her again how Pablo had suffered another stroke. This time it was a major one. There had been no chance of survival.

Samantha spoke in a whisper. "Do you think he suffered?"

"No. He won't have felt a thing – the doctors assured me of that."

Samantha felt a single tear escape from her eye as she listened to Pedro. "It happened when he was asleep, Sami. He was very lucky. He would have simply drifted off to sleep the night before the stroke and never woke up. There was no sign of a struggle or discomfort. I know. I was the one who found him in bed." His voice broke and Sam reached out as her big strong Riojan man succumbed to a fresh wave of grief. The staff that hovered near their table had the empathy to dissolve into the background and leave them in peace.

"I'm so sorry, Pedro. I'm here. I'll mind you." She held him in her arms and rocked him gently. "But we'll really miss that noble man."

"You'll see him in the next life," Pedro said as he regained some modicum of control. Then he paused. "Sami, I have to give you your copy of his will. He wrote you a note with it. There are four letters – one for me, one for you and one for your brother Ricky. There is also another letter for another man."

"Who?"

"In the one he wrote to me, he said that everything would make sense after you read your letter."

Sitting on a large sofa in the foyer of the hotel, Samantha snuggled into Pedro's arms as she listened.

"In my letter he told me to come over to Ireland and give you your envelope." He reached for the inside pocket of his wax coat and pulled out a letter. "That is why I am here," he explained simply as he kissed the top of her head. She took it from him with trembling hands. On the cover her name was written in Pablo's old, slightly scrawny handwriting. Her own hands shook as she tore it open. The first page was a copy of a legal-looking statement of just a few lines. Pablo was giving all his worldly belongings to Pedro. That was as it should be, she thought fondly. Then she turned her attention to the rest of the letter from the man she had come to know as her father.

My Dear Sami,

I am so sorry to be writing this letter to you but I know I have not got much time left on this earth. I appreciate that I led you to believe I had more time than I really do but forgive an old man his folly. As I write this letter you are heading back to Ireland for the party. We have had very good times together – you and I – and I believe that it was God who sent you to me. I will soon go to him willingly to thank him for the wonderful gift that is you. Excuse please my English! I have nothing of value to give you but my love which will go on even after I have gone. I hope you will treasure it as I treasured you. I am so sorry that I was not part of your life for such a long time. I now know that this was a mistake but you have to believe me, I thought I was doing right by you and Enrique.

For this reason I need your help for something. As I told you I too have mistakes in my life. I thought I was doing right to leave you in peace and now I must tell you, there is another child. Another poor soul who I have left alone. It was very bad of me and it was only one occasion but there is a woman in Ireland who has a child – a son by me. I would never have known but she told me one night after she had been drinking heavily – later she regretted telling me and made me promise to leave and never come back and I did as she requested. Now, having met you, I wonder if I did the right or the wrong thing. The woman's name is Rose Judge and the child I fathered was a boy, although, of course, he is a man by now. She called him Cameron. You need to meet this man and decide on whether it would be better if he knew about me or not. I gave her my word that I would not

345

approach him for the rest of my life but, now that I am no longer in this world, I have broken no promise. If you think it would be good for him to know, please give him the letter addressed to him. If not, burn the letter.

I leave you with all my love. Please mind Pedro for me.

Papi

Samantha didn't know whether to laugh or to cry. Just at the point where she thought nothing else could shock her, Pablo had rocked her world – again.

Cameron was fathered by Pablo and his mother was Rose. She herself was fathered by James and her mother was Kathleen. She began to giggle slightly then it turned into a full-blown laugh.

"Sami?" Pedro was concerned.

"We weren't related," she said as she kissed him on the nose. "All this hoo-ha and we weren't bloody related!"

"You and I?" he asked, misunderstanding. "But we already knew this. Sami, are you OK? You are acting very strangely."

Samantha smiled at him. "I have never been better, darling. I've been carrying around some stupid guilt and Pablo has cleared it all up for me, admittedly unwittingly but he has cleared my conscience. Jesus, this is crazy."

"How, Sami?"

"I will tell you – but later."

Pedro was being made decidedly uneasy by her new-found good humour.

"Will you come back to Spain with me, Sami?" he asked sombrely. Samantha sensed his unease and saw the insecurity in his eyes.

"Pedro," she took his hand.

"This is a no, isn't it?" he spoke sharply. "It's just as I said it would be."

"No, it's not a no," she smiled. "It's a yes. There are just a few things I have to sort out here first of all. Give me the other letters and I will follow you back out to Spain within the week. I promise," she smiled broadly.

"You promise?" He looked at her sheepishly from under his dark eyebrows.

"Really. I promise."

As soon as they parted, Samantha hit the road for Galway. She felt as if her life was hurtling along a predestined path. Were the gods just playing with her? How the hell did Pablo and Rose bloody Judge get together? How was it that Kathleen hadn't got wind of it? Did they have any scruples at all in the sixties?

Jesus, she realised, if Pablo had told her as soon as he met her that he was in fact Cameron's father, she would have rushed straight back and into her fiancé's arms – gloriously ignorant of the fact that he had been having a long affair with Gillian.

Sam still couldn't get over Gillian. Whatever about Cameron having a wandering eye – Gillian? The witch!

As she drove her powerful car towards Galway, her mind raced every which way. She thought about Ricky, her brother – how he had said that Cameron was like the brother he never had, and now it transpired that they had the same father. She thought about how she had always felt that Cam was different from the rest of the Judges because he had such passion – that was Pablo's passion that coursed through his veins. She remembered when she saw Pablo combing his hair back with his hands. Cameron always did that. Now that she knew, it seemed so bloody obvious. She remembered James once commenting that Cameron was more Rose's son than his. Was it possible that he already knew? Hardly. Then she thought about Cameron and Gillian again. It was the ultimate irony that Gillian had been trying to nab a Judge and ended up with a Garcia. Would she tell him? Pablo had left the decision to her – little did he know what a can of worms it was. Samantha reckoned it would destroy Cameron to discover that he was Pablo's son.

Of course, there was one other person who had chosen to keep that fact a secret for the past thirty-five years: Rose Judge.

Then it hit her like a twenty-ton truck. There was the answer –

the answer to why Rose Judge was still backing the marriage against all the odds.

She *knew!*

She had known all along.

She *knew* that Samantha was not Pablo Garcia's daughter, *was not Cameron's sister.* And so she could encourage the marriage.

The thought was so twisted it made Sam ill to rationalise it.

And by getting her and Cam to marry she was bringing the Judge blood back into the family. She was sorting out her own little dirty secret nicely and cleanly and nobody would ever be the wiser. While, of course, strengthening Judges' Whiskey by wedding it irrevocably to Gracias.

Then, in a flash of insight, Samantha knew with cold and absolute clarity that somehow Rose Judge had always known that Samantha White was Kathleen Garcia's daughter.

Samantha knew without a shadow of a doubt that both she and Cameron had been played like absolute puppets by Rose. She had engineered for them to be together – doubtless she had suggested to Cameron that he ask Sam out. It had always been her plan to get the two of them together, thus undoing her own faux-pas.

James once told Samantha that Cameron was a poor judge of character. He had said how surprised and delighted he was that Cam had been smart enough to choose Samantha. That was because Cameron hadn't chosen her, she realised with mounting horror. Cameron hadn't picked Sam because Rose had! How dare she, Samantha fumed. She would make Rose pay for this if it was the last thing she did, Sam decided as she neared Galway.

CHAPTER 33

Samantha was unexpectedly nervous as she pulled up outside the little house in Salthill, just outside Galway city. The last time she had been there was a few months previously when she attempted to tell her mother that she was going to marry Cameron.

What would her mother make of it all, she wondered as she got out of the car. To her surprise it was James Judge who opened the front door to her. His hair was now slightly less orange than it had been.

"What the heck are you doing here?" she asked indignantly.

"I could ask you the same thing but I'm too polite," James rebuked her. "Shall we start again?" He smiled patiently. "Hello, and welcome home!"

Samantha tried a slightly softer approach. "Hi, James. Is Mum around?"

"I'm right here," and Katie opened her arms wide to receive her daughter. "Oh, you're so welcome, Sam!"

They went into the kitchen together and there it was Samantha's sorry duty to tell her mother that Pablo Garcia was dead. She watched her mother weep genuine tears as she bid goodbye to her first love and she watched as James tried to console her. He was quite obviously very touched by her grief and not too jealous.

349

Copious amounts of sweet tea were served up as Katie talked about pushing Pablo away from her, admitting that alcohol had taken over her life by then. Samantha watched James tenderly hug Kathleen and realised what a positive influence he could be on her mother.

James then told them how Rose had admitted to forging his signature and sending the cruel letter. The world seemed to shift for the two women on hearing this. James admonished himself for his stupid crush on Gillian but Samantha insisted that he was a victim of her highly effective manipulation games.

Again Katie apologised for being such a poor mother. She vowed that she would never drink again and, for the first time in her life, Samantha actually wondered if this might be the time she succeeded.

Samantha also spoke about her dashed dreams, her disgust at being in love with her half-brother and her subsequent horror at discovering about Cameron and Gillian.

It was at this point that James yet again lamented being Cameron's father. Sam considered telling the older man the truth about Cameron's parentage but she held back. Now was not the time.

At teatime, James announced that he was going out to fetch fish and chips for their dinner. What he didn't say was that he wanted to leave the women a little time to talk alone. It didn't take them long.

"Well, Mum. What's all this then?" she teased gently. "You and James Judge?"

Kathleen chuckled. "He came to me last night when he walked out on Rose. He asked me to take him in. Said that he had nowhere else to go. What else could I do?"

"Oh, so you're just good friends?" Sam asked, tongue firmly in cheek.

"Yes, as a matter of fact. That's exactly what he is. He's just an old fool keeping your old fool of a mother company for the time being."

"So you don't think this is a long-term arrangement? Couldn't that hurt you?"

Kathleen stopped washing the teacups and looked at her daughter.

"It's one of the lessons in AA, Sam. I just take one day at a time. To be honest they're quite strong on not starting up relationships while you're on the road to recovery but I don't look at James as starting up a relationship. He is, after all, your father." Then she returned her attention to the soapy water.

"I just don't want to see you get hurt, Mum. You're very vulnerable."

"And so is he. We're well matched, for as long as he's around. What about you? Have you any idea what you're going to do?"

"I'm going back to Spain."

"What? What's in Spain for you now?"

Samantha's mind wandered back to the beautiful lush vines resting in the evening sun. She remembered the soft laugh of Pablo being carried on the gentle breeze and she thought of the horses whinnying contentedly from the distant meadow. Then she saw Pedro's face. His dark brooding eyes, glancing sideways as she said something to him. She thought of his face lighting up like a child's when they realised that they loved each other. Lastly she remembered the insecurity and uncertainty on that same wonderful face that very morning when she promised him that she would follow him back to Spain.

"Samantha, your eyes have glassed over. What are you thinking about?" Her mother reached over and touched her daughter's arm.

Sam snapped out of her daydream and continued drying. "I have to get back to Spain as soon as possible. That's where I belong."

"Yes but why?" Kathleen still didn't understand.

"Pedro, Mummy. The man I'm going to marry is there. His name is Pedro."

When James came back and found the two girls hugging each other and crying, he knew that it had been a good idea to leave them alone for a little while.

Later that night, when Kathleen had retired for the evening, Samantha spoke privately to James.

"Tomorrow I will hand in my notice, James. But I think you need to know that I am going to fight for my shareholding in Gracias."

"Couldn't agree more, girl. What's yours is yours. Don't forget that you have my 10 per cent at this stage too, so you hold 41 per cent of that company. Still, even after all that's happened, I can't believe you're leaving us. What about Gracias being your baby and what about the plans you told me about?"

Samantha's eyes glassed up. "Pablo's death has changed a lot for me. None of that old life matters to me any more. If he taught me one thing it was to follow your heart and my heart is not in Gracias any more. To be honest, I would quite happily sell my stake back to Cameron if he would take it. If you still want to part with your 10 per cent, please give it to my mother. I think she could do with the money."

"Surely you can't be serious," James was appalled. "Don't worry about your mother. Now that we have made our peace, I will see to it that she wants for nothing for the rest of her life."

"Now that you bring it up, James, what exactly are you doing here with my mother?"

"Isn't it obvious?"

"Not to me, it isn't."

"Why, Sammy, I'm stone in love with the woman. I always have been. I thought she walked out on me thirty-five years ago while she thought I walked out on her. Now that we've sorted that out, I don't plan to let her go again."

"She's not a strong woman. If you hurt her –" Samantha started but James put his hands up to stop her from continuing.

"I know, I know. Not to mention Ricky. I think he would kill me. Samantha, I have to tell you, my intentions towards your mother are truly honourable. I just want to be with her. She had the courage and love to give me another chance. Do you think you can too?"

She studied his face for a moment and saw nothing but absolute sincerity. Then she smiled. "OK, then. You're on trial!" she said but she laughed as she said it. James sat down at the table and took out a pen and paper from his inside jacket pocket.

"Now then, let's figure out your plan of attack."

Together they went through Samantha's objectives and James pointed out the pitfalls of various suggestions that she made. In the end it came down to one clear problem. Samantha wanted out but she wanted a fair and reasonable share price to let go of her stock. James's problem was that he didn't think Cameron would go for that. He knew that his son would try to bully her down in price and, even if he didn't, James wasn't sure that the company could afford that much capital outlay.

Then he went for another angle. "Would you consider maintaining a 20 per cent shareholding? It's a good pension plan, Sam, and you above all people know how likely it is to keep growing."

Samantha's eyes lit up. "I'll sell 20 per cent back to Cameron and keep an 11 per cent shareholding as my pension plan. You keep your own 10 per cent. I don't want what I haven't earned."

"But I want to give you something, Sam. It was a sort of a father-daughter present."

"There is something you have that I want," she said, grinning.

"Name it," he said.

Samantha looked at James and smirked. "You know your old Aston Martin?"

James laughed. "Take it, it's yours. The keys are in the key press in the library at Dunross and I'll post the registration book to you out as soon as I've transferred ownership to your name."

The following morning was Monday morning. The first thing Samantha did was phone Cameron and tell him she would be at the distillery at four. Next she phoned Rose. It didn't take long for the older woman to agree to meet. Samantha then had to bid her goodbyes to James and her mother.

"You're going to have a showdown with Rose and Cameron, aren't you?" Kathleen asked.

"It has to be done, Mother. Once that's over I'll meet up with Ricky to tell him about Pablo. Then I'm going back to Pedro."

"Phone me to let me know that you're OK, won't you?"

"Of course I will, Mum. As soon as I'm settled, you can come and visit if you like." Then she looked at James and smiled. "I meant both of you."

"We would love to. But wait . . ." Kathleen took her daughter's arm and drew her back into her bedroom. "Before you go, Sam, there is something I want to give you. I put it away for safe keeping a long time ago and I now know I'll never wear it again. Who knows, it might be just the thing for your showdown with Rose." Her eyes sparkled with mischief as Sam took the carefully wrapped brown paper parcel. She looked at her mother quizzically and then she opened it. Inside was the dress she had heard so much about – the white dress with the big black polka dots! It was just as she had pictured it.

"I don't believe you kept it all this time," Sam gasped, putting the dress up against her own body.

"I think it will fit you nicely," Kathleen laughed.

"Mum, would I? Could I?"

"Damn sure you could!" Her mother's eyes opened wider. "In fact if you really want to scare that old bat you should take my wonderful black hat and long gloves too. You'll look like Audrey Hepburn!"

"Mom, I'm blonde," Samantha giggled. "But I do have a spectacular pair of black sunglasses. I could certainly dress the part."

Kathleen beamed at her daughter. "I know it's not trendy by today's grungy standards but remember your enemy. I think that sort of look would certainly intimidate Rose Judge. If she sees you walk in with that little number on!" Kathleen went to her wardrobe and took out a huge hatbox. From this she pulled out a spectacular, jet-black wide-brimmed hat and elbow-length black satin gloves. She put them on herself for her daughter to admire. "What do you think?"

Samantha crossed the small bedroom and hugged her mother. "I say meet fire with fire, Mum. This gear is absolutely perfect!" She smiled as she realised that the old dear was a lot tougher than she was giving her credit for.

Thankfully, she had her knee-high black boots with her and a pair of black tights so she was able to change in a hotel toilet on the way to Dunross. The dress slipped on like it was made for her except that, being four inches taller than her mother, the dress looked shorter on her.

When she got to Dunross the house was strangely quiet. Before ringing the door bell, Samantha donned the black gloves and wide hat and a trench coat. Then she stood proud and reminded herself, "Fire with fire!" She pressed the doorbell button and Mrs Bumble let her in.

"Where is everybody, Mrs B?" Samantha asked, assuming more confidence than she really felt.

Mrs B looked morose. "Oh, Miss Samantha, what a time of it we've had. Poor Caroline Judge has left us. She won't come back to the house. She's gone off and moved into a house in the village. With the Delaneys she is and she won't come home. Stephanie is at work and so is Cameron of course. Mrs Judge is here though –"

"That's enough, Mrs B," Rose marched down the corridor from the study. "Do you blab to all our guests about the business of the family?" It was most unlike Rose to be sharp with Mrs Bumble but these were no ordinary times.

Then Rose looked at her guest. She almost stumbled when she saw the hat and gloves. "Samantha, hello. Won't you come in? Would you like a cup of tea?" She led the way to the library.

Samantha could hear the insecurity in her voice, however. Good, this was working. The old bat wasn't as tough as she pretended to be.

"No, thank you. What I have to say won't take long." Samantha followed Rose, privately resolving to be strong. As the older woman sat down at the desk in the library, Sam took off her coat and revealed the little black and white dress. The effect on the older woman was drastic.

"My God," she covered her mouth.

"So you recognise it?" Samantha leered at her opponent, placing her long thin gloved hands on her hips.

"It looks like – well, it just looks similar to one I saw a long time ago."

"No – it's not *like* a dress you saw once upon a time, it *is* the dress you saw a long time ago. It's the one my mother wore to your party, in this very house." Sam looked around her as if she had never seen Dunross before. "It was the party that I was conceived at, wasn't it?" She tilted her head, feeling very glamorous in the wide-brimmed hat.

Rose had gone white as a sheet. "Is this some kind of joke?" she trembled.

"Well, Mrs Judge, that would depend on your definition of a bloody joke, wouldn't it?"

"What are you talking about?"

"Now let's see. Was setting me up with your son a joke?"

"I don't know what you mean."

"Well then, what about Pablo being his father? Is that a joke?"

"I don't know what you're talking about."

"Don't even try that, Rose. I know everything. Pablo has told me. The way I see it, Kathleen had a fling with James and got pregnant with me, but what happened next? Did you get jealous? It couldn't have been Pablo's doing because he didn't know about them. It had to be you. What was it? Revenge? You managed to get pregnant by Pablo and hey presto – Cameron."

"Stop!" Rose covered her ears.

"So you have a real mess on your hands and then, even weirder, I arrive back into your life. Is that when the idea hit you? Because you knew, didn't you? Somehow you knew about the Garcia/White connection."

Rose snorted. "So I knew. Surely I was doing you a favour? I was getting you back under the Judge umbrella."

"After you tried to have me aborted. You did write that bloody letter thirty-five years ago?"

"Yes, yes, yes. I was so confused. I was terrified of losing James. If he discovered that Kathleen was carrying his child, he might have left me."

"So why did you seduce Pablo?"

"I admit it. I was so jealous of your bloody mother – she had it all! She was so beautiful and carefree. She had an amazing hunger for life that attracted men to her like anything. I only had James, and your mother –" she spat the words out with such hatred, "got him too in the end. So when I had a chance with Pablo – yes, I took it. He was working in the potting shed one day. I had heard the two of them fighting so I knew the timing was good. Damn it, he was just a man." Rose began to sob. "So, yes – I admit it. It was revenge."

"There's an old Chinese saying, Rose. If you want to seek revenge, better dig two graves."

"I am sorry, what more do you want? You're just like your mother, I hope you realise. You too have destroyed my life. Cameron is in bits. James has gone, Caroline has gone. Stephanie is moving out soon too. There's nothing left. You've ruined me."

"No, Rose, I think you did a pretty good job of that before I was even born," Sam said witheringly.

"It was all your mother's fault! She took James."

"She had a fling with your husband so you had a fling with hers. You're equally to blame – equally stupid!"

The older woman rose to her feet. She spoke in a furious trembling voice. "How dare you?" Her eyes blazed. "How dare you even compare me to that tramp?"

Samantha squared up to her adversary. "That's my mother you're talking about!"

But Rose wasn't finished. "We have nothing in common – your mother and I. She was a whore – a bounty hunter – but what I did, I did out of cold revenge. I didn't have a sordid affair. I was simply getting even."

Samantha's own bitterness began to melt as she saw Rose Judge for what she really was. "That's really how you see this, isn't it? Do you have any idea how much you're deluding yourself? You really think that you have some sort of high moral ground here, don't you?" Samantha's voice was full of sympathy. "Do you have any idea how sad you sound?"

Rose collapsed back into her chair. Her outburst had exhausted her. "Look, what do you want?" she asked miserably.

The fight was over.

Samantha continued in a more civil tone. "Well, the question is where does all of this stop?"

Rose's head snapped up. "What do you mean?"

"Well, do I tell Cameron that he's a Garcia or do you?"

"Oh God, Samantha, you can't do that." Rose stood up again and wrung her hands. "What do you want? I'll do anything but please don't tell Cameron or James or any of the children for that matter."

"What? So you can keep your sordid little secret to yourself?"

"How did you find out anyway? He gave me his word he would ·never tell anybody."

"For as long as he lived," Samantha added. "That was the promise." Sam glared at the woman who had tried to destroy her. "Pablo is dead, Rose."

The older woman fell back onto her chair again but Samantha would not let herself pity her and so she continued. "He left me the information in his will. He also left me this letter for Cameron and I have to decide whether or not to give it to him." She waved the envelope menacingly.

"Please, Samantha, what do I have to do?"

"Well, first of all I want the keys and the log book for the Aston Martin."

"James's car? You can't be serious?"

"I'm perfectly serious. It's a sort of a father–daughter thing, if you must know."

"What else do you want?" Rose asked shakily.

"Well, it's like this." Samantha walked over to the desk Rose was sitting at and placed her hands on it, still holding the letter firmly. "I'm going to meet Cameron now and we're going to resolve our differences and put them behind us once and for all. I am going to offer him most of my shares in Gracias at their current market price. If he accepts it, you need not worry. If he becomes difficult, I will get him to phone you and *you* can convince him."

"Are you going to rob him?"

"Rose, I just said I would expect a fair price. Now don't be rude, or else −" She waved the envelope again.

Within five minutes, Samantha was driving out of Dunross for the last time in the exquisite 1969 silver Aston Martin DBS V8. She left her BMW there for Cameron to worry about. It was a company car − his problem. As a memento for him, she threw the wonderful hat and gloves her mother had given her on the passenger seat. They had served their purpose. She wouldn't be needing them again.

Thrilled though she was, Samantha was shaking. She had won. She had beaten the monster, Rose Judge, into submission. Thankfully the old bat didn't call her bluff because the truth was Sam knew that she could never show Cameron his letter. This was not out of any moral fidelity to the Judge family. It was for dear old Pablo.

The meeting was not as scary as she thought it would be. Rose was so nervous that she had already phoned her son and told him to give Samantha whatever she wanted.

"Money's no object, just get rid of her," Rose had begged tearfully.

"Mother, whatever she has on you, I won't let her bully you," he tried to reason with her. But Rose had begged and wept enough to unnerve Cameron.

What hidden weapon did Samantha have over Rose, Cameron wondered furiously. When she marched into his office and asked for three million euro for 20 per cent he was pleasantly surprised. He'd had the company valued at fifteen million plus already, so this was, in fact, a very good price. The Judge Business Group could finance that.

"I can only tentatively accept pending approval by the entire board," Cameron stalled instinctively.

"Don't bullshit me, Cameron. You know that I already have your mother and father on side. Just take the deal and process the cheque."

She spat the words at him – which was a pity, he thought, because she was looking absolutely gorgeous in a short fitted black and white mini-dress. It really showed off her long legs and her slim figure.

"Samantha," he tried to ingratiate himself.

"Don't, Cameron. Just agree to the deal."

He shrugged and nodded. "If Mum and Dad are behind it, then so am I. We stand as a family."

She knew that he meant it as a dig at her illegitimate status but she looked at him with pity in her eyes. She couldn't tell him the truth – that he was really the gardener's son. If she did he would have a nervous breakdown, poor pathetic bastard.

Five minutes later, Samantha walked out of Cameron's life. She couldn't believe that she had actually done it. She had made herself a cool three million euro, she had acquired the Aston Martin and she even had her pension plan sorted out. Quite suddenly her mind returned to something Pablo had taught her when he was telling her about the cold winters and the vines fighting for survival. His words sailed back into her mind and into her heart. "If you have to fight for something, it's all the sweeter."

As Samantha walked out of Judges' Distilleries for the very last time she glanced skywards. "You're very clever, Papi. You're very wise!" she whispered.

Jean the receptionist ran after her to say goodbye and good luck. It was then that she spotted Samantha's new car.

"God, Sam, you look like Grace Kelly with the dress and car. All you need now is the little trench coat and the head scarf and you could be her double."

Samantha laughed and said that she thought it was a great idea. She already had the coat; she could buy the headscarf to look the part for her long drive to Spain. If she was going to drive back to Pedro, she might as well do it in style!

Epilogue

Paul and Wendy arrived two days before the wedding. Unlike her last attempt, Samantha had opted to go for a spring marriage this time round.

"Because the autumn is such a mad time for Pedro with the harvesting of the grapes," she had explained.

Sam was particularly thrilled to greet Wendy because they hadn't actually seen each other since the night of Victoria's ninety-fifth party. That had also been Wendy's first night with Paul which is why the girls hadn't crossed paths back at their apartment. Naturally they had spoken on the phone regularly but that just wasn't the same.

Pedro took Paul off to walk among the vines and to see his beautiful horses while Wendy and Samantha grabbed a bottle of wine and caught up on each other's news.

They sat at the back of Casa Garcia, where Pedro and Samantha now lived together. In the evening sun, the rays poured through the trunks of the pine trees. It was warm, incredibly calm and very peaceful.

The girls nattered as they caught up on each other's news and enjoyed the Spanish sunset. Even in the early spring, it held warmth and the promise of a good summer.

"Well, are you still deliriously happy?" Samantha teased Wendy.

"Never happier! Paul has set up his own chauffeur business and he has just branched out into the luxury and stretch-limo service too. You'd be amazed how many people in Ireland want to look like Hollywood stars."

Samantha winced. "Bit pricy to start up though," she said delicately, not wanting to offend her friend. But Wendy took no umbrage. "Well, Paul came into a slight windfall recently." Then she had the good grace to look a little timid. "He sold the video tape of your last wedding – well, half-wedding."

"He did what?" Sam spluttered her wine.

"Relax," Wendy laughed. "He sold it to Rose Judge. You can rest assured that she has destroyed it by now."

"Wendy, you bold girl! Wouldn't that be a little like blackmail or at the very least, extortion?"

Wendy pretended to look hurt. "After all his years of service, Rose let him go without as much as a gold watch. I think she reaped what she sowed."

"He quit!" Sam argued.

"That's not the point. They didn't give him anything by way of thanks and besides," Wendy brightened up a little, "it gave us enough money to buy a stretch limo and a very nice people-carrier. We even got the down payment for a house together too."

"Both of you – like together?" Sam squealed with delight.

"Yep, we're moving in together."

Another bottle of wine was opened.

Samantha eventually brought something up that had been on her mind. "Do you see Gillian much these days?"

Wendy looked horrified. "Are you mad? After what she did to you? I moved out a few days after you did. I read about her recently though. She's as big as a house but the baby isn't due until July. She's still seeing Cameron I think but no sign of a ring. I just got that bit of news from *VIP* magazine."

Then she glanced nervously at her friend. Wendy didn't want to upset her. "I think Cameron has moved to Barbados."

"What?"

"Yeah, he's bought a distillery or something. Caroline told Paul."

"Remind me to avoid Barbados," Samantha scowled but it didn't seem to perturb her too much. How could it when she was so in love with Pedro, Wendy realised with relief.

"What about Caroline Judge? I was appalled to hear about her attempt to commit suicide."

"Yeah, that was dreadful. Did you know she had a drug problem?"

"No, I had no idea. Cameron never said." Samantha sighed, "Jesus, he probably didn't even know – what a family!"

"Well, things are improving. She was incredibly lucky that the fall didn't kill her. Evidently the fact that she was half-stoned helped. She fell like a rag-doll into the water and nothing broke when she made impact."

"She didn't even break anything?"

"No, just got a few spectacular bruises, I gather. Paul still stays in touch with her. She's used our chauffeur service already. She took all the Delaney family up to her art exhibition in a stretch limo. Paul says they had a ball. He says the Judge girls are lovely. It was really the mother and Cameron who were rotten. Where was I? Oh yes, Caroline and her exhibition. It created pandemonium. She had a whole series of highly controversial oil paintings. Let's see if I can remember them . . ." She took another sip of wine.

Samantha helped out. "Well, I heard all about the Shepherd's Series. Mum told me about those. How much did she get for them?"

"That's right! Sylvester Stallone bought the three of them for one million euro. Not bad for a packet of Knorr! No, the one I was thinking about was one she had of Marcus, her ex – bonking her mother. I think she tried to call it Mother Fu–" Wendy stopped herself, and smiled. "Well, they wouldn't let her use strong language so when it sold it had the title Poor Judgement. She also had a painting of Gillian!"

"Our flatmate, Gillian?"

"The very same only she looked a bit like a ghost and she had a massively oversized nose. It looked like she was leering over somebody's shoulder, trying to snoop at something. It was called Gillius Interruptus. Caroline told Paul that it was because Gillian once rudely walked right past her while she was enjoying an al fresco bonk! Evidently Gillian made Cameron buy it at some extortionate price. It was hilarious."

"Do you think she's OK now? Caroline Judge, I mean."

"Paul says she's getting sorted out slowly. It's a long way back when you've got into the state she was in, I guess. The day Luke Delaney saved her life was the turning point. She hasn't been back to Dunross since."

"I don't blame her. Where is she living then?"

"Well, actually she and Luke are living together in a little house that she bought in the village. It's just a few doors up from his parents."

"No!"

"Yes." Wendy looked philosophical. "It's funny, isn't it? You'd think that she would be happy in that huge sprawling mansion of Dunross and yet she seems to have found herself in the simple surroundings of a little house in the village."

"Are you saying Luke and Caroline together – romantically?" Sam was enthralled. "Isn't he the guy that Gillian had an encounter with?"

"Yeah, lucky escape for him, what? Well, the gossip in Fiddler's Point is that Luke and Caroline are just good friends but who knows?" Wendy regarded Samantha. "You still haven't got over it, have you?" she asked gently.

Sam studied at her glass of wine. "How do you ever get over the betrayal of a best friend? I have come to terms with Cameron. He's just a bastard and I'm lucky I got to find out before I became his wife. But Gillian? How can I ever get over that? Take it from me, having lost a boyfriend and a best friend, losing a best friend hurts more."

Wendy came over and hugged her friend. "It will get easier with time. It has to."

"Papi used to say something very similar. "Give it time, everything will come good.""

"There you are," Wendy smiled.

Sam harrumphed. "Who says old friends are best?"

"You may not be able to forget but with time you might be able to forgive – eventually." In an effort to lighten the mood, Wendy changed tack as she sat back down again. "How are your mum and James getting on?"

"They're like lovesick lambs. They were here a few weeks ago and now they've gone down to the south of Spain for a bit of sun."

"I assume they'll be back for tomorrow?"

"Of course, James is going to walk me up the aisle."

"And your gorgeous brother? He's coming too?"

"Naturally. He's still breaking hearts and taking numbers," Samantha smiled. "He was actually pretty cut up when I told him about Pablo's death but it didn't occur to me back then that he and Pedro are actually first cousins. Pedro's mother and Ricky's father were brother and sister so even though he's upset at losing Pablo, he's delighted at getting to know Pedro."

"That's terrific," Wendy agreed. "And how are you two getting on with the locals in Haro? Have you cleared up the confusion about you two being related?"

"More or less," Sam laughed. "We still get the occasional odd look but sod them!"

"Oh Sam, this is so exciting. You're getting married!" Wendy gushed with genuine excitement. Then she asked gently, "Are you going to wear flowers in your hair?"

Samantha flashed her a broad smile. "Of course. Wendy, you remembered, how thoughtful. Do you also remember telling me that night in the Wicklow Arms that I would be married within the year?"

"I said that?"

"Yep, I think you might have been talking about Cameron but leaving that aside you were right! What else from home?"

"Oh yeah, I was telling you about Caroline Judge. Did you hear about the oil painting that she did called Ashling?"

"No, I don't think so,"

"Well, it's the most haunting and beautiful painting of a young woman. Evidently when she was drowning, Caroline maintains that a mermaid guided her up to Luke's hand. Even though they were under water, the girl told her that her name was Ashling and she was Luke's sister. She was to tell Tess Delaney that all was well and that they would meet again sometime."

Samantha suspended her glass mid-air, so transfixed was she by the story.

"Creepy," she whispered.

"Well, it is because Luke had a sister called Ashling who died when she was a baby. Evidently Tess Delaney is over the moon about it and she claims that a short while before it happened she had asked God for a 'gift from above' to help Luke get better. The only thing she's not sure about is whether the gift from above was Caroline falling from the chopper or Ashling coming down from heaven to lend a helping hand!"

"Wow," Samantha was transfixed. Then she felt a shiver go down her spine. "I wonder if Pablo is near us now," she whispered. The trees rustled as if on cue despite the fact that there was no wind. Both girls blinked at each other and burst out laughing.

"Well, if he is I'm sure he's very happy for you and Pedro, Sam." Wendy spoke with conviction.

"That's if he understands that we're not related."

"But you yourself said that you think he had his doubts, Samantha."

"There was one day he said that he would have loved Pedro and me to be together if we weren't related," Sam conceded.

"And you're not, so he has got his wish," Wendy encouraged.

"I hope so. He also told me that I must always follow my heart and that's exactly what I'm doing. I got to tell you – it works." Sam looked at her best friend as her eyes glassed up slightly. "He was a good man and he gave me something nobody else was able to."

"What was that?"

"A home," Samantha smiled and looked around her at the growing vines.

"Does that mean you're going to stay here?"

"Absolutely."

"What about Pedro's plans for the horses?"

"With the money I brought from Ireland, we have been able to buy a good deal of land around us here. He can breed his horses. Centella is in foal already and I can run the vineyard."

"You know, speaking of bringing money over from Ireland, I still haven't got over the shock of discovering that Gracias was an anagram for S Garcia. You never even told me about that."

"To be honest, I was a bit shy to tell you. Remember, back then everybody called me Samantha White so the Garcia thing was pretty private."

"Not any more. I never saw an argument won so conclusively in such a short amount of time," Wendy added, fantastically proud of her friend. One of the resident squirrels scampered up to them looking for some food, much to the girls' delight. "This place really is wonderful, Sam. Is this what you're going to do with your life now – tend Pablo's vines?"

"Heck no. I was thinking, what I really need to do is to buy my own *bodega* so we can make our own wine. Casa Garcia has a certain marketing appeal, don't you think? I have this idea, you see, with a couple of hundred acres of good vines, I could –"

Wendy slapped her forehead. "And I thought you were coming over here to slow down and live the simple life. You have too much drive, girl."

Samantha giggled guiltily.

"You know," Wendy continued. "I reckon you could really do anything you want. You have amazing ability and willpower. All you really need is the will to win and you have that by the shedload."

Samantha laughed at the praise. It was grossly exaggerated of course but her friend was right about one thing. She thought about the other sort of will – the one that Pablo had left for her after his death. It had unlocked so many secrets for her. If she hadn't had that, she would never have been able to bargain with Rose Judge.

It had also helped her to forgive her mother because she realised Kathleen wasn't the only misguided party in her parents' marriage.

The men returned from their walk around the land. They each went to their respective women and kissed them hello. Samantha felt the butterflies flutter in her stomach yet again on seeing and kissing Pedro. She knew that she had found her soul mate. In that regard, Wendy was correct. Sam would fight through heaven and hell for the things she wanted on this good earth. She looked over at Wendy who was still smiling at her.

"Well?" Wendy asked again. "Do you realise how impressive your willpower is, Miss Garcia?"

In her mind's eye, Samantha pictured the will which was safely tucked away in the back of the bottom drawer in her bedroom.

"Perhaps you're right," she laughed. "I'll concede to one point. Thanks to Pablo," she raised her glass and eyes towards heaven as if to salute him, "when I really needed it, I guess I did have *The Will To Win.*"

THE END

The Woman he Loves

SUZANNE HIGGINS

"I'll give you anything you want," he tried again, "money, holidays, diamonds."
"Out!" she shouted as she shut the door in his face.

Saskia Dalton has her hands full. She has four uncontrollable daughters, a missing lover, an over-affectionate ex-husband and now somebody is pregnant! Richard, her ex, had an affair with their au pair and has paid the ultimate price – now he reckons it's payback time. Her neighbour, Sue Parker, has an equally complex life. Feeling just a little neglected, she accidentally seduces her GP while her husband is away on a business trip. But he's cruising down a lot more than the Nile . . .

Meanwhile, a mystery developer moves into their stunning village and builds 10 luxurious mansions, attracting a motley crew. When the most exciting newcomers turn out to be the drop-dead gorgeous and totally shameless Condon twins, Maximilian and Sebastian, it looks like Saskia may have to lock up her daughters.

But, in Ballymore, when life gets this complicated there's only one thing to do . . . throw a party, invite everyone and hope that every man gets . . . the woman he loves.

ISBN 1-84223-107-3

www.poolbeg.com

The Power
of a
Woman

SUZANNE HIGGINS

*'I am not some pawn of destiny,' she thought
in fury. 'I can and will control my own future.'*

Richard Dalton, mega-rich proprietor of Rock FM is gorgeous and
ruthless! Saskia, his wife, is loving and obliging until she discovers a few of
her husband's darker secrets.

With their three daughters, they live in the beautiful village of Ballymore,
where the arrival of a mystery celebrity causes ripples of excitement as
rumours spread of his radical plans for the run-down Rathdeen Manor.

Meanwhile, Sue, breathtakingly beautiful wife of the famous clothing
chain-store entrepreneur David Parker, is slowly being destroyed by a
dangerous secret that she cannot share with him.

As Richard's business empire continues to grow, so too does his depravity.
Facing despair, Saskia realises that for her sake and that of her children she
has no choice. She has to fight back, but can she find the power?

ISBN 1-84223-093-X